BRUTE FORCE

The Rachel Peng Books

Digital Divide
Maker Space
State Machine
Brute Force

Also by K.B. Spangler

A Girl and Her Fed
Rise Up Swearing
The Russians Came Knocking
Greek Key

BRUTE FORCE

K.B. SPANGLER

A GIRL AND HER FED BOOKS
NORTH CAROLINA

Brute Force is a work of fiction. Names, characters, and events are the creations of the author. Settings are either fictional or have been adapted from locations in and around Washington, D.C. for purposes of storytelling. Any resemblance to actual persons, living or dead, is entirely coincidental. All characters, places, and events are set in the world of *A Girl and Her Fed*, found online at agirlandherfed.com. Additional information can be found at kbspangler.com

Copyright ©2016 by K.B. Spangler.
Cover art by Rose Loughran of *Red Moon Rising*

All rights reserved. No part of this book may be reproduced or distributed in printed or electronic form without permission from the author.

This edition was printed by CreateSpace,
an Amazon.com company.

For Andy, Demia, Tobin, and Fletcher

ONE

Two hours past naptime and all hell had broken loose.

The toddler had reached that transcendent screaming phase of a tantrum, the one that could only be found after fifteen minutes of warmup weeping. The little girl was not *quite* upside-down in what was not *quite* a fireman's carry, but the woman holding her had the determined look of someone who had accepted that reason, begging, and loving threats no longer applied, and that the screaming would only stop once they reached the car.

The second woman, slightly shorter than the first and deliciously curvy, marched a few steps in front of the others, leading the way. She kept turning towards the toddler, then back towards something unseen ahead of them, her attention divided.

His men waited, hidden behind cars and the stony twisting structure of the parking garage itself, their heads down as they pretended to play games on their phones, just in case.

Even so, the woman carrying the little girl paused.

He saw her eyes search the dark corners of the parking garage, knowing there was something wrong but unable to find it.

The little girl also paused, and in that moment of stillness, he saw months of planning fly apart.

He breathed out, slow and relieved, when he saw the girl had been gathering strength for the ultimate stage of a toddler's meltdown. The screaming returned, but now she also began to pummel the woman holding her with tiny fists.

The girl's mother—and even if he hadn't planned this day down to the smallest detail, he still would have known the shorter woman was the girl's biological mother from the way the child's face was a smaller, softer clone of her own—spun towards her.

"Avery," she said, in the universal tone mothers used when they had Had Enough, "you do *not* hit!"

The child, utterly inconsolable, wailed on.

The taller woman pushed forward, oblivious to the child's fists banging against her face and shoulders. "It's okay," she said. "C'mon, we gotta move. The paparazzi will be here soon, this is like blood in the water for—"

She stopped dead in the center of the lane, and he knew he was caught. He thumbed the button on his phone which sent the text to his men: *GO*.

"Carlota," the taller woman said, as she lowered the screaming child into her mother's arms. "Call for backup, and get yourself and Avery behind those cars. Right now."

"What's happening?" The girl's mother glanced about the parking garage, not seeing anything other than the usual orderly mess of concrete and metal.

"There's nobody around." The taller woman pulled her dark hair into a ponytail, and then quickly cracked every knuckle on her hands in order of smallest to largest, like a pianist warming up before a concert. "There's *always* somebody around."

"The security cameras are dead. There are… There are cell phone signals all around us!" The shorter woman glanced around, knowing his men were there but unable to see them. Her daughter caught her mood; the screaming stopped, replaced by frantic sniffles and arms wrapping tight around her mother's neck.

"Get behind the cars," the taller woman said again, and pushed the girl and her mother towards a nearby pickup truck. "Hell, break into one and lock it behind you. I'll keep them away from you until backup gets here."

The woman moved back towards the center of the lane as she shrugged out of her jacket, leaving her arms bare. "Hey!" she shouted, and her voice ricocheted around the garage. "Wanna get this over with? We've got a little girl who needs a nap!"

He stepped out from behind a nearby support pillar, no

more than ten feet away from her. He saw her take him in—the camouflage clothing, the enormous hand cannons holstered at his waist, the hunting knife in his boot—and judge him in that same moment.

"Howdy, Try-hard," she snapped. "Militia men travel in packs. Where're your buddies?"

There was a sharp cry from behind her; the taller woman's eyes widened at the sound of a body hitting the pavement, followed by the piercing plea of *"Mommy!"*

"Shit," the woman hissed. She turned to find one of his men holding a gun very near the toddler's temple, her mother crouched beside her, pressing her hands to her head. "Carlota?!"

The first man grinned at her with a movie star's perfect smile.

"The Agent will be fine," he said, as he knelt to roll a glass vial towards the woman standing in the road. It bumped into the tangle of her jacket, and she snatched it up before it could spin under the cars.

"Brevital," she read, the liquid swirling around the vial as she shook it at him. "Holy fuck, did you use this on her? Do you know what too much of this stuff can do?"

"I'm okay," the other woman said, her voice muffled by her arms. "They didn't... I didn't feel an injection..."

"See?" he said. "She's fine."

He tossed a baggie after the vial of sedative.

She picked it up: a fresh plastic hypodermic syringe.

A large sedan pulled up beside her. Its trunk opened, slowly, on silent hydraulics.

The woman looked from the baggie to the terrified toddler to the dark recesses of the trunk. "Ah," she said in a quiet voice.

"You're a doctor," he said to her. "I'm sure you know the dosage. So do I. Show me before you inject yourself."

In reply, she tore the package open with her teeth.

"I'll make a deal with you," she said, as she filled the syringe and tapped the air bubbles out. "Leave the kid and her mom here, and I'll be the best-behaved hostage ever."

"I'll make *you* a deal," he said. "I bring the kid as insurance, and anything you do to me or my men? We'll take it out on her."

He nodded to the man holding the gun on the child. The gun vanished as he lifted her into the back seat of the sedan. The toddler couldn't quite remember how to cry: fear was layered over the old tantrum tears on her face, and then the door shut her away from her mother.

"Avery?" The girl's mother tried to stand on unsteady legs. "Avery?!"

"I'll keep her safe," the woman promised her friend. "It'll be okay."

She held up the syringe. The liquid pressed against the plunger; a small amount, but still enough to put her out. He nodded at her to proceed, and she tapped her own arm until she found a vein.

He didn't let himself blink as she injected herself, just to be sure.

Once done, she threw the vial and the syringe at his feet. The glass vial broke, spraying droplets of surgical anesthetic across the parking garage floor.

"If you please," he told her, gesturing towards the black hole of the sedan's trunk.

She snatched up her jacket and climbed into the trunk. When she vanished from view, the other woman's face went blank, her gaze distant, as if lost in a critical conversation.

He gave the Brevital another ten seconds to work before he looked in the trunk.

The woman's resiliency was amazing. She was still conscious, and her eyes managed to focus on him.

"You better pray I'm the one who kicks your ass," she said softly. "Because if I don't, my husband is coming for you."

"I'm counting on it, Doctor Blackwell," he told her, and he slammed the trunk closed.

TWO

Rachel Peng was doing yardwork.

Resentfully, yes, but she was fairly certain nobody in the history of the civilized world had ever done yardwork without some resentment. She would not call a landscape company and spend good money to get out of doing her household chores. She would not call Santino and roar about how he had turned her backyard into a veritable Garden of Eden and then all but moved out. She would not reach up into space and see if a top-secret defense satellite was in the right place at the right time, because she would not nuke her own home from orbit because it was not the only way to be sure…

"And I will *not* shoot you to *shut you up!*" she shouted at the neighbor's bulldog on the other side of the fence.

The bulldog blinked at her before it resumed snarling and throwing itself against the chain-link mesh.

She tore great armfuls of winter-dry honeysuckle down from the fence and hurled them aside. The fence, hidden under layers of vines, began to appear. It was old, but sturdy and well-suited to keep the bulldog out, at least until those vines really got some summer into them and their weight would start to bring the whole thing down—

A man's silhouette emerged from behind the vines.

"Aw hell," Rachel muttered to herself, flipping frequencies to see which of her neighbors was creeping up on her today. She expected the washed-out reds of the bulldog's owner, or maybe the bright urine yellow of his brother. Both of them liked to poke at the neighborhood's favorite freak, and they tended to make an appearance whenever she was outside.

A rich light brown came back to her.

Sandalwood!

Her gun was in the house. She knelt, her scans never leaving the center of the man's chest, as she picked up the garden shears lying beside the mountain of honeysuckle.

Her scans locked into the frequencies she used to see facial features, and her heart stopped pounding in her ears as she saw a stranger on the other side of the fence.

"Hey there!" she said, forcing a smile as she lifted the shears like a sword.

The man nodded at her, and knelt to scratch the bulldog's ears. "Mornin'," he said. The bulldog leaned against the man's legs, tongue lolling out the side of its mouth.

Rachel waited.

And watched.

The man was perfectly calm, his conversational colors looping across themselves in slow, peaceful waves. A strong streak of her Southwestern turquoise ran within these, but that wasn't unexpected—everyone knew who she was.

She saw nothing else. None of the dangerous reds or professional blues that accompanied that particular color of brown within her memory. He was the right height, the right weight, and had the muscle tone of a professional athlete, but…

Sometimes sandalwood is just sandalwood, she decided, and began to apply the shears to a large clump of wisteria that was competing with the honeysuckle for possession of the fence.

She didn't bother to ask if he was friends with the bulldog's owner. The same beast that attacked the fence if she so much as dared step into her own backyard was lost in the joys of a belly rub, squirming on the ground like a wiggly puppy.

"New to the neighborhood?" she asked.

"Got a place about five blocks over," he replied in a heavy Southern drawl that reminded her of home. "I've been here about two years."

"Me, too," she said, as she hacked through the wisteria. It wasn't yet full spring, and the wisteria was still dry and woody from the winter freeze. "What brings you by?"

He didn't reply as he rubbed the bulldog's belly.

The silence began to itch.

She dropped her shears and turned her back on him as she dragged the vines off to the compost heap in the corner of her property, her scans fixed on him the entire time. He was calm, his mind at rest; there was no hint of red lust chasing her turquoise around in his emotions, or an awkward orange as he searched for something to say, or any of the other colors she had come to associate with too-long silences.

Rachel took a quiet breath before running her scans along the deep contours of the skin on his face. She didn't entirely know what she was looking for—would she recognize the signs of plastic surgery if she saw it?—but her mind tripped over unfamiliar bumps that might have been scar tissues.

She marched straight from the compost heap into the house to get her gun.

When she came out, the man with the core the color of warm sandalwood was still waiting by the fence.

Rachel walked back to where she had left him, the cold grip of her gun warming in her hand.

He glanced up at her, and they stared at each other through the metal diamonds.

"Why are you here, Glazer?" she finally asked.

"That's not my name any more," he said. His normal voice was steady, all trace of Southern drawl gone. The bulldog came alive at the sound of it, lunging to its feet and scrambling across the grass to hide beneath its owner's porch.

The man who used to be Jonathan Glazer stood, slowly and carefully, and brushed off the knees of his jeans.

"Who have you called?" he asked. He placed both hands on the fence, fingers curling through the chain link. He gave the fence a quick jerk, as if testing its strength, as if he hadn't expected her to do yardwork today and the loss of a layer of vegetation meant she might be able to get over the six-foot fence faster than he had planned.

"For backup? Everybody," she lied. "Better start running."

"You'll just shoot me," he said, nodding towards her gun.

"No one would blame me," she said, grinning.

The psychopath on the other side of the fence returned the grin. "Maybe not at first," he said. "But give it a week, and you'll kick yourself for it."

"I really don't feel too much guilt when I kill murderers, Glazer. My conscience has convenient blind spots."

It was an intentional turn of phrase, and his grin grew slightly honest.

Fuck, she thought. *He knows. Or, at least suspects...*

"That's not what I meant. I'm here on loan," he said, and then reapplied his slow drawl to his speech, easier than she ever could, even when she was thoroughly saturated with the South after visiting her hometown back in Texas. "I'm your new best friend."

"Sorry, I've already got a couple hundred best friends. I don't need another one. It's already too crowded in here," she said, tapping her skull. "But don't worry—you'll get to meet them soon. They've been watching us chat."

"No," he said, "they haven't."

He leaned towards her and the chain link squealed beneath his weight; she planted her work boots against the earth and moved her index finger to her gun's trigger.

"Do they know you helped me escape?" he asked. "Do they know you let a mass murderer blow up a police department? Don't think so."

"*Mass* murderer?" she asked, cocking her head like a curious sparrow. "You getting braggy on me, Jonny-boy? I only caught you for that one."

"Don't play dumb. You knew what I was. And I," he said, moving close to the fence so his eyes cut through to hers, "know that this conversation is between you and me."

Rachel stared straight back at him.

In her brief but ongoing experience as a blind woman, she had yet to meet someone who could match her in a staring contest. Glazer was no exception: his conversational colors began to quiver around their edges, but instead of dropping his gaze and backing away, he lunged forward, rocking the fence until metal sang up and down the line.

She had her gun out and as close as she could get it to the center of his forehead before the chattering song of the fence had faded.

It took her a few moments to convince herself her voice would be steady before she said, "Are you finished?"

The conversational colors of the man who had been Glazer changed, becoming a wild ruby red made from crazy edges. He responded by pushing his head against the barrel of her gun, hard, twisting it just a little bit, just enough so she felt his force run from his skin, up through her gun, into her own body—

Rachel made her gun vanish under her hoodie. "Why are you here?"

"I'm on loan," he said again, the jagged red madness leaving his colors as quickly as it had appeared. A dark blue the color of a business suit replaced it, wrapping around him as he set himself to work. "I'm yours for the week. Maybe ten days, if things get complicated."

She blinked. "What?"

"I'm your new assistant, *Agent* Peng," he said, his false Southern drawl crawling all over her title. "I'm here to do the things you can't be caught doing." The man who used to be Jonathan Glazer leaned against the fence again, spreading arms and legs wide, turning himself into a large, convenient target. "Things are about to get bad for OACET, and he sent me here to help you."

"*He?* Who's *he?*"

Glazer didn't say anything, but a soft bluish-gray came over his colors, twined into the red affection and deep teal Rachel associated with close-knit families.

Oh goodie, she thought. *The psychopath loves his daddy.*

"I don't think he's willing to do me any favors," Rachel said. "Last time I saw him, I nearly killed him."

He cocked his head at her. "Telepathic," he said, a note of orange surprise working its way into his mood. "There are rumors about you, but we didn't believe them. Why are you telepathic?"

"I don't need to be psychic to read a one-note nutjob like you," she said.

The man nodded. "True."

He stepped away from the fence, and his hands went towards his pockets. Rachel didn't react; he wasn't carrying weapons.

Then again, he doesn't need to, not him, not a man who can escape from a police lockdown using nothing but office supplies.

A cheap cell phone came out of one pocket, its battery out of the other. The man who had been Glazer powered on the phone and held it up like a tiny trophy.

"Got it?" he asked, after he had given her a few moments to register the phone's unique signal.

"You think you're walking out of here?" she said, touching the bulge of her gun beneath her hoodie.

"Smile," he said, pointing towards the house behind him. "You're not on camera."

He was right—Rachel couldn't feel any of the relentless directed chatter in the digital ecosystem that meant she was being monitored. Instead, she noticed the dull red and the urine yellow of her neighbor and his brother, along with a handful of other core colors she didn't recognize. They were watching her and their good friend Not-Glazer from behind the dubious safety of a sliding glass door.

One of them was eating cake.

"You're crashing a birthday party as an alibi?" she asked. "Cute. Real cute."

"You shoot me as I walk away," he said, "and that'll go over great for OACET."

"Didn't you just tell me you're here to help us?"

"Yeah, I am," he said. "So don't fucking shoot me."

She weighed the situation: the witnesses; the time it would take for her to clear the fence versus the time it would take for her to run around the block; the complete lack of any police presence…

Now, *that* was strange. Rachel threw her scans out as far as she could go without giving herself a headache, and came back with nothing using police scanner frequencies except the occasional bored trucker.

"There're usually at least two or three patrol cars within a quarter-mile of my house," she said. "What did you do?"

"Nothing serious." The man who used to be Glazer shrugged. "Nothing that would let you justify shooting me."

"If you hurt a cop, Jonny-boy—"

"Don't get in the habit of calling me that," he said, as he turned to leave. "These days, I go by Marshall Wyatt."

"Marshall What—like hell you do!"

He popped the battery out of the phone, and waved as he walked away.

Rachel fixed his new face in her mind. High forehead, a receding hairline…very, very British. She cast back through her memories to the real Marshall Wyatt, a man long gone from her life.

Yes, it could be Wyatt's face with ten years of weathering stamped into his skin.

"New best friend, indeed," she muttered to herself.

She watched the mass murderer let himself through the neighbor's front gate, and then followed him through her scans as he strolled down the road. Unhurried, unworried, just another neighbor out for a walk on an early spring afternoon.

Rachel wanted to hurtle down the street and intercept him before he got out of range. She'd start by tackling him to the ground, and then see where the fight went from there. It'd be a great one, she was sure of that. No matter whose face he wore or whose name he hid behind, he carried himself with the confidence of a man who had spent much of his adult life in an elite military unit.

But…

"Let him go," she whispered, and forced herself to break off her scans. Jonathan Glazer—*No, he's Marshall Wyatt now*—disappeared from her expanded senses as completely as if he had never come close to her home.

Rachel found herself standing in her kitchen, checking the locks on her windows, and wasn't quite sure how she had gotten there.

"Stop," she said aloud. The sound of her voice echoed back at her, a hollow reminder that she was alone. "Stop," she said again, more quietly. "Get your shit together."

First things first. She reached out through her implant and activated her security system. Santino had installed it in spite of her protests, declaring that a cyborg should have complete control over her own home. She had laughed at him and gone to clean her gun, saying that anyone who was stupid enough to break into this cyborg's house would get what they deserved. Now she was grateful for the cameras that covered every corner of her property, the contact elements which assured her that every door was sealed. If Wyatt was going to murder her, it'd have to be with a sniper's rifle—

"Shut up, brain!" she growled.

The urge to run around the house and draw the blinds surged within her, and she had to talk herself down by running over the many, many ways that Wyatt could shoot her without needing to see her. Thermal imaging. Tracking her personal GPS. Using a goddamned rocket launcher.

Her hands unclenched.

She paused and took stock of her kitchen. Empty plastic bags that had held takeout food were thrown across the counters, and the glass contraption her erstwhile roommate used to brew coffee hadn't been cleaned in almost a week. Behind this light layer of filth was an explosion of paint which (she had been assured) was an offense to working eyeballs, the multicolored rainbow of acrylic swatches that Rachel had slopped across every available surface with her fingers, names and moods and other descriptive labels written next to each color in thick black Sharpie...

Her home. *Hers.* And no psychopath was going to drive her to panic when she stood in her own home.

"Okay," she said, and this time her voice didn't echo in the kitchen. "Okay. Wyatt's wrong. I'm not alone in this."

She cleared her mind, and concentrated on a dark gray the color of an expensive wool overcoat.

When that didn't get Jason's attention, she reached out through the link to locate him. Jason Atran was in his digital imaging suite at the D.C. Metropolitan Police Department's own Consolidated Forensics Laboratories. She kept the link light and conversational; when Jason opened his end of their connection, she made sure to hold back from spying on his work. Thus far, they had never needed to testify on the same case for the MPD, but if they kept moonlighting with the city's police, it was inevitable. As inevitable as a defense attorney accusing the two cyborgs of collusion or whatever straws were within grasping distance at the time. Better to play it safe, forever and always.

"Jason!"

"Busy."

She sent him the image of a man made from warm sandalwood, then painted the man in a red the color of blood.

Jason appeared beside her a moment later, shaped in the bright greens of OACET's digital projections. His avatar looked like a male French model, lean and haughty in a buttoned-down shirt and slacks, the perfect copy of Jason's physical self on the other side of the city.

"Didn't you hear me calling you?" she asked.

Jason's avatar rolled its eyes. "I saw a dark gray," he said. "I know that's supposed to be me, but you always call direct when you want to talk. I thought I was just on your mind."

She pushed the sandalwood towards him again.

Jason's avatar gestured for her to pull out a chair from the table for him. Avatars might be mirror images of their owners, but they were nothing but electrons dancing on a spectrum that other cyborgs could see and hear. Rachel pulled out two chairs, and sat, cowboy-style, her chin pillowed on her hands.

"He's back," she began.

Jason sat beside her, his face tight. "Tell me."

She did. It took a long time, much longer than if she had used the telepathic connection that cyborgs used as their primary means of communication, or even something as clunky as spoken English. Instead, she passed Jason the colors and images that defined her world.

Rachel was, according to all legal definitions, blind. Macular degeneration had reduced her own eyes to nothing but useless collections of cells and fluids. Her implant allowed her to mimic many of the regular processes of normal vision. When she used the right frequencies, she could read, or recognize strangers by their faces, but her expanded senses couldn't duplicate the exact mechanisms of the human eye.

The closest she could come to normal vision was to project her own digital avatar at head level, and watch the world through her duplicate's eyes. The effect was similar to watching a horror movie shot with a handheld camera, and tended to trigger her motion sickness something fierce. She used this overlapping perspective only when she was applying makeup, as lip liner needed extra attention or it tended to make a break for it.

She found it much easier to go without normal vision entirely. For Rachel, people had become human-shaped core colors. Over these was a surface layer of colors that shifted to match the person's mood. Core colors tended to be unique to each person, and unchanging. The conversational colors that covered these were in a continuous state of flux, and were reasonably universal among those who shared the same mood.

It had been hard enough for her to learn this new language of colors. Anger was red…but so were other emotions, like love and lust and pride. Teaching the nuances of the emotional spectrum to someone like Jason had been next to impossible. But they had realized that colors would allow them to talk without worrying that they'd be understood by the rest of the collective, and so Jason had forced himself to learn.

Despite nearly a year of practice, he wasn't very good at it.

She stuffed her impatience down the rabbit hole and showed him a human-shaped blob of sandalwood entering a threshold of Southwestern turquoise. That sandalwood came with a bloody red stripe which whipped around like a barb at the end of a leather tether, the red barb seeking to bury itself in flesh but finding no target. Then, it left the turquoise, shrinking until it vanished into the edges of their shared consciousness.

Jason's avatar closed its eyes. "I think I understood that," he said, and then pushed sandalwood back at her, along with the hue of yellow-orange that went along with questions and curiosity.

Rachel felt confident enough that they could talk through the rest, as long as they hid the names behind the colors.

"He says that something nasty is about to happen," she told him.

Jason replied by showing her the vivid chartreuse green that OACET had claimed as their official color, and Rachel nodded.

"How does he know?" Jason asked. "Is he setting something up, like last time?"

"I didn't get that impression," she said. "More like he knows what's coming and he's here to help keep us from getting hit."

The digital man sitting across from her shook his head. "He's got to know you're gunning for him. Coming here puts him at risk. If you arrest him—"

"—I finally put things right," she finished.

Secrets were next to impossible to keep within a hivemind. While she knew that some of the other cyborgs had secrets of their own, Rachel was absolutely sure that she and Jason shared the biggest one between them: Rachel had helped the man who used to be Jonathan Glazer escape from police custody.

It had been a matter of cost versus benefit. He would have escaped on his own, and probably would have killed a whole lot of people on his way out the door. In exchange for her help, he had provided OACET with leverage over a prominent politician, and had left everyone in the MPD untouched.

Rephrase: relatively untouched. He had given Jason a

concussion, and several of her coworkers would always carry the scars from where they had come into contact with flashbang grenades. It could have been much, much worse.

Jason knew. And Jason thought she had made the right choice.

If the others in OACET found out…

Well. She was sure that most of them would share Jason's opinion. But they still would hold her accountable. Catching the man with the sandalwood core had been on Rachel's to-do list for nearly two years. She needed to put things *right*.

"But why?" Jason asked. "Why risk it?"

"He said that he was sent by—" She sent him another image of a human-shaped blob: this one was slightly stooped and squishy when contrasted against the one the color of sandalwood, and drawn from a gentle bluish-gray.

Jason's green fingers knitted together in a facsimile of fidgeting. "He doesn't owe you any favors," he said after a few moments. "In fact…"

She nodded. "I think they're—"

That's as far as she got before Josh Glassman appeared beside them.

Rachel reacted on instinct. She seized an empty beer bottle from the pile of trash on the table, and swung it at the intruder's skull. It was only when the bottle passed through Josh's head that Rachel realized she had overreacted: not only had she failed to recognize her friend's digital avatar, she had greatly misjudged the force needed to club a skull with a bottle, and she ended up face-down on the kitchen floor.

Josh didn't notice. "Penguin," he said to Rachel, his voice tight. Then his avatar's eyes slid to the side, and he spotted Jason. "Good, good. I was going to track you down after talking to Rachel. You both need to get down to the Batcave, right now."

Rachel took a breath, and let herself feel Josh's tension, tight and hot, as he sat in OACET's downtown headquarters a couple of miles to the south. She had no idea how Josh had found out about Glazer (*Wyatt!*), but she picked herself up off of the floor and fell into parade rest, readying herself for the reprimand.

"We can explain—" Jason began, but Josh cut him off with a hard wave of his hand.

"Hope has been kidnapped," he said.

And, before Rachel could burst out laughing, he added, "Avery, too."

THREE

The Office of Adaptive and Complementary Enhancement Technologies finally had a permanent office. The old postal hub near the Judiciary Square Metro Station had been fully gutted and repurposed for the cyborgs. Rachel thought it was a nice enough place, and much easier to reach than the Agents' old headquarters out by the Potomac River. But it was a long run from her house to the center of Washington, D.C., and her subconscious took it as an opportunity to act the asshole again.

They hate you.

Rachel pushed on and tried to focus on her feet, the feel of the rough layers of asphalt layered over concrete layered over gravel cutting through the cold earth beneath her...

They hate you. You've been out for nearly three years, and they still hate you. You're nothing but machines to them. They won't be happy until you submit. Become tools. Like they planned.

"Shut up," she said through gritted teeth.

You thought you could get used to this? You thought you could have a life? Even if you did, they'd still be there, in the shadows, waiting for you to slip up, to think you were safe, to steal your children—

"Shut up *shut up **shut up!***"

She threw herself into an all-out sprint, but her subconscious had sunk its teeth into her fears and was shaking them apart.

The worst day of her life had been the one when she had woken up with second- and third-degree sunburns across most of her body, a pair of dying eyeballs, and an endless waking dream of meetings and rote tasks as her only memories of her mid-twenties. That was until today, when her niece had been taken—No. Had been *stolen*. And with her went the peace of mind they had tried to shape around themselves. Even if Avery toddled through the front door of OACET headquarters right now, right this second, before anything worse could happen to her, nothing would ever be the same again.

They hate you.

Well, maybe they were right to hate her, to hate all of OACET. Or at least not wholly wrong.

It had been nearly two years since three hundred and fifty cyborgs had told the world that the U.S. government had discovered a way to control all networked machines, and that these controllers happened to walk and talk and celebrate birthdays.

Nearly seven years since Rachel had a teeny-tiny quantum organic computer chip implanted in her parietal lobe.

Nearly eight years since a certain U.S. Senator had offered her a place in a new federal program that would be, in his words, "revolutionary."

Her footsteps sounded like lost moments.

They hate you.

I know, she assured herself. *I know.*

The sounds of heavy traffic and random car horns joined her footsteps as she crossed into the city. Around her, pedestrians and drivers turned an uncertain orange at the sight of the tall Chinese woman running at full speed in dirty jeans and work boots.

Jason caught up with her after she crossed into Dupont Circle. He popped the locks on the passenger-side door of his Mustang, and she swung herself inside as the traffic lights turned green.

Neither of them spoke until they pulled into OACET's private parking garage. Jason killed the motor. He slumped over the steering wheel, his shoulders rounding in on themselves.

She reached out and touched his hand. Skin contact between Agents deepened a link, bringing the organic aspect of those computers in their heads more fully online. The emotions she felt at the periphery of their conversation—*panic, loss, fear,* **hate!**—crossed over and joined hers.

"I'll say this once," he said quietly. "If he—" Here, Jason flashed an image of a human figure made of sandalwood. "—is responsible for taking Avery, I'll kill him myself."

"You won't have to," she said, as she wrestled their shared bloodlust under control and shoved positive emotions—*calm, control, reason*—across their link until they both believed it. "He's my responsibility."

They left the quiet of the parking garage and walked the half-block to the front entrance of the Batcave.

It was a lovely building. It had started out as a beautiful piece of neoclassical architecture, with thick columns and thin black windows spaced out beneath ornamental friezes. Mare Murphy, OACET's Agent in charge of administerial tasks, had made sure the repairs had been performed by restoration experts, and the sandstone veneer of the old post office shone a light gray in the light of the Sunday afternoon. The front doors were huge metal monsters covered in a bas-relief mural of Roman gods, and wore their age well. Bronze rings the size of Rachel's head served as knobs, with the metal of the right-hand ring polished to golden and rubbed thin beneath a million different hands.

She paused as she picked up the ring. Jason laid his hand over hers, and they steadied each other before they opened the door on its well-oiled hinges.

The Batcave was cold, the heat turned down to save on energy over the weekend. She sent her scans into the large central lobby to take stock of what the others had done with the place. Her own office was over at the MPD's First District Station, and she only dropped by OACET's headquarters when her physical presence was required. Normally, she'd delight in the small changes around her, signs that the other Agents were adapting their new headquarters to their needs. Today, she moved straight through the entrance hall, past the gymnastics spring floor that had been installed in the lobby (*When did we get a spring floor?* ***Why*** *did we get a spring floor?*), and up the stairs that led to Patrick Mulcahy's office.

An FBI agent at the front reception desk checked their

badges. Jason glanced around, his colors moving towards grays.

"Nobody's here," he said aloud.

His comment earned him a pointed glare from the man from the FBI, but Jason was right. The building seemed empty. Even on Sundays, there was always a skeleton crew of cyborgs roaming the halls, tugging on the digital aether of the collective's link. Now, the alarm systems and WiFi signals of the building twitched and moved around them without guidance.

Rachel reached out through her implant to tweak a perimeter alert system and make sure it was active; it slapped her mind away, focused on its task.

Good, she thought. There was no better security system in the world than the one that OACET had designed for themselves. Even without supervision from the security teams, it was still humming along, still protecting itself from intrusion.

The Agents didn't take chances.

No, that's wrong, that's so wrong, Avery's gone, we didn't do ***enough***—

Jason placed a hand on her shoulder, and the two of them moved to where the minds in the building came together. A cluster of core colors had gathered in a conference room on the second floor, surrounded by electronic fields that burst into life as unfamiliar equipment came online. Rachel didn't recognize many of those colors. She assumed they belonged to the FBI: kidnapping was a federal crime, and OACET wasn't going to shoulder the responsibility of getting Hope and Avery back.

Shouldn't, she corrected herself, as she finally spotted the cerulean blue that was Patrick Mulcahy. *We **shouldn't** be the ones who try to get Hope and Avery back.*

She wasn't sure how that was going to play out—the Cyborg King had taken control of the Batcave.

The head of OACET was a quiet flurry of commands. Under his direction, the FBI agents were setting up shop. They bustled about: here, they set up their own computers; there, they linked the FBI's computers into OACET's own systems. Rachel watched as Mulcahy reached over and yanked a power cord on an anonymous piece of machinery, handing it back to its owner with a strong warning about making sure the equipment stayed out of OACET's private servers.

Over by the windows was a woman with a core of blue slate. She radiated deep red sorrow as she answered questions from a stranger in a suit. A gigantic man with a core of forest green stood behind her, his hands resting on her shoulders, carrying his own share of misery.

A trace of wooly charcoal and Southwestern turquoise appeared in his conversational colors: Mako Hill had noticed their arrival. He gave his wife's shoulders a gentle squeeze, and came over to meet them.

"Guys…" he began, his voice a heavy rumble, his fingers twisting aimlessly as he tried to find the words.

Rachel hugged him.

Mako was the largest man she had ever met; her head barely came up to his sternum. She wrapped her arms around him and hugged him as hard as she could, letting him go only when she felt the dampness against her forehead and realized he was crying.

She and Jason steered the grieving father out of the conference room. Mulcahy's office was across the hall, and Rachel popped the digital lock so the two of them could move Mako to a nearby couch. He dropped, sobbing, onto the overstuffed leather, Rachel and Jason to either side of him. They covered his hands with their own. The force of his anguish was unreal: the two of them might love Avery as their niece, but their own concern was nothing in comparison to what a parent experienced when a child was missing.

Not missing, she reminded herself. *Stolen.*

There was no such thing as a happy ending in a kidnapping. Even if the victims were rescued or returned unharmed, there would always be the knowledge that it had happened, and the fear that it might happen again. Rachel and Jason could offer nothing except their presence, holding Mako with the shared knowledge that he was not alone in this. It was enough, and it wasn't, and he was angry and grateful to them, all at once.

No, kidnappings didn't have happy endings, but if you were lucky, you found peace.

When he had calmed down enough to pass through the worst of his sorrow, Rachel asked him: "What do we know?"

"Multiple men," Mako said. His voice hitched, and he unconsciously fell back into the cyborgs' version of telepathy as Jason passed him a box of tissues. *"The security cameras in the garage were disabled. Carlota began recording once she realized what was going on, so we've got the leader's face on file."*

"On it," Jason said. He snapped his side of their three-way link and left the room.

"He's got this," Rachel assured Mako. "Nobody's better with digital images than Jason. If Carlota got anything useful on tape, he'll pry it out."

"They had it all planned, Penguin," Mako said. She tugged on his shirt until he allowed himself to lean against her. He was all heavy muscle, and it was somewhat similar to comforting a rockslide. *"They wanted Hope, but they... They took my daughter! She's **nothing** to them!"*

She began rubbing her friend's back as his fury rose, pushing calm, control across their link as hard as she dared. The last thing they needed was a three-hundred-pound, six-foot-eight-inch weightlifter on a rampage.

"Easy," she told him. "Easy. They took Avery because they knew it was the only way to control Hope. Hope might have been the target, but Avery's wellbeing is their priority. If anything happens to Avery, Hope will bring Hell itself down on them."

Mako's rage ebbed as she got through to him. Hope Blackwell was violence incarnate. The woman was a psychological hot mess, held together by decades of rigorous training in judo and a massive daily dose of Adderall. And, while not public knowledge, Hope was also one of the handful of normals able to perceive the Agents' digital projections. Abducting Hope was stupid on so many levels that—

Well. If the kidnappers were willing to risk abducting Patrick Mulcahy's wife and his oldest godchild, Rachel was sure they must have planned for the fallout.

The door opened, and the head of OACET walked into his office.

Mulcahy moved like a boxer before a match, tight with unspent energy and ready for the fight. Rachel had turned off the emotional spectrum so Mako's heartbreak and fury didn't overwhelm her senses. She flipped it on again to read Mulcahy, expecting to find the same mournful reds worn by Carlota and Mako. Instead, she saw his core of deep cerulean blue, and... nothing else.

Nothing. No emotions at all. No red-white blur of sadness and shock, none of the deep blue of professional suits to go along with his negotiations with the FBI. Not even the uncertain yellows of hidden fear.

Her confusion must have jumped across her link with Mako, as the big man sat up. "What's happened?" he asked.

"Nothing new," Mulcahy replied. "Could you step out of the room? I need to speak to Rachel."

Shit, she thought to herself.

Mako caught it, a small smudge of curious yellow appearing in his conversational colors.

"It's not about the kidnapping," she assured him. *"I'm just going to get my ass handed to me before he puts me to work finding your daughter."*

He nodded, not convinced but too preoccupied to care, and left without a word.

Mulcahy waited, the two of them watching through the wall as Mako walked down the long corridor to the nearest bathroom. Rachel counted her heartbeats—*ten, eleven, twelve*—before Mulcahy turned towards her.

His shields went up. Rachel blinked: Mulcahy had taught her the trick of twisting electromagnetic fields around them to block out all electronic surveillance, but she had never seen him use it in the Batcave. OACET's new headquarters was, by design, a private sanctuary, and no Agent would dream of spying on Mulcahy while he was in his own office.

This was going to *hurt*.

She sighed and stood, falling into her reliable Army habit of standing at parade rest, and waited for him to burn her to ash.

"Have you called Santino?" he asked.

Rachel shook her head. "I didn't know how far you wanted this to go, but he's spending most of his time at Zia's," she replied. "If she knows—"

"She doesn't," he said. "We're trying to keep this as quiet as possible. We've got maybe an hour left before the media realizes the abductions are connected to OACET." He was silent for a long moment before adding, "Hope and Avery weren't the only two who were kidnapped."

Rachel fell out of parade rest at the news. "Who—"

"Nobody else associated with OACET," he assured her. "It seems as though they grabbed another dozen people at gunpoint as they made their getaway."

"Hostages?" she guessed, and when Mulcahy nodded, she nearly gasped in relief as she realized she had been stupidly selfish, that he still didn't know about Wyatt, that he needed her to get his wife and godchild back... That she needed to pull her head out of her butt and concentrate on the bigger picture. She slumped down on the couch and raked her fingers through her short hair to hide her face. "That's not good," she said. "Hope and Avery might not be expendable, but random strangers? They could kill them, use them as armor or decoys, anything."

"That's what the FBI thinks," he said.

"Do we have any suspects?" she asked.

He shook his head. "Nobody," he replied. "The only current threat on OACET radar is the China faction."

The China faction... Possible. Slim, but possible. Last week's security briefing had contained a credible rumor that a paramilitary organization in China had begun work on its own version of the cyborgs' implants.

Which made nothing but sense. Rachel may have used her

implant as a substitute for her eyesight, but it had been sold to Congress as a means of networking all branches of the U.S. government, with a wink and a nod to its use in espionage. By this stage of the geopolitical game, it was widely presumed that other intelligence agencies were playing catchup to OACET, with Israel and China leading the pack.

But the data that had led to the development of the implant was gone, in no small part due to Rachel's own actions. She had already gotten a certain U.S. Senator removed from office because of what he had done to OACET, and she had no intention of stopping with him. Those who had been responsible for those five lost years needed to pay.

Is this a way for the Chinese to get their hands on— No, she decided. *Just no.* China might be trying to build their own version of OACET, but there were better ways to get information than by stealing Mulcahy's wife.

"You want me to get my team together and start doing what we can?" she asked.

"Yes," he said, his face turned towards the conference room across the hall. "The FBI is excellent, but I'm not taking chances."

"What are my limits?" she asked.

Usually he'd raise an eyebrow at that, an implied *You should have learned this by now, Rachel, really,* and follow it up with a martini-dry joke. Today, all he did was say, "When this hits the media, everything we do will be dissected. Play it like you already know you'll be on the witness stand."

"Better than at the defendant's table," she said, the slightest push.

Mulcahy ignored her; she shivered at that, glad they weren't sharing a link tight enough for him to feel it.

"Call Phil, too," he said. "I'm pulling him off the MPD's Bomb Unit and assigning him to you. We're going to need everyone you've trained on this."

"The MPD's not going to be happy," she said. She had taught Phil all she could about deep scans and how to see through walls, and the MPD had snatched him up and assigned him to their bomb squad. With Phil on their team, injuries and other unsavory incidents had fallen to nearly zero. The MPD wouldn't want to go back to their old methods, no matter how temporary. "Hell, I don't know if I have the jurisdiction to pull my guys and have them run an OACET case."

"You know you do," he replied.

"No. No way," Rachel said. "I'm not invoking the charter unless I absolutely have to."

"Agreed. Ask first," Mulcahy said, "but get it done."

She nodded.

A blur of yellow-white energy came over his surface colors. Not an emotion, not exactly, but it showed Mulcahy's attention had shifted from her to something unseen. It was gone as quickly as it had come—he had dealt with it and moved on—but was the only color she had observed in him, so she chased it down.

"What happened?"

"The FBI turned on another piece of equipment," he said. "Every time they boot up something new, it tries to get onto our network. I've been running security all morning."

And managing personnel, and setting up a response plan, and freaking out about your wife and godchild... She checked his colors again to be sure; there was still nothing resembling anger or concern. Or fear. Or any emotion at all.

Or not.

"You doing okay?" she asked him.

They weren't close, her and her boss, but they were in each other's minds often enough that she knew what his reaction should have been. There should have been a wave of red anger at the question, held in check by his professional blues; anger at those who had stolen his wife and godchild, anger at her for asking such a stupid question...

Nothing.

"As well as can be expected," he replied, and turned to rifle through the stack of papers on his desk.

Dismissed.

"Do I salute you or smack you?" she asked.

"Good luck, Rachel," he said as he flipped through a notepad. "Work fast."

She paused. What would happen if she really did smack him, just haul off and crack him across that steel jaw—

Mulcahy looked up from the papers and stared at her.

"Right," she snapped, and went to look for Josh.

He had to be nearby. OACET's second-in-command handled their major media appearances. Something like this would require his full attention. But...

She couldn't find him.

All Agents had their own GPS, and they kept these open and available unless they wanted privacy from the collective. When Josh wasn't on duty, he tended to play games with his GPS, setting it to rotate through multiple locations. Finding him became a game of hide-and-seek, when you knew he was within spitting distance but spitting distance could be anywhere from the local coffee shop to OACET's office supply closet.

You didn't want to barge in on Josh when he was in the supply closet. Not unless you wanted to join in on whatever— or whoever—he was doing.

Rachel wasn't in the mood for such shenanigans, and she was willing to bet that Josh wasn't, either. She sat down at the top of the stairs and scanned the building from roof to foundation, looking for the person with a core color the blue of fresh tattoos.

She found him two floors down in the War Room, surrounded by the glowing green avatars of other Agents. Rachel had no trouble picking out the details of those avatars: she recognized Ami and the two other members of OACET's internal team of wetworks and demolition specialists. Mulcahy didn't allow his former assassins to practice their old trade, but the Cuddly Hippos were more than just mindless killers. If stealth and information gathering was required, the Hippos would fit the bill.

Rachel went downstairs, tossing polite words back and forth with the personnel from the FBI she met along the way. *Not right,* her subconscious nagged, *not right at all, get them out of here, they don't belong.*

She told herself to shut up, that there was a huge difference between a crumbling mansion on the Potomac and a state-of-the-art government facility in downtown D.C., and that the FBI were only here to help.

Her subconscious rolled over and went back to sleep, muttering to itself.

When she reached the basement, she found the door to the War Room had been gaily painted in ponies.

Not horses. Ponies. Cartoon ponies with large eyes, and rendered in colors that spoke to the back of her brain. She took a moment to absorb this cartoonish mutiny against federal regulations before she knocked; the ponies weren't photorealistic (thank goodness) but they had been painted by an expert hand, and appeared to be sliding down an iridescent rainbow into a sun-drenched pond.

On the other side of the ponies, Josh's surface colors flickered. A strong thread of Southwestern turquoise appeared, and this chased away the core colors of the Hippos. As Rachel watched through the wall, Josh said something to the Hippos, and the three avatars winked out of the air.

"Come in." Josh's mental voice wasn't exactly weary, but it did carry with it the sense of things getting much worse before they got better.

"What's up with the door?" she asked.

"Shawn," he replied. "He said he wanted to do something quick and fun."

As she entered the room, he moved to retrieve a file from one of the ubiquitous filing cabinets that lined nearly every vacant space in OACET's new headquarters. In this post-Agent age, paper trails had taken on new importance; the War Room had been named for its files, most of which held the names and last known locations of those whom OACET considered viable threats to their organization.

Rachel threw a scan through the filing cabinets on the west

side of the War Room, double-checking the hidden safe secreted away in the wall behind them. It was a smallish safe, about the size required to store a decent collection of shotguns. That safe held the really dangerous files, the ones that had the names of senators and congresspersons and the other powerful folks who were responsible for OACET's creation. Not the sanitized story that had been sold to Congress in exchange for funding. That story was a happy tale of government agencies coming together to work for the Greater Good, an alignment of young professionals from different federal agencies to smooth out the problems inherent in complex bureaucratic systems.

No. The files had nothing to do with that story.

In the real story, the one hidden in those dangerous files, networking the Agents had only been the first step in building America's new cyborg army. The next step had been five years of intense mental conditioning. Brainwashing, really, a thorough deconstruction of personal autonomy. The technology which allowed them to access any networked machine was bioorganic in nature, and needed a human host to function. The politicians, though, didn't need those human hosts. No, they didn't need them at all. Those who were involved in this part of the plan didn't want cyborgs; they wanted robots in human bodies, ready to act and react as directed. So they had planned that the five hundred young people who received the cybernetic implant would be broken down, slowly, until nothing was left but the willingness to follow orders.

It hadn't worked out that way.

Rachel knew she could never repay Mulcahy and Hope Blackwell for what they had done to break the surviving Agents free. If it hadn't been for them, she would still be in California, living alone in a cold apartment, blind from staring up at the sun for *days*—

Nope.

Rachel scanned the edges of the safe again, making sure that it was invisible to any members of the FBI who might need to run a security sweep. She was one of the few Agents who knew Mulcahy and Josh had copies of those files somewhere else, backups kept in yet another secure location that wasn't on government property in case the worst happened, but they had never told her where and she hoped she'd never need to learn.

Josh's conversational colors moved in and out in varying shades of orange as he searched through the files. She flipped frequencies to look at him, and found he was fairly neat and tidy: his too-long-for-government-work dark brown hair was neatly combed, and his clothing looked less rumpled than usual.

"You okay?" she asked. His colors glazed over with orange-red irritation, so she quickly added, "You're too organized."

He glanced up at her, and she pantomimed running her hands through her hair.

"Shit," he said. He used his hip to slam the filing cabinet drawer closed, and began to finger-comb his hair so it fell across his eyes. "Thanks. I've got to go on camera soon."

"Your clothes, too," she said.

"Yeah, this suit came straight from the cleaners. I didn't expect to work today," he replied, as he stripped off his pants and handed them to her. "Here. Mess these up a little."

Rachel wadded his pants into a tight ball and sat on them. Her friend did the same with his suit coat.

They faced each other across the War Room's small table, and she gave him an anemic smile.

Josh knew her too well. "What?"

"I think—" That sickening sensation in her stomach rolled into the back of her throat, and she paused to bite down on it. "I think I've got another problem for you."

"It's the right day for it," he muttered, as his digital barrier sprang into place. "Shoot."

Josh's shield differed from hers or Mulcahy's. Where Rachel took strands of frequencies and wove them into shining chainmail, and Mulcahy forged them into an impenetrable fortress, Josh's shield looked like a glowing plate of spaghetti. His barrier contorted and writhed, a mess of frequencies that seemed to have no purpose other than to clutter up the EMF.

Except anything that touched this mess got tangled up within it.

It had taken a few light pokings before Rachel had realize that Josh's barrier was as intentionally sloppy as the rest of him. When he was under his shield, any targeted contact was bundled up and moved aside, its information registered so Josh could follow it back to its source at his leisure. Josh was as safe as she was behind her own shield, and had the additional benefit of trapping the signal of anyone stupid enough to snoop on him.

She felt him reach out and tug on the ends of a few loose frequencies, pushing them into an order that must have made sense to him. "There we go," he said. "I don't like how this place is crawling with the FBI. Better safe than sorry. What's on your mind?"

Rachel wanted to tell him—she started to tell him!—but her mouth sidestepped the inevitable one last time by moving to the newest problem on her list. "What's wrong with Mulcahy?"

Josh's colors shot towards an anxious orange. "What do you mean?"

She thought about the best way to describe what she meant and came up empty. There was no good way to describe the lack of Mulcahy within Mulcahy. Vagueness would have to do.

"He's *here*," she said, tapping her head, and then laid her hands across her heart. "But he's not all *here*."

Blue relief came over him. "Christ, Rachel, you see too much," he said. "Leave this one alone."

"Josh—"

"This is how he's getting through it," he said. "He's fine."

They weren't sharing a link, but her reaction to the dimples in his conversational colors—*Liar!*—was so strong that it jumped between them.

"He'll be fine," Josh amended. "Once he's done what he's got to do. Leave it alone.

"Please," he added. "This'll just waste time we don't have."

It wasn't as clear a dismissal as the one she had received from Mulcahy, but coming from Josh, he might as well have taken her arm and escorted her to the door. She told herself to stand, and couldn't.

He moved to place a hand over hers; she yanked her own hand away before he could touch her. Skin contact would be the end of any secrets. *Jason,* she reminded herself. *There's Jason.*

He closed his eyes as the sorrow and stress strengthened within his colors. "Tell me," he said, softly.

She sighed, and did.

Rachel told him nearly everything, all about Glazer—now Marshall Wyatt—and helping him escape, about what had happened in the police station. About the psychopath who had practically turned up on her doorstep and had offered to do the things she couldn't. About how this might not be just a kidnapping, not if he was involved.

She let the words run together, fast and sometimes in the wrong order, and even though she couldn't help but think about Jason, she managed to keep his wooly gray fixed in her mind. *Gray, gray, gray, gray...*

Never his name.

Through it all, Josh kept his fists pressed hard against his temples, his colors frozen and yellow-gray from shock and sickly horror. "You realize..." he began.

"What I've done? Oh, yes. Absolutely."

"No." He shook his head, his brown hair sliding over his knuckles. "This is... This goes way beyond..."

He stopped. She counted along with him—*ten, nine, eight, seven*...the simple grounding technique that all Agents used to keep themselves in the here and now—and he tried again when his colors finally unwound themselves from their tangled knots. "I knew the police station had been booby-trapped, but you think they did that just to facilitate an escape?"

"Yeah."

"That's disturbing," he said. He stood up, and swung his suit coat over his shoulders. "Almost epically disturbing. How long had they been planning for Glazer to be captured?"

Rachel shrugged as she handed him his pants. "Best I can tell, as soon as they learned I was to start working at First District Station. The building renovations were mostly finished by the time I was finally cleared to work."

"Right. So, how'd they learn you'd start working there?"

She blinked.

"They didn't learn it from us," he continued. "Our internal security is too good. Nobody has ever been able to break into our systems and snoop around, and they've tried. Hard."

She began to run the options around in her head. The idea of a spy within OACET wasn't even a consideration, and she trusted Josh's knowledge of their digital security. Two options emerged, neither of them all that pleasant.

"Someone on the MPD," she said. "Or someone....a private party with connections to Congress."

"Let's consider the MPD option first," he said, as he ran his fingers along the surface of the nearest filing cabinet. There wasn't much dust, but he smudged what he could find along the collar of his white dress shirt. "Why would they think to have connections at the MPD on the off-chance that they could get a shot at OACET? That's bullshit. That's too much ground to cover for any two people, no matter how smart they are."

"Could have been coincidence," she said. "Somebody from the MPD said something to someone, and it got back to Wyatt."

"Except now he's back," Josh said. "The moment before things got bad."

Now it was Rachel who was rubbing her temples. "Oh shit," she muttered. "Yeah, that's definitely not coincidence. Shit shit *shit*."

His hands slammed down on the table beside her. "Find his source," Josh said, his colors picking up in a red whirlwind. "Your *only* job is to learn who's feeding him information. Because there's a huge difference between your part-time job and this kidnapping, and if the information on both of those came from the same place—"

"—then the kidnapping was protected information," she finished. "He only found out about it after enough people got involved to create a leak."

He opened a link, and the sensation of close-kept terror crashed into her. *"And if it's protected information, we're screwed."*

Rachel nodded. The idea of protected information made her feel sick. Bad enough that Avery was taken; worse—unimaginably worse—if she had been taken as part of a professional operation.

She pushed back against their link until it broke. "Say this is protected info. Who do we want running it, a government op or private party?"

"Either comes with its own special brand of fuckery," Josh said, electric blue energies running across his conversational colors. "Did Wyatt ever say that he knew what was about to happen? Did he even hint at kidnapping?"

"No." She shook her head. "Just that something bad was about to go down."

Josh began pacing the length of the War Room. "So he's probably not in the loop," he said. "Not directly. He probably just got word of mobilization when whoever's in charge hit the switch and the plan went into action."

"Could be something simple," she said. "Maybe he's monitoring email, phone calls… Has an active keyword search, like the NSA."

"That wouldn't be enough reason to go to the effort of booby-trapping a police station," Josh said. "It'd have to be a sure thing. You've got to find his source."

"Right," she said, and stood to leave. She kept herself closed tight, and tried to crush her relief into a tiny ball to be played with at a later time.

Josh placed a hand on her shoulder, high enough so his skin brushed against hers as he opened a link. *"Not so fast,"* he said, anger flooding her mind.

Busted.

"Yeah," Josh agreed. "You are. There's going to be a hell of a reckoning for what you did. But, unlike Mulcahy, I have to prioritize. Holding you accountable for something two years gone is on the bottom of my list."

"Listen—" Rachel began aloud, and then gave up on trying to keep him out of her head. She knocked his hand off of her shoulder and turned to face him. *"You weren't there. Mulcahy had just finished telling me that Hanlon was pushing the Senate to get us forcibly impressed into military units! He told me to buy him time to keep Hanlon off of us. I did my job, Josh!"*

He stared at her, weighing her Southwestern turquoise against OACET green, a slip of sandalwood moving through these dominant colors as he tried to figure out where it should fit.

"Mulcahy told you to buy time, not blow up a police station and let a murderer go free," he replied. *"If you had gotten caught, that would have been the end of us. Not might—**would**."*

She wanted to hit him. She wanted to cry.

She settled on nodding.

"It's in the past," he said. *"We got lucky. Things turned out for the best—that was our first big break, and you made it happen. But that was a gamble you shouldn't have taken."*

Rachel couldn't find the right words to sum up impossible choices. What she could do was grab his hands with her own, and shove every ounce of those moments into his head. All of her fear, her panic… Forcing him to relive those moments when she knew that Wyatt *would* escape, and that he *would* commit a whole boatload of murder on his way out, and she was the only one who *might* be able to mitigate that damage.

No, not might. *Would.*

"Fuck gambling," she said, as she felt her friend's mind squirm beneath the onslaught. *"I made a bad call, but the alternatives were worse. I did what I had to do. I've gone over the options a million times, and I'd do it again.*

"And," she added, as she gave him the image of Wyatt on the other side of a fence. A psychotic, a killer…and there to help. *"Whatever else he is, Wyatt helped us once before. He's here to*

help us now—he wasn't lying, Josh! Do you want me to turn him away, or turn him in, before we know what comes next?"

She gasped as he pulled her into a hug. Fear, both remembered and all too recent, tried to come inside, and they held each other to keep it at bay.

"No, you're right," Josh said, all but whispering into her hair. "You're absolutely right. They took one of our children, Penguin! Do whatever it takes to get her back."

FOUR

Detective Matt Hill was waiting.

For who or what, Rachel couldn't tell. She was on her way upstairs to find Jason when she caught a glimpse of his forest green core standing just inside those huge bronze front doors. She raced down the stairs again to find him staring down at the FBI agent running security. The FBI agent was on her com, chattering nervously about needing clearance for a Metropolitan Police detective who wasn't saying much but also wasn't leaving…

"Hey, Hill," Rachel said, as she circled around the FBI agent. "Guess you heard. I'm so sorry."

He cocked an eyebrow, and his conversational colors moved towards curious yellows.

Rachel's own eyes widened. "Oh shit," she hissed, and grabbed him by his arm to haul him aside.

He humored her: she didn't have much chance of manhandling any member of the Hill clan. Matt Hill might have been nowhere near as broad as Mako, but he was just as tall and nearly as solid. She maneuvered him around the protesting FBI agent and deposited him in a nearby chair. "Okay," she said, as she stood over him. "Who called you down here? Your cousin?"

Hill's colors moved towards Mulcahy's cerulean blues.

He was here officially, then. Good.

"Gotcha," she said. "Promise you won't freak out?"

"Peng—"

"Promise me!" Hill was standing again, the reds of alarm and panic beginning to surface. She pushed an index finger against his sternum until he returned to the chair. "Avery's been abducted."

His colors froze in place, white shock bursting within them.

"No."

"They took her and Hope Blackwell. Mulcahy's told me to get our team together and start turning over rocks. *Now*. I bet the others are—"

One of the bronze doors opened with a bang. Raul Santino, his cobalt blue core nearly lost beneath layers of orange and red, blinked a few times to accustom his eyes to the dim light of OACET headquarters. Something in his jacket pocket began to beep, and he peered into the gloom. "Rachel?!"

"Here," she called out to her partner.

Santino sprinted over to her and Hill, nearly knocking the FBI agent down on his way. The beeping grew louder; Rachel reached out to his phone and told it to shut the hell up, and the proximity alarm cut out mid-tone. It was replaced by the squeak of sneaker rubber on polished stone, followed by the semi-awkward half-hug shared by troubled men.

"Where's Zia?" Rachel asked.

Santino and Hill broke apart. "I told her to stay at home," Santino said, concerned reds and worried yellows growing more intense as he thought of his girlfriend. "It's—"

"Perfect," Rachel cut in. After her partner had fortified her own security system, he had then all but turned Zia's house into a castle. Surrounded by a moat of lava. With an aerial defense grid of drones, and starving tigers roaming the grounds. "Best place for her. What do you know?"

"Nothing," he said. "There are rumors that—"

Hill put a hand on Santino's shoulder.

"Okay." Rachel put both of hers up in surrender. "Hill just now found out about Avery. Let me run through what I know."

It took her all of a minute. By the end, Santino had gone pale and Hill…

Hill was fiery, fiercely red.

Shit.

"Hey," Rachel said, "don't go getting any ideas."

He glared down at her, the barbed tips of his anger beginning to point towards her.

"Be pissed at me all you want," she told him. "Better that than a cop going off like some half-cocked bullshit action hero. Or do you think you can rescue your cousin's kid all by your lonesome self?"

Hill's fists clenched and unclenched a couple of times; his reds snapped and tangled with the blue of a police uniform. The blue won.

"Thanks," she said.

"Zockinski?" Hill asked.

Good question. Rachel reached out to trace the cell signal of the fourth member of their small team. Detective Jacob Zockinski was halfway across town, his signal immersed within others she recognized, as well as hundreds she didn't. Next to Zockinski's signal was the silver-bright pulse of Phil Netz.

"He's already at the parking garage where Hope and Avery got ganked," she said. "Phil's with him.

Washington D.C. being what it was, it took them nearly thirty minutes to travel ten miles, and that was with the police strobe light affixed to the top of Santino's tiny hybrid.

None of them spoke, but Hill's reds looked like the caldera of a volcano.

When they finally reached the garage, they found it crawling with cops. The majority were FBI, but a few other federal agencies and the local MPD had a strong presence. Enough of them knew the team from First District Station well enough to let them on the scene.

Rachel ignored the flashes of OACET green that popped up as she walked through the checkpoints, Santino and Hill following close behind. Those flashes of green were usually a warning to her, and anyone with OACET in their thoughts received her full attention. Today, considering the victims, the green was to be expected.

She led the men straight through the crowd, to the colors of autumn orange and bright silverlight that stood together on the edge of the active zone.

The source of the silverlight was Phil Netz. Barely a hand's width taller than Rachel, the other Agent was pulsing with energy. As soon as she was close enough, he reached out to shake her hand. As they touched, his mood spilled into her: nervous, anxious...*eager*. Ready to fight.

Her adrenaline rose in response. The sounds of the crowd clarified, the edges of their colors crisp and sharp. The mingled scents from all of those people slammed into her like a sledgehammer, body odors and shampoo and food and a hundred other smells that went along with cars and cities.

She stepped away from Phil, reminding herself she couldn't start punching strangers for the hell of it.

"News?" Santino asked.

Jacob Zockinski was just over forty, broad and brooding, with hair beginning to go to salt-and-pepper at the temples and a razor for a jawline. "Nothing to go on," he said. "The FBI's on Forensics. MPD's out patrolling, interviewing witnesses, the usual."

"Nothing?" Rachel wasn't surprised. Anyone who could steal themselves a Hope Blackwell and survive had done plenty of prep work.

"Nothing," Zockinski replied. "Or, at least they've told me nothing."

Phil turned towards her. "Run the crowd?"

"Guess we have to," she sighed. "Boys, we'll go high."

"We'll go low," Santino said. The three men from the MPD each had a small carbon fiber case in their hands, and were fitting earbuds into their right ears. "Ping us when you've found something."

"*If*," Phil whispered as they moved into the shadows of the parking garage. "*If* we find something."

Rachel cast a scan behind them, to where Hill was pacing angrily under dark, hateful reds, and didn't reply.

Phil fell silent as they went deeper into the garage. He was somewhat out of his element: as an explosives expert, he was used to a certain type of crime scene, one which was typically soggy, smoky, or still on fire. Kidnappings were alien to him—

rather than hunting for clues from what had been left behind, they instead sought to find what was had been taken. Still, he kept his back straight and his steps sure as he tailed her through the garage, his silverlight core visible beneath cloudy layers of professional blues and orange-yellow uncertainty.

Rachel took the stairs. Somewhere below, a man shouted at the FBI to let him get his car and go home.

"Another hour, if we're really lucky," she said to Phil, as the push of yellow curiosity that preceded a question reached her scans. *"We probably won't be, though. The media's already down there."*

"Stop that," he replied. *"Or at least wait until I've asked the question."*

"Hey, it's on my mind, too," she said aloud, and pointed towards the streets four flights down. A crowd had gathered, mostly shoppers from the nearby mall who were beginning to demand answers. Further down the street, a van with a startling array of antennae was crawling through the checkpoints. "The clock's ticking."

They left the stairwell at the top floor of the garage, emerging into bright afternoon sunlight. Phil winced in mild red pain and adjusted his sunglasses. She picked a convenient flatbed truck and hopped into the back, then stretched out to get comfortable. Phil did the same, brushing aside a few leftover autumn leaves before settling down beside her.

"Ready?" he asked.

"Let me run some scans of my own," she replied. "Then we'll get funky."

"Sure," Phil said, and closed his eyes so he could do the same.

Up here, Rachel could take in everything. The sun was warm on her face as she flipped off the visual frequencies she used to see, and began to run the garage from the top down.

Structural elements came first. She probed the interlocking network of concrete and rebar which formed the shell of the garage, looking for anything out of the ordinary. Then, the utilities: she traced conduits and pipelines back to their sources.

Basic police work, really, or basic for all OACET Agents working with law enforcement. Start by checking off the fundamentals to make sure there's nothing hinky about them, and then proceed to those areas of the scene most likely to have been involved in the crime. Necessary, but it was also time-consuming, which is why she and Phil had retreated to the empty fourth floor for privacy.

Her scans found nothing unusual about the structure, so she moved on to the security system. It was a decent mid-range system with the usual collection of cameras and motion detectors. As she poked around the system's digital storage unit, she felt Phil's mind moving along with hers.

"Anything?" she asked. Phil was better with computers than she was; if there were hidden secrets within the system, Phil would be more likely to find them.

"No," he said. Then: *"Ready?"*

She took a breath to steady herself, and then reached out to twine her fingers through Phil's.

Her world exploded.

Rachel had introduced Phil to the finer points of scanning the physical environment, but that had been more than two years ago, when they were both new to cyborgery. Since then, their abilities had gone their separate ways, with Phil teaching himself how to recognize the trace components of bombs—chemicals, molecules, and the like—and Rachel continuing to focus on the little details that made up the strangeness of human nature.

Together, their scans could pry the fabric of the world apart.

Her version was full of color and textures and movement entwined into one; his was of sights, smells, and strands of music, each holding its own space in his mind. She reopened parts of her brain that were rarely used and let herself take in everything that existed below, and she stopped existing in the single body that housed the majority of what she knew as Rachel Peng.

Hive minds were...complicated.

Their shared link was mostly Rachel and Phil, but along the periphery of their joined minds were the others in the collective. The presence of the others was felt rather than seen or heard—if they had wanted, Rachel/Phil could have reached out and asked if others wanted to come along for the ride as they plunged themselves into their scans. They didn't: adding more minds would just make a mess out of things. Skin contact kept them contained and focused.

Together, they knew what this mess of senses below meant, where reds and the heavy bass of OONCH OONCH OONCH had meaning. They understood that the repetitive beat of dance club music signified a null state in which no chemical traces stood out as significant, that the orangey-yellow that was the dominant color of the crowd meant confusion and uncertainty, with a large dose of the grays of boredom as they waited.

Their minds swept down and out, tracing the building, the people…

Is that Bryce Knudson?

They paused and determined that, yes, it was indeed Knudson's raspberry core standing beside the FBI at the crime scene. The Homeland Security agent was more red than yellow, anger radiating from his body in whiplike threads. OACET green lay trapped within the reds, the vivid green all but choked beneath Knudson's emotions. The music that came from his body in steady streaming pulses was reminiscent of mid-90s acid metal.

He doesn't like us very much.

There was a flicker of guilt between them. The part of Rachel/Phil that was Rachel had come up against Knudson on more than one occasion, and had won every time.

Not our fault, they reminded themselves. The same memory from two different perspectives: Rachel dodging Knudson's fist, both from within her body and from Phil's perspective on the ground a story below. A hand clenched: Rachel's, stiff from scar tissues from where the man from Homeland had allowed her to cut herself to pieces on a broken window pane. *God save us from those who think we're unstoppable machines.*

Down, down, into the crowd, to look for those who knew more than they should.

These were close scans, almost intimate. They kept themselves on the outside of clothing, scrutinizing every inch of what each person chose to show to the world. They found traces of blood and fluids, poorly-concealed weapons…one woman's jeans were coated in a chemical agent they dismissed as household fertilizer; a man had apparently spilled gasoline all over his boots several days before.

Many of those gathered near the parking garage had handled firearms recently. Their hands fluoresced in a busy disco beat, an indicator of trace amounts of gunpowder. The singular being that was Rachel/Phil swept low, scouting, paying close attention to anyone whose hands blinked in a steady rhythm.

There!

A man in a suit, his emotions a nervous yellow straining against a professional blue. The suit was the right size and a decent cut, but he wore it with resentment, tugging on the tie between attempts to find a place to house his hands.

Those hands pounded in the yellow-white drumbeat of someone who had recently fired a gun, and within that professional blue was a melody of OACET green.

Curiouser and curiouser… Why would an innocent bystander have us on his mind?

They inspected him. He was chatting on a cell phone but didn't have any other electronic devices. There was nothing in his pockets which gave off an RFID signal, and he carried an old automatic pistol in a well-worn shoulder holster.

But the damning factor was his shoes.

They were polished leather, shiny and new. So new that the soles hadn't even been scratched up with more than a block or two of walking.

Somebody remembered the suit but forgot the shoes, they agreed, and then they reached out to Raul Santino's earpiece.

Rachel's partner in the MPD answered as quickly as if he

was an Agent himself. "What have you got?" he asked, his voice muffled as he pretended to cough into his shoulder.

"White male, standing by a blue Volvo. Brown hair, brown eyes, gray pinstripe business suit."

They had never asked how their mental voice sounded when they were joined. Not good, apparently; Santino paused, then rolled with it. "Anything we can use to bring him in?"

"No. He's got a weapon, but he's carrying concealed. You won't be able to notice unless you're lying on the ground, looking up under his jacket."

"Damn," their partner said. "Time to take a fall. Got it. Stand by."

Rachel/Phil pulled back from Santino's earpiece. They tracked him with their scans as he joined up with two other men. Santino was the one who didn't look like either a cop or soldier. He was tall and lanky in jeans and a dark blue windbreaker, with dark hair swept back from his face and pinned behind his ears with a pair of thick-rimmed glasses. His body language changed, falling from confident into awkward in a single step.

Behind him was a man so obviously a detective that he could have been typecast in a procedural: Zockinski, moving like a bull through cattle.

And behind Zockinski was a black man built like a basketball star, who was carrying himself like a predator on the hunt—

Shit, they thought, as they spotted the reds seeping into Matt Hill's conversational colors again. They reached out to Hill's earpiece.

Beneath them, Mako's cousin paused as he touched his ear. "Go."

"Stand down, Hill."

"No."

"Yes."

Hill's head snapped up towards the upper levels of the parking garage. "He's got my niece," he said, and Rachel/Phil shivered at the menace in his tone.

"Which is why you need to fall back. We'll give him to you,"

they promised. *"We just have to take him down first. Legally. Or he walks, and Avery stays where she is until we catch another break."*

Hill paused. Again, they saw the red of his anger weigh itself against professional blue. There was more red this time—much more red, and moving like a tornado around him—but the blue slowly engulfed it.

"Thanks."

Hill didn't answer. They watched as he stalked off towards the road leading out of the perimeter to cover the most likely exit.

Three hundred feet away, Santino and Zockinski pinned the man in the gray suit between them.

They had the element of surprise on their side, and not much else. All they could hope for was that the man in the gray suit would spook and give them a valid reason to arrest him.

Or…

Rachel/Phil sighed to themselves as the suspect spotted Zockinski. His apprehensive orange deepened, and he began to slowly move away as he pretended there wasn't a cop in plainclothes nearby.

That's when Santino tripped and stumbled against the man in the suit.

It was a hard fall, and clumsy enough to look accidental. Santino went down and came up holding the hand that he had smacked against the barely-there lump on the man's lower back.

"Sorry, dude!" Santino was flat on the ground but was smiling worriedly at the man in the gray suit, the stereotypical nerd desperately trying to make friends with the class bully before the ass-kicking began. He winced, rubbing one hand with the other to try and shake the pain out. "Whatcha got there? A metal spine? Like tripping into a rock!"

Out of instinct, the man's eyes shot sideways towards Zockinski, and found the detective watching him.

Zockinski began moving towards the suspect in a big-shouldered cop's walk, pushing through the crowd as if they were merely objects in his path.

Rachel/Phil held their breath.

The man in the suit was good. He wrestled his orange under control, and bent to help Santino stand.

Shit, they thought, but the part of them that had boundless faith in Santino's cleverness added: *Wait. Just wait.*

Santino kicked the man's legs out from under him.

It was quick. Even Rachel/Phil wouldn't have noticed if they hadn't seen that blue-lined streak of white that went with Santino's trickier schemes. One soft-heeled sneaker pushed against the closest leather-soled shoe, and that took the man in the suit off-balance just long enough for Santino to pull him down.

Judo? Curiosity, brief, asked and answered in the same thought: *Santino's been sparring with Hope Blackwell.*

The man in the suit didn't hit the ground. He took a knee, then came up with a hard shove against Santino's chest. It was nothing but a testosterone bump, but Santino cried out as he fell backwards and sprawled against the pavement.

"Hey!" Zockinski had nearly reached them. He pointed at the man in the suit. "You! Stop!"

The man broke and ran.

Rachel/Phil felt themselves jerk sideways as their bodies tried to follow their mind. On the ground, the man cut across the parking lot, straight towards an opening between the police vehicles. There was an embankment on the other side, and a highway behind shallow hurricane fencing beyond that. They saw what was about to happen…the mystery man would go over the fence, into a car, and would disappear—

Matt Hill stepped out from behind a news van and shot out one long arm.

The man in the business suit didn't see Hill until it was too late. There was a brief flash of yellow-white surprise, and then he was on the ground, hands pressed to his throat as he tried to rediscover the ancient art of breathing.

Hill bent down and seized the man by his lapels, the spectrum of anger and fury covering him in a burning red halo.

"Don't."

"Fuck off," Hill growled. The man in the suit cringed.

"You need another lecture?"

They had stalled him long enough. Zockinski arrived, full of pointed questions about concealed weapons and gun permits. The questions came so fast and hard that the man in the suit had admitted to carrying before he remembered that silence was the better part of a legal defense, and was bundled into the back of Zockinski's unmarked sedan in handcuffs.

As Zockinski and Hill drove towards First District Station, Rachel/Phil did one last low sweep. The song of the crowd had changed with the commotion: the onerous beat of the dance club was still present, but there was a new strain of electric guitar shooting through this beat. Adrenaline, they knew, the hormones heavier in the air thanks to the slow generation of cortisol and the arrest of a stranger.

No new threats, they decided, and their joined minds flew back up to the roof.

Separation came in stages.

They were too deeply entwined to simply break apart from each other's psyches. A puddle of motor oil was their doorway to their own bodies. The stain on the pavement of the parking deck was an electric melody of rainbows moving in a slick jazz melody. Motion and tempo began to separate; the feeling of a shoe skidding across oil came apart from the percussive smell of petroleum. A spark of unique thought came through—this spill is a chemical hazard—and the mind which thought of spilled oil as merely an unattractive blotch pushed itself away from the mind which had been trained to think of errant chemicals as the seeds of destruction.

Then, their joined selves broke apart, and they found themselves in their own skins.

Reorientation involved lots of wiggling, an unconscious survey to make sure that all of the right bits were still in their remembered order. Bodies were strange. They stretched and moved and meant everything until you went out-of-body, and then they meant nothing.

(It was more likely that bodies meant *everything*, as entwined deep links were an anomaly within the collective. It was more likely you'd accidentally trip over someone else's mind and find yourself in two places at once, or ten, or a hundred. Limbs and knees that were intimately yours, with scars you remembered collecting in childhood or an ass you've wiped each day of your sentient life, suddenly becoming as much a part of the collective as the mind itself. What a nightmare.)

Rachel stretched. Her right elbow throbbed; the injury wasn't hers, and she shook out her arms until the pain went away.

"Overextended it while boxing," Phil explained, tucking his own arms around himself protectively as he settled himself back in his own body.

"Getting old is going to suck," Rachel grumbled aloud as she snapped their link. She hopped down from the bed of the truck, and began brushing the dirt from her pants.

"Yeah," Phil said. He followed her down, favoring his bad arm. "All the problems of aging, and we won't even need to complain about them."

"We'll still complain," Rachel said, taking point and leading them back down into the dark recesses of the parking garage. "But it'll be by shoving our sciatica into each other's heads."

"Or Alzheimer's," he said.

"Jesus!"

"You haven't thought about that? If someone in the collective gets dementia or worse… There are enough of us so the odds are really good it'll happen."

Dementia within a hivemind… Rachel had to stop and lean against a nearby sedan. "Fucking ray of sunshine, Phil. That's what you are."

"Yeah, well," Phil shrugged and kept walking, moving his right arm gingerly to test its range. "We're still young. Maybe we'll get lucky and they'll cure old age by the time we get there."

She wasn't too sure about that. OACET Agents tended to live fast. No one had died since the collective had been fully activated, but Rachel figured it was only a matter of time before the good-looking corpses began to pile up.

Knock on wood.

They backtracked through the parking garage. The relative peace of the upper levels gave way to the chaos of the crime scene, and the two of them plunged into the mess.

"Want to see if they've learned anything new?" Phil asked, nodding towards the local and federal crime scene techs.

Rachel paused and checked their colors: yellow-orange frustration was beginning to blur into gray stress, with none of the complex colors of hope within them. It wasn't a pretty picture.

"Nope," she replied. "They know less than we do. Plus we've got a suspect to question, and they don't."

"Point."

They kept their heads down and crossed to a staircase safely away from the yellow crime scene tape. Rachel's attention was on the grounds below, so she was just as surprised as Bryce Knudson when she opened the door and walked straight into him.

The Homeland Security agent recoiled from her, but as he leapt backwards, he started grinning. His mouth was in no way involved: the thick line of smug pink split Knudson's conversational colors like a smile.

"Hi, Bryce!" She waved at him with her left hand like an eager child. He saw the mass of scar tissue and his colors flinched towards red shame. She felt no qualms whatsoever about poking him. Twice a day, she had to massage lotion into that hand and run it through a physical therapy program, just to maintain flexibility. In her opinion, Knudson could deal with some reminders of the consequences of being an asshole.

"Peng," he said with a nod, and tried to push past her.

"And Netz," she said, cementing herself in his way. "Agent Netz. You've worked with him about a half-dozen times, I think? He's with the MPD's Bomb Unit? Has probably saved you guys from big booming painful death?"

Knudson's colors were already bright with OACET green, but they took on some of the greens of guilt and Phil's silverlight. "Yes," he said. "Good to see you again."

Liar, she thought, even before she spotted the dimples across his shoulders. She stood to the side and grinned back at him.

Knudson stared at her as his smug pink grew until it swallowed the rest of his conversational colors, and then the door slammed closed between them.

FIVE

Rachel loved interrogations.

She especially loved running them with Hill. The detective saved up a week's worth of words and honed them to arrowheads, then used them to pierce his suspects until they were all but bleeding to death on the floor. But today, Hill was pacing on the other side of the one-way glass, his murderous reds whipping towards the man in the too-new suit.

Instead of Hill, it was Santino who sat beside her in the interrogation room, the two of them watching the man across the metal table squirm.

"Really?" Rachel asked him. "You're a Staff Sergeant? What unit?"

The man glared at her with deep-set eyes. He could have been anywhere between his late twenties and his early forties, depending on how well life had treated him; Rachel guessed he was much closer to twenty.

"John Smith, Staff Sergeant, eight-four-eight."

"This is hilarious," she said to Santino. "He couldn't come up with anything better than John Smith?"

"Could be true," Santino said, as he nodded kindly to the man. "There're a lot of John Smiths out there. I heard there's even a John Smith convention."

"I don't believe you."

"Google it."

She cocked her head to the side and stared off into space as they let the man fidget in his suit. He had removed his tie and opened the buttons on his collar, showing off an impressive bruise where Hill had clotheslined him.

"In case you're wondering," she told him, "we're trying this new thing in interrogations. We're all friendly-like nowadays."

Santino nodded. "The Obama administration sponsored an investigation into police interrogations, what works, what doesn't. Turns out that when we treat you like a buddy, you're more likely to talk."

"Ideally, we should be holding this conversation in a neutral location, like a coffee shop or a hotel room," she said. "It's been shown that police stations aren't the best place to build a friendly rapport. But we've got to follow protocol."

"Takes protocol some time to catch up to the science."

"So true."

"People hate change."

"Preaching to the cyborg choir, brother."

"Amen."

The suspect's conversational colors twisted in on themselves in the grays and oranges of stress and annoyance.

They were lying, of course. Not about the research, but about having to keep the man in the suit in that particular interrogation room. The cops at the MPD loved that room. Two years before, Jonathan Glazer had picked his handcuffs and escaped from that very room, leaving a trail of smoke and flash bombs behind him. The cops had decided the damage made a lovely backdrop for their routine harassment of criminals. The linoleum floor was puckered from the grenades, charred streaks of soot marred the paint around the doorway, and, if you knew where to look for it, there was a dent in the metal tabletop the exact size of Jason's forehead.

Rachel drummed her fingernails against that dent, glancing from the man in the suit to the tabletop as if to say *Your Head Goes Here*.

"Would some coffee help?" Santino asked him. "Some studies have shown that you're more likely to trust us if you're holding a hot beverage."

"Oh, no no *no*," Rachel cut in. "I'm a little too angry at this guy. Let's not give him something that I can throw at his face."

"We've got no proof he's part of the kidnappings," Santino said. "So what if he's giving us nothing but name, rank, and serial number? He could just be an antiestablishment nut."

"Well, I do my best to be all righteous law and order."

"Chung-chung."

"Exactly. So while I'm happy to question our alleged Mr. Smith, I'd rather not push the limits of my tolerance. After all," she continued, as her eyes began to bore into the suspect's, "I don't know what I'll do—this is the first time anyone's kidnapped my niece."

The man's colors blanched, then flashed shock-white as someone pounded on the other side of the one-way mirror with a large fist.

"Sorry. De facto niece," she said. "But Avery Hill is Detective Hill's cousin's child. I still don't know what that makes them, exactly, except that Hill is very likely to beat the everlovin' shit out of you if you don't start giving us answers."

Santino cleared his throat.

"If we let him," she amended. "Which we won't. Because we're all friends here."

Hill pounded on the mirror again.

"We're just thinking of your safety," Santino said.

The man in the suit took a deep breath. "John Smith, Staff Sergeant," he said. "Eight-four-eight."

Rachel stood up so quickly that the man in the suit jumped in his chair. She leaned forward and gave him a big toothy grin before she moved to the door.

"Ah…" Zockinski was on the other side, one hand raised as if to knock. Rachel grabbed a file from his other hand before she slammed the door on him. She dropped the file in front of Santino, and resumed smiling at the man in the suit.

"Ah, Mister John Smith?" Santino said, skimming through the papers with the perfection of a professional scholar. "Your prints came back. Says here your real name is Damian Brady. Also known as Lobo, last seen with the Sugar Camp Militia in Pennsylvania.

"FBI's got a hell of a file on you," he added. "They're sending it over. Until then, we know that you're mushrooming us."

"Keeping us in the dark and feeding us bullshit," Rachel clarified, then shouted: "It's a *joke!*"

The man in the suit jumped again, ever so slightly.

"This is a good time to start talking, Mr. Brady," Rachel said.

"Maybe he only answers to his alias," Santino said. "You could start calling him Lobo."

"No, I can't. Not ethically."

Santino stood and left the room.

Rachel began to whistle. She was terrible at whistling. Santino had told her on more than one occasion that he wanted to stuff her inside a tea kettle to see if she could learn anything. Today, she was working on a nautical medley, with lots of high, shrill notes.

Santino's phone number flashed through her mind. She opened the connection, still whistling.

"Rachel?" Her partner's voice wasn't muffled, as it had been back at the parking garage. It was as clear as if they had been joined in a link, with none of the emotions that came with contact with another Agent.

"Go."

"How's he look?"

"We're not going to break him. He's fighting stress and anxiety, but he's got those under control."

"Yeah, Hill says he's jumpy but locked down."

She cranked up the volume on her whistled sea chanty, and watched AKA: Lobo begin to turn green. *"Does the FBI want him?"*

"No. Hell no! The guy Zockinski talked to? He said the Sugar Camp Militia is one of those sovereign citizen organizations. You arrest one of their members, they bury you in claims and litigation. He recommended holding Lobo as long as possible, but that we should avoid actually arresting him."

"Too late for that," Rachel said. She had never gone up against a suspect who subscribed to the common law doctrine before, but she had known she'd trip over one of them eventually. It was too easy to use the legal system against itself. The legal system

was a bureaucratic labyrinth of procedural items that needed to be *just so!* in order to function. Sovereign citizens walked up to this labyrinth and dumped enough paperwork into it to drown anyone unlucky enough to be inside at the time. *"He was carrying concealed and tried to flee the scene."*

"Yeah, that's what I told the guy at the FBI. He said we should turn him loose before the militia's lawyer gets involved. Said the lawyer's a real shark."

"They have a lawyer?" Rachel's sea chanty hit four false notes in a row; the man in the suit began to grind his teeth. *"Militias don't have lawyers. How the hell did that happen?"*

"They might not respect the law, but they have no problem using it to their advantage," Santino said. "Think of it as a DoS attack on the legal system."

"DoS?"

There was a long pause. "Are you *sure* you're a cyborg?"

"Right!" Rachel said aloud. Blue relief appeared in Lobo's conversational colors as the whistling ceased. "New deal, dude," she said. "We're going to hold you for forty-eight hours. If nothing else comes up, we'll let you go."

The suspect glared at her, then nodded.

"Anything else?" she asked.

The man in the suit shook his head.

"You're okay with this? With sitting on your ass in a police station? During what I assume is a very exciting time for your militia buddies?"

The man sat motionless.

"Anyone you want to call?" she asked, her hands knotting into fists. "A person who might be able to help get you out of here, perhaps someone in a legal capacity…?"

Nothing.

"Lawyer, motherfucker, do you *want* one?!"

This time, when she lunged forward, the man jumped away hard enough to fall out of his chair. The door opened with a crash: Zockinski grabbed Rachel around the waist and hauled her out of the room, with Rachel thrashing and shouting obscenities at the suspect the entire time.

"That was fun," she said, after the door was firmly shut and Zockinski had tipped her onto her feet. "I never get to play the crazy cop."

"I'll take another run at him in a few minutes," he said. "Why'd you go at him so hard?"

Rachel shrugged. "He's not going to break," she said, "or call that lawyer. But if he really is a sovereign citizen, I don't want anybody claiming I didn't try to cram a lawyer straight up his butt."

They entered the observation room. It was dimly lit, with a couple of comfy chairs and a twin to the metal table in the other room, minus the head-shaped dent and the rings welded to its face to hold the handcuffs. Hill was leaning against the one-way mirror, both palms pressed flat against the glass as if trying to mentally compel the man on the other side to talk. Beside him, Santino was on his phone, and Phil had the thousand-yard stare of an Agent talking through a link.

"We need to find that lawyer," Rachel said.

Santino held up his phone, one hand covering the receiver. "Already on it," he whispered. "The FBI's getting Lobo's recent history for me."

"Got it," Phil said, his eyes snapping back to the interrogation room. The cardinal red that belonged to Joie Young, one of the Agents on loan to the FBI, was beginning to fade from his conversational colors. "Joie says the lawyer's moved around a lot recently. Started in Pennsylvania, but moved down to Maryland this past year. I'm tracking his mobile phone number, and it puts him in Maryland right now."

"It's a short drive between Washington D.C. and Maryland," Zockinski said.

"Yeah," Rachel replied. "If I were the lawyer for a militia involved in something shady, I'd like to be within shouting distance when the cops come knocking."

"Yeah," Santino said. "Now, if we could…"

He trailed off.

"Can anybody think of a legal reason to track that lawyer's phone?" Zockinski asked.

"Nope," Rachel said. She felt the finger-light touch as Phil tried to open a direct link, and she shook him off. "Don't," she said aloud. "I can't know that phone number—I've run too many traces and might run his without meaning to."

"I've already run it," Phil said.

"Yeah," she said, "but you're not the Agent who'll get dragged into court over this."

Hill banged a fist on the glass so hard that it shook in its frame.

Beside him, Santino's surface colors turned yellow-white with excitement.

"What?" she asked him.

"He came in with a phone, right?" Santino replied.

"Shit! Yes!"

Santino ran down to Intake to grab the phone, and Rachel started the long, tedious process of unlocking it.

Worst part of the job, she thought as she reached out to her golfing buddy. Access to Lobo's phone would have taken her all of a thought, but she was carrying the judicial system around her neck. At least today there was less of the usual hullabaloo that came with getting a warrant: Judge Edwards had heard about the kidnapping.

"What can I do?" he asked.

"I need to crack a suspect's phone," she told the judge. *"I'll be honest, we don't have anything that isn't circumstantial—he's a member of a militia, and the abduction was carried out by men who were wearing militia gear."*

"What did you bring him in on?"

"Carrying concealed at the parking garage and trying to flee the scene."

"That's slim. Can you make a case for resisting arrest?"

"Nope," she replied, remembering Hill's long arm across the suspect's throat. *"He didn't get much opportunity to resist."*

"Try to make this easy for me next time..." Rachel heard the sounds of a keyboard from the judge's end of their connection. "All right. He's got an established history with militias?"

"FBI says yes."

"Since there's a child involved, I can plead urgency, but you'll be limited to call histories and contact files on this go-around. No photos, no private files unless you get something more. Send me the details so I can write up the warrant," Edwards said. "It's Sunday, so I'll fax a copy to you. Just have someone drop by my house and pick up the original file.

"Oh," he added, as if the thought had just occurred to him, and wasn't the reason he had answered her call on the first ring. "Should we cancel Wednesday's game?"

"Absolutely not," she said. *"But maybe ditch the other members of the foursome? I've got the feeling someone will want to catch a round with me between now and then."*

"Gotcha," the judge said. Then, because Edwards was a sharp cookie and the two of them spent entire afternoons wandering across well-manicured fairways while talking about every little thing, he asked: "Anything else I should know?"

"Well..."

"Rachel?"

"The militia might be a sovereign citizen organization."

"What?! Those guys have it in for judges! Son of a bi—"

Rachel hung up on him.

Sovereign citizens. She had heard them described as ants with guns. Alone, a sovereign citizen was one person who had decided to live outside of the law. Tax evasion was their siren song, with members of the movement aligning themselves with the idea that the U.S. government was illegal, and therefore any taxation was likewise illegal.

Not much of a threat, really. Yes, the movement tended to collect racists, misogynists, and anti-Semites like lint on tape, and yes, there had been the infrequent hyper-violent ant who took up his private arsenal and blew away those who stood in his way. Terry Nichols had been a sovereign citizen, after all. But dangerous lone sovereign citizens tended to be outside the norm: violent actions summoned cops, and cops had guns, and escalation played hell with everybody's plans for the weekend. (Besides, who didn't secretly sympathize with those who had the stones to tell the IRS to go fuck itself?) But, together, sovereign citizens could pool their resources, and woe to the idiot who kicked their anthill.

As she went to the nearest printer to pick up the judge's warrant, Rachel had the feeling that most of her immediate future was going to be spent stomping around in anthills.

By the time she returned to the observation room, Santino was back with the suspect's phone. Rachel made everyone wait while she futzed around with her vision and struggled through the dense language of Edwards' warrant.

"All good?" Santino asked when she dropped it on the wooden table.

"Yeah," she said, rubbing her eyes in reflex. "All the Ts are dotted and the Is are crossed—"

Zockinski reached for the warrant. She shot him a Look, but slid it across the table for him to double check. Once done, the five of them gathered around the table.

The phone lay in one of the ubiquitous small plastic Tupperware boxes that First MPD kept on hand. An evidence bag rested beside it, ready for the phone's official indoctrination into the judicial system. It was an iPhone, shiny and new, a recent model fresh from the production line.

"Remind me to join a militia," Rachel muttered. Her own phone, used for emergencies when she wanted to stay out of the link, was nearly three years old and scratched to hell from swimming in the sea of trash at the bottom of her purse. She thumbed the button, and when the passcode screen popped up, she told the phone to accept her print as its owner's.

She grinned as the phone unlocked itself. There was always some minor enjoyment when a locked piece of technology broke open for her. Sidestepping passwords had been her first job at the MPD: for months, she and Santino had done nothing but manage warrants and open password-protected electronics.

Small reminders helped keep life in perspective.

Once unlocked, she turned the phone over to Santino. Her partner's thumb moved as he scrolled through its call history.

"Who was he talking to when we busted him?" Zockinski asked.

"Wasn't the lawyer. At least, not the number registered to the lawyer," Santino said. Then, to Rachel, "Run it for us?"

"Yup." She did, but… "Whoa."

She opened a link with Phil. "Can you double-check this number?"

"Sure…" he replied, with the press of an unformed question underneath his thoughts. This vanished as his conversational colors changed to a complicated mess of oranges, with stray colors spinning off as he found a new puzzle. There was some royal purple, but none of the red she associated with pride; something had impressed him but he wasn't happy about it.

"I'm not crazy?" she asked.

"Nope," he said. *"I'm still following the signal. It's…bouncing?"*

"Yeah." Rachel nodded. *"I've tracked it all over Maryland and Delaware. I can't—"*

Hill pounded on the window again.

"Sorry," she said automatically. "We can't track it. It's got a… thing…happening.…"

Phil hopped in. "We can't get a fix on it. Its GPS is bouncing all over the place."

"What happens if you call it?" Zockinski asked.

"The signal will probably settle down, but the guy on the other end will know something's happened to his buddy," Santino answered. "This is a one-shot deal."

Zockinski looked from Rachel to Phil, his colors an uncertain orange with the sickly greens and yellows of someone who wants to be polite but needs to ask an impolite question.

"We'll have someone else at OACET look at it," she said, and Zockinski's colors changed to blue relief.

"Too much time," Hill said from the other side of the room. "That'll take…"

She was too focused on the phone, and didn't see Hill's colors snap into the hard stony blues of resolution until it was too late. The detective turned and snatched the phone in its Tupperware box away from them on his way out of the room.

The other men tried to rush him; Rachel held them back. The whipping fury of reds that had defined Hill for the past two hours was gone. Clear bright white purpose, shining like a lance and aimed straight at the man at the suit, was coming through his usual professional blues.

They watched through the one-way mirror as Hill—calmly, *so* calmly—entered the interrogation room.

He didn't bother to sit. Instead, he stood, arms crossed, and stared at the man in the suit until Lobo's colors began to twist and run.

Then, Hill began to talk.

"I got burned pretty bad a few years back," he said, as he slid out of his jacket. He pushed up the sleeves of his shirt to show Lobo the pale wrinkled skin where the flashbang grenades had hit him during Wyatt's escape. "Needed some surgery, couple of skin grafts. Hurt like hell.

"Not as bad as when I served in Afghanistan," he continued. He stood and put his left leg on the steel chair. He tugged on his pants cuff, and the man in the suit blanched white at the sight of the holes that dotted Hill's shin and calf muscle. "Could have been worse, but it was bad enough."

Hill smoothed down his pants again, then sat. "You've got my cousin's kid," he said. "That's a whole different kind of pain for me. It hurts. I can't push it down, I can't take drugs to shut it off. It's there in my head and my heart, like I've been shot and left to die.

"If it's this bad for me," he said, leaning forward, "I don't know what it's like for my cousin. His kid is gone. He doesn't know where, or why, or if he's gonna get her back. But you do."

Hill tapped the Tupperware box on the table. "The Agents say that whoever's on the other end of this phone? They know how to duck a trace. All the usual shit we do when a kid goes missing? We can't do it. Not here.

"There's pain, and then there's *pain*." He rolled down his shirt sleeves, the white scars disappearing beneath the cloth. "You know this—it's why you took her. To get results. So, you've got them. We'll help you out, okay? Just…help us get started. Point us in the right direction. Give us something that'll help us get her back. You don't have to give up the person on the other end of that phone, but you can tell us what they want. Maybe we can give it to them, maybe we can't, but we won't know unless you give us something.

"You've got to," he said. "'cause if it's this bad for me? This pain of not knowing what comes next? I can't imagine what it's like for a kid who's not even three years old."

Rachel knew that was as close to begging as Hill would ever come in his entire lifetime. She also knew it couldn't work, not with a member of a militia. Threats worked. Coercion worked. Reason and empathy didn't—men who branded themselves with stupid-ass nicknames such as "Lobo" couldn't be reached by pleas for basic humanity.

And yet…

Well, fuck me sideways, she thought to herself, as the man in the suit's colors slowly turned a sympathetic wine red. *What did Hill see in this guy that I missed?*

"It's actually working?"

Rachel jumped: she had forgotten she was still linked with Phil. *"Yeah,"* she replied. *"The guy's starting to…"*

Starting to…what? Not crack. Not cave. Just…

He's thinking about Hill, she realized. *Hill's become a real person to him.*

The man in the suit nodded, very slowly.

"Can I ask you where she is?"

The man in the suit didn't reply. To Rachel, his conversational colors showed strands of a careful, cautious orange-yellow, each strand working to turn Hill's core of forest green around and around in his head.

"Why OACET?" Hill tried a different approach. "Is that why

you took Hope Blackwell?"

"We didn't take anybody." A moment later, Lobo added, "But if Blackwell went with us willingly, Mulcahy'd be more… He'd listen. Help us out."

"Help you do what?"

The man in the suit sat, silent.

Hill wasn't done with the OACET angle. "Why would Mulcahy help you?"

Lobo stared at Hill, not fully understanding the question. "Guy's a hero."

On the other side of the glass, there was a rush of emotion between Rachel and Phil. Confusion (*Mulcahy's a hero to these assholes?*) turned to clarity (*Oh. Yeah, I guess that makes sense.*), followed by teeth-grinding frustration. There had been rumors that Mulcahy was the new patron saint of wingnuts, but OACET's research team had said they should focus on how that played in Washington rather than profiling how those outside the political sphere might respond.

"Fuck," whispered Rachel.

It did make sense, in a crazed roundabout way. Rather than participate in an ongoing cover-up, Mulcahy had taken OACET public. He had said the world had the right to know that the U.S. government had funded a weapons-grade cybernetics program. Going public had made OACET some powerful enemies, yes, but now, two years after the fact, they had more allies than enemies. Most politicians now admitted that what Mulcahy had done was better than if the world had learned about cyborgs who could control everything from refrigerators to nuclear weapons from a WikiLeaks article.

If you were antigovernment, if you wanted to lionize a powerful man who had successfully stood against a system you saw as inherently flawed, you could do worse than Patrick Mulcahy.

"You think he'll help you?" Hill asked the man in the suit.

"Can't," Lobo shook his head. "Not publicly. Got his image to protect."

"But if his wife and godchild are on the line…"

"They're not. They went with us—"

"Willingly. Yes." Hill's bright patience was beginning to dull around its edges. "If they're with you, you think he'll use that as an excuse to start fighting for you."

Lobo started smiling. "We know how the game is played," he said. "All about image. All about how strong you are. He's too good at it, too careful. Helping us won't help his image. Not like taking down a Senator. We get on his radar, let him know we're here, give him a good reason to fight for us? Then he'll help."

On the other side of the glass, Phil tapped Rachel on her shoulder, then nodded towards her clenched fists. *Let it go*, she reminded herself as she shook out her fingers. *Assholes be assholes.*

"You did this for him?" Hill asked. "Took Blackwell and the girl to…protect Mulcahy?"

Lobo was starting to glow with red pride. "Think I'm done talkin'," he said. "But now you know, that girl of yours is as safe as if she was in her own bed. Nobody'll do nothin' to hurt her, promise, even if they wanted to."

"Why would they want to?" The detective's voice was quiet.

"You know, the kid's a—" The man in the suit remembered where he was and who he was talking to just in time, but the word he didn't say still hung in the air between them. "She's black," he said instead.

—Rachel was sure the whole world had stopped, waiting, wondering if Hill would lash out and choke the man in the suit to death—

"Thank you for telling me all of this," Hill said, *ever* so politely. He gathered up the Tupperware box and left the room.

Hill didn't stop at the observation room. He dropped the box outside the door and kept going, moving as fast as he could without running, moving down the corridor and…away.

"Rachel?" Zockinski asked.

"On it," she sighed, and broke her link with Phil as she left the room.

The fresh green of a forest in springtime was out of place with the reds raging across it, and became her beacon through the halls of First District Station. Once she had figured out where Hill was going, she stopped at the nearest vending machine and grabbed two cans of soda before she resumed the chase.

She found him in his usual spot on the roof. There was a corner between two ventilation shafts and a wall, a three-sided hole that Hill sometimes used as a retreat when he was exhausted of having to deal with other people. From within the nook, Hill had a clear shot of the stairwell door leading to the roof and an eagle's-eye view of the street below.

Rachel had never asked what Hill had done when he was stationed in Afghanistan. Before she had found his nest, it had never come up; after she had found it, she hadn't needed to ask.

She came out of the stairwell, shaking one of the soda cans as vigorously as she could.

Hill pointed at the other can. She lobbed it at him, slow and easy.

"Watch this. Saw it on YouTube." Rachel began tapping her own can with her fingernails. She turned the can around, tapping its metal skin the entire time, then sat it down on the roof and pulled the tab.

Soda bubbled out and ran across the roof in tiny streams.

Hill smiled, a little purple humor edging through the reds.

"Shut up," she said. "Mister Wizard said it would work."

She carefully picked up the can to avoid the stickiness, and moved to stand just outside Hill's nest. The two of them watched the traffic below: him, the cars and pedestrians in the street; her, the half-organized muddle of those who worked within First District Station.

"They think Mulcahy took down Senator Hanlon," he said.

"Let 'em," she said. It didn't sting, Mulcahy getting the credit for something she had nearly broken her neck to accomplish. Nope, it didn't sting at all.

"No." Hill shook his head. "It's important to them, to think Mulcahy's fighting the system."

"Yeah. At least we know this means Hope and Avery are safe," she said. "They want to stay on Mulcahy's good side."

The strange two-toned blues and blacks of Hope Blackwell's core appeared in Hill's surface colors, weighed against orange uncertainty.

"Hell if I know," Rachel replied. "Hope's hard to predict. She might fight back—she might sit quietly and wait for rescue. She won't do anything to endanger Avery, though."

"Not intentionally."

Rachel shrugged.

He glared at her.

"No, I'm not worried," she told him. "OACET's got ways to talk to Hope, even if she doesn't have her cell phone. Whatever she does, it won't spill over on Avery. Promise."

Hill went back to watching the street below.

"Guess the next step is learning what they want Mulcahy to do," she said, almost idly. "Got to be something big. If they're sovereign citizens, they probably want him to step in and solve a legal problem of theirs."

Hill's colors took on a pigheaded iron gray with red gilding its edges; Rachel filed that unfamiliar combination under: *"I will go downstairs and resume being a detective when I am good and ready and no longer a danger to others, thank you."*

"Nope," she told him. "This is a big-boy-pants day. Time to buckle up and ride."

An ember of red anger caught fire, just a little bit, before Hill stomped it out in a surge of professional blue. He stood and stretched in the manner of all athletes, his body coming fully on-line and readying itself for action.

They were most of the way to their office when Hill finally said, "Scary as fuck."

Rachel double-checked his conversational colors. The reds of sadness and anger and sympathy, the grays of hopelessness and depression, the oranges and yellows of anxiety and an inability to comprehend... All of these were bundled into an enormous tight knot that rode on his shoulders and chest like a weight, and trailed behind him until it dissipated into colorless energy.

"I can't read that," she admitted. "There's too much going on in your head right now."

Hill didn't reply. It wasn't until they reached their office door that he said, "They think they're doing the right thing."

"Most people do."

"Think they believe it?"

"Like, committed to the cause?" She paused, one hand on the cool metal of their office door. "Probably. This wasn't an impulse kidnapping."

Hill's grays grew deeper.

"I need some words, man. I'm not a real psychic."

"Martyrs," he said, as he pushed past her. "Scary as fuck."

SIX

Sometimes, when Rachel was feeling especially grumpy, she'd kick herself about how she never realized how Chief Sturtevant had set her up. Set all four of them up, actually—it had seemed a normal course of events when she had begun working with Santino, and then later had picked up Zockinski and Hill, but now she knew that Sturtevant had been steering them all together. Why else would he have given Santino a private office large enough to house four people comfortably?

Not to mention a pinball game.

Their office at First District Station changed with their mood. Santino kept it full of plants, all of them thriving despite Rachel's best efforts to thin them out by leaving the windows open during January. Two recliners were pointed towards an oversized television hanging on the east wall, a small beer fridge serving double duty as a side table between them. The four of them had agreed on long plastic folding tables instead of desks: these were pushed against the bank of windows to the south, their steel legs squeaking at the hinges from the weight of their computers and peripherals, with Santino's and Hill's books crammed into milk crate shelving below.

The wall across from the television was kept bare. Half of it was covered in corkboard, the other half painted in glossy white, with a wire rack holding a prism of dry-erase markers drilled into the cement blocks at waist height.

That wall got a good, solid glare from Rachel as she stomped into the room. Santino and Zockinski had already tacked up pictures of Hope Blackwell and Avery Hill on one side of the corkboard, with Damian Brady (AKA: "Lobo" and no, she would never stop thinking of that as the *dumbest* alias, why in the *world* would someone choose—) on the other. Santino was typing away at his computer, running searches as quickly as he could. Zockinski was on the phone.

Phil was playing pinball.

Phil had been to their office on many occasions, but the pinball game was a recent addition. He was shooting metal balls at plastic monkeys, racking up points with each flick of the flippers. She watched the flashes of kinetic energy burst from the machine before she reached out to him through a link.

He allowed the connection, but took one hand from the pinball paddles to wave her off. "Busy," he whispered.

There were others in his head with them; Phil was catching up with the home office. She felt Josh in there, along with a distracted Mako, but pulled herself back before she disrupted their conversation. Phil would catch her up once he was done.

She headed over to Santino. Her partner nodded to her, but his fingers didn't pause as they banged away at his fluorescent-green keyboard. He was murder on computer peripherals, and anything less than a keyboard designed for professional-level video gamers tended to break within a month.

He was also much better with online searches than she'd ever be. Or Phil. Or Hill, or Jason, or…

Or anyone.

"Whatcha got?" she asked as she dropped into the desk chair beside him.

"What do you know about sovereign citizens?" A few extra browser tabs joined those open on his monitors as he chased rabbits through their digital warrens.

"Magical thinking meets white supremacy," she said.

"Why?"

"They're wingnuts who've convinced themselves that there are multiple layers of government," Rachel replied. "There's the surface government, which is laws and taxes and whatever, and then there's the real government beneath it. Most of their interactions with government are done to try and get access to that shadow government. They think if they use the right pen colors, or write their name in capital letters, or… If they discover the right combination of any one of a billion small details, they can join the secret society of real America."

"Wrong," he replied.

"Bullshit. OACET knows its fringe groups."

"Not very well, apparently," he said with a sad grin and a nod at the whiteboard. She winced as she marked up a point for her partner in the air between them.

"No, seriously," he said, stretching. "That's the stuff that's cute and wacky enough to get played up in the press. And yeah, there are some sovereign citizens who're invested in that myth. But if one person files the same lawsuit several hundred times, making tiny changes to each file, there're practical repercussions."

"Right," Rachel said, drumming her fingernails on the plastic tabletop. "The fog of bureaucracy."

"Exactly. For them, it's not about gaming the system. It's about forcing the system to shut down. And since they stand behind their claims that using multicolored pens is a legitimate political belief, any resistance from law enforcement or the courts can be framed as persecution. These guys can turn any single interaction with the government into an endless paperwork nightmare. The best part? Some of it is completely legal. Not all of it, but enough of it so they can say they're doing their best to comply within their understanding of the law."

"Legal system logic bombs," she said. "Like South Korea airdropping anti-North Korea propaganda that's been printed on the back of photos of Dear Leader. Must destroy the propaganda! Can't destroy the propaganda! That's really pretty brilliant."

"Yeah. Honestly, I'm surprised more people aren't doing it," he said. "Seems like any defense lawyer worth a damn would advise their clients to claim to be secessionists."

"…um…"

"Well, any defense lawyer with zero ethics. And I haven't cross-referenced sovereign citizenship against the professional code of conduct for lawyers in Maryland, Delaware, and D.C., so there might be prohibitions against—"

"What *have* you found?" she asked quickly. Santino's rabbits sometimes simply plummeted headlong into endless space, and could take her with them if she wasn't careful.

"Lobo's militia?" He turned the monitor towards her. A series of digitalized mugshots were displayed, with relevant case files attached to each one. "Splinter group from a larger one in rural Pennsylvania. They relocated to Delaware a couple of months ago. Seem to be relatively recent converts to sovereign citizenship, too: before then, they were typical antigovernment isolationists. They started displaying sovereign citizen traits after they relocated."

"Militias don't relocate," she said. "They're almost pathologically territorial."

"These guys did," Santino said. "Got themselves a lawyer and everything."

She threw up her hands. "Militias. Don't. Have. Lawyers!"

"These guys do." He tapped the monitor. "Most of the casework they've filed has to do with property ownership. There are thousands of files... I'm still working to find the core case that spawned them."

Rachel blinked.

Santino's face went blank. She knew that expression: if she had been running emotions, his conversational colors would have glazed over with crystalline irritation. "What I'm looking for is the one case that started—"

"No, no, I got that," she said, and turned away so she could hop back into Phil's link.

"Guys," she said by way of greeting. *"We're looking for one man. He'll be white, educated, between the ages of thirty to fifty, and is currently involved in a property dispute somewhere in Maryland, Delaware, or the D.C. area."*

"Hello to you, too, Rachel," said Josh, bemusement crossing from him to Phil to her. *"Explain?"*

"Phil told you about the militia angle? Good. This militia got religion a few months back, and the new pastor took his converts south. We're looking for that pastor. And there's a cause out there,

too, a catalyst which caused that pastor to go looking for a ready-made flock."

"Or a general who needed an army."

"I'm analogizing off the cuff here, Phil. But yeah, looks like their leader has a legal problem, and he's gotten astonishingly creative in solving it."

"What's the rationale behind thinking this is all because of a land dispute?" Josh asked. He felt distracted: Rachel pinged his GPS and found him standing in the same room as Mulcahy, as well as several cell phone signals that came from a block of numbers used by the FBI. Carrying on two active conversations at once would do that to most Agents. Josh was normally exceptionally good at it, but today was anything but normal.

"Santino says most of the documents filed by these militia members are in some way related to property ownership. Who wants to bet that if we find that property, we find Hope and Avery?"

"No bet," Josh said. *"Good work."*

"Rachel—" Mako began, as a wash of emotions came through their link.

"Let's get them back first, big guy," Rachel told him, and broke away from them before he could feel how his gratitude had brought her close to tears. She reached out through her implant to caress the steel-reinforced cement support posts running beneath her office. Concrete and cement were her touchstones, and these support posts were so familiar that she wondered if her scans might eventually wear them down, like water across stone.

Once grounded, she stood and went over to the whiteboard.

The others stopped to watch: since Rachel could read text written with a dry-erase marker without too much effort, most of their best work was done on windows and whiteboards. Her marker squeaked across the board as she drew out the timeline of known events, beginning with, "Leader Arrives at Pennsylvania Militia," and ending with, "Current Location Unknown".

"What am I missing?" she asked Santino.

You think a single person's responsible?"

"Yeah," she said. "Probably a white male under fifty, with more education than the average militia member. It helps to know how the game is played before you jump in and grab the ball."

Zockinski came up beside her and tapped on the first point on the timeline. "There's a story here," he said. "How did he find that militia, and how did he manage to split it? Those guys are tight. Brothers to the end."

Rachel scowled. "Let's try and get lucky with court records before we decide we've got to drive out to Pennsylvania. God, interviewing fundamentalists? That'd be a horror."

"Rachel."

Josh's presence was quick and strong, the link much tighter than the communal link they had just shared. She glanced over at Phil to see if Josh was talking to him, too... No. Phil was still head-down in the pinball game, and she couldn't feel him ride along. Apparently this was a private call.

"Josh?" There was anger on his end of the link. *"What's happened?"*

"Hope's regained consciousness."

"Where is she?"

"Maryland. An old warehouse near the ocean." GPS coordinates suddenly appeared in her mind; she scribbled these on the whiteboard and pointed at Santino. Her partner nodded as his gaming keyboard began to clatter and sing.

"Safe?" She had to ask. Josh was too angry for something to not have gone wrong...

"Hope is groggy but otherwise okay. We're still searching for Avery—they've separated them."

"Fuck."

"And they've called us. They don't want ransom. They want Mulcahy to... Listen, I'm on my way over to pick you up. There's a news report that you should watch first. It'll save time. Ping me as soon as it's done."

"*Sure,*" Rachel agreed, and he vanished from her mind.

She snapped her fingers a couple of times until the men were looking at her, and then pointed towards the television. It was an older model, and burst on in a cascade of noise and light before the signal stabilized. She flipped channels until she landed on the local news. An Indian woman with shoulder-length hair was talking into an old-fashioned microphone, the channel's call sign stamped onto a plastic square on its side.

"—Blackwell, wife of OACET Assistant Director Patrick Mulcahy, has allegedly been kidnapped, along with a two-year-old child who is reported to be the daughter of two OACET Agents."

The woman stepped to one side. The camera zoomed in on a gigantic factory, a small wedge of ocean behind it, and all of it beginning to glow pink from the sunset. The building was in the middle stages of chronic decay: the structure appeared to be solid, but most of the windows had been replaced by blue film, and whatever paint had been applied to the exterior was peeling into the wind.

"How did the media learn where they are before OACET?" Zockinski asked, as he ran a hand beneath the minifridge.

Rachel shot him a Look.

Zockinski wasn't mollified. "Shoulda told us, then," he said, as he shook lint balls from his personal notepad. "I thought they were still missing."

"I can find the three of you whenever I need to," Rachel said. "You better believe that as long as she's awake to tell him where she is, Mulcahy can find his wife."

The sound of knuckles cracking; she looked towards Hill. "Hope just woke up," she added quickly. "They're still looking for Avery."

On screen, the reporter was walking towards the factory. "We've been granted an exclusive interview with the man who claims to be responsible for these alleged abductions—"

"Exclusive?" Santino said quietly, as the white noise from several competing news crews reached the reporter's microphone. "I do not think it means what you think it means."

"—and he's promised to address these rumors. Stay with us for more—"

Rachel muted the reporter as the channel cut to commercial. "Fuck," she said, as she fell into one of the natty armchairs. "Fuck fuck *fuuuuuck*."

Phil poked the back of her head, and she glanced up at him.

"*What?*" she asked.

"*I asked you a question.*" Curiosity came through their link. "*You're not running emotions?*"

"*Oh. No, I don't do that when I'm in the office. The guys think it's invasive.*"

"They're getting a guided tour of part of the kidnappers' lair," she explained aloud. "Which means… I don't know what it means. Nothing good."

"Could be overconfidence," Zockinski said.

"Which's better?" she asked. "An overconfident kidnapper or a paranoid one?"

"Paranoid," Hill said.

"Agreed." Santino nodded. "A paranoid kidnapper knows things will go wrong. An overconfident one thinks they won't, and when they do…"

He held off on finishing that thought, but there was the quiet shriek of metal on linoleum as Hill leaned too heavily on a filing cabinet.

Rachel waved the television back to normal volume as the dancing slices of pizza faded to black and were replaced by a shot of the abandoned factory. The reporter had resumed walking towards the main doors, repeating her earlier comments about the kidnapping and an exclusive interview.

"We're about to meet the man responsible for the events of this morning. While OACET has confirmed that Hope Blackwell and a minor in her care were abducted from a parking garage, the man claiming responsibility has said that no abductions have occurred—"

"Anyone else starting to hate parking garages?" Rachel asked aloud. Three of the men raised their hands; Hill didn't move.

On the screen, the reporter had reached a loading dock. Chattering away in the near-meaningless babble of time fill, she walked up a readied ramp and into the belly of the factory. Her cameraman was good at his job. The scene was straight out of a movie, crystal-clear and panoramic. A factory, old and rusty, full of gears and gigantic machines that Rachel couldn't put a name to. Dusty light streamed down through windows covered in blue film, giving the scene an unearthly blue glow, and spray paint covered every inch of the walls within arm's reach.

"No trash," she murmured aloud, noticing the generally clean floors. Santino nodded; they had been in enough abandoned buildings to know that most of them collected teenagers, junkies, and their castoffs.

The camera pulled back to focus on a youngish man with perfect teeth. He was wearing military camouflage, well-worn and patched, but clean. The man smiled for the camera, a wistful smile; Rachel thought he looked like Clark Gable in his more outdoorsy roles.

"I'm Jeremy Nicholson, and welcome to my home," he said. "This factory has been in my family for generations. If you're over thirty and you grew up on the East Coast, you've probably used metals that were smelted in this very plant."

He turned slightly, and began to walk towards the center of the factory. The camera followed. "The government forced us to close in 1986," he said, placing a paternal hand on a monstrous piece of equipment. "They claimed we hadn't done enough to meet environmental regulations. They lied; my father had complied with every code on the books. I'll make a long story short and say that if you look up a man named Arthur Bennett, you'll find that he was an inspector who went to jail in the late '90s for accepting bribes."

Hill stood and walked over to the white board, and the names *Jeremy Nicholson* and *Arthur Bennett* went up in green marker.

"Is that true?" Zockinski asked the room at large.

Santino, fingers still clattering away at his keyboard, nodded.

"Bennett's name turns up in multiple news stories about bribery and corruption. Looks like some of the good folks in the regional EPA were living large for a couple of decades before they got caught."

On the screen, Nicholson resumed his slow tour of his family's factory. "My father refused to pay Bennett, and tried to go through legal channels to keep the factory open and get Bennett investigated for corruption. The system failed him. Twice. By the time Bennett was convicted of bribery, my father had spent most of our family fortune just trying to hold on to the factory.

"Ironically..." Nicholson paused for effect before he continued. "My father wasn't able to reopen the factory because environmental codes had changed during the time it was closed. It would have cost millions to bring the facility up-to-date."

He pressed on, one arm sweeping out to take in the factory. "He filed a civil suit against Maryland. He filed another against Bennett. My father lost those cases. But through it all, he paid his taxes on this factory, and never gave up the dream of reopening it."

Nicholson's winsome movie-star smile fell. "Sadly, my father passed away before he could realize his dream. I've followed in his footsteps, trying to secure finances to invest in the factory, to invest in the *community!*

"I was making progress, but a couple of years ago, the banks began turning me away. It took some digging, but I found that True Ally, a local real estate company, had been snatching up every piece of property in the neighborhood. I approached them and offered to sell them the factory, thinking I could rebuild my family's legacy in a new location.

"No." Nicholson shook his head. "Instead of negotiating, they laughed me out of their office. I didn't know why, until the notices came... The government is demolishing the property and reclaiming the land for development."

"To be fair, I was offered money," Nicholson said. "But pennies on the dollar, and not nearly enough to rebuild."

"True," Santino said, reading documents faster than either Rachel or Phil could have located them. "Or true enough... I think if I dig deeper, some of this won't hold up. There are time stamps on some of these that look a little hinky—"

Hill shushed him as Nicholson moved closer to the camera.

"Tell me, friends, what was I supposed to do? My father and I followed the law—*all* of the laws!—that were supposed to protect us. I'm a lawyer myself; I went to school to study property law, to find some way to preserve this valuable part of the local community."

"And we just found Lobo's lawyer," Rachel murmured. "That was easy."

On screen, Nicholson pressed a hand to his face, as if it hurt to talk. "Nothing has worked," he said. "We are days away from demolition, and my land has been seized under the guise of eminent domain. They aren't building a highway or a power plant—they're claiming my land has been abandoned and are selling my property to True Ally.

"So," Nicholson said, holding out his hand. The camera turned, taking in a large number of men dressed in various shades of urban camouflage. They were armed, each of them carrying a minimum of two weapons. Some of them appeared to be wearing body cameras. "Here we are. My friends and I have occupied my own building ahead of demolition, peacefully, to ask the government to reopen my family's case. I have followed all legal channels to the fullest extent of the law; the least I expect is the government to do the same.

"I need to emphasize that this occupation is not a military movement. It is a peaceful protest. Every person on site is here willingly, and no one will be harmed. In fact, we met some people today who were glad to join our cause…"

The men stepped to the side, and there was Hope Blackwell.

She was furious. There was no doubt about that; she glared into the camera with the burning hatred of someone who was ready to tear the world apart with her mind alone. But her hands weren't tied and she was standing on her own two feet.

"We came voluntarily," Hope said, rolling her eyes and sighing like a teenager caught in a lie. "Because *of course* we came voluntarily, because this man none of us has ever met before is just *so freakin' amazing* that he won us to his cause as soon as we met him, because there's nobody holding a gun to—"

A little girl's whimpered cry came from somewhere off-camera.

Hope shut her eyes. When she opened them, she was somewhat calmer. "We are in no way restrained," she said, her voice still as sharp as razors. "These men are occupying this structure as part of their ability to exercise their constitutional rights. They are willing to negotiate."

"Thank you, Dr. Blackwell," Nicholson said, draping an arm over the woman's shoulders companionably. Phil sucked in his breath; Rachel's skin went so cold that she thought her heart had seized. It was only after Hope allowed herself to be steered away that they let themselves relax.

The reporter's face filled the screen and she resumed chattering, dragging out a summary of what everyone had just heard to prologue her time. Interview, over.

"Okay," Rachel said, thoughts racing. "Okay. This isn't a hostage situation." Hill's chin came up, and she hastily clarified. "Not a normal hostage situation, anyhow. Unless there's proof they're under duress—"

"Bullshit!" Phil snapped. "Blackwell was coerced. That speech was so obviously fake that she might as well have been waving the cue cards around."

"I know that, you know that, but it's probably not enough to stand up in court," Santino said. "Not without additional evidence."

"Video of the abductions?" Zockinski asked.

"The kidnappers had shut off the cameras in the parking garage," Santino said. "Everything we've got came from Carlota's perspective, and there haven't been enough court cases involving testimony from OACET Agents to set precedent."

"They weren't the only ones abducted," Zockinski said. "What about the other hostages?"

"Jason's working that angle," Phil said. "He says that all of the footage they've located so far shows a van pull up to a person on the street, and that person gets into the back a moment later."

"At gunpoint?" Santino asked.

"Probably, but unless we can get a clean view of the gun, there's no proof." Phil shrugged. "Jason's running the videos. If there's anything there, he'll find it."

"So what have we got?" Zockinski asked.

Hill rapped the butt of the dry-erase marker on the painted side of the wall. *Jeremy Nicholson* and *Arthur Bennett* had been joined by the words *True Ally (real estate company)*.

"And the Sugar Camp Militia," Rachel said. "And that shark of a lawyer the FBI warned us about, except I'm betting Nicholson is playing that part, too. Do we have his name yet?"

"Not yet," Santino said. "But you're probably right."

The printer in the corner began to spit out high-resolution photographs. Rachel flipped frequencies until she saw Nicholson's face come rolling off the tray, followed by those of men she recognized from the militia in the background of the interview.

"Jason's work," Phil said, as he moved to gather up the prints. "He's made stills of the men from the factory. He's running facial recognition through the usual databases."

"Good," Zockinski said, and stood to help Phil tack the printouts to the corkboard.

Busywork, Rachel thought, but couldn't quite bring herself to join them. She was sure that this same wall was being duplicated in at least ten different law enforcement offices throughout the city. *We need to work on something new. Something different. Some angle no one else would think to check out—*

"Rachel? I'm outside."

"Shit!" she exclaimed aloud, as Josh's voice broke into her mind. "Guys, I've got to go. I'll call... Phil?"

"Go, go," Phil said. "Tell us what you learn."

She grabbed her purse and jacket, and ran out of the room.

There was another heavy bang! as the metal door to their office flew open a second time. Rachel reactivated the scans she used for the emotional frequencies and saw Hill's forest green core pounding down the hall behind her, angry reds twisting within the oranges of confusion and the grays of anxiety.

"I don't know what's going on," she told him.

"Find out."

She reminded herself that, no, this was certainly not the best time to punch Hill.

"Why do you want to punch Hill?"

"Because I want to punch everybody today, and he made a good point," she told Josh. *"Tell me what's happened. Where are we going?"*

"You saw the broadcast?" He was anxious: more than his emotions were spilling over into their link. She felt a steering wheel gripped by hands that were too large to be her own.

"Yeah."

"Jeremy Nicholson called OACET right before that news report aired," Josh said. *"They wanted Mulcahy to come and meet with them in person, but they settled for me. I've been allowed to bring one other Agent. You're it."*

There were stairs: Rachel pulled herself away from Josh until she and Hill reached the bottom. Stairs and too-tight mental links made for twisted ankles. It was as good a time as any to catch Hill up on Nicholson's phone call to OACET.

"I'm coming," he said once she had finished.

"Yeah, I got that," she said. "But you need to stay in the car. Josh is negotiating this mess, not you. Not me, either—I'm just his portable mind reader."

Hill's reds knotted around themselves once more.

Rachel stopped dead in her tracks and spun, putting the flat of her hand against Hill's chest. "Listen to me," she said. "If this was a normal situation? You could get Avery back yourself, no doubt in my mind.

"But this isn't normal," she continued. "Nicholson's got

something planned, and we need to learn what it is. They're not going to give us anything today—not even one of the other hostages. It's too soon. This is a fact-finding mission, not a rescue mission. Got it?"

He made as if to push past her. Rachel set her heels and pushed back, staring him down as hard as she could.

Hill had no problem meeting her eyes.

The moment before she toppled backwards down the stairs, he relented. The wall of reds that was towering over her like a tidal wave eased into itself.

She turned away first, and led them outside and into the fading daylight.

SEVEN

"Stay in the car," Rachel said.

Hill's knuckles were tight as he gripped the handle of his car door, dark skin going pale from the strain. He was violent reds, layer upon layer of them, each distinct hue whipping around and giving him the appearance of being wreathed in flame.

"I mean it," she told him. "You come in with us, this'll be nothing but a bad joke. A Jew, a Chinese woman, and a black man walk into a militia standoff? Josh is already going to be dancing in there. All I'm going to do is keep my mouth shut and read the crowd. Unless you've suddenly discovered you've had an implant all along, you'll just be an extra liability."

Hill's conversational colors twisted around the handle.

"Thanks," Rachel said as he mentally bound himself to the car. "Um… If you hear gunshots…"

He pulled down his shirt collar to show her the ballistic vest beneath, then nodded towards the news crews. There were other officers there, both local cops and the FBI, all of them standing around and waiting for things to go sideways.

"I'll tell them," she assured him, and went over to have a few words with the officers so they'd be aware of the giant with the gun in OACET's unmarked sedan.

It was twilight, with a cold breeze moving off of the ocean through the factory yard. The air smelled like dead fish and old iron, and was an unearthly bright beneath the banks of LED light towers. Everyone—reporters, law enforcement—was gathered a safe hundred yards outside of the building. The local police department had established a barrier for crowd control another twenty yards past that, and the leading edge of what would likely become a massive public mob of looky-loos was butting up against it. Nobody was allowed to approach the building, not unless a member of the militia was there to escort them.

Jeremy Nicholson had decided to keep Josh Glassman waiting.

That was quickly turning into a mistake.

Or, Rachel corrected herself, *an orgy.*

Forcing Josh to stand around in a parking lot was a power play, the sort of thing that businessmen pulled on their rivals to show who was in control. Josh had responded by letting down whatever mental shields he used to keep his libido in check. He was radiating lust like the sun, and a whole solar system of men and women had fallen into orbit around him.

Rachel wasn't sure how he did it. It wasn't pheromones; she would have seen those. In fact, it didn't seem to be physical at all. It was more like he was broadcasting *sex **sex** SEX!* across a mental link that had nothing to do with cybernetics and everything to do with biology. He was leaning on the bumper of a news van, sipping coffee and telling a story of That One Time When That Funny Thing Happened. It was exactly like every other time when he had needed to entertain a crowd... Except his conversational colors were deep red with (*Throbbing? Ew!*) lust, and everyone around him knew it.

The Indian reporter from the news swept her black hair away from her neck and oh-so-casually placed a hand on Josh's arm...

He put a gentle hand on hers and brought her in close so he could whisper in her ear; her mouth opened and her eyes lost focus as her own red lust wove itself into his. Josh smiled at her, then stared straight at the nearest windows of the factory where indistinct shapes bobbed behind blue film and broken glass.

You see these people? The ones you think are here for you? that look said. *Better do something if you want to keep them.*

Someone walked past Rachel, and she glanced behind her to see that some of the officers from the local police force were starting to gravitate towards Josh. Rachel rolled her eyes and set out in search of her own cup of coffee. She found a large pump thermos by the crowd control barrier. It was manned by the youngest cop she had ever seen, a boy no older than eighteen. Or nineteen. Maybe twenty. All right, maybe twenty-five, tops. God, she felt old today.

"What's happening over there?" he asked, nodding towards the mob surrounding Josh.

"Evolution," Rachel replied.

She dumped a stupid amount of sugar into her coffee and headed back towards Josh, stopping just outside of what seemed to be his blast radius. The attention of the crowd shifted, red lust and Josh's core color of tattoo blue swinging to professional blues and…

Blood? Uh-oh.

A man in urban camouflage and a core the color of raw blood was walking towards them. She flipped frequencies to put a face with that unfamiliar color, and saw that Jeremy Nicholson himself had come out to say hello.

Interesting, she thought. *I guess the bad guys do color-code themselves. Sometimes.*

The crowd gathered around Josh were shaking their heads as if reeling from a sudden punch to the face: whatever he had done to draw them in could be turned off as easily as he turned it on. Rachel saw the flash of embossed type as Josh slid a business card into the pocket of the reporter's pants, followed one last ripple of lust between them as they broke apart, their conversational colors uncoupling.

Then came the pressure of another's mind just staying outside of her own senses, a cyborg's version of coughing politely before knocking.

She opened their link as carefully as possible, ready to step back and slam it shut if Josh was still in full-blown Lothario mode. His mind flowed into hers, as crisp and sexless as an irradiated mountain stream.

They fell into step as they walked towards Nicholson, their coattails whipping in the half-rotten wind blowing up from the ocean.

"Bad cop?" she asked him.

"Invisible cop. I want their full attention on me. Make them forget you're here."

She dropped a few feet behind him.

"Can you tie me in? I want to see how they read for myself." His request was half caution, half politeness. Josh could read people better than she could, but for him, it was because he understood them. He was the human equivalent of the mechanic who could diagnose the cause of engine failure from the sounds the customer made over the phone, the baker who knew from a glance at the recipe that the cookies would benefit from another half-pinch of salt.

But he couldn't see through walls, and if someone was standing behind him and thinking that this meeting was turning into a joke, that life would be more exciting if they unslung their semiautomatic machine gun and started blasting holes in those irritating Agent-shaped targets…

"Not right now," she told him, as she swung her scans back through the building. *"Not when I might need to move. Let's get to somewhere safe."*

She felt him nod through their link, and then they were standing before Jeremy Nicholson.

Rachel didn't bother to flip frequencies to see his face again. She had gotten all the physical details she needed from the initial news broadcast. Now, she put herself at parade rest behind Josh, and stared through the layers of Nicholson's emotions. His colors were confusing and confused. The professional blues of a man in control were whipping like a flag across his body, but there was a cloak of sickly yellow beneath this, and he wore a crown of sharp reddish-orange spikes. These spikes burrowed in and out of his temples like serpents through sand: Rachel's brain hurt from watching it.

"Ping," Josh said through their link, as he shook Nicholson's hand and greeted him with the same courtesy he used for visiting heads of state.

"About how you'd expect a man in his situation to look. He's

stressed out and knows he's not fully in charge, but he's not an immediate threat."

"Let me know if that changes."

"Yup."

Nicholson was talking, some prepared speech, probably, playing to the cameras as he welcomed Josh Glassman to his home. His voice was strong in that old-fashioned Marlboro Man way, but his words were nothing to her. What he said? That was Josh's job.

What Nicholson felt? What he meant beneath his pretty well-planned words? That was hers.

She turned part of her scans back towards the building. She had spotted Hope Blackwell's core colors as soon as they had arrived. Mulcahy's wife was being held in a lofted office with clear sightlines of the factory floor below.

Avery wasn't with her.

Nicholson's men were keeping Avery on the other side of the factory compound. She was surrounded by people wearing a terrified blend of yellows, oranges, and grays. Around them, another layer of people in professional blues, all of whom held guns.

The little girl's core color was losing the pastel blues that were the ambiguous hues of early childhood, and was transitioning towards a stony green. She was also the only hostage who wasn't scared out of her mind. Where the others were frightened, Avery was…wary. Her colors shone yellow-white: she was alert and watchful, somewhat eager. Vivid blue flashes the size of dimes darted around her in unpredictable patterns, as if keeping her safe within a web of light.

Someone with an unfamiliar core of copper was sitting beside Avery, reading to her. The person with the copper core had the same frightened coloration as the rest of the hostages; as Rachel watched, Avery patted them on their leg to comfort them.

Rachel turned her scans away and kept her hands well away from her gun.

She followed Josh, who followed Nicholson, up a loading

ramp and into the near-blackness of the building. The lamps from the cops and the news crews had turned the parking lot as bright as day; inside, the light was transformed into an otherworldly blue from the tinted film across the windows.

The building was huge. Whole football fields long, maybe a quarter-mile or more from one end to the other. The light couldn't keep up with them, and it wasn't long before there was nothing before them but the dark. Nicholson didn't acknowledge it; he walked the halls with the surefootedness of a king who had grown up in his castle. This was why he had waited, Josh mused through their link, and she agreed. With the sun almost down, the factory was dark, strange, dangerous. Nicholson had assumed he would take the lead and keep the Agents off-balance as they struggled to keep up with him in the factory's great hostile voids.

Rachel chuckled to herself as Josh slowed down to walk beside her. She brought her scans down to their most basic settings, and let her friend use her senses as his own.

Josh began to point out interesting elements within the factory—the large pipes crisscrossing overhead, the woven metal catwalk beneath their feet—and Nicholson's conversational colors picked up some orange-red irritation around the edges.

They walked for what seemed like forever through the bones of the factory. The walls, mostly cinderblock and veined in girders of steel, were the same sturdy ones she had seen from the news report, but now she could also see the water damage seeping into them, the rust and rot beneath... There were holes in the ceiling, and the concrete floor was beginning to crack from neglect.

This place is dying, she realized, and wondered what kind of music Phil would bring to her scans if he were here. Something sad, maybe, or classical, or both. Chamber music for a funeral.

Josh pulled his senses away from hers; there was light ahead.

"Hope's in the office," she said, and used her mind to direct him towards the room on the catwalk above them.

"*I know. Pat and I went out-of-body to check in with her as soon as she woke up and let him know where she was," he said. "There were two men standing guard."*

There was just one man now: he was keeping well away from the windows, and had a core of fresh-made iron. Hope's core of twisting blue-black was beside him; she was seated on the floor, her arms and legs bound together.

Nicholson stepped into the single pool of light.

There was a meal waiting for him. Waiting for him and Josh, rather, a small table draped in white linen and set in matching fine china for two, with a main course of steak and potatoes kept hot beneath silver covers. Rachel picked a spot a few feet behind Josh and settled into parade rest, and tried to not think about what kind of person would host a candlelit dinner as part of hostage negotiations.

"Can you tie me in now?" Josh asked.

Rachel took a quiet breath, and gave herself over to poetry.

As she let down her walls, her friend's mind came into hers. It was a different kind of link than the one she had shared with Phil. There, they had become a single mind. Here, she and Josh maintained their separate senses of self. And those two identities? Their competing self-awareness? They caused problems. No one else in the collective could do what she could do: no one else had had cause to learn. A deeply merged link would have allowed Josh to have access to her full range of senses and the knowledge that came along with it, but he would have no longer been Josh. A shallow link would give him access to both senses and knowledge, while also allowing him to keep his own personality. She just had to get the hell out of his way.

Poetry helped. On the drive over, she had chosen "Prayers of Steel," a lesser-known poem by Carl Sandburg. It was a tiny piece barely nine lines long, and no less beautiful for its length and obscurity.

Lay me on an anvil, O God.

Simple. Image of metal, raw. A plea from something that wanted to become more than it was. She felt her mind slide sideways as Josh inspected the room. Beyond the halo of candlelight, there were men everywhere, crouching in the dark like predators. They used the machinery as cover. They were all heavily armed, their guns trained on the Agents.

Beat me and hammer me into a crowbar.

Becoming more through hardship. No pain—metal didn't feel pain—but it took shape through fire and strength and skill. Without the hammer and the anvil, there would be no tools. Without tools, there would be nothing... None of the men were an immediate danger. She wouldn't have allowed Josh to enter the candlelight if they had been. They crouched over their guns and radiated hope.

Let me pry loose old walls.

Hope? Yes. Not the blue-black core color of the woman in the office above them, but real hope, the kind that Pandora had managed to slam the lid on. The most complicated emotion of them all. Yellow, red, blue, all primary colors, braided into each other, supporting each other. Yellow for joy. The blue of relief. Passionate red. And through these ran strands of OACET green. Colors that wanted a purpose. Wanted to be validated... Although maybe that was just the crowbar talking.

Let me lift and loosen old foundations.

Tools were needed to shake off the old. To break up what no longer worked. To make way for the new. The hostages were at the other end of the structure. Not in a different room, not really: factories were single rooms with partitions, office furniture for giants. The hostages were uninjured but scared, so scared, yellow fear pouring from them in great sick blobs, with Avery at their center.

Lay me on an anvil, O God.

Back to the anvil again: Sandberg loved the syncopation of repetition. Nicholson was yellow-white energy now, excited and excitement both as his plan unfolded, cutting into his steak and drinking his wine as if he and Josh were dining at the best table in Mastro's.

Beat me and hammer me into a steel spike.

A spike this time, a tool of a different kind. The spike

comes after the crowbar. Making comes after breaking. Josh, passing through the introductions, starting to test Nicholson's boundaries, little pokes and prods to see how committed Nicholson was to his plans.

Drive me into the girders that hold a skyscraper together.

She hadn't given much thought to collectives outside of her own. Small parts that make a whole. That's what buildings were—that's what this factory was. And the militia stationed around them? A collective of a different sort. One that looked to Nicholson.

Take red-hot rivets and fasten me into the central girders.

What would happen if she took out Nicholson? Right here, right now, one shot between his eyes. Brains everywhere. Dinner ruined. Would the militia collapse around them? No. Take out that one steel spike and the building would still stand.

Let me be the great nail holding a skyscraper through blue nights into white stars.

But what happened if the great nail was gone? The collective wouldn't be the same. The weight carried by that great nail would be pushed out, the others around it forced to carry the strain. If that great nail was important enough, if that nail had been a keystone made from steel, the collective would sag and collapse.

The center must hold.

As her meditation ended, Josh pulled away from her mind.

"Got what you needed?" she asked.

"Yeah. Nobody's going to attack us, and this guy's about as deep as a puddle," he replied. *"He's a rich kid who was never told no."*

Rachel turned her attention back to the small dinner table, where the head of the militia was…pontificating? Yes, that worked. Nicholson was pontificating at Josh, all preaching and no point.

Josh, who lived for verbal jousting with a decent opponent, had begun to turn an irritated orange-yellow around his edges.

There's something not right here.

She couldn't tell if that was Josh's thought or her own.

"We're missing something." That came from Josh; his mental voice was beginning to take on new flavors of concern. *"Scout around."*

The request took her by surprise. *"I have to watch your back,"* she reminded him. *"I'll come back and scout when we're done."*

"These guys aren't dangerous. Not right now. You agree?"

She did, but…

"This is probably the only time you'll have physical access to this building. I need your detective's brain working. Get the feel of this place while you can."

"Fine," she said, and shoved her friend to the margins of her mind so he wouldn't get in her way.

Walk the scene. She had learned this early on in her career with the MPD. Walking the scene allowed her body and brain time to process what her scans perceived. She couldn't move around the factory, not without drawing attention to herself, but…

Rachel stepped out-of-body.

It was her least favorite cyborg trick, this business of projecting her consciousness into her bright green avatar while leaving her body behind. Out-of-body…itched.

Not physically. Some of the others swore that out-of-body came with sensations of its own, but she never felt anything except a general sense of wrongness, that she had been given one body and her soul should stay in it, damn it! She could scan whatever she wished, she could throw her mind across the planet if she wanted, but walking around in a digital copy of herself? Her scans at least kept her somewhat honest; they didn't allow her to pretend she was physically present when she wasn't. A New Age-y friend of the collective said that going out-of-body was merely astral projection, and assured them that monks had been doing it for thousands of years. Rachel thought that "merely" and "astral projection" didn't belong in the same sentence, and that the cyborgs should have left it to the monks, who had probably trained for the stomach-churning weirdness of walking around without having bothered to bring your stomach along.

Her avatar pushed off against the cement floor and flew straight up in the air.

(Okay. That part was cool.)

Below was the table, with Josh and Nicholson staring at each other across their meals. She had no access to the emotional spectrum when she was out-of-body: Josh's posture was screaming boredom, with his head propped on one hand; it was the opposite of the vivid electric whites and professional blues he had been wearing a moment ago.

Up, up. The darkness around the candlelit table wasn't an issue for her avatar. The men stationed around the table appeared to be sitting in broad daylight. They had had some training; they held their posts around the table in silence, their weapons close at hand but not ready to be used. Some of them wore body cameras, recording everything that happened. She saw the uneasy glances among the militia members as they watched their leader lose face in front of OACET's second-in-command, and Rachel told Josh to dial the disrespect down a notch. Josh's head came up off of his hand as he pretended to agree with something Nicholson had said; the men noticed, and were pleased.

She allowed herself to be drawn over to a stack of crates positioned near the exterior wall. New crates, nearly two dozen in number, made of fresh wood with score marks across the top from where they had been pried open. There were no markings on the crates, no way to tell exactly what was in them, but she had seen hundreds of featureless crates when she was with Army CID, and they always held the same things.

Up again, and over to another stack of boxes. Smaller boxes this time, cardboard instead of wood, with an American flag and the initials MRE stamped on each surface she could see. Nearby was an open trash can; she peered inside to see familiar plastic bags, and the stomach she had left behind churned at the remembered taste of prepackaged slices of cafeteria pizza covered in moon dust.

Up, one more time.

Rachel landed on the stairs just outside the office door, and peered through the glass. The room inside was spacious and freshly scrubbed. There were walls up here: the front office had the only view of the factory floor below, but behind it was an entire second story. A china setting identical to the ones downstairs was on a cafeteria tray and had been tucked to the side of the door, dotted with the usual inedible shreds of steak and the skin of a baked potato.

She forced her avatar to walk through the office door, and ignored how passing through solid matter didn't feel like anything. On the other side, Hope Blackwell was sitting on a pile of clean blankets, staring at her guard with eyes like lasers. The guard was also sitting on the ground, but the fresh finger-shaped bruises around his neck explained why Hope had been bound at her wrists and ankles with nylon cord.

"Hope?" Rachel said. She pitched her voice low out of habit; Hope was one of those rare people who could see and hear her without needing an implant of her own; for the guard, Rachel's avatar might as well not exist.

Hope jerked, then settled herself. The guard spun his handgun towards her in a practiced movement before he realized she wasn't about to squirm free and lunge for his throat again.

"How's Avery?" Hope asked. She was looking at the guard, but her question was meant for Rachel.

"Shut up," the guard growled, one hand pressed against his throat as if it hurt to talk.

"Eat a dick," Hope snapped at him. "Hell, eat two. In your case, they're probably small."

The guard came up off of the floor, his gun snapping up to point at Hope's head.

"Coward," she said, grinning like a wild animal. "Untie me and we'll do this all proper-like."

The gun went down.

"C'mon, asshole!" Hope shouted. "You're the only one here who's not a waste of my time! C'mon!"

"Can't fuckin' wait 'til I get to kill you," he muttered, and turned away.

The guard's attention was elsewhere for all of two seconds before Hope—*She's untied? What? **How?***—was up and moving. Hope was right; the guard was decent in a fight. He saw Hope coming and met her attack with an arm block, then another while he tried to bring his gun into play, but she was coming from above and had the advantage of surprise. The weird woman grabbed him by the top of his too-long hair and then it was merely a matter of banging his head against the closest metal filing cabinet until his body went limp.

Hope stood, kicked him once in the balls for good measure, then sighed and knelt to check his pupils.

"Your mouth's open," she said to Rachel.

"Hope, what the shit?!" was all Rachel could manage.

Hope yanked the door open and began to descend the metal stairs. Rachel watched her from two sets of senses until she remembered to drop her avatar and put her mind back in her own body. She pinged Josh and updated him as quickly as she could, and he was standing and pulling out his chair for his boss's wife as soon as Hope's feet touched the ground floor.

"Thank you," Hope said to Josh, and tucked into what was left of his meal. Then, to Nicholson: "Got any more wine?"

It took Nicholson a moment to recover. "Doctor Blackwell?"

"Yeah," she said around large bites of mashed potatoes. "Hi. The wine?"

When Nicholson didn't respond, she reached over and took Nicholson's plate from in front of him, and scraped its contents onto her own. She started shoveling food in her mouth with the efficient practicality of someone unsure of when she'd get another opportunity to eat.

"The lady asked for wine," Josh said to Nicholson.

"Of course," Nicholson said, and gestured towards his men. Another bottle of wine appeared, carried by a man with a core of swimming-pool blue.

Hope took it from him and gripped the bottle like a baseball bat. For a moment, it seemed as though she was going to take a swing at Nicholson, but she read the label on the bottle and the bottle went from weapon to prize. "A 1990 Dalla Valle red?" she asked, her colors changing to a rather pleased pink. The bottle went onto the table, right side up. "This is some good stuff."

"Only the best—"

"Yeah, whatever," she said, and had the foil and the cork out of the bottle with a single practiced twist of her wrist. She set the bottle on the table to breathe, then returned to her steak. "Have you…hey, this is pretty good, too…have you realized you're completely out of your depth yet?"

Nicholson chuckled. "Doctor, please. This—"

"You're dealing with people who've been forced to take a stand against the U.S. government. For *years*. And they've *won*. The government keeps trying to break them, get them to fall in line and be good little civil service robots, but guess what? OACET loves it—they live and breathe politics! You push them, they push back. And my husband? The worst. Seriously, the *worst* of them. Total control freak. Going up against him is like kicking a nuclear missile in its junk." She paused. "You should probably send an ice pack up to that tossmunch in the office, by the way."

Hope wiped her mouth with the back of her hand and glared at Nicholson. "Here's how this is gonna go," she said. "You tie me up? I break out of it. You chain me down? I break out of it. You drug me? I'm out of action, but my husband's gonna start calling surprise press conferences and he'll ask to see me on camera."

"True," Josh said, nodding.

"Bet it'd look bad for you if your star hostage can't testify that she's here of her own free will."

Orange annoyance started to drip from Nicholson's pores.

"Now," Hope said. "Here's the part where I cut through the red tape and offer to buy this factory."

The orange evaporated.

Could it really be this easy? Rachel thought.

"Nope," Josh said. *"Wait for it..."*

Nicholson smiled. "I don't think that'll work."

"Seems like a plan to me," Hope replied. "You've already established the cover story. I'm your friend now, right? You made me say so in front of God, the media, and everyone. So how about I buy the factory from you, or... Hell, how about I just pay to get it upgraded? I write the check, you cash it, we all go home, and next April I write this bullshit mess of an afternoon off as a failed investment."

The men in the dark began to stir at this. Not at the offer itself—Hope was a genius at day trading and was famously wealthy—but at...

At what?

Rachel couldn't tell, but the conversational colors of Nicholson's men kept growing brighter as they waited for Nicholson to strike.

"Josh, the natives? Getting restless."

"Dangerous?"

"Not yet, but wrap it up? Hope's walking straight into a trap."

"I'd like to meet Agent Mulcahy before we make any deals," Nicholson said.

"And I'd like a million dollars and a pony," Hope snapped back automatically. "Wait. Okay, maybe just the pony." She paused. "Nah. Too much work, and I'd have to put in a barn. The rezoning alone would—"

Josh placed a hand on her shoulder. Hope made a sound halfway between agreement and a grunt, and dove back into the potatoes.

"This sounds like a viable option, Mr. Nicholson," Josh said. "If you're willing to treat this like a business transaction, I can be back here in an hour with a contract."

Nicholson reached for the bottle of wine. Hope's fork came up; Josh moved his hand to her own and gently lowered it to the table.

The militia leader refreshed his glass, smiling.

"This isn't about the factory, is it, Mr. Nicholson?" Josh said quietly.

"The factory is a symptom of a larger problem, Agent Glassman," Nicholson replied. "OACET is in the unique position of having the power to address that problem." He settled back in his chair. "I'd like to meet Mulcahy now."

"You know how this has to go," Josh said. "You're not meeting him. Not until we get something first."

"Doctor Blackwell may leave whenever she wants to, of course."

Hope's conversational colors blurred white in shock; Rachel was sure her own colors matched.

Josh merely went orange in annoyance again. "Of course," he said. "And Avery?"

"She's having a good time with us," Nicholson said.

Hope's colors fell to grays. "You asshole," she whispered.

"She's a child," Josh said. "She can't consent."

Nicholson spread his hands, an almost sheepish *What, me worry?* grin taking over.

Hope stood; the small sounds of metal brushing against metal came from the darkness around them as Nicholson's men readied their guns. She grabbed the bottle of wine, stomped up the staircase, and into the office.

Then, as if part of an afterthought, the unconscious guard was shoved through the doorway and left to lie facedown on the stairwell's landing as the door slammed shut behind him.

Nicholson turned to Josh. "I hope you'll tell Mulcahy that his wife is staying with us willingly?"

"You can be sure I'll tell him everything," Josh replied. "Such as how you've denied her food."

Nicholson's colors shifted and came up in a wall in front of him, a motion that Rachel recognized as part self-defense, part protest, but all he said was, "Oh?"

Josh tapped the now-empty plate in front of him. "Let's not pretend that you've been treating her like a friend instead of a prisoner."

Anger roared into Nicholson's colors. "I'll make sure she's

well-fed from here on out," he said, his tone as mild as possible.

Shit, Rachel thought to herself.

Josh was there. *"What?"*

She sent him the memory of the empty plate on the tray in Hope's office prison cell.

"Oh, that's just great," he replied, and stood. "We'll be in touch," he said to Nicholson. "Thank you for your time and your hospitality."

"Leaving so soon?" Nicholson asked.

Rachel pressed her palms against her thighs and sent her mind into the concrete floor beneath them. *Do not,* she told herself, *go after this condescending little shit. Not yet.*

"You've given us a lot to consider," Josh said. "I'd like to extend an invitation to visit us at OACET headquarters."

"I'd be delighted," Nicholson said. "Shall we say the day after tomorrow? Sometime later in the afternoon? My schedule is quite tight."

"Ping."

"He expected this," Rachel told Josh. *"He's fine with the idea of not playing on his home turf. And he's stalling—he's not going to budge on the time. He doesn't want to rush."*

The men shook hands, all smiles, and Nicholson waved one of his men over to escort them to the front door. The militia man made them walk in front of him, one hand on his flashlight and the other on his assault rifle.

The Agents ignored him. *"What did you see?"* Josh asked.

Rachel thought back to those brief minutes when she had gone out-of-body. *"I think they've got enough arms and armor to wage a small war,"* she said, and threw her scans into the featureless crates to be sure. And, because she had been in Criminal Investigation Command and such searches were second nature to her, she checked the equipment itself. *"Yup. Guns. Lots of them, and their serial numbers have been removed. I could probably dig the numbers out of what's left of the metal if I had enough time."*

"How close do you have to be?"

Rachel rubbed her temples. Her implant had limitless capabilities; she didn't. Small, intense scans gave her crippling migraines; add in some distance and she was useless. *"I'd have to go into the metal and look for trace impressions,"* she said. *"Closer than I was tonight."*

"What about this guy's rifle?"

She sent her scans out and tried to scrape away at the impressions deep within in the steel. *"No dice. It's delicate work. I want to be sitting and able to concentrate."*

"I'll figure something out," he said. *"What else?"*

"They've got military rations," Rachel replied. Her stomach twisted as it readied itself for mutiny. *"Same supplier for the meals we had over in Afghanistan. We didn't eat them unless we were out in the field, but they're not something you'd ever forget."*

"Are they common?"

"Hmm?"

"Say I wanted to buy some. How hard would it be?"

"Oh." She thought about this. *"Procurement wasn't my department. I investigated a lot of MRE thefts, though. They used to be treated as a commodity. It's probably different back here."*

"All right. Put that on your list, too."

As they approached the door, the factory began to glow in that unearthly blue light. The militia man stopped walking; Rachel and Josh didn't.

They reached the door. When they stepped through it, the air was suddenly tight around them, claustrophobia within a wide open parking lot. Behind the barricades, the news crews and cops launched into action at their reappearance.

"We can't just leave," she whispered.

"Hope's safe, Avery's safe. Now we're just discussing terms," Josh whispered back as he waved merrily to the cameras. "You spend the next twenty-four hours tracking down Glazer or Wyatt or whatever he's calling himself. Find out how he ties in to the kidnapping. Get access to his sources. I'll work this end with Pat and the others."

"You saw how Hope was eating," Rachel said. "And I saw how

Nicholson reacted! Her guard ate her meal in front of her, and Nicholson didn't have a clue. He doesn't have full control over his own men, Josh! How is that *safe?*"

He pushed her out of his mind so quickly that she swayed on her feet, and turned to walk away.

Rachel was too quick for him. She snagged his hand; bare skin against bare skin, with Josh's mind squirming sideways to stay away from hers.

"Level with me," she said, and pushed against Josh's mental walls as hard as she dared.

He sighed. "We can get Hope and Avery out any time we want," he said in a low voice. "Safely. Quickly. They'd be fine in a couple of days. But…" He glanced behind them, towards the dark factory and its cracked windows running along the top floor.

"You can't get everybody out," Rachel whispered.

"Not safely," Josh said. "Not at the same time. We could try to get as many out as possible, but those who would be left behind? They'd be targets. Whatever happens to them? That'd be our fault.

"Nobody else can know about this," he continued. "Pat's got it all worked out, just in case the worst happens. But if it does…"

"Yeah," Rachel said, throwing her scans back over her shoulder to the building behind them. It loomed, dark and brittle, and with it the superstitious fear that it might all come tumbling down around them if they weren't careful. "Yeah. I know."

EIGHT

They were *not* spending the night in Becca's condo because of Wyatt.

Really.

The building may have been home to bankers, lawyers, and politicians, and had its own four-man security team walking the halls at all hours of the day and night, but that wasn't why they had decided to sleep there.

Really.

It wasn't the flash of sickly yellow fear that had nearly knocked Becca to the ground when Rachel had told her that Wyatt was back in town—

—and that he had shown up at her *house*.

…really…

The first thing Rachel had done when she got to her girlfriend's home was to walk around the condo and yank the curtains closed. Dinner was a quiet affair, Chinese takeout with a bottle of red wine, usually a mutual favorite except Rachel had insisted they move the table away from the windows before eating, and after that each bite seemed to be made from Szechuan-flavored clay.

They had gone to bed unforgivably early, mostly for something to do, and had made love in the manner of people who couldn't go to sleep before midnight. It didn't work: they were still awake and slowly going mad from not acknowledging the psychopathic elephant in the room.

(And doing their best to keep the conversation light and merry. They had been together for over a year, and, like all couples who were testing to see if they were truly in it for the long haul, they knew that bad situations could become worse with very little effort.)

Rachel had found a paperback detective novel in Becca's study, and was forcing herself through the stilted, self-aware prose. Reading through her implant was awkward. She could make out printed text, but it took conscious effort. Softboiled detective novels were perfect for her: she could never take them seriously enough to get lost in them, and this particular author liked to add taglines about the perils of sexism after every interaction between the woman detective and her male coworkers. There was no other option than to read the choicest passages aloud, and snark as she went along.

"'Laulinda'—who names a character Laulinda anyway? I mean, you get the choice of any name you can imagine, and you pick Laulinda?—'Laulinda ignored Paul. He could never understand the perils of girls in the world.'"

"Perilous," Becca muttered. Her fingers slid around the glass surface of her tablet. "So perilous."

"Does the author mean the world is full of perils faced by girls, or that girls themselves are perilous? Like frail feminine sharks?"

"There's a reason I stopped reading that book, you know."

"You shouldn't have stopped. This book is a printed atrocity. It should be framed and mounted on a prison wall as an example to other books... Here! 'Laulinda zipped her jacket tight across her high breasts—'"

"Oooh," Becca said, as she scrolled through an article. "High breasts. Kinky."

"—and confronted Paul. 'How can you not see the dangers these precious girls face?' she wailed. Wailed? Perfect!"

"You don't talk like that with Zockinski?"

"If Zockinski decides the best reason to pick a fight with me is because of my gender, I've completely failed at pissing him off. Oh God, this one character keeps referring to women as 'chippies'. Is the author British?"

Becca yanked the book from Rachel's hands and flung it across the room.

"Way to kill my fun, Dorothy Parker," Rachel muttered.

"That wasn't hurled with great force. I don't have the time to wait around for a guy to come in and replaster."

"You have a maid."

"I'm not going to ask—" Becca began, then shut her mouth tight. Rachel was sure that if she had the emotional spectrum turned on, she'd see Becca wrestling with orange frustration.

Rachel sighed and moved closer, wrapping her arms around her girlfriend as best she could with a bed and a stack of pillows in the way. Becca relented, her legs stretching out beneath the blankets as she snuggled tight against Rachel.

"What are you going to do?" Becca whispered.

"I don't know," Rachel whispered back.

"How dangerous is he? Be honest."

"I don't know that, either," she admitted. "He's a mystery. He came out of nowhere, and... All I know is he's a killer."

"Who's wearing your friend's *face*."

Rachel shuddered.

"Why would he do that?" Becca asked. "That's so..."

"Manipulative? Calculating? Completely fucked up?"

"Yes." Becca nodded. "Those."

"That's probably why he did it. That, and he couldn't show up wearing his old face. My team would have recognized him on sight."

"You're sure he's here to help? This isn't a...double-play or a set-up or...?"

"Could be," Rachel agreed. "I don't know. But Wyatt and his Daddy Dearest helped OACET once before, big-time, and he wasn't lying when he said he was here to help today."

"I don't know," Becca said, shaking her head. Her long brown hair fell in Rachel's face, and Rachel had a few moments of surreptitious tugging to get it all out of her mouth. "I don't like it. It feels wrong, and I hate that you're in the middle of it."

"Yeah."

Words felt wrong, too; they stopped talking. Rachel let her scans roam up and down the building, checking security points, running through air ducts and ventilation shafts, just in case.

"Is he here?" Becca asked quietly.

"I don't think so. Do you want me to leave?"

Becca's arms tightened around her in reply.

"If Daddy told him to help OACET, then he'll help. Wyatt's loyal to him," Rachel said. "I just don't get that. If he's a psycho, why should that matter?"

"Here." Becca rolled out of Rachel's arms to reclaim her tablet from the other side of the bed. "I've been doing some reading on psychopaths," she said, flicking a fingertip across the screen to call up recent articles. "Everyone assumes that they're cold, unfeeling monsters. But they're not—they've just got the ability to choose what emotions they experience. A lack of conscience doesn't mean an absence of humanity."

"I kind of think that's exactly what it means," Rachel muttered.

"Well, no. It means it's easier to avoid being human."

Rachel sighed. "Which means…?"

"There are a lot of psychopaths who say they've been hurt," her girlfriend continued. "Emotional abuse, psychological damage… They've made a conscious choice to avoid being hurt again. And they do. Like magic.

"Others? They choose to feel love or commitment. They want to be close to someone, but it has to be on their terms. That's why a lot of relationships with psychopaths go south—the other party turns out to have opinions of their own."

"Say you've got a really smart psychopath," Rachel said slowly. "One who knows he's a psychopath. He's got expert military training on top of exceptional impulse control. Could someone like that form relationships?"

"Absolutely," Becca said. "They don't have to have the training, either. I know a lot of psychopaths who've been married for years."

"Wait, what?!"

"Come on, dear," Becca said, leaning over to kiss her. "Everybody knows it's only the dumb ones who go to prison. Smart sociopaths and psychopaths go into business or politics."

An older memory: Mulcahy, pacing in his office, worried to

death.

A newer one: Mulcahy, stone-cold and unblinking to get the job done—

Nope, she told herself, as she pulled her thoughts away from that black hole. *That way, there be tigers.*

"Wyatt isn't crazy," she muttered.

"Oh no," her girlfriend said. "He's definitely nuts. He's just...a very stable kind of nuts?"

"I'll take that over the alternative."

"Me too," Becca said. "You know. If I absolutely have to choose between an ax-crazy psychopath and a congressman."

After that came the usual ruminations over which politicians were most likely well-disguised psychopaths (consensus: all of them), and then they found they were able to sleep after all.

The next morning, Rachel awoke in a cold fury. Not at Wyatt. She was furious with herself, because sometime during the night, her subconscious had finally gotten through to her—the psychopath hadn't been lying when he said he had owned a house in the same neighborhood as hers.

Once she had finally realized *that*, it took her all of fifteen minutes to locate it.

She started with online property records. She had bought her own home when she had relocated from OACET's office in California, six months before the Agents went public. To pull off his scheme at the police station, Wyatt needed to have been in the area for some time, but Rachel had found his original lair. Only one man had lived in Wyatt's apartment; his partner had kept his own place across the city. Both had been thoroughly searched by the FBI and the MPD after the raid on First District Station.

So. The house would have been purchased after the raid.

How long did plastic surgery take? Rachel wasn't sure. The Internet was of no help: reconstructing a man's face could take weeks to months to years, depending on the surgeon and where the surgery was performed.

Rachel decided to go with a nice three-month window

between when Wyatt had left the city and when he had returned. There were some excellent plastic surgeons in Europe and in Mexico who could swap out an entire face in that time. And three months was the bare minimum for the reconstructive surgery required to put Daddy Dearest's legs back together, allowing Wyatt to safely move him into the D.C. area again.

So. The house would have been purchased at least three months after the raid.

It wouldn't be close to her own home, she knew. Too much of a chance that she'd spot them by accident. They might not have known about her scans when they bought the house, but how awkward would it be if she were out for a morning jog and happened to bump into someone with a suspiciously familiar face from her Army days?

So. Something on the outskirts of her neighborhood and nowhere near a park, or between her house and the city proper, or on any of her familiar well-traveled routes. That still left several dozen houses, so she put on her best fake real estate agent's voice and started making calls to the agents on record.

Her fifth call in, and she learned that a charming bungalow in Forest Hills had been sold to a nice young man who had insisted on looking at single-level homes. He had family members with mobility issues, he had told the agent, and needed a place that didn't have stairs.

"That psychopath sure loves his daddy," Rachel muttered as she hung up.

She walked out of the front door of Becca's lovely centrally-located building and hailed a cab.

The cabbie took her to an address in the Goldilocks zone of stalking: not too near her own home, but not too far away, either. *Juuuust* right. When they were close enough so she could scan the house, she knew—instantly, immediately knew—it belonged to Wyatt. The security system was bonkers. There was video and audio monitoring, alarms on each entry point, some weird plastic wands that might have been used in thermal detection…and that's just what she spotted from the electronic fields surrounding the equipment.

She let her scans drop before she went into the system itself.

So. Rachel told the cabbie to take her back into the city, as she had business at the Bank of America branch on 15th Street. What? No, it couldn't be any other Bank of America branch, and yes, I know we're passing one of those right this moment. It's got to be the big building in the city. Because I'm paying you, that's why!

She then spent an hour at one of the largest, heavily-guarded banks in the city, telling the clerks she had seen an advertisement for an impossibly high-yield interest checking account, and allowing too-polite managers to pass her around as she played with the limits of the bank's security equipment.

The bank was her dry run on an unfamiliar security system. Rachel had tested her shields against OACET's own security systems months ago, and poking around the bank's systems was just to be sure she hadn't missed anything. She hadn't: nothing beat a security system devised by Agents (except, perhaps, another Agent), and while the bank's security system had shown her that she did register on some of their equipment when shielded, she was more of an artifact than a threat. Her shield allowed the light to bend around her, turning her into a blur instead of a person-shaped hole in the world. Managing audio equipment was easier: she usually told it she had the same audio register as a flock of noisy starlings, and it ignored her.

So. Once satisfied, she hailed another cab, and went to the local big-box hardware store.

Then, she went home to prepare.

She had assumed the approach would be the tricky part: the mission usually went as planned once you were safely behind enemy lines. Until she was inside Wyatt's house, she'd have to contend with the unexpected—nosy neighbors and the like—and she was so well-known around the neighborhood that there was no way she could go incognito.

So. Three in the afternoon, just before people started coming home from work, and a lovely time for a leisurely afternoon stroll to the local store.

So.

A few easy questions, and she had learned the man with the stunning front lawn kept normal business hours, except on those days when he worked a little late. He was rarely around on weekends, but when he was, he was friendly and generous. Over Labor Day Weekend, he had hosted a block party and let the kids play in his pool.

So.

Plastic grocery bag swinging from one hand and her oversized purse hanging somewhat lower than usual, Rachel kept to the sidewalk one block over from Wyatt's property. It was an effort to keep from whistling nonchalantly. She had wrapped her shield tight around her, making sure it hugged her physical form as closely as it could.

So.

Wyatt's house.

From here, with her scans fully active, the psychopath's house looked like a portal to Hell, all glowing reds from the early warning systems that blanketed it, and pulsating in a cold white light from the alarm systems within.

"Great," she muttered to herself. "The cyborg's version of a haunted house. Lucky me."

She turned the corner and began the long walk towards Wyatt's house.

Wyatt had a landscape company, she decided. He *must* have had a landscape company—she refused to believe someone like Wyatt could have maintained such a perfectly manicured lawn. Even after a hard winter, the grass looked crisp and green.

Too green. She prodded it with her scans and found it fluoresced at a rate consistent with paint.

"What kind of psychopath gets his lawn dyed green?" she muttered as she turned into his driveway. "I am dealing with a shitty psychopath. I *demand* a better class of psychopath…" And so on, until she was right there at the end of his driveway and couldn't pretend any longer.

The property was fenced on all four sides, with the front of the house filling the gap. It was a newish fence—she assumed Wyatt had installed it when he had bought the house—fancy-looking in tall white wooden slats. She ran her scans through it and found the wood was an engineered plastic, and went more than three feet down into the earth.

Wonder how they explained that to the fence company? she thought. *The world's biggest Digging-est Dog?*

She went straight to the gate and popped the handle.

There was a cold moment in which the sound of the gate latch coming open sounded an awful lot like the click of a landmine, but no, not here, not in suburbia, there was no way Wyatt would booby-trap the grounds around his own home and her scans were too thorough, besides.

Still.

She closed the gate behind her, every one of her weird and augmented senses ready for a trick, a trap, something. Anything. A homing pigeon to zoom out of the bushes and shoot towards Wyatt to warn him, maybe.

Nothing.

So.

The back yard was as diligently landscaped as the front: a series of boxwoods in a straight hedge provided excellent cover. Rachel scanned the area one last time before she scurried behind the bushes and allowed herself to breathe.

Once safe, she took out the circular saw she had bought at the hardware store.

Houses are like mollusks, she reminded herself as she slapped a fresh battery into the saw's handle. Phil had taught her this: it was a rule of any good bomb squad. *Get though the hard shell, and there's nothing but soft, chewy innards.*

She had picked a spot well away from the windows and doors; the contact points on the motion sensors wouldn't trip to minor vibrations. The saw's metallic rasp seemed louder than it had when she had tested it in the privacy of her own garage, but it ran through the masonite board like a knife through butter.

Frozen butter, admittedly, but it was just a matter of making a pair of foot-long cuts straight up, then another two cuts at the top and bottom, square between the studs. The entire process took less than a minute.

She had been worried about the next part—one mistake, and the masonite boards might fly off the plywood backing—but the carpenter who had nailed on the siding had done a thorough job of it and the whole thing popped off the house in a single piece. A little work with a short-handled crowbar, and she was through the layer of pink insulation. She sat, surrounded by fluffy clouds of spun fiberglass, as she cut through the drywall on the far side with a contractor's blade. Then, she rapped on the drywall until it popped loose and fell on the carpeted floor of the living room.

Three minutes, eighteen seconds... She stopped her internal timer before it began to slice time into incomprehensible fractions, concentrating instead on using her new electric screwdriver to put an overlong screw into each corner of the plywood backing of the piece she had removed. She hurled her power tools into the bag, followed by handfuls of fiberglass, and scuffed up the mulch to hide the sawdust before she tossed the bag through the small square opening she had made.

Rachel slithered headfirst into Wyatt's house.

Not yet, she reminded herself, as she gasped for breath, propping herself up against the wall of Wyatt's dining room. *Not yet.*

She reached through the hole, took up the plywood square by the screws, and yanked it back into position.

This was the tricky part. She projected herself out-of-body, her avatar positioned outside the house and staring at the hole. A seemingly endless amount of fiddling and jiggling later, and she had aligned the panel to hide the seams as best she could. A little caulk and paint, and nobody would be the wiser.

Now, safe inside Wyatt's wards, she relaxed.

She moved into the kitchen, and stayed there. Wyatt might not have layered his lawn in landmines on the chance of curious neighbors, but he could have booby-trapped other areas of his house. No reason to run that gauntlet unless she had to, and she was pretty sure that Wyatt's nice, normal suburban home didn't hold any useful secrets other than himself.

Rachel crept across the wide white floor tiles to the fridge, and gave it a good, solid staring. Once she was satisfied it wasn't a sinister fridge in disguise, she opened it and helped herself to a beer.

The psychopath drank his beer in cans, because of course he did. Still, it was either that or the open carton of orange juice beside it. Nope, beer it was: she trusted nothing in this house, including the tap water.

She carefully chose a kitchen chair, and settled in to wait.

Rush hour came and went.

Sometime after the sun had set, the noise of a car pulled her scans towards the road. A late-model coupe, gray and low to the ground, purred into Wyatt's driveway. A new thread was stitched into the local digital ecosystem, and the garage door began to climb.

Rachel took a deep breath and made one last scan of the kitchen.

Everything she had brought was tucked tight behind the angle of a wall. The breakfast nook showed from both entrances to the kitchen, but the chair closest to the garage was also the only one out of the line of sight. She made herself slump into it as if she couldn't care less about this insanity, her gun resting on the table and pointing at the door. A second beer, unopened, rested beside her own.

In the garage, an engine cut off, followed by the solid thump of a car door.

Through the wall, she saw Wyatt in dull, cloudy colors. Whatever job he was working as his cover story was boring him to tears, and perhaps normalcy.

He was carrying a briefcase. Rachel threw a light scan inside; it held papers, plus a .22 caliber automatic pistol. A matching gun rode in a nylon harness on his lower back, concealed beneath the folds of his almost-cheap suit. Business casual for psychopaths.

Wyatt paused at the door, his hand stalled above the keypad that deactivated his security system.

Rachel held her breath.

His fingers punched in a code, then tumbled two locks and a deadbolt using three different keys. Once done, Wyatt walked into his own home, no trace of Southwestern turquoise or OACET green in his emotions.

"Howdy," she greeted him, as she tapped one finger on the barrel of her gun.

Wyatt's colors exploded in yellow surprise. He froze for all of a full heartbeat before his colors relaxed into wary oranges.

"Peng." He nodded to her.

"Disarm," she said.

He took off the gun riding against his lower back, slowly.

"Put it on the briefcase and kick them both over here," she said.

Once he had done this, she used her gun to nudge the unopened beer towards him. He took it and circled away to a chair on the far side of the breakfast nook, keeping the wide belly of the round table between them.

"Where's Marshall Wyatt?" she asked. "The real one. My friend."

"Dead," the fake Wyatt replied.

Her world shrank around its edges. *Just because you already know the answer doesn't mean it won't hurt when you hear it.*

"You?"

"No," he said. "Not me. He died a few years ago. I didn't even know he existed until I went looking to become someone from your military days."

"How?"

He shrugged and popped the tab on his beer. "Homeless. Meth addict. Froze to death under an overpass in Chicago."

"You're lying." *He's lying, he must be lying, Marshall couldn't go out like that—*

"I can show you the files," he said. "The original copies. They're different now, of course."

"What's in them?"

"DNA verified by military record, the cemetery where his cremains were sent, and so on."

"Cremated? Nobody came to claim his body?"

"Shit, Peng, I don't know. I just took his identity."

She watched for any trace of dimpling or weaving, and her world got smaller still when she realized he was being honest with her.

"Why Wyatt?" she asked. "I served with a lot of men who never made it home. Why not one of them?"

"Right age, right body type. But," he said, as he crushed his empty beer can in one big hand, "You were close to him. That's the big thing. You've probably mentioned Wyatt to your friends in OACET, and that gives me some extra credibility."

"Joke's on you," she said, almost a whisper. She had never mentioned Wyatt. Not to anyone.

"How'd you break into my house?"

She pointed towards his dining room.

The false Wyatt shuffled around in his chair until he could see the hole cut through the drywall, and began to laugh. "Knew we needed internal security," he chuckled. "The best defenses don't matter once they're already inside. How'd you get past the perimeter?"

She glared at him.

"C'mon," he said. "We built this place to respond to anything you could throw at it."

"I'll give you a hint," she said. "I didn't need to throw anything at it."

The perplexed mess of yellow-oranges that sprouted up from his conversational colors like sickly sunflowers was delightful.

"So," she said, after a lengthy pretend sip, "who's your source?"

The confusion bled away in the greens of comprehension, and maybe a little too much smug pink.

"I'm not leaving," she said. "This is endgame for you. What

happens next depends on how well you convince me that you're of some use."

Wyatt laughed. He *laughed*. "Been spending too much time in the interview room, Peng?"

"Hard to improve on the truth, Wyatt. Your source."

"No."

"I've got all night. And a gun."

"All night?" he asked, slowly, running his eyes up and down what he could see of her body.

"Cute," she said.

"Yeah, you are," Wyatt said. He leaned towards her, grinning like a hungry animal. "I think we'd get along damned fine after a good solid fuck—"

She punched him.

She didn't hold back, and he didn't see it coming until the instant before her fist crashed into his jaw. Wyatt fell out of his chair, his head making the most delicious sound as it bounced against the white tile floor, a few flecks of blood falling soon after.

Rachel stood over his body, running her medical diagnostic autoscript over him as he sank into an unconscious stupor. Then, half-disappointed as the autoscript assured her he'd be fine, she walked over to his freezer and stuck her hand into the icebox.

Wyatt was out cold for nearly an hour. When his conversational colors began to crawl over themselves again in slow, unsteady loops, she pulled a fresh can of beer out of the fridge and dragged her chair into easy kicking distance.

He groaned as his eyes fluttered open. Rachel leaned forward, making sure that the first thing he saw was her looming over him, her gun resting on a knee.

Wyatt closed his eyes again. "Point taken," he said.

"Good boy."

He stayed flat on the floor, one hand exploring the new tender spot on the back of his skull, the other prodding his jawline.

"So," Rachel said. "Who's your source?"

He rolled to his knees, a smooth movement that made Rachel's finger jerk towards the trigger. "You don't want to know."

"Try again."

"No," he said, coming up on his toes and sliding into his chair as if he had never left it. As if she hadn't hit him hard enough to make him lose an hour. "You *don't* want to know. It took me too long to get into position. If I blow this, it's gone."

"I love how you think you've got room to negotiate," Rachel said.

Wyatt turned away and stared through the kitchen window. His conversational colors blurred to a sad gray, then shook off the sadness in a burst of professional blues and the burning white of excitement. "All right, you win," he said. "I'll show you."

"Tell, don't show."

"You won't believe me if I do," he said, straightening his suit. "I'll need my briefcase."

Rachel knelt and retrieved it, with her scans and gun aimed straight at Wyatt's center mass. The briefcase was locked. She sent her mind into the cheap combination lock until she found the grooves in the tumblers, and flipped the case open to retrieve the small handgun.

"Here you go," she said, as she shoved the sans-gun briefcase across the table.

"You're a fucking headache," he muttered, his hand moving to explore the lump on the back of his head.

"Thanks!"

He stood; her gun moved towards him again. "Calm down, Peng, I'm just getting my car keys."

"Put myself in a moving metal box, with you? No."

"Scared?" Wyatt squared himself in front of her.

"Smart," she replied, as she sent a text message to her usual taxi service. "Now, let's have another beer and you can tell me all about the nice company who paints your lawn while we wait."

NINE

Of all the places Rachel had thought that Wyatt might bring her, the Capitol Building hadn't made the list.

She had expected a chase across the city, maybe, or a tour of the seediest areas of town before he tried to lose her by sneaking out a back door and down a secret tunnel. She was ready for such shenanigans: the moment she had jumped in the back seat of her cab, she had flashed her badge at the driver and had hinted ominously about tax audits if the man in the new Honda Civic managed to slip away.

But there had been no such nonsense. Wyatt had driven along familiar streets, and had left his car in a parking lot she had been to many times before, usually when OACET business had required her to stand in front of a sea of angry faces to tell them no, you have neither cause nor reason to take control of our agency, but thank you for playing. Rachel had instructed the cab driver to follow Wyatt as he walked the two blocks to the Capitol, the taxi holding up traffic and blocking a good portion of the bike lane, and she grinned at Wyatt over the sounds of horns and cursing.

The Capitol... The back of Rachel's brain was churning through the options. *Posing as a Congressman's aide, and getting information by snooping through his files... Pretending to be a security specialist, and eavesdropping in the halls, or in meetings, or in bathrooms...*

When Wyatt reached the first security barrier, he bowed low, one hand extended like an usher's to show her into the building.

"Remember this," she told the cabbie as she shoved a fifty at him. "In case my corpse shows up on the news."

The cabbie fled, tires squealing.

Wyatt held out his arm for her; she walked past him towards

the first security checkpoint, scans fixed on him so she'd know if he was about to cut and run.

Nothing. His conversational colors were steady, with gray resignation resting against blue professionalism.

The entrance to the Capitol was layer upon layer of kill zones, spots where bystanders needed to gather in convenient clumps for processing before they were allowed to proceed deeper into the building. Her scans bounced off of the security guards: there were fewer guards than usual as the Capitol began to wind down for the night. Rachel was held up at the first checkpoint for the traditional OACET song-and-dance which allowed her to keep her gun, and wondered how she'd explain the fallout to Mulcahy when Wyatt used the delay to escape…

Again, nothing. Wyatt chatted with a guard on the far side of the security checkpoints until she rejoined him. He took her past the meeting rooms, the House and Senate Chambers, the offices of various staff members and persons of varying importance, each time waiting patiently when she had to pass through security.

(It did not escape her attention that not only was Wyatt familiar with the Capitol's security protocols, but the guards and staffers were familiar with *him*. They greeted him by his alias and, on one occasion, asked him about his father's health. And, when Rachel got hung up with a guard who recognized her from a previous visit in which several Congresspersons had threatened to defund OACET and she *might* have mentioned something about the status of their own campaign finances and a Congressman *might* have tried to have her arrested and she *might* have mentioned something about spotting that Congressman at a local club which *might* have caused the nearby reporters to scurry off in search of information about an extramarital affair… Wyatt intervened.)

After the last checkpoint, he led them down a deserted hallway and opened the door to a dark stairwell.

"Is this when you murder me and leave my body as an example to your enemies?" Rachel muttered as she scanned the space.

"These days, Peng, you're the only enemy I've got," he said, and paused before adding, "Left."

"Cute. Real cute," she said, but she made him lead the way down the stairs.

The back of her brain kept churning.

Despite her many visits to the building, she had never stopped to consider what might be in the Capitol's basement. She knew, in that abstract way in which facts were turned into mental scaffolding for reality, that there was a basement after she had overheard a tour guide say that there used to be a spa down there for Congressmen and their guests. And nothing the size of the Capitol Building could function without utility rooms, furnaces, and the like. But she had never bothered to toss a scan below the main floor.

The deeper they went, the fewer the opportunities. *Is he in housekeeping or maintenance? No, not while wearing a suit and tie... Security? No, we passed their office already...*

And the little voice in the back of her mind that never truly shut up was saying: *I've been looking for him for nearly two years, but I never thought to look in the cellar. Or did he know when I'd be in the Capitol, and he called in sick? Was he here? What if he sat in some of those public hearings? Did I just never bother to notice him?*

*Is it better for us that I **didn't** notice him?*

These thoughts smashed around her head, stopping only when Wyatt did, right beside a metal security door with lettering large enough for her to read:

INFORMATION TECHNOLOGY

And beneath that, a few printouts of cartoon robots. One was carrying a lightsaber.

"Oh Lord," she sighed. "You're on the Congressional Geek Squad."

"I was," he said, as he typed his security code on the electronic access pad. "Took me a long time to set up this alias, too. You're fucking welcome, by the way."

The lock released with a metallic *zwink!* Wyatt opened the door, and too-cold air poured from the room.

"Welcome to my home away from home," he said, as the fluorescent lights noticed there was a human being beneath them and flickered to life.

"Where's your home away from home away from home?" Rachel asked, her scans crawling over the edges and into the holes of the IT room.

"Let me have some secrets," Wyatt said, as he shrugged out of his suit coat.

"Nah." Rachel shut the door behind her and leaned against it, arms crossed and shoulders slumped with all of the boredom in the world weighing her down. Her mind raced: her scans kept searching the room, looking for guns or other surprises.

It wasn't a private office. Going by the sit-stand desks covered in the debris of different personalities, Wyatt shared the room with at least five other people. Around those—all around, in towering heaps that threatened to avalanche and crush them at the slightest sound—were electronics. Except for the empty hulls of desktop computers, she didn't recognize any of the equipment, knowing only that the stuff around her pulsed in wave after wave of data. *God, I wish Phil were here. Or Jason. They'd know what this stuff is.*

"Guns are at your twelve and eight," Wyatt said, pointing.

Rachel had already caught the gun at eight o'clock, a gigantic .45 taped behind a wall-mounted monitor. The second was its twin, buried beneath what appeared to be roughly sixteen million inert laptops and tablets.

Wyatt noticed the look of revulsion on her face. "Yes, Desert Eagles," he said. "It's called an alias, Peng."

"They're shitty overpriced hand cannons!"

"Ask if I've wanted to spend the last seven months here," he said, his colors freezing into cold dead blues.

"Then you should be thanking me for blowing your cover.

After this, you can get out of this shithole."

The blues brightened, running straight up the spectrum to that eager yellow-white of excitement as Wyatt's mood changed.

"You're welcome," she said.

He glanced at her, his colors darkening to professional blues which weighed her Southwestern turquoise against itself.

"Forget it. Just go ahead and tell me why we're here," she said. "Did you set up camp in the Capitol Building to help OACET?"

Red scorn flicked across his colors like a whip. "World doesn't revolve around you, Peng."

"Why, then?"

He gave a familiar tug to a nearby office chair. It was an ancient device from the Seventies which squeaked across the stone floor on plastic rollers, and complained by losing some stuffing as he sat down. "Adam and I got bored, chasing the money—"

"Who's Adam?"

"My partner. Your creator," Wyatt said. "You blew his old alias, and he needed a new one. He thought Adam was…appropriate, considering how much of his programming went into building OACET's implants."

Rachel sighed. "Lemme guess—you're not calling yourself Eve."

He grinned and leaned towards her, his colors a rich, bloody red as the office chair let out a small plastic scream beneath him.

"Your code names are shit, Cain," she said. "If Daddy Dearest sent you here to help OACET, maybe naming yourself after the son who murders his brother wasn't a smart choice."

"Cain had plenty of siblings," Wyatt said, still grinning in reds. "He just killed that one asshole who wouldn't leave him alone."

"Good luck trying to sneak up behind me to bean me with a rock," she said, and regretted the words as she spoke them.

"So are you really blind, or what?"

She pointed at the computers. "Didn't you want to get out of here? Permanently?"

Wyatt watched her for a few moments to see if she'd give in; when she didn't, he turned and started typing. "Sort of," he said.

"Hmm?"

"This place is a tomb," he admitted, "but it's a good spot to gather intel."

"Why? Not to help OACET."

"As I said, we got bored." He reached beneath the desk to plug something in, pressed a key on the keyboard, and she felt a new piece of equipment in the back of the room come online. "Setting complicated traps for rich guys at the request of other rich guys? Adam thought there were better things to do with our skills."

"Such as?"

He turned from the computer and leaned back in the ancient chair, his arms crossed behind his head. "You like the way the world works, Peng?"

"Most days, no. Not particularly."

"Nobody does," he said. "So Adam and me, we're making the world a better place."

Rachel laughed so hard she began to cough.

"No, no!" She waved him on. "Please. I want to hear how this plays out."

Wyatt's colors sank back into those cold blues. He turned back towards the monitor. "Come look at this," he said.

"Show me from here," she said, her butt still firmly planted against Wyatt's office door.

"Right." He grunted as sage green and red embarrassment appeared in his conversational colors as he remembered what she was. "So, nobody in this office works for Congress. Technically, I work for the Infrastructures Services Group at the Office of Management and Administration."

"You're a federal tech guy?"

"A heavily vetted federal tech guy who's got access to anything that goes through these servers."

She nodded. Pulling bytes from the data that was freed into

the wild would have been child's play for Wyatt, but Congress's own interdepartmental emails were another story. After the Great Benghazi Email Hunt, the government had cracked down on how email could be processed and stored. Working in the Capitol Building itself was probably the only way he could have gotten access to protected data.

"What else do you have?" she asked.

"Any time somebody loads data from an external source, I get a copy," he replied, typing. "Thumb drives, phones, hard drives... If I've serviced it, I've bugged it. It sends new data directly to my own personal servers."

Rachel chased down the connection to the piece of equipment she had felt come online. There it was: a server, a small one, with less data stored than she had anticipated, but Wyatt was talking directly to it and ignoring the other servers in the room.

Fooled you, Bert, she thought. *You just told me where you hide your gold.*

"You've got personal servers down here?" she asked. "That's risky."

"And two guns," he reminded her. "Which are more likely to get me caught than just another purloined letter in the stack."

"Why risk the guns?"

"Because Marshall Wyatt was a soldier in Afghanistan," he said. "He's got gunlust. Most of the guys in the office share it."

She flipped frequencies and gave a careful once-over to the personal effects on the desks. There were the usual plastic toys, mostly robots with a smattering of heavily articulated men in camouflage with guns stamped into their thighs.

"That's why you went with Desert Eagles," she muttered.

"Conversation pieces," he said. "They're what civilians expect to see in a gun. But they're functional, and I wanted to have something ready to go, just in case. The guys think I'm worried about another Weston incident."

A printer spun up and papers began to spool into a plastic tray.

"Those are for you," Wyatt said, with a nod towards the

printer.

Rachel kept her butt against the door, and raised an eyebrow at the psychopath.

His colors turned over to show an annoyed orange, and he went to gather up the papers. "Here," he said, holding them out as if they were laced with smallpox.

She stared at him, eyes hard, as she took the papers and wadded them into her purse.

"Not going to read them?"

"No," she said. "What are they?"

"Text messages, emails… It's the data trail that led Adam to believe that something involving OACET was about to go down, and was worth me breaking cover."

The stack of papers had been no more than ten pages thick. Her other eyebrow went up.

"If you were going after a tribe of technomancers," he said, "would you trust digital communications? It's mostly references to what was discussed at private meetings. That's the best evidence I've got for you, but none of it is enough to hang anyone."

"Makes sense," she said. "I got the feeling that Nicholson was somebody's puppet. Dude might have the charisma to hold a militia together, but the tactical know-how to run a long game on OACET? Nope."

Wyatt's colors flared in yellow curiosity at this; she took the opportunity to introduce Wyatt's private server to the server they kept at OACET for files labeled: "Suspicious, possibly swimming in viruses, might burn the whole place down."

His watch began vibrating. "Thanks for reminding me," he said, and pushed a button on the watch. A power supply across the room blew; the small server vanished from her mind.

Rachel shrugged. "Can't blame a girl for trying."

He waited, his conversational colors hovering patiently in stasis around him. She opened the door and pulled it with her as she stepped aside, keeping a goodly distance from him as he passed. He headed down the musty hallway, happy blues and yellows in his colors, a small balloon of purple inflating as he thought of a good joke—

Rachel gave a sharp whistle.

Wyatt paused.

"Get your briefcase and put on your coat," she said. "I've got better things to do than be called into questioning as a witness in your disappearance."

The purple burst.

"Now that I think about it," she said, "you should come into work tomorrow. Normal business hours."

Grays rose up and sank their claws into the blues and yellows.

"Peng—"

"And probably the day after," she added. "Just to be safe."

"Don't think so," Wyatt said, as he returned to the office to gather up his gear. "Don't much like the idea of you trapping me here."

"What are the odds that arresting you while you're at work will turn the Capitol into a bloodbath?"

"Point."

They retraced their path, except this time they managed to dance around the security checkpoints. Rachel watched the surface colors of everyone they passed, checking to see if Wyatt was signaling distress… No. So far, so good. The two of them left through the main entrance and walked down the steps, just another couple of federal grunts putting in some overtime.

When they reached the curb, Rachel hailed a fresh cab.

"Get in," she told him.

He touched his lapel, fingers resting near the bulge of the Desert Eagle he had slipped beneath his coat.

"Yeah, yeah, I know," she said. "Ask yourself why I let you pick it up. Now, get in the car."

She took them straight to OACET headquarters.

A gauntlet of reporters had entrenched themselves on the front lawn. Rachel plastered her best No Comment expression to her face and plowed through the thorny hedge of microphones and cameras. Wyatt followed, silent and glowering in reds and oranges. They paused at the old bronze front doors. Wyatt's sour mood had gotten its teeth in him, and he glared at the reporters as if he was thinking about doing damage.

"What's wrong?" she asked him. "I thought serial killers loved publicity."

"Only the dabblers," he said. "The craftsmen do it out of love."

Rachel stared up at him. "You are so fucking creepy."

He gave her that predator's smile again, and opened the doors for her.

The ground floor of the building was lousy with FBI and (Rachel noticed with some trepidation) the odd official from Homeland Security. Most of these were standing ready by the doors to keep the media at bay, but others had set up checkpoints throughout the building. Rachel asked the FBI agent who checked her badge why security had gone up: the agent told her that people kept sneaking in through the fire exits.

Once safely past the first checkpoint, Rachel shoved Wyatt into the same secluded niche where she and Hill had discussed the kidnapping.

"Here's the deal," she told him. "We both know there's no way in hell you're going back to the Capitol, ever. I'm going to make sure you're on camera when you leave this building. After you disappear, my story is that an old Army buddy of mine came to me with some suspicious information. I went to his place of business to check it out, and then brought him here to report to my superiors. If he vanishes on his way home? Well, that information must have been pretty important, right?"

"Except you cut your way into my house," he reminded her.

"My old Army buddy and I have some crazy prank wars," she said, before she realized the purple was back. "What?"

"Nothing," he said, smirking.

That purple smirk persisted all the way up the stairs and into Josh's office.

If Mulcahy's office had been designed as the crown jewel of OACET, Josh's office had been modeled after the offspring of a filing cabinet and a bordello. Nobody outside of OACET ever visited his office (at least, not without a very specific invitation), so Josh hadn't bothered to decorate. There were no windows, but light came through a skylight; after dark, the room was lit by a wall covered in mismatched sconces holding remote-controlled LED candles. His desk was an IKEA knockoff, pressboard in a faux-Swedish design, and leaning gently to one side under the weight of the computer peripherals and stacks of color-coded paperwork. The shelves circling the room were buried beneath law books and legal files. There was a floor—the logic of human residences required some form of floor—but a paper avalanche had come crashing down and hidden it a few months ago, and Josh had yet to dig his way out.

The only horizontal surface clear of this administerial debris was the queen-sized bed in the corner, with clean sheets turned down in welcome.

"Package for you," Rachel said, as she shoved Wyatt through the open door.

Josh glanced up from his keyboard, saw Wyatt, and just knew.

"Please tell me you didn't bring Jonathan Glazer here," he said through a new link, his conversational colors a sickly gray.

"I didn't," Rachel said aloud. "I brought Marshall Wyatt here. He's an old friend from the Army who reached out to me with a hot tip about the kidnapping.

"Here you go," she added, as she tossed the crumpled stack of papers on top of his keyboard. "Fresh from Congress's printers, and given to me by an employee dutifully hired and vetted by the…"

She looked at Wyatt.

"The Office of Management and Administration," he said.

"Them."

Josh's attention moved from the papers to Wyatt to Rachel before returning to the papers. He sighed and started reading. Wyatt stared at Josh for a long moment, then turned and began to explore the office.

Josh's colors went chameleon, shifting through excitement and anger as he flipped through the pages.

Her curiosity got the better of her. *"What is it about? I couldn't read it while watching Wyatt."*

"One sec... Okay. It's email communications between four people, and texts between those same four people and two numbers I've traced to a block of numbers sold to cell phones. The phones in question are inactive now."

"Burners?"

"Probably. The email accounts are under anonymous usernames. Looks like six people who are discussing a single holiday shopping list. It's definitely coded; there are different categories of what they want to buy, and discussion of a 'Comptroller' who controls access to the mall and who won't let them buy what they want."

"Is the Comptroller also named Mulcahy?"

A brief tremor of purple humor came and went through their link. *"That'd defeat the purpose of a secret code,"* he replied. *"There's also a long thread about friends in their holiday shopping network who're relocating to 'Steel City'."*

"Please tell me they're talking about Detroit."

"I doubt it," Josh said. *"The most recent message said that 'moving day' was a go. That message was sent mid-morning on Sunday. That's when Wyatt showed up at your house?"*

"Noonish, but yes."

"Okay. Is this all he gave you?"

"Yeah. Why?" she asked.

"There're no names, IDs, or other tracking data. These are just plain-text conversations with time stamps."

"Hey, murder machine?" Rachel called aloud. Wyatt looked up from perusing Josh's law books. "What are the names that go with these accounts?"

"Golly, Peng," Wyatt licked his middle finger and used it to turn a page. "How would I know that?"

"Oh, fuck you!" she snapped.

"You didn't check to make sure he included the names?"

"He's a goddamned psychopath, Josh! I could either read or make sure he didn't try to kill me. Not both."

Josh didn't move, but that shivery sensation of feeling

someone else nod came through their link again. *"I'd have done the same thing,"* he admitted, distracted, as he began highlighting text on the pages. *"I'll give this to our analysts. If their authors have any media presence, they might be able to track them through phrasing or content.*

"But..." His mental voice trailed off as his thoughts turned to the hidden safe down in the War Room.

Rachel agreed. The list of politicians who had been involved in the original OACET conspiracy was short. Mulcahy, Josh, and Mare had decided not to expose them, mainly because doing so would have destroyed the leverage the Agents held over them. These politicians were fish on the line, living with the knowledge that if they tried to come after the Agents, they'd be smacked with an oar and left in a cooler to rot. As threats went, it was a pretty good one: OACET had already taken down one of the most powerful senators in Washington. But this didn't mean those politicians were happy to leave things the way they were.

"Send somebody over to the U.S. Capitol, too," she said, as she showed him the location of the small server in the basement.

"Nice!" Josh brightened. *"If there's anything to be salvaged on it, we'll dig it out."*

Rachel had her doubts: Wyatt had a history of using thermal charges to nuke his computer equipment. But the tech side of OACET operations was, thankfully, none of her business.

"Neat," she said. *"Now, what do you want me to do with Wyatt?"*

Josh froze in mid-stroke and glanced up at her, yellow curiosity the same hue as his highlighter moving across him.

"He's your problem now," she said. *"I just burned him as a source, so he's of no use to us any more. You're my superior officer. It's up to you to decide what I do with him."*

"What?!" Josh exclaimed aloud, then: *"Come on, Rachel. I've got a million other things to deal with today. Handle him yourself."*

"Sure," she said, settling against an overflowing filing cabinet.

"Just tell me what I should do. Call the cops and turn him in? That'd be a fun confession. Or maybe we should wall him up in the basement. We're good at hiding people that might embarrass OACET, right?"

"I..." Josh's conversational colors were at war, professional blues in a pitched battle with OACET green, Wyatt's sandalwood caught between them.

"The ethics aren't so fucking easy when you aren't a Monday Morning quarterback, are they?"

"Jesus, Rachel!" Josh was nearly shouting, his professionalism gone and his colors turning red.

Wyatt coughed. It was a delicate sound, and existed for no other purpose than to remind them that he was in the room.

The Agents turned and glared at him.

"Don't let me interrupt you," he said.

Josh's eyes went towards the ceiling, as if evoking a higher power. Their link was tight enough for Rachel to feel the shape of his request, and she shivered.

He turned to Wyatt. "Where's your partner?"

"Around."

"We're calling him Adam now," Rachel said brightly. "And Wyatt is Cain!"

Josh stared at them until his colors ran gray and orange. He stood, and climbed over a stack of bankers' boxes to reach a nearby wine rack. An opened bottle of whiskey waited beneath the Chardonnays and the Bordeaux; he unscrewed the cap and took a good, long drink.

"Let's go over this again," he said, once he had come up for air and his professional blues had reasserted themselves. "You're here to help us?"

"Mostly," Wyatt replied.

"Why?"

The psychopath shrugged.

"He says they're the good guys now," Rachel added. "They're making the world a better place, one stupidly complex caper at a time."

Josh took another lion-sized drink of whiskey before returning the bottle to its place on the rack. "What's it going to take to get the names associated with these files?" he asked.

"I'd like to walk out of here," Wyatt said.

"Why?" Josh asked again, professional blues wrapping around himself.

Wyatt's colors froze in mild shock before they sped up to normal. "Seems the smart thing to do. For me."

"How long were you working at the Capitol?"

"Seven months," Wyatt said, some curious yellows beginning to appear as the conversation went wide.

"So you can hold down a job," Josh murmured, as if thinking aloud.

Wyatt laughed. "As part of a cover, yeah. You see me filling out a 401k?"

"I manage two trained assassins and a covert demolitions specialist," Josh said. "None of them seem to have problems obeying the tax code. We don't allow them to kill, but their lives are anything but boring."

Josh and Wyatt kept talking; Rachel stopped listening. She was trying to twist this new idea around in her head—*Is he actually trying to recruit Wyatt?*—and, like a cat held over a sink full of soapy water, it refused to let itself be placed anywhere of use. That idea kept bouncing between *It would solve the problem of what to do with him,* and *He'd officially be Josh's responsibility,* before spiraling down the hole and landing solidly on *But Josh might make me Wyatt's permanent babysitter.*

"Gentlemen," she said quickly. "Can we focus? Is there anything in that file that will tell us who's behind the kidnapping?"

Annoyed oranges pulled themselves over Josh's professional blues, but as he opened his mouth, Patrick Mulcahy entered the room.

Rachel jumped. She hadn't been scanning the halls, and the head of OACET was still missing his usual layer of conversational colors. He was nothing but a streak of man-shaped cerulean blue in the air, with a thick curtain of emotionless gray exhaustion around him.

He stared at Wyatt.

Rachel nudged a few files aside so she could make a seat from a stack of boxes, and curled up to watch the show.

"Wow, are you—" Wyatt went into charming mode, sticking on a good ol' boy smile and slumping slightly to blunt his edges. "Mulcahy! Wow! I've wanted to meet you for forev—"

Mulcahy didn't move as Wyatt came closer, hand extended, as friendly and as harmless as a big floppy puppy. When the psychopath was an arm's length away, Mulcahy said: "Stop."

The air went dead. Not cold; cold would have implied some sort of sensation. Just…dead.

"Why is this person here?" Mulcahy asked.

"You want the long version or the longer one?" Rachel asked.

"As short as possible."

"Josh asked me to find a source, and I did, and it happens to be attached to this dude."

"And you brought him here," Mulcahy said, an unspoken *"Where he could hurt our family"* lodged in the lifeless air around them.

"Long story," Rachel said. "Extremely long."

"Marshall Wyatt, Army CID," Mulcahy said, his facial recognition autoscript finally pulling the information out of the Army's database. "Except you're not, are you."

Not a question.

Wyatt straightened up and began to walk in a slow circle around Mulcahy. "I'm here with Peng," he said.

"No." Mulcahy turned as Wyatt did, slow and smooth. "She might have brought you here, but you aren't with her."

"You think so?" Wyatt asked. "You don't know her as well as you think you do." And he flipped open his suit coat to show the butt of his overlarge gun.

In a blur of motion, Mulcahy slipped a hand into Wyatt's coat. He stepped back, the Desert Eagle seemingly shrinking to fit comfortably in his palm, its barrel aimed square between the psychopath's eyes.

Wyatt went very still; Rachel grinned at him.

"Rachel?" Mulcahy asked.

"Now he's Marshall Wyatt," she replied. She took a deep breath, then added, "Before that, he was Jonathan Glazer."

Two heartbeats of silence, followed by: "Why is he here?"

Josh, who had been wholly orange until Mulcahy had taken control of the gun, began to get some color back. "It's complicated," he said. "He's—"

"You were sent to help us," Mulcahy said to Wyatt.

Wyatt nodded; Mulcahy lowered the gun.

"Can I get that back?" Wyatt asked.

The gun disappeared beneath Mulcahy's own suit coat.

"Or not," the psychopath muttered. He put some distance between himself and the Agents, and tucked himself against a bookshelf in the corner of the room.

"Don't. That was a gift," Josh said.

Wyatt paused, then removed a slim silver letter opener from his sleeve. He replaced it on its wooden stand, and resumed going through Josh's files.

Mulcahy turned to Rachel. When he opened a direct link, she felt her knees go weak. *"Start talking,"* he said.

TEN

"Rachel, I'd like you to stop running emotions," Mulcahy said. "I'd rather not be picked apart during this meeting."

"And let's do all of this on the verbal, please, Pat," Josh said. "None of us enjoy being anywhere near your head right now."

As Rachel turned off emotions and pulled herself out of the link she shared with Josh, the anxiety of those in the room seemed to fade away. It actually made her feel a little better: if she couldn't sense it, she could pretend everything was going to be okay.

OACET's in-house briefing room was as casual as they could make it. There was a kitchenette with a full-sized fridge on one side, and a fifteen-foot drop that ended with a basketball court on the other. The four members of OACET's administrative team were spread out along the table, with Rachel putting maybe a little too much space between herself and Mulcahy.

The old wooden conference table in the middle was a remnant from the building's past life as a post office. It had taken Pat and Mako the better part of an afternoon to move it from its former station in the letter-sorting room to the new conference room, and that was after the two of them had gotten so fed up with trying to move the colossal thing that they had torn its legs off.

Marshall Wyatt was handcuffed to a desk in an office down the hall. And the desk had been chained to a steam pipe. And, mostly for fun, Rachel had located a standard 60-meter coil of climbing rope in the gym and had wrapped it around Wyatt until his legs and torso had vanished beneath a cocoon of thick pink floss.

"Recap," Pat said. "Last twenty-four hours, starting after Josh and Rachel left the factory."

"I'm convinced Nicholson is somebody's puppet," Josh said.

"Even if he doesn't know it. I've spoken to him half a dozen times today, and his story changes each time, like he's getting advice from a third party."

"Any calls into or out of the building?" Rachel asked.

"No," Mulcahy replied. "No emails, either. But the factory is so large that somebody might be able to sneak messages in and out without us noticing."

"Or they're using something archaic and dumb, like homing pigeons," Rachel muttered. Mulcahy and Josh exchanged a glance. "You did check for homing pigeons, right?"

Josh scribbled something on his notepad.

Rachel changed the subject. "How are his men holding up? I haven't gotten a chance to drop in and look around today."

"Things are calm, but the first few days of a siege are the easiest," Mulcahy said. "I've kept a roster of Agents rotating through the factory to make sure that Hope and Avery aren't mistreated. The militia seems to be in good spirits; there've been no casualties."

"If we can wrap this up before the novelty wears off, we might be able to pull everybody out without a scratch," Josh said.

"That might be another problem." Mare Murphy, the fourth member of OACET's administrative team, was shuffling through her copious notes. Their organizational specialist trusted paper documentation and nothing else: Mare swore that the cyborgs playing with her data had managed to singlehandedly undermine the paperless revolution. (She had been the one to insist on adding the hidden safe to the War Room in the basement, saying that it was all fine and good that Josh and Mulcahy had a secret trove of documents somewhere, but that trove would be absolutely useless to OACET if, God forbid, the two of them were both shot in the head or something on the same day.) She tossed handfuls of paper and her own long red hair around until she found the page she was looking for. "Here we go—our analysts say that Nicholson is most likely operating on a timetable."

"Why?" Josh asked.

"Why do they think that, or why is he… Well, same answer to both questions," Mare said. "The incentives we've offered haven't made him budge. So, either we're offering the wrong incentives, or we're offering the right ones and it's not yet time to accept."

"Pat, I'd like to go to the media and tell them that Hope offered to buy the factory," Josh said, a pencil rolling across the backs of his fingers like a magician who was about to pull off a trick. "If I do this about an hour before tomorrow's meeting with Nicholson, it'll ramp up the pressure to negotiate."

"My contact at True Ally is willing to come public and state that they're willing to negotiate, too," Mare said. "All of this is just the worst possible publicity for them. They've decided to back off of the waterfront deal."

"Call them and see if they'll put something on the table," Josh said. "If they're willing to go on the record, I'll bundle them into the announcement and put a good spin on it for them."

"What about the local government?" Mulcahy asked. "Who's on that?"

"Me," Mare said. "The mayor pleads ignorance; so does his staff. Says that Nicholson filed a mountain of paperwork and most of it was nonsense. Now that the issue's gone public, they say they had no idea it was this bad, and of course they're willing to help."

"So if Nicholson is being honest about wanting to rebuild the factory, we can almost literally pave the way for him," Josh said. "Perfect. It'll be easy to kill any public sympathy for him if we offer him what he says he wants, and he still shoots us down."

Mulcahy turned to Rachel. "The investigation?"

"Right," Rachel said, and called up the documents that Santino and her team at the MPD had been sending to her all day long. "Check your tablets," she said. "I haven't had the time to print these out."

"*Always* print it out," Mare grumbled. "If it's not down on paper, we can fuck with it. You wouldn't believe how many of us think it's okay to screw around with the time sheets—"

Mulcahy didn't say anything, but the silence around the table grew deeper.

Mare sighed. "It's a *problem*."

Rachel tapped her tablet. "Santino and my guys have been busy. They've tracked down the original militia group in Pennsylvania. Their spokesman said the group's leader will be happy to sit down and meet with someone from OACET, but we'd have to come to him since he doesn't travel.

"They've also started to track Nicholson's movements since he came down to the Maryland area. It's going to take some time, but if there's any overlap with the investigations done by the FBI, we can speed it up."

"I'll see what I can do," Mare said.

"All right," Josh said, with a sideways glance at Mulcahy. "We should probably discuss…"

"Worst-case scenarios," Mulcahy said. "What are our options?"

"Our best option is rapid diplomatic resolution," Mare said. "We give Nicholson what he wants, retrieve the hostages, and let the lawyers sort everything out once everyone is safe."

"We all want Happy Fun Smile Time," Josh said. "But if we don't get it, we've still got choices. Including, but not limited to, turning this entire catastrophuck over to the MPD's ERT."

"Rachel?" Mulcahy nodded to her.

"Put a pin in that idea," she said. "The Emergency Response Team is great, really, just top-notch, but if they get involved in a raid conducted on OACET's behalf, they'll probably drag Homeland in after them."

"I don't think we can get away with running a full raid without involving the FBI," Josh said. "Homeland might try to weasel its way in if that happens."

"I know," Rachel replied, drumming her fingers on the desk. *Knudson in his pinks… Smug bastard's got something planned for us, I just know it.* Across the table, Josh glanced up at her. She shook her head, and shoved all thoughts of Knudson aside.

"I'd prefer to run our own raid," Mulcahy said. "I take the

Hippos in with less-lethal weapons, we take down Nicholson's team, and we secure the site."

"Pat, no." Mare said. "OACET doesn't have the authority to act as law enforcement. Not without invoking the charter. And if the raid goes wrong—"

Mulcahy cut her off. "We'd have to include the FBI," he said. "OACET doesn't have enough personnel with the training to run a true large-scale stealth operation; I'd have to join in. It'd be me, the three Hippos, and a handful of ex-special forces."

Rachel gave a little wave.

"And you," Mulcahy told her.

"You were special forces?" Mare asked. "I didn't know that."

"She wasn't, but we'd need her scans," Mulcahy said. "Rachel's the best advanced warning system on the planet."

"Well, me plus Phil," Rachel said. "But I'd rather not go into a dangerous situation while in a deep link."

"Next idea," Mulcahy said.

"Jeez, Pat, I don't know," Josh replied. "Diplomacy first and foremost, followed by a stealth raid if that fails… Then what? Magically teleporting—"

"Josh." Mulcahy stared at his friend. "We're wasting time."

"Right," Josh said, dropping his eyes to his notepad. "Right. Must stay within the realm of realistic outcomes. Okay… A full-out frontal assault isn't even on the table, I assume. That would go bad for everybody involved."

"We should block an assault option if any other agency begins to push for it," Mare added.

"Agreed," Mulcahy said. "Next idea."

Nobody said anything. Rachel moved her pen around her notepad in (what she assumed were) long aggressive loops.

"Can we talk about the real problem?" Mare asked after the silence began to stretch.

"My wife," Mulcahy said.

"Yes. Pat, she's not really… I mean…"

"Hope tends to treat all problems like nails that need to be hammered back into place," Mulcahy cut her off. "In this situation, she could easily become a serious liability. If she decides that she's done waiting—that she's taking Avery and leaving—it'll be a slaughter."

He wasn't cold, just impassive, as he spoke of his wife and godchild as if they were chess pieces to be managed on the board, and Rachel shivered.

Josh paused, then exhaled. "Exactly," he said slowly. "I'd want Hope at my back in any combat situation, but this can't become one."

"What about Hope's meds?" Rachel asked. "If this turns into a standoff that lasts a couple of days or more..."

"Non-issue," Mulcahy said.

"But if this lasts—"

"Non-issue."

Mucahy wasn't budging: there was no other course of action than to let it go.

"What about walking her and Avery out?" Josh said. "Both of them can see our projections, so we can communicate with them. That's a hell of a tactical advantage."

"Same problem as before. Hope's a warrior, not a commando," Rachel said. "Very different skill sets. I'd love to have her around in a bar fight, but she's likely to get me killed in anything that requires tactics or covert movements.

"Sorry," she added to Mulcahy.

"I agree," he replied. "It's too much a risk to rely on Hope to get herself and Avery out. Maybe if it was just the two of them, yes, but we can't forget the other hostages."

"Why did they take more hostages?"

They all turned towards Mare.

"Hope and Avery are the ones they wanted, right?" she asked. "Their abduction was intentional. The other hostages were picked up at random. Since they already had their key bargaining chips, wouldn't more hostages be a greater liability once all of this is over?"

Josh and Mulcahy exchanged a glance: Rachel had no idea what to make of that, and grumbled to herself about men and their insistence that she stay out of their heads.

"What do you mean, Mare?" Josh asked.

The tiny woman ran a pen across her notes. "Once this is over, the hostages would be free to talk," she said. "They'll say they were kidnapped against their will. More of them means that Nicholson won't be able to claim that everyone came along willingly."

"Shit," Josh said quietly. "I don't like what that implies."

"Okay, guys?" Rachel said. "Let's not freak out just yet. My team has been going through the literature on sovereign citizens—conventional logic doesn't even begin to apply to these people."

"Explain," Mulcahy said.

"Okay..." Rachel flipped around her tablet to locate one of the files Santino had prepared. Like everything else her partner wrote, it was a work of heavily cited and properly annotated art. She skimmed the digital text to refresh her memory, and mentioned the relevant details as she went. "Militias are usually groups of like-minded folks. They're almost always formed from volunteers who join up to train or to run missions—they call them 'ops'—and once the op is done, they go back to their homes. Almost like the National Guard. Most militias think they're performing a public service with these ops, like the Arizona Minutemen patrolling the Mexican border back in the mid-2000s.

"Sovereign citizens are different. They're more of an ideology than an organization. Most sovereign citizens aren't big into killing. What they want is to...okay, Santino says that the layperson thinks that sovereign citizens are all about chaos. They aren't. If they believe—sincerely believe!—in their movement, all they want is for the rules that they believe apply to people in power to apply to them, too.

"They can be dangerous. Not all of them, obviously, but sovereign citizens will kill." Rachel paused, her heart heavy with the next words. "And when they do, they almost always go after cops. The majority of assaults and murders committed by sovereign citizens happen during confrontations with law enforcement.

"Then we get into militias. Sovereign citizen militias tend to be less common than traditional militias. They're *new*. They're different and scary, and nobody has a solid handle on what they're capable of. They rarely run ops: when they do, they tend to be more confrontational, especially since their enemies aren't illegal aliens but the U.S. government itself. You remember the occupation of the Malheur National Wildlife Refuge? Some of those guys were sovereign citizens.

"Folks, this is important." Rachel tapped her finger on the tablet. "Santino cites authorities who claim that the more contact a sovereign citizen has with law enforcement, the more likely they are to snap—if they are militarized, the odds increase. Which means we all benefit if we keep contact between Nicholson's group and ours to an absolute minimum. Or, if we have to do it, we send Josh in and he doubles down on the goofy."

"We've got to work on Nicholson's background," Mare said. "Figure out if he's a true believer or just using the movement to work the system."

They all agreed, and then—

"All right," Josh said, trailing off. The pencil flitting across his fingers stuttered and fell. "Rachel—"

"Go ahead," Rachel said, as she realized her body had gone numb. She reactivated emotions and Southwestern turquoise sprung up in Josh and Mare, shadowed by guilt, sorrow, and more than a little depression.

Mulcahy was still a blank canvas.

"Rachel, I'd like you to drop out of the link," Mulcahy said.

Rachel stared at him. "You realize what you're asking," she said.

He nodded.

"Right," she said, and stood.

"You don't have to leave—"

"I do," she told Josh. "I honestly do."

She left them behind her and started walking.

She was shaking. Not a lot, just a little, hands trembling to the point where she had to stuff them deep in her pockets.

Karmic debt was such a bitch.

She didn't know this building. If this were the old OACET mansion, she would have known where to go (*hide*) to wait for the (*trial to end*) others to come to a decision. There was pressure building in her head; the others were starting to talk. About her. She felt their minds turn towards (*against?*) her own; she had to remind herself that they were thinking about her, not calling to her (*they might never call to her again—*)

She kicked open the nearest door and found herself in someone's office. Empty, slightly stale. Nothing interesting in the way of furniture or decorations. Probably the office of an Agent who, like her, who was out of the building more than they were in.

Rachel locked the door behind her and slumped down.

She searched (*not for the last time, oh, please…*) for concrete. When she couldn't find any within the range of her close scans, her fingers found the stainless steel leg of the desk instead.

She seized it with her fingers; it would have to do.

A flicker of thought to deactivate her implant.

The world went black.

The pressure of others' thoughts against her own mind disappeared.

(*alone in the absolute dark*)

The table leg was cold comfort. The part of her that didn't bother with things as trivial as panic wondered if the hammer and the anvil had been involved in its making, or if those tools were just relics, or if they were still a hammer and an anvil, technically, what with the pounding and the breaking, but had taken different forms for a different world.

(*…the absolute dark…*)

It had only been a matter of time, really. They all knew their collective wasn't a utopia comprised of perfect, flawless beings. They were just human. Imperfect, awful, miserable humans who stumbled and fell and sometimes let serial killers go free…

(…*alone*…)

It was inevitable that a member of the collective would fuck up. Fuck up bad. Fuck up in a way that not only required punishment, but deserved it.

Rachel had always figured it'd be her.

It didn't hurt any less to know she had been right.

They had talked about what they would do when it finally happened. They were both the watchmen and those who watched the watchmen, and there must be accountability. (She had been one of the loudest at those meetings, demanding policies that would go into effect as soon as an Agent's wrongdoing became known. You could take the Catholic out of the church, and even the Catholic out of the Catholic, but the guilt was born within the bones and it knew that payment would come due.) Somewhere off in the periphery, she was on trial, where nearly four hundred of her peers came together in that nebulous realm where thought met cyberspace, and discussed what must be done.

(*Alone.*)

How did time used to pass for her? She had spent most of her life without a clock in her head that blipped off the hours and the minutes and the seconds and the centiseconds. It shouldn't be that hard to remember how she lived without it.

The metal under her fingers had warmed, become familiar. So had the old stone floor beneath her.

How long did it take stone to pull that much heat from her?

How long are you going to allow yourself to sit like a useless shit on the floor?

Right.

She knew how to do this. She had taught herself how to do this. There had been months spent in this absolute dark. Months of living by feel and sound and smell, and trying to settle her mind on the fact that she either needed to start carrying a cane or get over her fear of dogs. She had learned how to use her implant as her adaptive device before that, but adaptation hadn't come quick or easy—she knew how to do this.

Rachel stretched out her other hand—carefully—and found a wall. *Desk on one side, wall on the other...* On the ground in front of her was a cheap area rug with a knotty polyester weave. There'd be a couch in here somewhere; all OACET offices had a couch for when the occupant needed to attend out-of-body meetings. She remembered it being near the far wall...

Three slow steps, arms outstretched.

A shin bumped against a padded surface.

The couch. Cheap bonded leather around an industrial-grade wood frame. A few papers on it; she piled these together and moved them aside before she nested.

Okay, said the part of her mind that dealt with homeostasis and didn't give one single whit for collectives or trials or psychopaths. *This is a good first step, but you better pick it up. Because you need to pee and that situation's not going to get any better on its own.*

The door was to her left. Up. Four steps to the far wall, so the door would be about three... One hand out to find the wall. One hand low, just in case.

The wall hand does its job. Follow the wall, the low hand turning into the door hand...

Door. Metal, good quality. Door hand turns into knob hand; the knob is solid and turns easily. Mare put this place together and she's good at her job—

Don't think about Mare. Or Josh, or Phil, or Jason—

—*Jason! Jesus! Jason, **please** have the sense God gave a gopher and keep your mouth shut—*

The hallway is cold. It's long after normal work hours and the heat is turned down at night. No jacket. Nothing but a short-sleeved polo shirt because today was supposed to be about getting the drop on a psychopath, and that's the dictionary definition of Casual Monday.

If only you had spent more time in this building—

She hadn't.

If only you hadn't chosen a room at random—

What's done is done. Move on.

One hand along the sandstone walls. Mason lines between the blocks of stone at regular intervals. Thirteen of those lines between door frames.

Door frames are easy. It's a federal building; federal buildings require braille labels on anything more public than an office. And Mare got a nice package deal on door plaques with raised type, so she can navigate by names.

If only you knew where anyone's office was beside Mulcahy's and Josh's—

Move on.

Footsteps. Someone else, a long way down the hall; they stop walking when they notice you. Male, by the sounds and smells of them. You face them, nod, and move on.

Water fountain. Ceramic, a vintage piece left over from before the building's rehab. Water fountains are almost always next to bathrooms, since the plumbing can be tied into the same lines.

Door frame. The handle is different; offices have knobs, but this one has a bar. Slide a hand up and down the sandstone wall to find the bathroom signage with its braille—

Men's room.

Fuck.

There's no privacy in a men's room. Just urinals and splash and stink, and that one sad doorless stall that might as well spend its entire life crying over abuse.

Right.

There's a symmetry to bathroom placement due to the water lines. Except there wasn't one on the other side of the fountain. That means the women's restroom is probably nearby. Might be directly across the hall, might be around the corner and butted up against the men's room.

Try across the hall first. One hand out, four paces forward.

—a man's smell? Is there someone watching—

Fuck 'em if they are.

Outstretched hand hits the sandstone wall, maybe a little too hard. Calm down, calm down. Turn left, count six blocks…

doorway. Office doorway. Turn right, count thirteen blocks... doorway. Another office doorway.

It's a doughnut layout, then: the restrooms share a central wall on opposite sides of a circular hallway. Back across the hallway. Men's room. Turn left. Thirteen blocks, door. Thirteen blocks, door. Thirteen blocks...

Corner? That's new.

Thirteen blocks, door. Over and over and—

*—that smell again there **is** somebody watching me and I swear to Christ I will fucking punch them in their goddamned throat—*

Corner.

If symmetry and basic math are her friends, it's two offices before she hits the women's room. And if not, there's always the men's room and an extremely thorough shower once she gets home.

Thirteen blocks, door. Thirteen blocks, door. Thirteen blocks...

Door frame. Handle instead of knob, and the braille says—

Oh, thank God.

She's inside the women's room with its comforting scents of industrial cleaners and basic sanitation, and it feels blessedly, mercifully empty. She whistles; the acoustics of bathrooms bounce the noise back to her. It's louder on her right side; the stalls are on the left.

Walk slowly; the floor might be wet.

Both hands out, and close together; bathroom stalls are nothing but edges and they have a way of jumping out at you.

Surface. Flat and cold, too cold to be plastic; probably a marble slab left over from the building's old post office days. Mare would have kept those, too. One hand along the marble until it ends, then a space of open air, then another flat surface (plastic?) that moves when she touches it, then more stone...

A bathroom stall.

Toilet paper is almost always on the right, with clearance between the edge of the door and the holder. Check to make sure the holder is full, or at least full enough for practical purposes. Take a bunch, wad it up, and *slowly!* find the toilet.

Flush first. Then, wipe down the seat, because failure to do so is a mistake you will make only once in your lifetime and the nascent germaphobe in you gets near-terminal heebie-jeebies when you think about That One Time At Burger King.

Shut the door. Slide the bolt home.

The rest is easy. In federal buildings, toilets are positioned in the dead center of stalls, with a minimum of seven inches of clearance on all sides. God bless standardization and regulations.

And then, of course, just as she's finally about to pee, her fucking owl shows up.

There's no visual barrier between her and her own avatar; it taps into her optic nerves, circumventing her eyeballs entirely. The enormous green bird flaps around (what Rachel assumes to be) the bathroom stall until it finds a perch on top of (what Rachel assumes to be) the left-hand marble slab.

It peers down at her and cocks its head in that owlish way, and opens its beak as if to hoot.

Instead, a very familiar human voice comes out.

"Rachel? You can reactivate now."

Josh's voice.

"Fuck you," she mutters to nobody in the absolute dark, and resumes her business.

The owl vanishes.

A few minutes later, while she's washing her hands in the sink, there's a quiet tapping on the door to the restroom.

"Rachel?" Josh's voice again, but this time there's a body attached.

"C'mon in."

The bathroom door opens, followed by footsteps against a hard floor.

She's found the towel dispenser by the time Josh arrives (*Not beside the sink, but over it? What the hell?*) and is drying her hands. There's a wall-mounted trash can, and it's an easy drop into it; she hears the paper towel hit the bottom of the nearly empty plastic bag.

"Did you get my message?" he asked.

"Yup," she said, a little too harshly. "Didn't want to reactivate without knowing what I'm walking into."

He waited before replying; her heart sank a little lower. "You've spent all of this time in the bathroom?"

"Nope," she said, turning to face him.

"Rachel—"

"Just tell me."

Sounds of shuffling feet.

(*Did they even stop to consider what it meant to her, to cut her off from not just the collective but from her fucking fake **eyes**—*)

"Damn," she whispered, and wondered how long it would take her to get used to the absolute dark.

"No," Josh said, "No, Rachel, you're… We took a vote. You're fine. We decided you did the right thing in how you handled the fallout from the Glazer incident."

He was too quiet. "But?" she asked.

"A majority isn't…comfortable…with how he's still hanging around."

She laughed. It wasn't the nicest laugh, and its echoes ricocheted around the bathroom like bullets. "*They're* not comfortable?!"

"Just reactivate," he said. "But you might have to, you know, say something."

"Right," she said, and activated her implant.

She kept her scans off, so the flood of *other-same-self* washed over her, into her, through her within the black… Gratitude? Yes, mostly gratitude, but anger, too, and deep within that was enough fear to chill her down to her bones.

—*the risk you took*—

"*I know,*" she told them. "*Believe me, I know. The only thing that's kept us safe is that we've convinced the entire world we can be trusted. If I got caught—*"

Terror, now, instead of fear. The gasp of four hundred people brought to the edge of a cliff and thrown into thin air, followed by the crashing fall to the rocks below.

"*I know. And I've beaten myself up over it a million times, but I'd still do it again.*"

—*yes*— came the reply from nearly four hundred mental voices, with all of the emotions behind it. Then: —*but*—

"*I know,*" she said again.

"*We shouldn't have this power,*" she added. The words were suddenly there, heavy and ready to be used, like a hammer that had always been waiting in her hand. "*But what I did, that had nothing to do with what we can do. That time, I didn't mess around with data. I just tossed the man a goddamned paperclip and let him see himself out. That was all me. **My** choice. It would have hurt all of us, but it was my choice.*

"*I didn't learn from it.*

"*Last year, I went into a suspect's cell phone and tampered with data.*"

Shock. A fresh surge of terror and anger. Outrage pounding against her mind in profanities and pleas and prayers.

"*I thought it was necessary,*" she said, holding up the mental version of her hands so the collective would let her finish. She poured her own emotions—*honesty, integrity, good intentions*—through the link until the others relented. With all thoughts of Jason buried behind a blanket of thick charcoal gray wool, she added, "*I thought that if I didn't, we'd get hit, hard. It was a set-up to catch one of us in an abuse of power, and I nearly walked right into it.*

"*I've done everything by the book since then. Not because it's the right thing to do—Christ, guys, we all know nothing is black and white in our world!—but because it's…easier. The law needs to determine how we act, what we do. Not us.*

"*That's how it should be. The law protects us from ourselves. I almost learned that the hard way—the fallout probably would have killed me. It'll be the last time I ever do something that selfish and stupid again. If we need an object lesson about risks and dumb-ass decisions, let it be me.*"

A moment for a deep breath, which spilled out throughout

the collective.

"I was hoping it'd all go away, but I guess I'm not that lucky. Yesterday, when Jonathan Glazer showed up, I went straight to Josh and told him what I had done. And then I tracked Glazer down, and brought him here. He's ours, now, and I have no idea what to do with him. He says he's here to help us get Avery back and…I believe him.

"And…" Here, the words that had come out like a flood began to fail. Instead, she reached out, into the link, and shone a light on fifty distinct minds. These grew brighter in return, and she felt the others acknowledge the complexity of the wrong actions for the right reasons. That sometimes, lying and hiding and ignoring the law? Those were the right actions.

Just as long as they didn't get caught.

—aren't we all just the biggest hypocrites—

Rachel let her role in the link ease; as she pulled back, the others came forward.

More discussion. More questions. And she couldn't ignore the anger coming from Josh…poor Josh, who had probably stood up for her and had then learned about her tampering with the cell phone at the same time as everybody else.

The collective picked her up and rolled her around their shared consciousness. She floated, adrift within their minds, as they weighed her actions anew. She moved from mind to mind, called by their will before another grabbed her and pulled her to them.

It's a dance, she realized, and felt a brief flash of amusement as someone pulled her identity against their own before spinning her away. Someone else took her into themselves; ideas, brief, here and then gone. Another seized her, weighed her… And another… Another… Another…

How long can this last?

Not a loss of identity, this dance. No, that would have been easier, to cast off her sense of self and just float around as nothing. Here, the relentless pounding of *Judgement! Judgement! Judgement!* came hard and fast against her mind.

This was an entire universe which contained her, weighed her, found right and wrong and confusion and hopelessness and fed all of this straight back into her soul—

Hands around her, holding her up, touching only fabric and no skin contact at all.

"Rachel!" A name—her own? Of course. "Rachel! Drop out!"

"Nobody," she said, and realized she was laughing. "Nobody knows what's right! Nobody! Nobody knows!"

Someone slapped her.

The arms which kept her standing hadn't moved: the slap came through the link and hurt all the more for that, bypassing flesh and bone and going straight for her nervous system. She rocked backwards, and the arms around her tightened.

"Penguin?" Josh's voice, eighty kinds of worried. "Drop out of the link. Please."

She did. It took a scream and every ounce of her willpower, but she broke away from the dance.

"Jesus," she whispered, her throat raw. "That was new."

"What just happened?"

Rachel rubbed the side of her face; the sore spot was huge. Whoever had slapped her thought of themselves as having hands as large as dinner plates. Probably even large enough to hold a Desert Eagle and not make it seem like a joke—

"Rachel?"

She opened her mouth to crack her jaw, carefully; it wouldn't surprise her if her bones had snapped in sympathy from the force of that imagined slap.

"Has everybody ever thought about you at the same time?" she asked. Her head was pounding. "And I mean *everybody*."

"Yeah," he said. She felt the rumble of his voice through his chest as he talked. "When I'm holding a linkwide session."

"Have we ever…judged you?" she asked as she thought back to all of the group meetings over the past three years. "I mean, have these sessions happened while we thought about you? What you've done, what we think you should do? How it could affect the rest of us?"

"No," he said. "I don't think so."

"You'd remember if we did." Rachel got her feet under her and pushed away from her friend. "Let me know when they've calmed down."

"They already have," Josh said. "Pat told everybody to go out, get drunk, and get laid."

Rachel glared at the space where she felt he was standing.

"Well," he admitted, "I might have been the one to tell them to get drunk and laid. What happened?"

"No idea," she said. The urge to find that anonymous office and curl up on the couch was almost overwhelming. "But if you're still looking for a good punishment for me, that was probably it."

He sighed. "We're not going to punish you," he said. "The majority agree with what you did. It's just…you shouldn't have made those decisions on your own."

She grabbed for the image of wool overcoats before she remembered they weren't linked. "Right."

"We'll have to talk about additional security precautions, though. After things calm down."

"Right," she said again. "Let's go see what we can do to make sure that happens."

ELEVEN

Her head was still throbbing.

No. 'Throbbing' suggested the pain came and went, however briefly. This was more along the lines of what happened when a sledgehammer was applied to the back of her skull at the same time an eggbeater was shoved into the semisolid goo in her cerebrum. Aspirin, coffee, coffee, and more coffee had done little other than turn her migraine down to a level where she could stand to be around other human beings.

But not when they were arguing.

"Nicholson is your all-American trust fund kid. There's nothing in his background to suggest he's radical, or radicalized, or militant. Not until he gets back from China."

"You don't go *to* China to become radicalized!" Santino said to Zockinski. "It's an authoritarian state!"

China again, she thought from her spot on the linoleum floor beneath the pinball machine. *How does that line up?*

At Mare's request, the FBI had sent copies of their case files and investigation notes over to Rachel's team at the MPD. Santino had fallen upon these and devoured them, and had managed to piece together a timeline which showed that Nicholson had been a good upstanding manchild before he went on a month-long sightseeing tour of China two years ago.

Once Nicholson had come back to the States, he had gone feral, so to speak. He had dropped off the grid for a time, resurfacing now and then in gun stores or to make sure the service fees on his various investments, holdings, and other properties were kept up-to-date.

(None of this made sense to Rachel, who was beginning to wonder if Nicholson was an alien hybrid of sovereign citizen and lawyer. Someone who had gone to law school and learned how the legal system worked, just so he could bend it over a judge's bench and give it a jolly good porking.)

Arthur Bennett, the regional EPA official who had been instrumental in tipping Nicholson's father towards the breaking point, was dead. Quite dead, dead from kidney cancer, dead and buried almost seven years ago. Records showed that after he had been released from jail in 2001, he had been living quite comfortably, financially speaking, up until the time of his death. Bribery had certainly been a viable retirement plan. Bennett still had family in the area, but he was so far down on their list of priorities that Rachel thought they could avoid searching the usual forgotten storage units for mildewed boxes of tax returns.

But then there was China.

"Guys?" Rachel said, more to cut through her team's protoshouting than because she had anything to say. Talking amped up the eggbeater. "Where did he go in China, exactly?"

"Beijing," Santino said, as he flipped through a file. "The Great Wall, the Forbidden City, the Yungang Grottoes... Tourist spots."

"You got connections over there, Peng?"

"I've got family over there, Zockinski. Not the same thing." She tried to sit up... Nope. The sledgehammer was having none of that. "China is diligent about tracking its tourists. Especially American tourists. Might want to see if we can get their version of Nicholson's travel itinerary."

"The FBI thinks the odds of Nicholson picking up a sovereign citizens' mentality while in China are—"

"Except he *did* pick up something in China!"

And then they were fighting, Santino and Zockinski, at a decibel which sent Rachel to stick her head beneath her suit coat and tug it tight around her ears.

Fighting is good, she reminded herself. *Different is good. Different is **priceless**.*

It was a familiar mantra, one that was often repeated when her team at First District Station was trying to close in on answers to especially sticky problems. The fights were annoying (definitely) and time-consuming (certainly), but they also forced the members of her team to change how they thought. For Rachel, that was priceless. Falling into the repetitive patterns of groupthink was a real possibility for members of a hive mind. Each Agent was still learning how to develop their own unique talents, but they all knew there could come a day when they all had the same autoscripts, the same abilities...and shared the same broad opinions about how OACET should be run. She was sure one of the reasons that Mulcahy had stuck her over at First District Station was to guarantee that she got constant exposure to strong-willed jerks who weren't part of the collective, to fight and learn and fight some more, and, above all, to avoid falling into the rut of sameness.

But oh, how her head hurt.

"Guys?" she said through her jacket's sleeve, just loud enough to be heard over the din. "Please. I'm dying."

She wasn't running emotions, so the brief glance shared between the two men was reduced to head shaking and eye rolling.

"I can see that," she reminded them.

Santino sighed. "Here's the FBI's working hypothesis," he said quietly. "Nicholson goes to China on a tourist visa. He's profiled before he gets there, tagged as a possible malcontent because of his father's financial problems, which he's inherited—"

"But he's still rich enough to take an extended overseas vacation?" Phil asked from his spot on the floor beside Rachel.

"I don't think anybody has ever accused Nicholson of having an abundance of common sense," Santino replied.

Rachel thought that probably wasn't the case, that it was more likely Nicholson had been born into the rarified socio-economic strata which thought anything less than fifty thousand dollars was pocket change, and that he had never needed to outgrow that mindset. But she was a government employee who grew up in a nice middle-class suburban household, so what did she know?

"The FBI thinks someone made contact with Nicholson,"

Santino continued. "Purpose of contact unknown, obviously, but it made him change his behaviors."

"This would have been long before OACET went public, though," Phil said. "So why's he targeting us?"

"He's not," Hill said.

"Yup," Rachel agreed. Above her, the steel underbelly of the pinball machine hung like a heavy metal sky. She reached up to poke it; her head stayed in one piece as she moved her arm. Progress. Maybe the suit coat was helping to hold her head together. "Whatever he's doing, we're a means to an end."

Zockinski moved to the whiteboard and uncapped a fresh marker. "Ideas, people. The crazier, the better."

Santino and Hill began to outline the tinfoiliest of tinfoil-hat concepts. Some of them were familiar. Movie plots, mainly, but Rachel recognized a couple of themes from their previous cases.

Phil recognized them, too. "You guys handle the craziest shit," he said quietly.

"Yup," she replied. "The world's gone weird."

"Can you link yet?"

She groaned, gritted her teeth, and reached out to him.

Much of the previous night was a blur. Rachel remembered going with Mulcahy to settle the matter of Wyatt, and then nothing at all until she woke up this morning in Josh's office bed with the shampoo-sweet smell of Mare's long red hair all around her. Beside her, Mare had stirred ever so slightly, and had told Rachel to go back to sleep until one of OACET's doctors could examine her.

Rachel had obliged.

Later, after her physician had put her through the usual battery of tests to prove her brain hadn't melted, Jenny Davis told her that, no, there seemed to be no viable health reason to prevent her from doing any of her usual activities, but yes, if it still hurt, maybe don't do them until your head feels better? Idiot.

But, idiot or not, today was a day when staying out of the link wasn't an option.

Joining a close link hurt, but the touch of Phil's mind was gentle. Too gentle, actually...

"Jason told you," she said.

"Last night." She felt Phil nod. *"You didn't give him up."*

"No reason to." Jason had kept her secrets; why shouldn't she keep his? And since his secrets boiled down to crap she had dragged him into against his better judgement...

"It matters to us," he said. *"Thanks."*

—an image, half-seen and half-felt, of Jason and Phil and a young woman who wasn't part of the collective sitting at a kitchen table together, the two of them pleading with Jason to keep his damned mouth shut—

"You told Bell?"

Curiosity and chastisement flavored his side of their link, a quiet rebuke over her objection to including the third member of their partnership. *"She's not going anywhere, Rachel."*

Her scans pulled themselves back towards Santino. He was ranting about the Chinese scattering thumb drives laced with viruses in coffee shops near government buildings, and what happened when nature took its course and the government employees found all of these free thumb drives lying around.

"Yeah," she said. *"I get it."*

"He promised to stay quiet," Phil said. *"But if the vote had gone differently, he would have spoken out on your behalf."*

Rachel grinned. *"Tell him this,"* she said, and showed Phil the color of teal, cut through with soft warm threads of deep maroon.

Confusion came back across their link: Phil's, growing deeper as he showed her Jason's reply of the same teal and red sitting across from gray and OACET green, with Rachel's Southwestern turquoise balanced in the center.

"What does this mean?" When they were joined in a deep link, Phil became semi-fluent in the language of her overly color-coded world, but this fluency didn't seem to stick.

"Ask Jason," she said.

"Where's Glazer now?" he asked instead.

"Wyatt," she corrected him. *"Marshall Wyatt. He's in a very safe place."*

That was something of a lie. Maybe. Or maybe not. Mulcahy had turned Wyatt over to the Cuddly Hippos.

Which made perfect sense: who better to watch a murderous psychopath than a team of professional assassins? They had left Wyatt in the Hippos' care, and Rachel had chuckled on her way out the door.

(She had made it clear to Wyatt that she would be extremely—nay, *extraordinarily*—displeased if anything unsavory should befall the Hippos. Then, she had made it clear to the Hippos that she would be perfectly okay if Wyatt should accidentally vanish from the face of the earth forever. She was sure that the four of them would work something out.)

"What's Mulcahy going to do with him?"

"Hell if I know," she replied. *"I'm just glad it's no longer my call."*

"Rachel?"

She waved to Santino.

"You ready to go?"

"No," she said, and reached down and out for the familiar concrete lining the old elementary school. The strength of manmade stone came back, steady and resolute, to her scans, and she slithered out from beneath the pinball machine. "Yes."

"Can't believe you're making the Quantico run," Phil said aloud.

"Yeah, well," she said, her hands pressed against both sides of her head to keep her brain in place. "They've got the nearest gun."

"Technically, the factory in Maryland is closer—"

"Don't," she said to her partner as she found her feet. "Just don't."

In a different time and place, Rachel would have asked one of the Hippos—hell, even Wyatt!—to slip into the factory and bring her one of those guns from the featureless crates. With the legal system looming over her like an iceberg, the next best option was to gamble on the chance that AKA: Lobo's handgun had been part of the same arms shipment. The handgun they had seized from him at the time of his arrest had been sent to the FBI's Laboratory at Quantico for processing. Their contact at the lab said there wasn't much evidence to get off of the gun using conventional methods, but if Rachel wanted to come down and check for herself...?

She and Santino had gone back and forth on whether using her scans on AKA: Lobo's handgun would be admitted in court. Two years out, and the legal system had finally begun to address the cyborgs in their midst. The most significant case thus far had ruled that Agents in law enforcement could register and track the cell signals of a person, or persons, who were suspects in an active crime. The precedent had been established by a ticking bomb scenario, something-something suspects fleeing the scene, and an FBI unit that had been lucky enough to have an Agent liaison ready to pull numbers out of thin air. The ruling had determined that the Agent had performed the same role as a standard IMSI-catcher... In other words, the Agent was just a pretty face stuck on a piece of technology that was already in widespread use among law enforcement agencies.

Professionally, Rachel agreed with that ruling. Personally, she thought it was bullshit, mainly because she was against imposing any legislation on Agents that categorized them as machines. But, since a large part of the legal system in general was bullshit anyhow, she kept her mouth shut and let the laws fall where they may. Whatever happened as the result of using her scans on AKA: Lobo's gun might be used by a defense attorney as grounds for a mistrial. It might further push the legal system to categorize Agents as "tools" instead of "persons". And it might also help put pieces of Nicholson's past in perspective, and help bring Hope and Avery home that much sooner. The tiny details that made up the ice and loose gravel covering the slippery slopes were hardest to see during the downward slide.

Getting to the parking garage was a long, slow walk. When

they reached Santino's car, a compact blue hybrid, he allowed her to curl up in the backseat without offering his usual harassment. They were well past the Virginia border when he finally asked: "What happened?"

"You have a rock tumbler when you were a kid?"

"I've got one now. It's in the garage."

"Shoulda guessed." Rachel winced as the car bumped across a pothole. "Well, I went through one of those last night. Metaphorically speaking. The others stripped me raw."

"Why?"

She gritted her teeth and flipped on her scans. Santino was swimming through yellow curiosity; short of cramming an implant into his head, she wasn't sure what she could do that would blunt his fascination with the collective.

"You remember Jenna Noura? I told them about how I hacked into her cell phone."

"Oh," he said. "Whoa. Why now?"

"It...came up," she said quietly. "I needed to do some penance."

"Oh." He paused. "You finally told them that you helped Glazer escape?"

"How the fuck did you—" Rachel slammed her head against the rubber armrest as she tried to sit up.

Santino started laughing. Hard.

"Pull over, asshole!" she shouted as the hybrid swerved into the travel lane and their fellow commuters turned red in fury.

He took the nearest exit and parked on a small patch of windburnt gravel. They were out of the car and running across the nearby field, Rachel swearing obscenities as they pounded through the scrub grass. Her partner's legs were longer and he was faster in a sprint; he finally stopped after she threatened to take out her gun and shoot him.

"How long have you known?" she shouted across the field.

Santino was still laughing, nearly bent double in purples with tears streaming down his face. "A year," he gasped. "An entire year!"

"Why—*how!?*"

He fell over, howling.

When she reached him, she couldn't help kicking him. Just a little.

"Not in the kidneys!" he managed.

"Get up, you…you asshole!"

"You used that one already." Santino rolled over onto his back. As he caught sight of her face, he started laughing again. "Oh God, totally worth it…a whole year…"

She gave up. "How?"

The gray of expensive overcoats floated through the purples.

"Oh, *fuck* Jason!" she shouted, and stormed off towards the car. She reclaimed her spot in the back seat, decided that made her look like a pouting child, and got out to walk around to the passenger's seat.

This process made Santino laugh all the more.

Fifteen minutes later, he opened the driver's side door and slid behind the wheel, weak and wheezing.

"Okay," he gasped, as he grabbed the steering wheel for support. "Okay. I can explain."

"Please," she said, and hoped the word came out as a lofty, *Well, I really don't care,* instead of the petulant, *Well, no, I really **do** care, quite a lot actually.*

"Did you talk to Jason yet?"

She crossed her arms instead of answering.

"All right," he said. "You know how you told me you hacked Noura's phone?"

"I remember you crawled straight up my ass and laid spider eggs when I told you, so I'm wondering why you're suddenly fine with Glazer—"

He slumped over laughing again.

Rachel dug around in her purse until she found a black marker. She popped the cap with a loud *click!* and held the marker over his immaculate dashboard.

Santino froze in whites.

"Sorry for the drastic measures," she said, as she recapped

the marker and slid it back into her purse. "You were saying?"

"Not cool," he muttered, his colors gradually recovering from the mild shock. "Jason didn't out you, by the way. Or, when I guessed that you had something to do with Glazer's escape, he tried to take the blame."

"How'd you guess?" Her partner was one clever son of a bitch, but she had thought she'd kept this from him.

"It was after the hacking incident with Noura. You were a little too shaken up by that. I mean, it was serious, yeah, but you've admitted you'd let the city burn to the ground to protect OACET. Wasn't much of a jump to connect that to Glazer giving you evidence to use against Senator Hanlon in exchange for an escape. I never could understand how he managed to get out of the building."

"Je-*sus*," Rachel whispered. "You could have told me! Or Jason could have, or..." As the purple in his colors faded to grays and uncertain oranges, she realized what he had done. "This was an *experiment?!*"

Burning fury, quick and hot, surged until she heard her pulse pounding in her ears. Not because of the experiment itself—Rachel was well used to being her partner's guinea pig. Santino was an academic above all else, and she had been the subject of various tests and observations as long as they had worked together. When she had first been assigned to the MPD, Santino had kept a little notebook. Each time she had done something especially cyborgish, the details had gone into the notebook, the end goal being some high-level academic paper depicting what it meant to fight crime alongside an Agent. The notebook had disappeared around the same time she had confessed to Santino that she had lost five years of her life to an experiment gone bad. The two of them had never mentioned it again, and all subsequent experiments had been done with her consent.

Except for this one.

"Not really," he said, scrambling. "Not at all. It's...well, you're always worried about how much the others can pick out of your head, right? I just thought this was the safest way to test whether you could tell if someone in the link could keep a secret from you."

"How does that work when you aren't in the link, idiot?"

"Not me," he said. "Jason. It's a secret the two of you share, so if you could pick that out of his head—"

"This is fucked up," she said. "You realize this is fucked up, right? Keeping this from me to test if I can keep it from others? And now it doesn't matter anyhow!"

"It'll always matter," he said. "Unless you're going to share everything with the collective from now on."

"Fuck!"

She slumped down in her seat and pressed her hands over her eyes.

They were fifteen miles down the highway before she had worked out what was bothering her. "Mulcahy and Josh are keeping something from me," she admitted. "They say they know how to get Hope and Avery out of there, but they won't say how."

"You running emotions?" he asked.

"No." Her head was a knot of competing drumlines, and half of them were keeping time on eggbeaters. She had gone dark in the hopes that some of them would get bored and go home. "Why?"

"Just that secrets aren't necessarily evil," he said. "Sometimes, they're just about personal things. Things that those who keep them aren't ready for others to know."

"Yeah, well..." Rachel sighed. She thumbed the release lever and pushed her seat back as far as it would go. "If they've got something that could end this, then... I dunno. I feel like they should just go ahead and do it! But they're bright guys, so if they aren't, it's probably yet another ticking time-bomb solution that'll blow up later. If I knew what they were thinking, maybe I could help. Find a different way to use it...or... I dunno."

Secrets.

Traffic in the Quantico area was always a bear. The roads leading into the city were in a perpetual state of construction, and the roads out hadn't been expanded to allow for congestion. Quantico was a bottleneck of bumpers as far as the eye could see; Rachel threw her scans down the highway and found that the traffic was nearly at a standstill for the next half-mile.

Santino glanced at her in curious yellows.

"We're screwed," she said. "Totally screwed. Stop-and-go for the rest of forever."

"There's no way you're getting back in time for that meeting."

"They don't need me," she said. "The only reason Josh wanted me along on that factory run was to watch his back. If Nicholson is coming to the Batcave, they'll be safe as…as a…"

She gave up and flipped off visuals again.

"How's the head?" Santino asked.

"Not getting better," she admitted.

He sighed, and Rachel felt the car begin to turn. She turned on visuals to find Santino moving off of the main road and into the parking lot of a local sandwich shop.

"This isn't going to get us to Quantico any faster," she said, as five cars went to war over the space they had just created.

"When was the last time you ate?"

"I don't know," she said. Eating hadn't been a priority since Wyatt had shown up, although Josh had crammed a heaping plate of spaghetti in her last night to help offset any energy loss from the link. "This morning, I guess? I had a bagel."

"Wait here," he said, and disappeared inside the restaurant. He returned fifteen minutes later with drinks and two greasy paper bags. Before she could stop herself, Rachel had grabbed the nearest one and was tearing into the first of three sandwiches.

"That's what I thought," Santino said, slightly smug in pinks.

"Shut up," she muttered, as she dove into the second sandwich.

"How much energy do you think you burned last night?"

"No idea," she said. Chicken salad? Usually not her favorite, but this one tasted like it had honey and spices mixed in. "It was exhausting, I know that."

"You know the brain burns more energy than any other organ in the body?"

"You've mentioned," she said. The third sandwich was a meatball sub, the bread and meat nearly lost under a slab of toasted provolone. "Mako has mentioned. Jenny Davis has mentioned. All of you, probably a hundred million times or more. Damn, this is good!"

"You know what housekeeping is?"

"Yeah," she said. "Especially since my roommate has all but moved out because he's shacking up with his girlfriend, and now I'm stuck doing all of the chores."

"Yeah, well…" He winced in orange uncertainty and green guilt, but those were offset against a pale soft blue she didn't recognize. "In neuroscience, housekeeping is what they call energy expenditure designed to maintain non-signaling functions—"

She held up a hand.

An opaque glaze filmed over his conversational colors. "You've heard of synapses, right? How the brain uses electric impulses to activate them?"

Rachel nodded as she fumbled with her straw. Mountain Dew? A king-sized dose of caffeine and high-fructose corn syrup sounded like just what a very shady doctor would order.

"Well," her partner continued. "When a synapse is involved, that's a signaling function. Those are responsible for the majority of energy consumed by the brain. Housekeeping tasks are what the brain spends the rest of that energy on—they're processes that the brain uses to clean up after itself. You remember me telling you about the research which is used to show that there are higher energy requirements after mental exercises?"

"Yup." She could practically hear the rabbit scream as it fell to its death down the tangent-hole. "But I ate last night, right after the link. Josh carb-loaded me."

"You loaded on the front end. Has your headache been getting worse all day?"

"Yeah," she admitted. That smug pink was getting fierce.

"I'm betting your brain has a lot of housekeeping to do after last night," he said. "That type of link probably needed a lot of cleanup. Josh made sure you replaced your reserves to recover from the active signaling functions, but housekeeping has been sucking you dry all day. How's your head now?"

"Still hurts," she said. She craned her neck to test it. "But getting better."

The smug pinks overtook him, as he pulled back out into traffic.

Rachel pointed at him. "No more experiments."

"Sure," he said, as his colors rolled over themselves in a saucy wink.

Eight miles and ninety minutes later, they showed their credentials at the FBI's first security checkpoint. The FBI Laboratory at Quantico was one of the most sophisticated buildings she'd ever visited. She was familiar with the general layout; Jason worked at the Consolidated Forensics Lab, and the D.C. Metropolitan Police had borrowed heavily from the FBI's design when they constructed their new state-of-the-art forensics department. While older, the Quantico building was similar in that it was steel, glass, and concrete, and above all, clean. The leather soles of Rachel's boots squeaked on the smooth composite floors as they walked to the first security checkpoint.

Elissa Smith was waiting for them. The FBI ballistics specialist had a core the color of a purple orchid, and was bouncing on her toes in eagerness. "Agent Peng!" she shouted, waving. "Officer Santino! C'mon down!"

Rachel waved back. Smith was small and almost flighty, except when she was handling weapons. Put any type of firearm in her hands, and she turned from a bubble-headed soccer mom into a calm, steady-handed professional with deadly aim. Rachel imagined her kids won every Bring Your Parents to School Day, especially if their mother showed up with visual aids. Say, oh, a bazooka.

"Come on, come on," Smith said. "Hey, Agent Peng, while you're here—"

"I can't," Rachel said, forestalling the inevitable. She liked

Smith, but the woman had an inexhaustible interest in ballistics science, and that made Rachel and her shooting abilities a treasure in Smith's eyes. Every time Rachel came down to Quantico, Smith took her out to a different firing range and put her through a dozen tests on different weapons. "I want to get back to the city after this. The kidnappers are coming to OACET headquarters later today. I should be there if I can."

"Oh." Smith's bright yellow anticipation of an afternoon at the firing range blurred in grays. "Yes. Yes, of course. Let's get going, then? Coffee first? Coffee later?"

Smith's prattling moved off to the edges of Rachel's consciousness as she handed her credentials over to the guard at the second checkpoint. His conversational colors sharpened to a point as he checked her ID, traces of cautious yellow and uncertain oranges appearing around OACET green.

Caution? Maybe. This wariness was new.

No. Not new, her subconscious reminded her, as it stretched and rolled over, ready to resume an already full day of nagging. *It used to be like this all of the time.*

As Santino moved to take her place with the guard, Rachel scanned the others in the main entrance hall. Most were going about their business, treating her and Santino as part of the background.

Others, a very few others, were watching her. They all wore that same cautious yellow.

Stupid woman, you thought things had changed.

She told her subconscious to shut up, and kept walking.

The Firearms-Toolmarks Unit was kept in the basement. As they descended via the usual chain of stairs and elevators, Rachel noticed familiar faces here and there, old acquaintances from past cases. When they spotted her, OACET green bloomed, followed by that same cloud of yellows and oranges. One man, caught off-guard as he turned a corner and nearly bumped into her, froze in shock before turning yellow and walking quickly in the opposite direction.

Santino had noticed. He bent low and whispered, "What's

going on?"

She moved her scans up and down the hall to be sure.

Yup.

She leaned towards her partner and whispered back: "They're scared of me."

TWELVE

AKA: Lobo's handgun was…simple.

She kept trying to think of a better description, but "simple" worked. Not cheap, not complex, just a decent all-purpose gun from the NORINCO factory in China.

"We're seeing more and more NORINCOs over here," Smith said, her colors darting back and forth as she searched through the FBI's firearms database. "They've been trying to break into the international market. Decent weapon. Inexpensive. This model is used by the People's Liberation Army as their designated sidearm. Ever fired one?"

"Hmm?" Rachel shook her head and broke away from her deep scan. "Yeah. In Afghanistan."

"Right, right, Afghanistan is the global clearinghouse of weapons," Smith said, tapping on her tablet's miniaturized keypad. "Used to be. Syria is catching up. Caught up, I suppose. 2012 was a good year for Syrian arms dealers. Not so good for the rest of us… Ah, found it! You're sure of the serial?"

"Yeah." Rachel was having a hard time following Smith's train of thought. The woman's conversational colors bounced from topic to topic faster than she could fire them off verbally. Smith's emotions didn't shift too much—everything stayed within the hues of professional blues—but the yellows and whites of intense concentration moved around like a laser light show across a dark navy sky.

"This is it." Smith flipped the tablet around and tried to pass it down to her.

"I'm good. I'll read it from over here," Rachel said. Her headache was back. Grabbing the serial numbers from AKA: Lobo's handgun had been relatively easy, but she had gone through every pore of the gun to make sure she hadn't missed any evidence. Her scans had come up with black dirt, a different kind of black dirt, granite dust, gun oil, and yet another kind of black dirt, for all the good it did them. She rested her head on the cool steel tabletop of Smith's office workstation and began reading. Her head came up a moment later. "The PLA reported this gun as stolen?"

"Yes, along with a larger shipment of firearms," Smith said. "Much larger. Several thousand guns. All makes and models from NORINCO. What was in those crates?"

"Not several thousand guns," Rachel replied. She had told Smith about scanning the crates. (Had scanning those crates been legal? Santino had argued that anyone knowledgeable about Agents should assume that an 'in plain sight' standard applied to hidden objects as well as objects left in the open. He felt that since Nicholson and his men had obviously done their research on OACET, they should have expected Josh and Rachel to poke around in the figurative medicine cabinet. She'd have to talk to Judge Edwards at their golf game tomorrow to see if this would fly in court, or whether it should be introduced at all since very few other Agents had her capacity for scanning; doing so might unnecessarily complicate the already-complicated discussion of Agents and the legal system with the assumption that what one could do, they all could do, and damn them all for differences. For the time being, she had cloaked it in the chaos of the kidnapping. Smith had accepted that excuse at face value, and Rachel had to resort to her old fallback of crossing her fingers and hoping that everything she did wouldn't spin around to bite her in the ass.)

There was a knock on the door to Smith's lab. Rachel tossed her scans over her shoulder to see Santino let himself in, three bottles of soda stacked on top of each other like a precarious tower. His core of deep cobalt blue was covered in a shifting layer of gritty gray sand.

Rachel raised an eyebrow; her partner mouthed "Later," and passed out the drinks.

"What have we learned?" he asked.

"Another arrow pointing straight towards some level of Chinese involvement," Rachel said, poking the handle of the NORINCO pistol.

"How convenient," Santino said, as he nudged aside a few papers on the lab table and hopped up beside her.

"Occam's razor," she reminded him.

"Occam needs an update," he said. "If the simplest answer gets blamed for everything, anything even slightly complex gets a free pass. It's why we've been so busy."

"Apparently..." Rachel sighed. "...Lobo's gun was part of a large theft of Chinese weaponry. Since when is major weapons trafficking considered slightly complex?"

"If the last few years have taught us anything, it's that a conspiracy is just a bunch of assholes with access to resources," Santino said.

Rachel twisted open the cap on her soda and didn't bother to answer him.

"All right. Try this. Which makes more sense? That Nicholson went to China and became indoctrinated in a militia mentality that's unique to the United States, or that he picked up the sovereign citizen ideology first and went over there to start laying the groundwork for a false trail? Or, hell, maybe he just took a vacation."

Smith, who had been watching this exchange like a cat following butterflies in the garden, added a slight, "Um?"

"Yes?" Santino said, rather sharply.

"Sovereign citizens? We're—the FBI, I mean—we've classified them as domestic terrorists. To be honest? Nicholson scares us. The movement doesn't have many charismatic leaders. If he manages to unite them? He gets an army of about a hundred thousand soldiers. And most of them? Gun owners who hate us."

Smith's voice moved up and down as she went from question to statement, and her hands fidgeted around her tablet. That, along with the threads of uncertain oranges that kept tearing themselves away from the whole cloth of her conversational colors, drew Rachel's attention from the handgun in front of her.

"Nicholson's just a rich kid," she said to the ballistics specialist. "I've seen him. He's got no experience in leading an army."

"He'll find someone who does," Smith said quietly, the oranges beginning to wrap around her in futile self-comfort. She ran her hands along the pieces of a disassembled assault rifle lying across her work station, then began to put it back together. A metallic *shink shink shink* echoed around Smith's office as she slid each piece of the weapon into its place. "The smart ones always do."

"Yeah," Santino said. "They know they can't handle everything on their own, so they delegate responsibility like any good manager. If Nicholson has a good second-in-command, he'll do his job and let his second manage everything else."

(Rachel's subconscious took an older memory out of storage and blew off the dust. An OACET Administration meeting in the War Room, Josh and Mulcahy planning strategy for the coming week, Mare telling Mulcahy that he needed to lay off and let her and Josh manage more of the administrivia of day-to-day operations…)

"Yeah," Rachel said. "I can see that. But, guns and hair triggers for cops aside, why does that make him a threat?"

Smith's hands were flying, with *shink shink shink* chasing each piece of the weapon home.

"The smart ones might start out leading militias," Santino said. "If they're lucky, they end up leading countries."

Smith nodded as she completed her task, and set the assault rifle on the table. "We're not saying that will happen," she admitted. "Armed rebellions can be put down. But, you know, it's not that we'll win, but that we'll have to fight. Right?"

(Her subconscious whispered again, not a memory this time, but a threat about martyrs and blood in the streets.)

"Gotcha," Rachel said. She stood and placed AKA: Lobo's gun back in its evidence bag. "Thanks," she told Smith.

"Good luck," Smith said, one hand resting on the assault rifle, her colors now set in steady blues.

Smith's office opened into the main floor of the Firearms-Toolmark Unit. The hallway was wide and painted in industrial beiges, with the intermittent muffled sounds of gunshots coming from behind the thick steel doors.

"So, what happened?" she asked Santino.

"This way," he said, and set out down the hall.

He led her back the way they had come. At the top of a stairwell, a man with a core of pea green was waiting.

"Hey, Campbell!" Rachel brightened.

Special Agent Campbell flushed in reds and the same gritty gray stress that she had seen in Santino. "Peng," he said. "How you doing?

"Busy. We've got to get on the road," she admitted. "Nicholson's coming to OACET headquarters this afternoon and I want to be there."

"I'll walk you out," he said, his colors flashing OACET green.

Rachel glanced at Santino. Her partner nodded.

"Yay, intrigue," she muttered, as she and Santino followed Campbell through the door.

She had worked with Campbell on several occasions. The FBI Special Agent was one of the best crime scene technicians she had ever met. He and his team specialized in homicides; she assumed this was why he hadn't been called in on the Nicholson case at the parking garage.

Santino picked up his pace. With his long legs, he put a few lengths between them, all the while pretending to be immersed in his phone. Campbell waited until he and Rachel were halfway to the parking lot before he stopped talking about his kid's softball team. "We've been waiting for someone like Nicholson to come along," he said quietly. "You guys have to wrap this up, and fast."

"We're trying," she promised. "What have you got?"

He glanced behind them, as if looking for shadowy men with microphones. Rachel sighed and tried to direct him over to a nearby bench.

"Listen, I can't—"

"Cyborg," she reminded him, as she began to weave her shield around them. "I won't mess with any snooping devices, promise, but they won't be able to hear us either."

"That's no good," he said. "Not for me, not here. That'd be as bad as if you tampered with them."

"All right," she said, and let her shield drop. "Can I ask a question?"

Campbell's conversational colors wrapped around himself, like armor. It was a reflexive gesture she associated with interrogations, and it was disconcerting to see it happen in someone she considered a casual friend.

"Sorry," she said, hands up and empty. "Forget I asked."

"It's weird when you do that, Peng," he said, as a good-humored purple appeared beside an uncertain orange.

"Telepathy's a timesaver, but I can't read minds. Not really." She turned and started walking towards Santino. "Call me if you decide you want to talk."

"Fine," Campbell sighed, going just a little red around his edges as he hurried to catch up. "We're all wondering when you're going to take over."

Rachel stopped. "What?"

"Not you," he clarified. "OACET. Well, maybe you, unless there's someone else at OACET who'd be better at running a criminal investigation."

"No, that'd probably be me," she admitted. "Trust me, this is the first I've heard about taking over. Do you know something I don't?"

Campbell's colors shied away from her Southwestern turquoise.

"Hey, I'm not lying," she said, as she turned to face the FBI agent. "Why would I kick you guys out?"

"No, you'd keep us around," Campbell said. "We'd just be…" He shrugged, and gestured towards the FBI Laboratory behind them. "I guess we'd be *yours*."

"What's wrong with that?" she asked. It was a gentle tap to his equilibrium; she waited to see how he'd spin.

His surface colors weaved in and out of themselves, OACET green warring against professional blues and the burnished gold of a special agent's shield, but he pulled away from answering.

"Campbell, listen," she said. "There's no reason why OACET would want to bundle you into our assets. The FBI is the best there is when it comes to kidnappings—it's not like we could tell you how to improve on what you're already doing."

"You say that now," Campbell replied. "But what happens if we haven't made progress by this time next week? Your charter—"

"Oh shit," Rachel groaned, as she finally understood the wariness in the FBI agents that she had passed in the halls of the Laboratory. "That *fucking* charter!

"I hate that thing," she said, more quietly. "Sorry. Shouldn't have taken your head off. It just…"

"I get it." Campbell nodded. "But we're worried, okay? We deal with enough inter-agency bureaucratic bullshit without OACET crashing down on us."

"Where'd this rumor come from, anyhow?"

"It's just been going around," Campbell said, without a trace of dimpling. "Everybody's talking about it."

"I'm not going to take over," she said. "You've got my word. I can't speak for my boss, but I know he doesn't need any additional complications right now."

"But it's already started." Campbell began walking towards the cars again. "Mulcahy's already begun locking us out."

"What?! What do you mean?"

"At OACET headquarters—Mulcahy's not allowing our tech team access to your database."

Rachel had thought her headache was gone, but it had just been napping. It woke up with a nervous shriek and started kicking the back of her eyeballs again. "Honest to Christ, Campbell, you guys are just dying to see monsters. If you had to solve the kidnapping of the head of the CIA, would you expect them to give you full access to their internal files? Same damned thing."

"We'd insist on it." The gritty grays around Campbell deepened. "If we thought it was relevant to the case? Yeah, we'd go through every file we could."

"Do you think Mulcahy and Nicholson have planned this?" she asked. A hundred yards away, Santino had reached his car. "Does the FBI think we're running some kind of scam on y'all?"

"We don't know what to think," Campbell said. "We've suspected something big was going to happen with the sov-civ movement, eventually. Stack it with OACET, and you've got two big unknowns going up against each other."

"Right," she said, as the headache kicked around her skull like a ninja. "Thanks for telling me this."

"You're good people, Peng. You've always been honest."

Ouch.

Some more small talk, mostly for closure's sake. After that, she said goodbye to Campbell and escaped into the relative safety of Santino's car.

"When did he get you?" she asked, as Quantico fell behind them. "Cafeteria?"

"Yup, cornered me while I was buying the drinks. He's worried."

"No shit," she said. Campbell was at the limit of comfort for her scans, his colors still warring between orange and blue. "He says the FBI thinks that OACET's going to invoke our charter and take full control of the investigation."

"What?" Santino's colors shifted towards white. "That'd be the stupidest thing you could do."

"I know," she said, and yanked on the seat toggle. "Give me a minute. I want to rest before I call the office."

She turned off her implant, and felt the collective disappear from the periphery of her senses.

Blessed silence.

*...that **fucking** charter...*

She supposed that, once upon a time, the charter for the Office of Adaptive and Complementary Enhancement

Technologies would have made sense. In that fairytale time, a bamboozled Congress believed OACET would bridge the many different organizations within the federal government and was not, in fact, a mad Senator's scheme to take control of modern civilization. If OACET was to provide a networked infrastructure of high-level leadership, a charter which allowed Agents to come in and take control of various committees, procedures, and actionable events was logical.

There were limits to the charter, of course. Even the most cunning madman couldn't convince Congress that the Agents should be able to seize control of the Supreme Court, or the office of the President. But if Rachel wanted a criminal investigation to call her very own, she could have taken over this one with a word and her signature on a document she kept folded into a tiny square in her wallet.

Fuck the charter, she thought. It was good for nothing except causing friction between OACET and other agencies. She had never officially invoked it, and only once had dangled it as an implicit action against stonewalling. Better to pretend it didn't exist than flaunt it.

In her opinion, OACET should have gotten rid of the charter entirely, gone to Congress and begged them to take it away, or at least revise it so the level of power an Agent could wield on a whim was hamstrung to shreds. But no, Mulcahy had decided they needed every ounce of leverage they could hold, even as he advised them to avoid using it whenever possible. As a result, the charter—or at least the threat of the damned thing— remained intact.

"Could I take over the FBI if I wanted to?" she asked Santino.

"Thought you were resting."

"I am. Could I?"

"Nope." Santino had read paragraph and verse of the charter, and had an undergraduate's degree in procedural law besides. "Best you could do would be to insert yourself in their organization in a supervisional position of authority."

"Right." That made sense: that madman had sold OACET to

Congress as a form of government-wide Internal Affairs. "But OACET could take over the Nicholson case."

"No question," Santino said. "Why?"

"Why am I asking, or why would OACET do that?"

"Why are you asking? There's no logical reason on earth for OACET to take over this case."

"I know. Something's clicking around in my head," Rachel said. "It feels as though we've gone back to the bad old days when OACET first came out, and nobody trusted us because they didn't know what we'd do."

"You've only been out a few years."

"Yeah, but we've established ourselves," she said. She flipped her implant on again and felt the asphalt bleed and squeeze beneath them. Asphalt was so useless, plastic pretending to be stone. The car wobbled slightly. "Our media guys say the public trusts OACET more than they trust Congress."

True: they had built their walls piece by careful piece, shaping their image within the public as reliable. Credible. Trustworthy.

Will they still think we're trustworthy after this? she asked herself, as her mind wobbled down its own road.

Probably? This wouldn't be the first time their image had taken a hit. It had all but been shot and left to die in the street the previous spring, when the media had broken the story of what Senator Richard Hanlon had done to them. The public had already known that Hanlon had developed the program where five hundred young federal employees were turned into cyborgs, but the news that they had been slowly brainwashed into mindless machines? New information. They learned how Hanlon had introduced an intentionally buggy AI interface, and that this AI had been programmed to break down the Agents' resistance. Triggered not just by action but by thought and emotion, the AI had slowly conditioned them to obey. Unconscious, immediate responses replaced critical thinking. Hobbies, personal relationships, all of the finer things? Also gone—the AI was always there, and there was no reason for it to recognize the boundary between work and home lives.

Five years of this. Not living. Not death. A mechanical existence, office drudgery punctuated only by consuming enough food to survive, maintaining enough comfort to sleep, and the infrequent screaming fit during the morning shower when the bubbles of how wrong it all was made it to the surface of your dull routine and popped.

When Mulcahy had broken them out of it, they didn't even realize what had happened to them. Not at first. But the conditioning hadn't been completed, and they slowly came back to themselves.

(Most of them, anyhow. But those who hadn't weren't anybody's business but their own, and OACET kept its secrets.)

After the brainwashing story had broken, there had been some loud discussions over whether OACET should have disclosed this part of their history when they first went public—didn't the public have the right to know the risks posed by these obviously unhinged, psychotic cyborgs?

Mulcahy had responded by unleashing the psychiatrists. The psychiatrists had torn through the Congressional subcommittees, and had left no foe unassessed. When the Rorschach tests had settled, the Agents were found to have acted within the standards of the HIPAA Privacy Rule, and, more importantly, were judged to be clinically sane.

(Rachel watched the road run beneath them and wondered about Shawn, and Adrian, and Sammy, and the others who had left but might come back, and what might happen if they did, or, worse, if they wanted to come back but *couldn't—*)

"Your tires are low," she said, as her scans finally placed the wobble.

"Bad?"

"Getting that way."

They pulled off the highway at a gas station. It was a newer place, built after the gas companies realized that travelers were more likely to stop at a building that didn't look as if it were home to multiple homicides. Rachel sprinted inside for the bathroom and a sandwich or eight.

When she came out, Santino was on the phone and staring at two flattish left tires.

"What the hell?" she asked.

He covered the mouthpiece and said, "Look."

Rachel ran a scan through the flats, and found small perforations along both inside tire walls. "When did this happen?"

"I don't know. Maybe when we pulled off the highway on the drive down. We're lucky you noticed and got us to pull off before they went." His attention snapped away from Southwestern turquoise to the nondescript beige of the service industry, and he stepped away to talk to his insurance company. "Yeah, two flats… I've got roadside assistance coverage…"

"Of course you do," she muttered. She went back inside the gas station and bought a fistful of candy bars as sandwich chasers.

Santino joined her at the lone convenience table in the gas station. "They said they'll be here in an hour."

"So, five hours. Maybe three, if we're lucky." Rachel shook her head. "No way I'm getting back to D.C. for that meeting."

"Honestly, Penguin," Santino said as he took out his phone again.

Ten minutes later, she was in a northbound Uber. The driver was a college kid and the car stank of dirty clothes, but they were making deadly time. The kid drove as if she were competing for post time at a rally, and when Rachel managed to gasp out that she was a cop and maybe obeying the speed limit was a good idea? *Please?* the girl gave an exaggerated sigh and put the car into the travel lane.

City traffic was bad—it was always bad—but the driver darted through it like a water bug across the surface of a pond. By the time they had pulled up at OACET headquarters, Rachel's fingernails had cut little half-moons in the dashboard. The limestone steps of the old post office were warm from the afternoon sun and welcoming, and Rachel collapsed on top of them to watch the girl in the Uber speed off, another passenger already waiting in her queue.

Rachel wasn't alone; the reporters were setting up camp in preparation for Nicholson's arrival. Rachel fended off questions as she waited for her heart to decide it was safe enough to climb down from her throat.

"Peng."

Sandalwood.

"Wyatt."

The psychopath grinned down at her, then gently ushered the reporters back to the far side of the yellow sawhorses that OACET used as crowd control barriers.

"Sweet Jesus, they've got him doing chores," she muttered. She sent her scans up, to where they caught on Ami's core of meadow green high above in her hidden sniper's perch. She pressed on Ami's mind until the assassin opened a link.

"Has he been a good boy?"

"He's been really useful." Ami was…chilly. Polite, but the emotion behind what she said was restrained. *"He's helped out around here all day. Pointed out a few flaws in our security, actually."*

*"Well, he **is** a trained killer, Ami."*

"So was I," Ami said, and snapped their link.

A little too much wistfulness in Ami's last words, and Rachel lied when she told herself she didn't know why.

Up the stairs and through those grand metal doors, leaving the reporters and the man with the sandalwood core behind…

…strangers everywhere…

…through the first checkpoint, the second, and the third, and then left waiting until someone from the FBI was available to escort her upstairs. Rachel allowed five minutes to pass, and then gave the FBI agent at the last security checkpoint a good hard staring until the woman agreed that, yes, this was OACET's headquarters, and yes, since Rachel was undeniably a member of OACET, maybe they were being a little overcautious? Yes?

Rachel agreed, and trudged her way upstairs.

Mulcahy's office was the only room on the entire floor that

was empty of FBI agents. She opened the digital lock and let herself inside to wait for the other members of OACET's administration.

If Josh's office was the center of a bureaucratic sex tornado, Mulcahy's was the sound stage for a docudrama about contemporary politics. The office smelled of wood polish and leather. There were expensive Persian rugs and paintings by contemporary American artists, their straight lines and orderly patterns offset by the clutter of the awards and mementos that OACET had acquired along the way. Near the door was a TIME magazine cover with Josh and Mulcahy smiling at the camera, white and black typefaces chasing each other across the page in varying sizes of "men" and "year."

And the desk.

That fucking desk.

The mahogany executive's desk in the center of the office was a relic from a Roosevelt administration; she didn't know which one, and didn't care enough to find out. It was a massive piece of furniture, with elephants, lions, giraffes, and the rare stork in flight carved across its front and sides. It was ugly as hell, reeked of ostentatious wealth, and everybody in OACET despised it—the desk had been a much-publicized gift from ex-Senator Hanlon. A peace offering, Hanlon had claimed, a little piece of history to show that he wanted to improve his relationship with Mulcahy.

Peace offering, my skinny ass, Rachel thought. That desk was nothing but an insult. Every time an Agent entered Mulcahy's office, that desk loomed before them, a memento from Hanlon to remind them that he was still around, that what he had done to them would always be around.

She planned to set fire to the desk around Christmastime. It was the best she could do for Mulcahy. Her boss was impossible to shop for.

Rachel ran her scans across and through the desk, a familiar exercise as she searched for hidden bugs that she already knew weren't there. Any surveillance equipment would be a valid reason to get rid of the desk, and Hanlon didn't want that desk anywhere but in Mulcahy's office. Four hundred pounds of dead tree, gleaming in knots of browns and reds, to show up on camera whenever Mulcahy hosted a small press conference or entertained a visiting dignitary.

That fucking desk, indeed.

As she picked out a spot on the leather couch to wait, she decided that since Mulcahy's birthday was coming up in a couple of months, she'd just have to order the kerosene and find him an alternative Christmas gift instead.

She let her scans wander away from the desk and across the room. Not much changed in Mulcahy's office: it was a backdrop, with each piece on display carefully chosen to tell a story. But there, on a shelf that was in direct line-of-sight from the desk, a new photograph rested in an antique silver frame. A candid photograph from Mulcahy's wedding, taken late in the day when everyone was feeling the hours press down on them: Hope Blackwell resting in her new husband's arms, her dark hair swept back and tamed beneath her veil; Mulcahy in his tux, his jacket open and his boutonniere missing. The two of them were staring at each other as if they were the only two human beings alive, with enough love and lust crackling between them to survive the challenge of repopulating the entire planet.

Rachel stood and moved to examine the photograph. The old frame was heavy; sterling, not plate, and freshly polished.

Mulcahy was smiling down at his wife.

She set the photo down, carefully, and returned to the couch.

The factory in Maryland was more than thirty miles away, and her headache was still kicking the back of her brain's chair. She resigned herself to another six hours of misery, and closed her eyes.

Her avatar opened them, and the sight of the factory floor greeted her.

Green was her first thought, as she spotted the digital avatars of other Agents keeping watch throughout the factory. *Blue* was her second: the afternoon sunlight was pouring through the filmed windows, and the place glowed in false neons.

The avatar of the nearest Agent nodded to her. He was standing over a small group of militia men as they played cards. Rachel pushed off of the floor and glided over to him, and the two of them watched as the dealer started a fresh hand.

"...gin rummy?" she asked.

The other Agent shrugged. "They're pretty good, believe it or not."

She walked around the table. "Why are they wearing so many guns?"

"They think they might be raided while Nicholson's at the meeting." He pointed towards the windows. Men were stationed along the catwalks, staring into the parking lot below, rifles bristling across their backs like porcupine quills.

Rachel swore. "This isn't dangerous in the slightest."

"Nope," he said. "Not in the slightest."

"Avery?"

He pointed towards the far end of the factory. She followed the line of his finger, but her avatar's limited range of vision crashed into the wall before she could spot the little girl. "She's fine. Mulcahy stationed a team around her, and Mako and Carlota check in with her every hour. Kid thinks it's a game."

Rachel doubted that: Avery was one sharp cookie. She nodded goodbye and flew skyward, towards the second floor of the factory.

The windowed front room where they had held Hope was empty. Rachel steeled herself to a sensation that she knew she wouldn't feel, and walked through the door.

Sounds of a television, somewhere down the hall. She followed the noise of the laugh track to another door. Someone had moved a refrigerator in front of it, and had braced a desk between the refrigerator and the hallway wall to hold the refrigerator in place.

"Yup," Rachel whispered to herself, and pushed her avatar through the second door.

She found herself in a windowless office, large enough for a desk and a few filing cabinets. Faint blue specks of light chased themselves around until her avatar's eyes made sense of a room lit by nothing but a sitcom. A man, different from the one with the core of fresh-made iron who had guarded Hope on Rachel's last visit, sat with a shotgun aimed at Hope's head.

Hope was roped to a chair.

No, not just roped, but chained, with layers of duct tape wrapped around her arms and legs for good measure. The chair itself was an industrial steel contraption that had been bolted to the floor. Her face had been beaten to hell and back. Some of the beatings had been recent, too: there was fresh blood oozing from a shallow cut across her forehead.

As Rachel stepped into the space beside Hope, the woman's eyes moved reflexively towards Rachel's avatar, then returned to the man standing guard over her with the gun.

The man with the gun caught the gesture, and his body snapped tight. "What?!" he exclaimed, jerking his body sideways to see what she had been looking at.

Hope coughed. The sound twisted Rachel's stomach; it was dry and raspy, the sound of a woman gone too long without water. But the look she gave the man with the gun held as much venom as if she was well-fed and thoroughly rested.

"Paranoid much, fuckhead?" Hope snarled at him.

He hit her.

Hope rolled with the punch as best she could. It wasn't much—they had lashed her down so tightly that she could barely move. Her head rocked backwards and smacked against the metal crown of the chair.

The woman spat blood and laughed.

"That's nine," she said. "Wanna make it an even dozen? I've got time."

He backed away from her. "Crazy bitch."

"Kill the cameras," Hope said to Rachel.

"What?" The thug pulled back, head bobbing around to see who Hope was talking to.

In a single fluid move, Hope stood up and slammed the ball

of her foot into his chin. The man's head whipped backwards before he fell to the ground, solidly unconscious, the chains that had bound Hope to her chair crashing down around him.

"Asshole," Hope muttered. She knelt and checked his pulse, then turned him to lie on his side, before she began peeling the pieces of duct tape off of her arms and legs.

Rachel gaped at her, amazed. The tape that had bound Hope to the chair was shredded into tiny strips, the shackles on the chains unlocked. "Hope, what the hell?!" she shouted. "How do you keep doing that?"

The other woman shrugged as she walked around the tiny room, stretching and whipping her limbs around to get her circulation going. "Would you believe it's an old martial arts trick?"

"Really?"

Hope stopped dead and stared at Rachel. "Oh shit, that's right. You're out-of-body," she whispered, then said, almost hesitantly, "Yeah. They can't keep me tied up. Anything they use to hold me down, I can escape or break.

"Which is why they moved me," she added, as she gathered up the duct tape and began unpeeling it from itself. Her fingers flew as she began to bind the pieces back together into the shape of a flower. "All right, catch me up on what's happening before they notice the cameras went dark."

"They didn't," Rachel said. "I backed up the recording so it's playing on a loop."

"That doesn't work," Hope said. "Sparky tried that. They notice inconsistencies, but it'll take them a while to get in here. That barricade works both ways."

"Damn," Rachel said. She pushed her avatar through the doorway to check the hall. "We're good," she said, as she bobbed back into Hope's cell. "Nobody's coming."

"They've started checking in on me every fifteen minutes," Hope said, as a second duct tape flower joined the first. "And they bring Avery to me on the hour. I think they're reminding me that I shouldn't try to leave this room."

"Why do they only post one guard? They've got plenty of men."

"Probably because I can take down three men as easily as one," Hope said. From anybody else, it would have been bragging; from Hope Blackwell, it was a statement of fact. The weird woman finished another flower, and began to twist them together into a sticky daisy chain. "This way, they only lose one at a time."

"No," Rachel said, as she peered back into the hallway again. Still empty. "That's beyond stupid. Why lose any at all?"

Hope shrugged.

"They have access to sedatives," Rachel said. "So if they're now okay with beating you instead of keeping you fresh for the cameras, why aren't they keeping you drugged?"

"No idea. Hell, why kidnap me at all, while we're at it? Everybody knows you can't make my husband bend. Even if they kill me, it'll just piss Sparky off and he'll come after them that much harder."

"Maybe," Rachel said, but she had her doubts. That photograph from the wedding was too fresh in her mind. "I think it's more likely they're testing your limits,"

"Fuuuuuck," Hope groaned. "Shit. You're probably right."

"Yeah. Stop breaking loose," Rachel told her. "Next time they tie you up, let them think they finally got it right."

"Aww!" Hope rolled her head backwards and sighed. "Rachel, this place is soooo boring!"

Rachel squashed the urge to slap her. "You sound like a kid," she said. "A whining child. Avery needs you."

"Sorry," Hope squeezed her eyes tight. "I know, I know." She knelt over the unconscious man and began to attach the daisy chain to his hair, twisting his locks into the sticky clumps of duct tape. She gave the daisies a savage tug; the man's head followed, and then banged against the floor as she shook them.

"I hate to ask, but are they keeping you up on your medications?"

"No, not so far," Hope said with a shrug. "I haven't been

here long enough to know for sure, but they haven't given me anything."

"Oh boy."

"Don't worry about me. I'm good for a couple more days, at least. If this standoff lasts for more than that, I think we'll have bigger problems."

Rachel watched the man's head jiggle beneath its duct tape crown and didn't reply.

"Listen," Hope said with a deep sigh, "nobody wants me off of my meds. I'm a fucking menace. Two days of sitting in a chair is gonna be bad enough, but…" She dropped the man's head and stood. She resumed moving and stretching, trying to burn off what energy she could in the tiny room. "I'll be fine," she said quietly.

She rounded on Rachel. "I'll be *fine*," she said again. "And don't you go running back to Sparky, telling tales of his poor wife going violent, okay?"

"Don't go violent," Rachel said, "and we've got a deal."

Hope glared at her. After a moment, her face softened. "What's wrong?" she asked.

Rachel sighed. Somewhere, miles away, her fingers knitted together. "Would you believe I'm just here to check on you?"

"Nope." Hope paced across the room to check on the unconscious guard. "Sparky has OACET's foresters and tax consultants watching me and Avery. Everybody who's in law enforcement is working to get us out."

When Rachel didn't answer, Hope read her face like a book. "You think something's wrong with him."

"He should be freaking out," Rachel admitted. "We're all freaking out! Everybody in OACET has been quietly panicking since you and Avery got snatched. But your husband… Hope, there's nothing *there*."

"God damn it all," Hope muttered. "He said he wouldn't let himself go that far any more."

"What?"

"Sparky…" Hope paused, her head cocked to the side to

listen for footsteps. After a moment, she went back to making her silver flowers. "You remember how you all got turned into zombie-robots for a few years, right?"

Rachel didn't bother to reply. Hope glanced at her face again, and grimaced.

"Yeah, sorry," she said. "Of course you…sorry. Anyhow, Sparky—"

Shouting—distant, at first, but moving towards them, followed by the sound of running feet. A *Crash! Bang!* from the other side of the door, and the scraping sound of furniture being moved away.

Hope scrubbed the last of the sticky residue into the hair of her captor. "Later," she promised Rachel.

"Hope—"

The door opened with a crash. Four men rushed in, but froze in place when they saw the wild woman in the center of the room. They started to fan out, trying to push Hope into the corner.

There were no guns, but two of them had Tasers.

A brilliant grin lit Hope's face. "Talk to Josh, Peng," she said out of the corner of her mouth. "I'm gonna have me some fun."

THIRTEEN

Jeremy Nicholson breezed into Mulcahy's office like a conquering hero, his blood-red core neatly contained within a cage of yellow-white excitement.

The man with the core of freshly minted iron followed behind him, blending seamlessly with the four other henchmen in militia camo. Rachel wouldn't have paid him any mind at all, had not his colors been snapping across the office in professional blues as he weighed personnel, security, tactics…

"Found you," she whispered to herself as Nicholson's second-in-command weaseled his way over to a windowless corner with clear line-of-sight to Nicholson. He all but vanished in that corner, looking like nothing more than another silent sentry, and one who didn't want to be there.

Nicholson was dressed in his best camouflage business suit. An oversized semi-automatic rifle (not a NORINCO, of course, because why would a sovereign citizen who claimed to be trying to cut to the heart of the problems with America's legal system carry anything other than a gun made in the good old U.S. of A?) dangled like a prop from his shoulder. He flashed his movie star's smile at the reporters who had been invited to attend the meet-and-greet phase, and walked up to Mulcahy all a-grinnin', with a wink and a nod for the reporters as he offered his hand to the man whose wife he had stolen.

Mulcahy took it.

The man with the iron core watched the exchange, his attention focused in laser-bright whites, as if waiting to see if Mulcahy would break Nicholson's hand off at the wrist. No. Instead, Mulcahy escorted Nicholson to a pair of club chairs, and let the kidnapper choose his throne. Nicholson took the chair closest to the lights and cameras, the wide windows with their near-panoramic view of Washington behind him, and made a big deal of passing his rifle to Mulcahy as a peace offering.

Rachel scanned the rifle and found it empty. Unlike Mulcahy's own service weapon, which was fully loaded and lay like coiled death against the skin of her palms as Mulcahy instructed her to lock it up for the duration of the meeting—

As she moved, Southwestern turquoise and yellow-white surprise flared across the room.

She kept her head down and her face pointed towards the digital locks on Mulcahy's desk as Iron Core recognized her. As she watched him, an equal dose of her turquoise joined the cerulean and tattoo blues within his conversational colors.

If Nicholson doesn't give two shits about me, why would this guy rank me up with Mulcahy and Josh? she thought, and began to scan him in earnest. Hidden weapons, of course: as leader of this fiasco, Nicholson's impractical-in-close-quarters metal phallus had been granted an exception by the FBI. They had searched the other militia members (snerk!) and had gone over them with metal detector wands besides, but plastic knives had come a long way and held a fabulous edge. She went deeper, past cloth and into skin and bone: the contours of Iron Core's face had the same lines as Wyatt's, where skin and muscle had been parted and stitched back together to form something new.

"Oh, I am very interested in your tragic backstory, sir," she said quietly.

Beside her, Josh flared in curious yellows, and she felt the press of his mind against hers.

Rachel opened a link. *"That guy,"* she said, gesturing towards Iron Core with her thoughts as she showed Josh his conversational colors.

She felt Josh nod. *"Got him?"* he asked.

"You sure you don't need my scans for the meeting?"

"No."

"Then I've got him," she said. She snapped her head up and towards Iron Core, and broke away from the other OACET

Agents to stand beside him.

Iron Core did his best to ignore her, so she snuggled up beside him and draped her arm around his waist.

"Hey, cutie!" she said, her fingertips brushing against the handle of the knife he had concealed inside his waistband.

"Get away from me." He tried to sidle away.

"Don't be rude," she said, tugging him towards her. "We use the buddy system here. You're my buddy! Don't you want to be my buddy?"

He twisted; she countered. His hand went to where he had left his knife, and found it missing.

"You *don't* want to be my buddy?" she asked, as she pressed the resin blade against the back of his camouflage windbreaker. Its tip was aimed at his left kidney; his colors blanched slightly as it pricked him through his jacket. "Lots of reporters here," she said, waving her free hand at those who had overheard their scuffle and were watching them with the black-eyed stares of sharks. "Lots of FBI, too. Did you want them to pay attention to you? If I were you, I wouldn't want them to wonder why an Agent's getting all chummy with me…"

Iron Core crossed his arms and let her curl her arm around his waist.

"You're such a good buddy," Rachel said quietly, tugging him towards her. "So good. So polite. So willing to play along, even though you know about me…about what I can do…"

He stayed dumb, but his colors twisted towards uncertain orange and the green of disgust. *Good,* she thought. *Prime the pump until the red pours out.*

"Microexpressions," she said. "The little details of the face, the body…" She grabbed his arm and pulled him close enough to whisper in his ear. "…all laid out for me to see.

"You were hiding, weren't you? When I came to the factory with Josh? Volunteered to guard Hope so I wouldn't make you as the brains behind this shitshow?

"And I wonder why you were so surprised to see me today?" she added, running her free hand along his arm. "Did you think

I'd be stuck at a gas station on I-95? Got a buddy of your own who knows how to slash tires?"

The orange darkened towards annoyance, but now the sage green of comprehension was beginning to thread itself through the orange.

"There you go, that's exactly what I needed to see," she whispered, as she laid her hand over his. "What a good little buddy you are!"

The man with the iron core shuddered in green revulsion.

She felt positively filthy. *Avery,* she reminded herself. *Hope and Avery and a whole bunch of other people, huddled together in the dark.*

Across the room, Nicholson told the reporters he was done with them. He was more polite, of course, with broad statements about resolving issues quickly and how he would be happy to set up an interview with each and every one of them.

The reporters left: if they hadn't been charmed by Nicholson, they were willing to pretend they were in exchange for their exclusive. As the door shut behind them, the militia's nominal leader turned to the FBI agents.

"Shoo, flies," Nicholson said to the FBI. "The grownups need to talk now."

Professional blues took on the dark shine of gunmetal, and the FBI agents looked to Mulcahy.

"We'll call if we need anything," he said.

"It might get loud in here," Rachel said in her sultriest voice, as she pulled Iron Core against her. "Just ignore us."

There's the red, she thought, catching the embers of hate within Iron Core's conversational colors, and began to stroke his hand. Her scans showed the FBI taking position down the hall, close enough to come running but not close enough to overhear.

"Nothing to drink?" Nicholson asked, as he draped his feet on top of Mulcahy's coffee table. The table was fairly new—at least, its current iteration was new. The round top was made from slabs of reclaimed pine from Germany's Black Forest;

the aluminum legs had spent their last lives as ribs inside a decommissioned Sea Harrier. In Rachel's opinion, it was the nicest gift Mulcahy had ever received from a British Prime Minister.

"No," Mulcahy said.

"You're a poor host, Mulcahy. I put on the nicest dinner for Glassman—"

"I…" Mulcahy said, as he leaned forward and put both of his plate-sized hands flat on the coffee table. He pressed down; the coffee table began to groan under his weight. "…am not Agent Glassman."

He stood and hurled the coffee table across the room with one hand. His aim was perfect; the table hit the door—that one spot in the office that was empty of shelves, tchotchkes, or people—and clattered, spinning, to the floor.

Rachel didn't miss how the militia members turned to Iron Core for permission to react, or how Iron Core held up two fingers, ever so slightly.

She pulled him close to her again and stage-whispered, "Your pets are *so* well trained!"

Angry reds and oranges flared like fire across the room, and she leaned against Iron Core and tittered like a drunken cheerleader.

"Back off, girls!" she said, as she drew her hand up the center of Iron Core's chest. "He's mine!"

The FBI agents in the hall kicked open the door in time to see Iron Core grab her by her hair and drive her face straight at the mahogany abomination of a desk. Their guns were drawn; they were shouting commands.

Rachel screamed as she let her weight come down on her hands with a *Wham!* and pretended to collapse. She rolled to the side and beneath the desk, the world's slipperiest sack of potatoes.

Iron Core did not, despite her dearest wishes, puddle on the floor beside her in a disgusting rain of blood and bone and tacky camouflage pajamas. Through the desk, she saw him with his hands up, calling for peace, while the surface colors of the FBI whipped around the room, plucking colors off of different surfaces and fitting them together like a puzzle—

Damn, she thought, as the iron gray slid into place beside an electrified (but non-threatening) reddish-blue. *So close.*

Well, there was more than one way to deprive Nicholson of his second-in-command. She reached out to an anonymous burner phone two floors below.

Wyatt answered on the first ring. "Peng."

"Got a job for you," she told him, and flipped frequencies to take in Iron Core's physical details. *"I'm chasing a man out of the meeting. White male, early thirties, brown hair, about six feet, two-ten."*

"What's he wearing?"

"Camo."

"Ah," Wyatt chuckled. "What's the job?"

"I want DNA or clean fingerprints. Make sure he knows you're just extra security hired by OACET, and not an Agent."

"Yup," he said. "Tell your friends with the sniper rifles that I've been cleared to leave the grounds."

"Nope. Do a chump bump when he passes," she said. *"I'll tail him if he leaves the building."*

The connection closed with a sharp beep.

"Goodbye to you too, asshole," she muttered, and took stock of the room. The FBI had moved over to Iron Core and were making the kind of threats that could only be made when they were in someone else's home. But Iron Core was so nice and polite and sorry and it would never happen again—

Oh hell, they're letting him stay.

She sighed, and bit the inside of her lip until flesh crunched beneath her teeth. She gave herself a few moments to let the blood trickle down her face before she came out from under the desk, groaning. As soon as she appeared, the FBI agents helped her to her feet and hustled her as far away from Iron Core as the room allowed.

"I want him out of here," she said groggily, running her hand through the blood so it smeared across her cheek. "Just…get him gone…"

"I agree," Mulcahy said to Nicholson. "Ask your man to leave the room."

Nicholson was panicking, the sickened yellow in his conversational colors panting like an overheated dog. "He's—"

"Now!" Rachel cried, her voice tapering up to its breaking point. She pushed away from the FBI and found an empty space near the wide windows.

"This meeting is over," Mulcahy said.

"No!" Nicholson's colors twisted over themselves as Mulcahy's cerulean blue started to slip away. "No," he said, more calmly. To Iron Core: "Ethan? Would you mind?"

Ethan most certainly did mind: Southwestern turquoise burned within hateful reds. But once he began to move, he walked straight out of the door without stopping.

"Can you control your men?" Mulcahy asked, standing in the hole where the coffee table once was.

"Can you control *her*?" Nicholson pointed at Rachel. "She provoked him!"

Mulcahy raised an eyebrow. "By flirting?"

"I'll stay right here," Rachel all but whimpered, curling into a small ball on the window sill. Pity emerged in deep reds across the FBI agents who had seen her take the hit; with the exception of Mulcahy, everyone from OACET was riotously, uproariously purple.

As the FBI pressed Mulcahy for permission to stay for the duration of the meeting, Josh watched as she carefully tucked Iron Core's knife behind a set of thick curtains.

"I probably wrecked any fingerprints on that when I disarmed him," she said.

"We'll see what we can do," Josh replied. *"You okay?"*

"Bad headache," she said. *"But that's nothing new."*

"Are you going after him?"

Her scans, tight on Iron Core, watched as a man in sandalwood crashed into him in the hallway. Iron Core, already nothing but red fury, closed in on this convenient target for his rage.

"Definitely," she told Josh. *"He's so mad he's making mistakes."*

"Good luck."

"You too," she said, as Mulcahy won and the FBI left the office again.

Silence, broken after a moment when Rachel opened the catch on the new windows in their old wooden frames.

"Bye, fuckers," she said to the militia men, and, with a wink to Nicholson, she jumped.

Mulcahy's office was on the top floor of what was undeniably a very short building. It was only three floors, and one of those a basement. Still, she was thirty feet up when she leapt into space.

She was twenty-eight feet up when she grabbed the trellises that covered the front of the building. There were no plants to get in her way, not yet: below, OACET's gardeners were training tangerine crossvines to climb up the side of the building and cover the ironwork. For now, there was just metal—hot metal, she realized, soaking in the full heat of the afternoon sun—bolted to the stone.

As quickly as her too-hot hands would allow, Rachel spider-walked around the corner and hid beneath a convenient cornice. Above, several members of the militia had reached the window and were looking for her broken body in the street below.

She let Mulcahy call them to order before she began the climb down.

The trellises were solid. They were new, installed at Mulcahy's request during the recent renovations. Rachel was sure that if they could hold his weight, they'd hold hers, easy. The hand that Bryce Knudson had shredded kept complaining, pain surging across the scar tissue as she lowered herself from bar to bar, but she pushed on.

She got within nine feet of the ground before anyone noticed her—the trellises ended there, and she had to pause and dangle before she let herself fall. By the time her boots hit the pavement, a swarm of reporters had moved from covering the front doors over to where Rachel stood, questions locked and loaded. She ignored them and walked across the street, hailed a cab, and let it take her away.

"Stop here," she said, after the cabbie had turned the first corner and had removed itself from the reporters' blast zone. The cabbie, accustomed to the habits of politicians on the run, didn't even bother to nod before dropping her on the curb.

There was a coffee shop, doors open to let in the breeze of the warm early spring afternoon. Rachel bought a cup of iced tea for the price of admission, and tucked herself on a stool by the window.

Her scans, still fixed on Iron Core's distinctive colors, watched as he pushed his way out of OACET headquarters and into the bustle of city traffic.

Now, buddy-o-mine, Rachel asked herself, *where do you go from here?*

There was nothing she could do if he took a car. If that happened, she'd grab the number off of the license plate and turn the tail over to Zockinski. But if he was on foot...

Nope, he'd be on foot, no question. A guy like him knew that in a city, a car was basically a slow-moving prison that could turn right on red.

Iron Core didn't disappoint. He set out on 5th Street, heading north, his surface colors dead-set on orange annoyance beneath a layer of mottled grays and greens; he must have known, in this era of mass shootings, that he stuck out maybe just a little too much in his camouflage onesie. Anywhere else but downtown D.C. and he would have blended in fine, maybe gotten a free coffee or two out of it besides, but the locals knew the difference between a soldier's uniform and off-the-rack hunter's gear.

Rachel left the coffee shop, the plastic cup full of iced tea pressed flat against the palm of her (mildly) burned hand.

She was whistling: this was the part of the job she *loved*.

Running tails as a cyborg was like an adult playing hide-and-go-seek with a toddler, lots of "Wherever could he be?" and "Surely those feet sticking out from under the curtains mean nothing," with a dose of "Why is that closet giggling?" besides.

Rachel put herself one street over from Iron Core and watched him through the buildings. She turned when he turned, as if they were connected by a string the length of a city block.

There was purpose in his colors, professional blues with a white center of bright attention. Her own Southwestern turquoise was in there, along with a fading dose of sandalwood: Wyatt had gotten under his skin.

North and east, through the city, towards Columbia Heights and the ruckus of the rougher neighborhoods. He was leading her towards an edge, she realized, a place where the different sides of the city came together. She was a recent arrival to D.C. and had heard the city was greatly changed from its Mayor Barry days, but the smooth roads still gave way to cracked pavement, and the faces of the buildings began to blur beneath a patina of graffiti.

He turned down an alleyway and kicked open the door to an abandoned storefront. Rachel flipped frequencies until she could read the signage: an old tire dealership, long gone to ruin. She watched from the relative safety of a bodega as Iron Core chased two people out of the building, then sat down on the skeleton of an upholstered chair.

"Buying anything?"

"What?" Rachel blinked, her scans moving away from Iron Core to the bodega's owner. A slight woman with an unknowable accent was staring at her in suspicious oranges. "Yes," Rachel said. "Got anything for a bad headache?"

The oranges eased into wine red. "Aisle Three," the woman said, pointing.

Calling it an aisle was generous: cough drops and other mild pharmaceuticals drooped in cellophane packets from a wobbly wire rack. Rachel searched the rack until she found an assortment of headache medications, and, after admitting to herself that her doctor's advice hadn't gotten rid of her headache, decided to go with a powder endorsed by a prominent race car driver. She poured this into a cup of coffee so old that its surface shone like an oil slick, and went to pay.

"Not healthy," the woman said, nodding towards the coffee.

"It hasn't been a healthy day," Rachel replied. She flipped up the tail of her coat to give the bodega's owner a glimpse of her badge. "Can I stay here for a few minutes? I promise I won't make trouble."

The woman nodded, giving Rachel the shy smile of someone who was grateful that she was no longer responsible for anything bad that might happen, even if was just for the length of time that the cop was in her store.

Iron Core still hadn't moved. He seemed to be waiting. She stood by the window and watched as the clock in her head counted the minutes, while strangers came and went around her.

Half an hour later, he began sorting through the piles of trash around his feet, his colors sharpened into a point as he searched for something. He came up with a loose piece of paper, and reached into his pocket for a pen.

(She was somewhat offended that Iron Core would think to carry a pen, but placated herself with the knowledge that whatever he was, he wasn't really a member of a militia.)

He wrote for what seemed an eternity, and, from the Southwestern turquoise and OACET green in his colors, she had a pretty good idea what he was writing about.

"Thanks," Rachel said to the woman behind the counter, and dashed out the door.

The tire dealership was worse than abandoned—it had become a trash dump, with black plastic bags piled up against the broken windows as a wind block. Some of the local homeless community had carved out a large space on the other side of the building where the walls came together and the wind couldn't reach. Iron Core stood in that hollow, still writing.

He set his pen down and moved to the wall. There was a hole in the cinderblocks, and he shoved the paper into it, so deep that Rachel was sure he'd come out with a rat where his hand had been. Then, he left the way he had come, moving up the street towards the heart of D.C.

What to do, what to do… Follow Iron Core, or stop and read the letter?

Not much of a choice, really. Either option started with grabbing that letter for safety's sake—no telling what might happen to it after she picked up Iron Core's tail.

She gave him a whole block's lead time before she snuck into the building. It was…ripe. Overly ripe, to the point where her scans started to pulse with the airborne signals of decomposition.

Phil wouldn't be able to scan in here, she thought to herself. *Too many different chemical signals.*

It was a stray thought. A nothing thought, the kind that usually came and went without leaving its mark. But her mind snatched at it and caught it, and suddenly she was down a rabbit hole of her own.

—maybe he could, maybe he's worked out which chemical signals go with bombs, and which go with this amazing bouquet of liquefied foods and dirty diapers and God knows what else—

Rachel's scans hit on the dead body of a pigeon and she froze, nauseated at the thought that she and Phil could probably find corpses by the chemical traces of decomposition alone. The MPD had used her scans on cadaver searches before, but it was one thing to run a scan through clean soil and find a skeleton, quite another to know that the silent signs of the dead hung in the air. The urge to run home and scrub her skin until it bled rose up and she started to move—

No! She forced her feet to anchor themselves to the floor. *Stop. You're no stranger to dead bodies. You've seen, smelled, touched, and even **caused** them, so just stop and get your shit together, okay?*

That didn't work. Apparently, reminding herself that she was a killer on occasion wasn't much of a comfort. She started chasing logic instead.

It's a trash heap. It's unsanitary, yeah, but you've been in worse. The latrine outside of Ghazni? Remember that? You've got a job to do, and the faster you get it done, the faster you can get out of here.

The overwhelming urge to flee and scrub herself raw dissipated into the stinking air, and Rachel allowed herself a cautious first step.

Her legs went where she wanted them to go. Good.

Everyone in the Office of Adaptive and Complementary Enhancement Technologies struggled against obsessive-compulsive urges; it was a natural side effect of having a quantum-organic computer chip grafted into their brains. Rachel had been assured that their implants lacked the capacity to learn, but they did adapt and evolve through a feedback process—as the user experienced their environment, the implant acquired data that could be used to enhance the user's performance within that environment.

Rachel was fine with having an improved sense of balance, or completing the daily Sudoku puzzle a little more quickly than she could have before she had been recruited to OACET. It was the gestating germaphobe in her skull that worried her. Thanks to her scans, she was aggressively aware of the microbial world around her. The kicker was that she couldn't tell if she was being overly cautious, or if her implant was warning her about environmental risks her conscious mind didn't recognize. All assurances that the implant wasn't a tiny sentient mind lurking within her own didn't help when some part of her was shrieking about danger. Instinct was a bitch, augmented instinct doubly so. Not being able to tell which of those was in control at any given time was infuriating.

She knelt beside the hole in the wall, gave it a meticulous scanning, and went after the letter.

It wasn't just a hole: it connected to a pipe, which sloped downward. Iron Core's arm was longer than hers; her fingertips brushed the paper, but it was in too deep and there was a risk of pushing the paper further down the pipe. She sat back on her heels and sighed.

Hurry it up, she reminded herself. Iron Core was at the edge of comfort for her scans, still retracing his steps to OACET headquarters. She had to lose track of him now for the sake of her aching head, but she didn't want to let him go for longer than absolutely necessary. Instead, she turned her scans to the trash pile around her.

Something long. Something sturdy...

There wasn't much left of the old tire dealership. The car lifts were gone, either removed when the shop had closed, or stolen for scrap. All that was left were blocks of concrete, crumbling from age. There was a pile of old tires that had been picked over, with mostly shredded rubber scraps left behind. The tools were long gone.

Something long. Something sturdy... Bingo!

A crowbar, long forgotten between a wall and crack in the floor. Easy to retrieve, too—she moved a few trash bags and was able to pry the crowbar out of the crack without needing, oh, say, a smaller crowbar.

Back to the hole again. Careful work, this... The paper was thin with age and misuse. She used the crowbar to pull it a couple of inches forward, then shoved her hand back into the hole.

"Vic-toh-reh," she said in a dreadful Schwarzenegger, and carefully unfolded the paper. She flipped frequencies until the handwriting showed her name in prominent block letters at the top of the page. *Rachel Peng is on to us...*

"Oh boy," she said quietly. She smoothed out the letter so the creases wouldn't register as text artifacts, and began to read.

> *Rachel Peng is on to us. You were right to try and stay away from her. She says she reads microexpressions. I don't know if it's true but she got me thrown out of the meeting. Nicholson can hold his own without me there.*

"Hello, active self-delusion," she muttered. Nicholson had as much chance of holding his own against the mouth of a loaded cannon as going one-on-one against Mulcahy. She pulled the letter flat again, and tried to make out the next lines.

It's time to move up the schedule. Catch the train to the third rail. The flowers will be waiting. The bagels are on the counter. Repeat: the bagels are on the counter.

"What the hell is this supposed to—" she began, and then a slip of cold metallic gray was her only warning before Iron Core crashed into her like a runaway truck.

FOURTEEN

Rachel was flying again, but in her own body for once, and only briefly before her head struck the wall. The nonsense thoughts of surprise and shock stopped as she landed, face-down, in the pile of rubber castoffs from stripped tires.

Get up. The icy part of herself that navigated through a crisis took over. *Move or you're done.*

She tried to get her hands on her gun, tried to roll to the side, but her body wasn't listening, the rubber kicked out beneath her as she tried to find a purchase—

"Bitch." Iron Core glowed above her, haloed in red rage. He had her crowbar and was holding it over his head, a pause in her murder while he took aim.

The crowbar came down.

Halfway through its arc, the crowbar jerked sideways as Marshall Wyatt tackled Iron Core around his waist.

Get up, she told herself. *Get up.* ***Now!***

The two men tumbled across the floor, grappling in reds.

Iron Core was a good fighter. Strong, smart… He closed with Wyatt, grabbing the other man's shirt for leverage. Wyatt broke the hold with an elbow across his face, then took Iron Core by his other shoulder and threw him to the floor. Iron Core rolled with the throw and came up with a brick in his right hand.

Wyatt had a knife. A short silver combat blade. No, it was—

Rachel blinked. A butter knife?

"Get up, get up, get up…" she muttered, as she fumbled around in the scrap rubber to find the floor below. Her fingers brushed against something hard and stable: not the floor, but enough to put her back on her feet. She tried to clear her head of a new and suspiciously sloshy sound as she staggered towards the two men, drawing her gun on the way.

Wyatt closed, the butter knife held point-out. Iron Core swung the brick towards Wyatt's leading hand. There was a sharp *tink!* as the brick met the butter knife, then another and another, small sparks leaping into the air when the stone came in contact with the metal. Their free hands went from fists to claws and back again; they fought filthy, with eyes and genitals both up for grabs.

They tripped over something that went skittering across the floor—the crowbar, just out of reach. The brick came up; Wyatt stabbed down. Iron Core roared as the butter knife bludgeoned its way through fabric and skin, and sank into the meat of his forearm. Wyatt put his foot into Iron Core's shin and kicked off, diving towards the crowbar. He came up spinning, the crowbar in his hands.

Rachel put a bullet in the ceiling.

The two men froze.

"Children," she said. "Behave."

Iron Core glanced between her and Wyatt, his colors churning.

"He's thinking about rushing me," she told Wyatt.

Wyatt nodded and swung the crowbar. The curve of the hooked end cracked off of Iron Core's jaw with the sound of a baseball tagged by the sweet spot of the bat. The militia man's eyes rolled back in his head, and he fell backwards on the reeking garbage heap of a floor.

Wyatt pulled the bar back for a second swing, this time with the business end of the hook aimed right between Iron Core's eyes.

"Don't kill him!" she shouted.

Wyatt lowered the crowbar. "Right," he said to himself. The red bloodlust began to seep back into his sandalwood core like water soaking into dry earth. "Right. You need him alive."

"That, and you don't *have* to kill people," she said.

"Maybe *you* don't," Wyatt said in a low voice. There was some bubbling as the bloodlust fought to reclaim his focus.

"Gimme that," she snapped, and took the crowbar from him.

"Were you raised in a murderbarn or something?"

The psychopath had the decency to look embarrassed.

"Why are you here?" she asked. Sirens in the distance; the call she had placed to the MPD after Iron Core had clocked her had been given priority.

He tilted his head towards the sirens like a hound.

"Hurry up, man."

"After I tangled with this guy, I told the Hippos he was the real deal," he said. "They had to stay and monitor the meeting. Ami sent me after you as backup."

There were too many implications stuffed into that package. Rachel shook her head. "Get out of here," she snapped.

Curious yellows appeared in his conversational colors.

"Go," she said. "Just go. There'll be questions, and I don't want you anywhere near First District Station. Hill will know who you are the minute he sees you."

"Maybe," he said. "Maybe not."

"Go!"

When he didn't move, she sighed and went to collect the note that Iron Core had left for her.

"Go," she said again. The paper was old, thin from abuse and feather-light in her hand. She tucked it into the inner pocket of her suit coat for safekeeping.

"What's that?" Wyatt nodded towards the paper.

"Bait."

She didn't reply until the sirens turned onto their street. "He would have killed me," she said. "You saved my life."

It hurt to admit it. Both of them knew what would have happened if Iron Core had swung that crowbar, but it still hurt to say it aloud. (Not as much as that crowbar would have hurt, true, it was the principle of the thing.)

"I'm here to help OACET," he said. It was the mildest of comments, but his colors were thick in smug pinks, with the purple of riotous laughter popping throughout.

"It's not funny, and don't be such a smug asshole," she snapped. "You look like a little girl's bedroom."

"What?" Yellow confusion chased the other colors away.

"Oh, dear Lord," she muttered, as the first police car pulled up outside. "Last chance. Go."

"Your story will be stronger if you say you had help," he replied. "Especially since you're bleeding pretty bad."

"What?" Rachel was suddenly aware of the sticky mass of hair drying flat against her forehead. She touched it, and winced when she found the lump underneath. "Aw, damn it."

The police rushed in. Rachel and Wyatt stood, hands up, with Rachel shouting her bona fides until everyone's colors turned blue. An ambulance was called for Iron Core: Rachel's diagnostic autoscript put him with a broken jaw and a fairly serious concussion.

One of the EMTs treated her head wound while she gave her statement to the officer. Straightforward stuff, and pretty much the truth: Rachel had thought something was hinky when the militia man was in the meeting, so she had gotten him thrown out and then followed him to see where he'd go. Unbeknownst to her, an old friend (*cough*) that OACET had hired to work security had tangled with the militia man in the hall, and when he spotted Rachel tailing him, he had followed along as backup.

"Good thing he did," Rachel said, as Iron Core was loaded into the ambulance on a stretcher. "Otherwise, that'd be me."

Wyatt, lurking about the EMTs as if waiting to make sure his friend was okay, was thoroughly pink and purple again.

Once the cops had left them alone to manage the endless bureaucracy of modern crimefighting, she leaned towards Wyatt. "Is he military?" she said quietly.

"You know he is."

"Ours?"

Wyatt shrugged. "Somebody's."

"You recognize the fighting style?"

He shot her the mustardy yellow of scorn. "It's not a movie, Peng."

"I'm a detective," she sighed. "Systema? Krav Maga? Anything?"

"You talk a lot."

"Blame it on the head wound."

Wyatt pushed off of the ambulance and disappeared into the crowd. No one moved to stop him. Rachel wondered if she should, then saw that OACET green and the soft browns of sandstone had moved into his colors: he was headed back to the old post office.

She bummed a ride from the EMTs and rode shotgun with them to the hospital. Howard University Hospital, as luck would have it, and several members of the staff recognized her as the person who had torn up a good part of their landscaping the previous year. Rachel declined a thorough examination on the grounds of "Because I'm a cyborg, that's why!" and said her own doctor would check her for a concussion after she made sure the prisoner was secure.

The doctors weren't happy about that. They made her fill out *forms*.

By the time she was finished signing away her right to sue, Santino had arrived. He pulled her away from the desk and the two of them tracked down Iron Core. He had been moved to the Intensive Care unit, just in case—doctors didn't take chances with concussions, as she had just notarized in triplicate.

"Do me a favor," she said, as she handed her partner the paper. "Take a photo of that and send it to Jason."

"Sure," Santino said. He laid the paper flat on the reception booth and jiggled around with his phone until he got the lighting right. "Whoa," he said, as he checked the clarity of the photograph and started reading. "What's this?"

Rachel tried not to hate all things everywhere as her partner took ten seconds to skim something that had taken her five minutes to read, and had nearly gotten her killed besides. "He knows about me," she said quietly, as Santino finished absorbing the balderdash in incredulous oranges. "He set this out as bait."

"Does he know you're…" Santino left the last word unsaid, but his colors turned opaque over his eyes.

"Maybe? I don't think so," she said. "But he knows it takes

me forever to read, so he left this for me, gave me enough time to lose track of him, and then came at me as hard as he could."

"That's a compliment, I guess," Santino said. "Trying to take you out, instead of interrogating you."

"You can't question an Agent," she said. "Not without bringing the rest of OACET down on you like a load of dynamite.

"Whereas we," she said, as she took the paper back from Santino, "don't have that problem."

Two uniformed officers were stationed outside of Iron Core's hospital door. Rachel didn't recognize them; the assault hadn't happened in the First District. The cops knew her and Santino by sight, though, with Southwestern turquoise and cobalt blue moving into their conversational colors.

"We'd like to talk to him," she said to the first officer. "What's his status?"

"Conscious. Doctors cleared him. They're gonna watch him for twenty-four hours to make sure his concussion doesn't get worse, and then he's off to Holding."

"Great," Rachel said. "Hear anything from the FBI?"

"You'd know before us." He was a slight man with a core of soft, fluffy brown, and gave the impression of a determined teddy bear piloting a human suit.

"Orders?" Santino asked them.

"Hold the room, make sure he doesn't leave, keep the media out," the second officer replied.

"Is he restrained?"

The officers looked at each other and shrugged in oranges. "Don't think so," the first one said.

"Oh, that's a mistake," Santino said. "This guy's lethal. Can you get that started?"

The second officer nodded and stepped away to make the call, and Rachel headed towards the door.

The first officer moved to block her, but in the nicest of ways, his professional blues holding her back until he was sure she was aware of procedure. "This on the record?" he asked.

"No," Rachel said. "Detective Hill from First is going to

handle the interrogation. I'm just his warmup."

"Hill?" the cop said, his colors brightening in excitement. "Sure. Just leave the door open."

"Right," Rachel replied, before she cranked the knob and opened the door to the hospital room as hard as she could. The door slammed against the rubber bumper hard enough to shake the walls. On the bed, Iron Core winced in streaks of red pain that showed through the white bandages holding his broken jaw in place.

"Headache?" Rachel said. "Yeah, me too. Even before you gave me this." She pushed back her blood-soaked hair to show him the bandaged abrasion across her forehead.

"Forgive me for monologuing," she continued, "but it's not like you can chime in and set me straight." She accidentally kicked the foot of his bed as hard as she could. It set her own head to pounding, but it was worth it—even with the drugs in his system, Iron Core went bright red around his jaw.

"So…" she flopped down in the armchair beside the bed, and dropped her boots on the arm that held Iron Core's IV drip. The man in the bed made a noise like a whimpering kitten as a needle twisted somewhere. "Oh, sorry. So careless of me. Head wounds, you know how it goes."

Outside the door, the uniformed cop coughed once, politely.

Rachel moved her feet to the floor. "Ethan Fischer," she said, and his colors jolted towards yellow-white focus as he heard her use his name. "You were fingerprinted while you were unconscious. You've got no military record, which we both know is bullshit. You do have a criminal record that's very suspicious, in that it's got the right number of arrests but we haven't found anybody who remembers arresting you. Or prosecuting you. And that time you spent in jail? Well, you have prisoner IDs and room numbers and all sorts of data, but so far you haven't shown up on the security footage. At all. Our digital specialist still has a couple of years to process, but we're guessing…"

She looked over her shoulder to where Santino was standing

in the doorway. Her partner said, "Nope."

"Yeah, we're guessing nope," she said.

"Oh, right," Rachel said, as Fischer's colors took on some of the colors of confusion. "You're dealing with cyborgs now. We move really fast when properly motivated."

"Future of law enforcement, you know," Santino said. "Ideally, we'll use the same legal processes as we have in the past. They'll just be performed much, much faster."

"Yeah, I don't want to be Judge Dredd. Judge, jury, and executioner? No thanks."

A flicker of red anger, and the twist of colors away from her Southwest turquoise that meant he didn't believe her, oh, no, he didn't believe her one bit.

"Ah," Rachel said, leaning in close. "There we go."

"Oh?" Santino asked. "Whatever do you see, Agent Peng?"

"He thinks I'm lying," Rachel said. "I don't know if he joined up with Nicholson because he's a true believer, but he definitely thinks I'm up to no good. I wonder if it's just me, or all of OACET…

"How about it, buddy?" She propped her chin on Fischer's bed and stared at him with puppy-dog eyes. "Is it me in particular, with these freaky things I can do, or is it OACET in general?"

"Can you tell the difference?" asked Santino from beneath the world's worst poker face.

"Ask him some questions," she said. "I can figure it out from there. It won't be admissible in court, of course, but this will never get to court, will it, buddy?"

Fischer's stare was hard enough to take on her own in a cage match.

"Too bad we don't know who he is," said Santino, holding his hands palms up and pleading for divine assistance. "Well, who he *really* is."

"Yeah," Rachel said, and stood to leave. "He's covered his tracks pretty well. Too well for someone working alone. But however will we learn who those mysterious partners are?"

She stopped and turned before she reached the door, and

imagined she could feel a dirty trenchcoat swirl around her as she added, "Oh, just one more thing..." She reached into her pocket and retrieved the letter. "You gave me this," she said. "A handwriting sample."

Fischer's eyes widened as orange-yellow confusion crashed down on itself in sage green comprehension.

"See, I'm guessing you're military," Rachel said. "From the way you fight, I bet you're special forces. Ours, theirs... Who cares? Whatever. It means you've been part of the system for forever. Whoever set you up with this cover didn't go through and delete every document you've ever signed, every form you've ever filled out..."

He lunged.

This time, she saw the attack coming—the yellow-white intensity of a man determined to confront her narrowed itself into a lance made from furious reds. The bed flipped sideways as he bore down on her, medical equipment raining down behind him as the tubes tore from his arms. Blood ran from his wrists and elbows, but still he came, focused on nothing but Rachel and the paper in her hand.

She punched him.

She expected Fischer to black out from the pain of a second hit to the face, especially a solid shot to his broken jaw.

Then—too late—she realized she had never fought a special forces operative pumped up on painkillers before.

Fischer rocked back on his heels from her punch, but didn't go down. He recovered, twisting away to block her follow-through before he sprang at her like a wounded tiger. She swore and went for her gun, but he had already closed the distance. Her breath shot from her as he crushed her against the wall, both hands wrapped around her neck.

Santino and the officers were shouting at her; the cops had their guns out, Santino had his trusty Taser... There was no clear shot. Not at that angle. Not with him pressing against her throat with his full weight.

Things were getting awfully sparkly around their edges.

She finally got her gun out; he slammed his knee against her hand until she dropped it. She brought her own knee up; he was off-balance and she brought him straight down to the ground. Air—*glorious* air!—chased the blackout away, and she took a page from Hope Blackwell's book by grabbing a handful of his hair and using it to slam his head against the floor.

He rolled, one arm out and moving to throw her. As she fell, she reached out and grabbed the nearest weapon, and used her momentum to swing it at his skull.

There was a sound like a plastic window cracking. Rachel turned the cheap flower pot over and began to bash it into Fischer's face, dirt and begonia petals flying. He hissed, one hand across his eyes, as the edges of the pot began to cut his skin to ribbons.

"Rachel, move!" Santino shouted, and she abandoned the flower pot to throw herself clear.

Fischer lit up in whites as Santino's Taser tagged him. The militia man seemed to hover on his knees for a mild eternity before collapsing face-first on the floor.

Rachel pulled herself to her feet. Her headache was roaring in bloodthirsty vengeance, and the crowd of new arrivals—doctors, hospital staff, the stray patient who had suddenly gotten a ringside seat to a beating—who kept shouting at her wasn't helping. She stood over Fischer and ran her diagnostic autoscript over his unconscious body.

"What's craniofacial dissociation?" she asked her partner. When he winced in yellows, she added, "No, don't answer that. Just tell me if it hurts."

"Definitely."

"Good." She gave in to the tickle at the back of her throat and coughed up potting soil. When she could breathe again, she knelt to gather up Fischer's note and what was left of the begonias. The first went into her pocket, the latter to her partner, who started making the miserable noises of someone who has been handed a badly beaten puppy. "Sorry."

"I can fix it. I hope."

A glass of water entered her scans; one of the officers had found the sink. "Thanks."

"Listen, Agent Peng—"

She cut him off. "Get him in restraints," she said. "Have the lawyers talk to me if they give you any shit."

With that settled, her headache decided it was as good a time as any for her to black out.

FIFTEEN

Mulcahy's office wasn't nearly as vivid as usual, but the humans had faces, with eyes and ears and all the pieces in between. They wore clothing that was more than just fabric, color, and folds, and stood in a room where the books had titles on their spines. The scents of the room were less distinct than she was used to, but sounds were sharper; she wondered how Josh could go through life when every little noise sounded like the beginnings of something serious.

Smell... Musk and gun oil, standing out in equal parts, with a little bit of leather wafting up between them as Josh leaned to one side and his nose came closer to the couch. All masculine smells, which surprised her—she would have assumed Josh's senses would have been cued to the women in the room.

"I was working," he reminded her, a small measure of irritation coming into their link.

"I've seen you multitask," she said, and he laughed aloud.

She tried to swing her perceptions around to check for other differences, but experimentation hadn't been Josh's priority when he made the recording. His attention was on Nicholson and the militia men. Anything else was peripheral information that had made it into his memories of the meeting by exposure, not intention, regardless of its interest to Rachel.

(Case in point: Memory-Josh finished resettling himself on the couch. Rachel, riding along in the sensations of his body, felt the unfamiliar relief of testicles freed from the weight of a nearby thigh. Weird!)

Mulcahy picked up the coffee table and threw it across the room.

"That's when you started recording?" she asked.

"Yes." In the memory, Josh's focus swung towards a tall

Chinese woman with short black hair. Rachel couldn't place the woman's face until she heard her taunt the man in the camouflage jumper beside her.

"Oh Lord," she said, as the man in camouflage—Ethan Fischer—grabbed Memory-Rachel by her head and drove it straight at Mulcahy's mahogany desk. Memory-Rachel screamed like a movie starlet as she landed with a crash. *"Why did anybody buy that? I phoned it in."*

"Everything was moving too fast," he said. The perspective of the memory swayed from Fischer to the door. FBI agents swarmed into the office, shouting commands. Most of Memory-Josh's attention was on two of the FBI agents with their fingers on the triggers of their guns; out of the corner of his eye, he watched as Fischer put up his hands and played the part of a good submissive minion.

"That's a tipoff right there," Rachel said. *"Everything we've got on sovereign citizens says that when law enforcement pushes them, they make a stand and fight back. This guy's got to be a plant."*

"Yeah, but why?" Josh replied. *"And who put him here? Did you get a read off of the FBI?"*

"They're legit," she said, as the FBI agents stood down. *"Real reactions. None of them were playing along with Iron Core."*

"Who?"

"Sorry. Ethan Fischer. Nicholson's second. The guy who's hogtied in the hospital as he waits for them to reset his face."

Fischer wasn't literally hogtied in his bed, but only because Rachel had been unconscious when the officers did the tying. Her body had decided it was done getting clubbed in the head for the day, and the hospital floor was comfortable enough. Santino had saved her from the doctors and whatnots by insisting that no, she didn't need a CAT scan, and did you need to reread those forms you made her sign? He had still been shouting when Rachel's personal physician had arrived: Jenny Davis had thrown around the proper medical terminology until everybody had calmed down, and woken Rachel up long enough to get her out of the hospital and back to OACET headquarters.

Jenny had told her to lie down and rest until her headache went away. So Rachel had ordered an extra-large pizza and asked Josh to brief her on the meeting while she stuffed herself with pepperoni and cheese.

Rest was relative.

To be fair, nobody was resting this afternoon. It was getting on towards sunset, but the building was still full of Agents, agents, and others. The guys from Homeland weren't even trying to be subtle about their presence anymore, and were lurking openly in the halls. Worse, the FBI said some randos had jumped the barricade and snuck in while everybody's attention was on Nicholson and the media in his entourage. They had torn through the old post office, grabbing souvenirs whenever they could. There were signs of snooping everywhere.

Mulcahy had let the FBI know that this would not be tolerated. To their credit, the FBI had taken this to heart—the only places where they hadn't set up guards were in the private offices. Hence, this briefing on the couch in Mulcahy's office, as Josh was firmly believed that a recorded memory should be viewed under circumstances as close to the original conditions of the recording as possible.

It was an odd experience, to be sitting in the same place across time and in two different bodies. Rachel would have been happier sitting in one of the comfy club chairs, but nooo, she had to sit right here where Josh had sat when he made the recording, and deal with the phantom discomforts of anatomy.

Not so much of that at the moment, though. She shuffled around on the leather couch as the top layer of Memory-Josh shouted around her, waving his arms and doing everything he could to make the stand-off in the office as bad as it could get. He kept telling the militia men to *back off, Back Off!* his voice cracking from panic. The militia wasn't nearly as well-trained as Fischer; they began to press forward—

"*So close,*" she sighed through their link, as Fischer soothed the room through calm assurances. "He knew exactly what to say to get everybody back under control."

"Yeah," Josh said. *"Thanks for getting him out of there."*

"No matter what else happens, Nicholson's lost him. Did you see anyone else who could take over for him?"

"No, but that doesn't mean that he didn't have a fallback waiting at the factory."

They watched as Fischer left the room. Then came Mulcahy's assurances that there would be no more misunderstandings, and the FBI followed him out. The woman standing by the window opened it, and Rachel watched herself leap from the third story.

"At least that looked believable," she said.

"Heart-stoppingly believable," her friend muttered.

In Josh's memory, the militia men gasped and rushed to the window.

"Stop." The remembered version of Mulcahy's voice was as hard as the original. "Calm down, or the FBI will come back. You won't be able to get rid of them again."

This time, the militia men looked to Nicholson, then to each other when he offered no guidance.

"Stand down," Mulcahy told them, and they moved away from the window. The memory of Josh shook as he tried to keep from laughing, his quiet puffs of air lost in the shuffle of combat boots on expensive area rugs.

Mulcahy turned towards Nicholson. "You wanted to talk to me," he said, standing in the space where the coffee table had been. "Talk."

"Yes. Yes, well…" Nicholson squirmed as the blond giant in front of him walled him off from the rest of the room. "OACET… Your organization has been… Yes. Three years ago, when OACET—"

"No," Mulcahy said. "No sales pitches. No prepared speeches. Tell me why you kidnapped my wife and oldest godchild."

"Listen—"

Mulcahy held up his hand. It appeared to be a call for silence, but a glowing red dot appeared in the center of his palm. Nicholson's mouth snapped shut at the sight of it.

"This isn't yours," Mulcahy said, as he moved his hand through the air. The dot tracked the center of his palm, pulled together from fluid motes of light which seemed almost alive.

"What?" Nicholson couldn't pull his gaze from that red dot.

"My team took down your scouts before the meeting," Mulcahy said. "Don't worry, we didn't hurt them. They'll be released when we let you leave."

"I don't know what you mean," Nicholson said loftily as he tore his gaze away from the laser.

"It was a cute workaround." A voice—a very close, very loud version of Josh's normal speaking voice—dominated the recording. Rachel felt her cheeks contort as the memory of Josh grinned at Nicholson. "You can't use normal communications when OACET's involved. We'd yank a cell phone signal or an email out of the air, just like *that!*" Their fingers twisted and a *snap!* shot through the room. "We had to watch the EMF around the warehouse until we figured out your communications strategy."

"A ten-milliwatt laser can be seen from over three miles away," Mulcahy said. "You've been running Morse code with someone in a local high-rise. That line of communications will be closed by the time this meeting is over. We've located your contact and we'll have her taken into custody as soon as you leave this building, and we are very interested to learn who *her* contact is."

"I don't have a contact—"

"We thought you'd double up on the same strategy to let your men back at the warehouse know we didn't screw you in this meeting," Memory-Josh said. "You didn't disappoint."

"Your spotters took a position where they could see into my office from the roof of that building," Mulcahy said, pointing towards a nearby skyscraper. "They planned to signal another spotter in position on the east side of the city. The go-between is the one with the phone, and he's the one who'd call the factory if the spotters saw us take you down."

"Same way you've been getting messages in and out of the factory," Memory-Josh said.

Nicholson was shaking his head. "That's not what I've done," he said. "The spotters, yeah, I put them in place for this meeting. Can you blame me? I need to stay in contact with my men back in Maryland. But I'm not getting Morse code messages… I'm not sending them, either! I don't have to!"

"You don't," Mulcahy said. He put his hand down, and the red dot vanished. "Someone else does. Who gave you the idea for the communications setup for this meeting?"

Nicholson's eyes darted towards the corner where Fischer had stood, but he didn't reply.

"You're being played," Mulcahy said. "Someone is manipulating you, and they're using…Ethan, I believe? as their mouthpiece. You've got five minutes to convince me that you've got enough control to salvage this situation before I take all choice away from you."

Nicholson stared up at Mulcahy, dumbstruck.

"Get him out of here—" Mulcahy began.

"It's too big!" Nicholson blurted.

Mulcahy took another step towards him.

"I know what we said, but you should always have your elevator pitch locked and loaded, no matter what," Memory-Josh said. "Otherwise, you'll miss the best opportunities."

Nicholson just shook his head, but another member of the militia spoke up. "No!" The other man paused, as if shocked that he had opened his mouth, but he pulled himself together and added, "Not…not the plan. He means the government."

Nicholson tried to stand; Mulcahy laid a hand on Nicholson's shoulder until he sat back down. "We want the same thing," Nicholson tried. "We—everybody here—just wants to be free."

The head of OACET didn't respond, but Nicholson pushed on through the silence. "This country has lost its way," he said. "The government is too powerful. Not the elected government—the one that exists behind the bread and circus. The people don't have power anymore! That's why Hanlon tried to take control of you—he knows that politics isn't power. I mean, the guy decided he wanted to be a Senator, so he became a Senator. But he did that to get control of OACET. If politics was power—*real* power!—he could easily have become President. But why should he want to? The so-called most powerful man in the world is just a figurehead who gets five years older for every one that he's in office."

Nicholson paused to catch his breath. "That should mean something to you," he continued. "That to him, political office was just a means to get control of OACET."

Mulcahy didn't respond. Neither did Josh, or any of the other Agents in the room.

The militia leader tried again. "The government doesn't exist anymore," he said. "Not in the way that was guaranteed to us by the Constitution. The system is set up so there are no more winners or losers, just an endless status quo.

"You can't let them do this," he said. "They could hurt—No! They do hurt too many people. OACET can change that. You have the power to wipe the slate clean. Everything's gone digital. You can dump it. Dump it *all*. Wipe out this system of lies so we can start from scratch."

"If what you're saying is true, you've admitted that OACET is in power," Mulcahy said. "What makes you think we'd be sympathetic to you?"

The militia man who had spoken before called out: "Hanlon."

Nicholson nodded. "You've been hurt," he said. "He tried to break you, but you fought back and broke him instead. He gave you power and you used it to take down a Senator—Why not take them all down?

"Listen, America might not have started out as a feudal society, but that's what it's become. As it stands now, the system is set up to profit from the people. The system is broken—irreversibly broken! We're here…" he said, as he gestured towards his men, "…because we love our country. We don't want to see it destroyed."

His men were nodding. The brave one said, "You have to help us."

"No," Mulcahy said. "We don't."

Nicholson stood and tried to stare Mulcahy down. It was like watching a Honda Civic drive straight at a canyon wall. "Yes," he shouted, "you do! You're obliged to help your country!"

"Obliged?" said Memory-Josh.

"Morally obliged! Ethically obligated!" Nicholson shouted. "You've got the power to help us break free of this system, and if you can't recognize that, we'll *make* you!"

"Fuck!" Rachel broke her link with Josh and leapt off of the couch. "Fuck fuck *fuuuuuuck!*"

Josh rubbed his temples as the recording snapped into fragments of light and sensation. "Yeah," he said. "I know."

"Jesus H. Christ!" Rachel's voice sounded high and strange in her own ears. "What I wouldn't give to go back in time and sit on Chuck Palahniuk until he comes up with a better plot."

"He's not completely wrong," Josh said. "Nicholson, that is. Not Palahniuk."

"I know," she said. Then, more quietly: "What do we do?"

Josh didn't reply.

The memory had faded away and had taken the sharp details of the room with it. The familiar soft forms of her world weren't nearly as welcoming as usual: the room still stank of agendas and frightened men.

"We're trapped," Josh finally said. "We can't negotiate with Nicholson. Not at all. If we do…"

"…he'll be the first of thousands of anti-government conspiracy nuts," she finished for him. "All of them looking to OACET for salvation."

He nodded. "The terms have changed. It doesn't just end with getting the hostages back. We've got to have a decisive victory, real scorched-earth. No survivors, figuratively speaking. Or we might as well not win at all, because others will see us as sympathetic to the cause and they'll keep coming."

Rachel flopped back down on the couch; the smell of leather

puffed around her. "Fuck Hanlon," she said. "He knew this would happen."

"No, he didn't," Josh said. He stood and moved to search a spot high on a bookshelf, nudging framed photographs aside but coming up empty. "He's not a god. All of us together are four hundred times smarter than he is… Where'd Pat hide his brandy today?"

She pointed to a drawer in a nearby cabinet. "Check the shoebox behind the legal briefs."

"Thanks." He returned to the couch with a squat glass bottle, and they took turns passing it between them until they began to feel marginally better.

She didn't realize she had sighed aloud until Josh said, "Penny for your thoughts."

Rachel burst out laughing.

"I know, right?" he said with a grin.

"Oh God, we were such sweet summer children," she said, and opened a new link. She sent him her own memory, of a stairwell and a tall man made of forest greens, with a complicated mess of colors stitched over that green. The man-shape said, in Hill's voice, "Martyrs. Scary as fuck."

Josh took another drink, and asked, *"Is Nicholson a martyr?"*

"You tell me," she said. "You're better at reading people than I am."

"Couldn't tell." He wiped his mouth with the back of his hand. "He seemed sincere, but not to the point of sacrificing himself for the cause."

"Where's the woman? The one on the building who was sending the messages to Fischer?"

He shrugged. "We don't know. She slipped her tail."

"Great. Just great. Is there more to the meeting?"

"Yup."

"All right," she said, as she resettled herself in Memory-Josh's position on the couch. "Let's do this."

"Where were we?" Josh asked, as images and sounds moved themselves around.

"You didn't pause it?"

"You can't pause a memory."

"But you can record one?"

She felt him push aside the bundle of complex answers before saying, *"Ah, we were here. Ready?"*

She consented, and the feeling of being crammed inside a body larger and heavier than her own crushed her down against the leather couch again, as the physical details of the room took on edges, letters, and faces.

Nicholson was shouting: "Morally obliged! Ethically obligated! You've got the power to help us break free of this system, and if you can't recognize that, we'll *make* you!"

"Obliged and obligated?" asked Memory-Josh in his too-loud voice. "Those who can do, must do, for the overall good of society? Sounds like communism to me."

The members of the militia shot weighty glances at each other at the mention of communism, but Nicholson wasn't about to back down. "Not communism," he said. "Far from it. I'd call OACET the perfect weapon for true democracy. You have the ability to make sure that government plays by the same rules for all people. Not just the rich and powerful."

"That's wishful thinking," Memory-Josh said. "If—*if!*—we could equalize the playing field, there's no guarantee it'd stay that way. And once we took steps against the government, we'd be removed from office so damned fast—"

"It's a—" Nicholson tried to move around Mulcahy, but the head of OACET pushed him back down in the chair again. "Could you back off? You're not in this alone!" Nicholson snapped at him.

For the first time since he had hurled the coffee table, Mulcahy took a step away from Nicholson. The militia's leader took this as a triumph. "You wouldn't be removed," Nicholson said, a smile beginning to turn his mouth. "Everyone would be too focused on me and my men. The obvious threat. You work behind the scenes, and we do the hard work on the battlefield. By the time they figured out what was really happening, there'd be so little left of the establishment that there'd be no choice but to start anew. With both of our groups in positions of influence."

The memory of the same cold sweat that had broken over Josh prickled over Rachel's skin, and blended with her own. *"Holy shit,"* she whispered across their link, as if Nicholson might be able to hear her. *"Is he saying what I think he's saying?"*

"Watch," Josh told her.

"Battlefield?" Mulcahy asked, as calmly as if he were inquiring as to whether Nicholson wanted sugar in his coffee. "That implies you have an army."

"There are thousands of us!" Nicholson said proudly. "Tens of thousands! And more will join once the fighting starts. They've—*we've*—been waiting, Mulcahy. All of us waiting for a leader to step up and do what needs to be done."

"And you'd lead this fighting force?" Memory-Josh asked.

Another involuntary glance at the corner where Ethan Fischer had stood, but Nicholson nodded.

"What you're suggesting is treason," Mulcahy said.

"I'm sure you're familiar with the Founding Fathers," Nicholson said.

Mulcahy closed his eyes and exhaled, ever so slowly, and Rachel wondered if he had finally reached the limits of his seemingly infinite self-control. A moment later, he opened them to stare down at the militia leader. "I'm a Constitutional scholar," he said. "And I very much doubt the Founding Fathers would perceive the current government as a worthy target of open revolt."

"Only because the current system would benefit them," Nicholson said. "If they were down here in the trenches with the rest of us, they'd want another revolution. No, they'd *demand* it! The tree of liberty must be refreshed from time to time with the blood of patriots and tyrants!"

"Don't quote Jefferson out of context," Memory-Josh said. "Just...don't."

"I'm not," Nicholson said. "He addressed the necessity of rebellion to preserve an informed society."

"And claims that lives lost in the process are nothing in the grand scheme of time, a point with which I personally disagree."

"What do you propose?" Mulcahy asked Nicholson.

Nicholson brightened, as an almost palpable sense of eagerness moved among his followers. "The sovereign citizen movement isn't perfect," he said. "But it's founded on a core of truth. I need you to help us get to that truth, where the rules for the powerful are also those that apply to the general population. All we want is to bring the government that exists in line with the version that's been promised to the people."

Mulcahy closed his eyes again, as if considering. "It's difficult to hear you talk about moral and ethical obligations when you've abducted the same people you claim you want to protect," he said. "Including a very young child."

"They haven't been harmed," Nicholson said. His smirk had returned. "I've made sure of that."

"Have you seen my wife's face today? How many of your men have taken turns beating her?"

Nicholson seemed dumbstruck. "The cameras," he said softly. "That's right. You can look through the cameras."

"With that in mind, you must appreciate that I'm having a hard time trusting your word," Mulcahy said, his eyes still closed.

"Your wife is...difficult," Nicholson said. "She's resisted. When she attacks my men, they hit back."

"You kidnapped a world-class martial artist who's renowned for her short temper, and you expected her to play along," Memory-Josh said. "I see a few flaws in this plan right out of the gate."

Mulcahy opened his eyes. "I've heard you out," he said. "Now, let the hostages go."

"It's not that easy," Nicholson said. "We need assurances that you'll help us before you get them back. And you have to make sure that nobody takes this as an opportunity to come after us before the uprising."

Rachel felt the press of smooth top-grain leather on both

sides of a hand that wasn't hers, as Memory-Josh snuck his hand between the couch cushions.

"I apologize for the misunderstanding." The head of OACET opened his eyes and stared down at Nicholson. "We won't be helping you. Not now. Not ever."

"What?!" Nicholson tried to rise to his feet again, and this time Mulcahy let him. He stood, furious. "You *have* to help. And it has to be soon—this is an opportunity that won't come again! Congress will force you to join up with Homeland Security or the CIA soon, and then you'll be watched too closely to act!"

"Work behind the scenes to pull down the government while you set yourself up as the new General Washington?" Memory-Josh said. "Don't think so."

There was a scuffle around the room as the militia men protested. They began to move, closing in on Mulcahy from all sides—

A small *pfft!* sound, about as loud as a glass bottle breaking. Nothing loud. Nothing remotely like a gunshot. The men still froze where they stood—they knew a silencer when they heard one.

"Easy," Memory-Josh said in his too-loud voice. A semi-automatic pistol hung in his hand, the silencer on its muzzle pointing at nowhere in particular. There was a new hole in the thick wood of the monstrous mahogany desk.

"This meeting is over," Mulcahy announced. "Go back to your factory. Get your affairs in order, release the hostages, and give yourselves up."

Nicholson was turning red, the tips of his ears burning in anger. "Who do you think you are?!" he shouted. "I've got your wi—"

Mulcahy reached out one giant hand and, as gently as if he were plucking a peach from a tree, wrapped that hand around Nicholson's throat.

"Gurk?" said Nicholson, eyes wide.

"Indeed," Mulcahy said.

There was a rush of movement as Mulcahy picked Nicholson

up by the neck. Nicholson clawed at Mulcahy's hand with both of his own, strangled *gurks!* slipping through his lips as he tried to breathe.

Mulcahy bent his arm and brought Nicholson in close, so close that Memory-Josh with his poor sense of hearing couldn't make out what he whispered in Nicholson's ear…

"He asked Nicholson if he wanted a demonstration of true abuse of power," Josh said, as the memory hung within the moment.

Mulcahy lowered Nicholson to the floor and released him.

"There will be no negotiation," Mulcahy said. "Here are our terms: abide by them, or we will come into your house and tear it down around you. Release the hostages. Give yourselves up."

"We'll say you've cooperated," Memory-Josh said. "We'll spin this so you guys will play like princes! Freedom fighters so committed to the idea of fixing this country that you were willing to do anything to call attention to its problems.

"Hell," Memory-Josh said, "Why don't we make it a party? We'll call a huge press conference, give you guys all the media time you want. You can turn yourselves into heroes after this, you know. You'll be booked on all of the talk shows. I bet some of you can get movie deals."

The militia men shuffled in place. Heroism and royalty payments seemed to have some universal appeal.

"Thirty-seven hours," Mulcahy said to Nicholson. He took a cell phone from his pocket and pushed it into Nicholson's trembling hands. "Talk it over with your men. Reach a deal. There are more effective ways to make your case than open revolt."

"Trust us on this," Memory-Josh said. "We've gotten really good at working the media angle."

The memory faded. Mulcahy's office was darker, now—the sun had finally gone down, and the streetlights outside weren't able to pick up the slack.

"After that, it was just logistics," Josh said. The bottle of brandy was more than half gone. *"We gave them thirty-seven hours to*

surrender. Deadline is nine in the morning, day after tomorrow. In the meantime, we offered to provide meals and entertainment. If we're lucky, they won't recognize this as prep work for a raid."

"Are we that lucky?"

"Yeah," Josh sighed, as the weight of the world moved between them. *"Sure we are."*

"What's wrong with him?" Rachel asked aloud.

Her friend severed their link as his thoughts spun away from the image of Mulcahy, standing with one hand around—

"Nothing," he said, as he went to return the bottle to its hiding place. "He's fine."

"Josh!" Rachel stood and began to move around the room, feeling like Hope Blackwell trying to burn off her captivity. "We've already had this discussion. He's not fine. You've admitted it, and Hope told me to ask you about it, so hi, Josh, I'm asking you again—What's wrong with him? He's not…" She groped for the right words. "He's not acting human!"

"He's *not* human," Josh said, as gray stress and the pitted textures of depression swirled around him like a cloak. "Not right now."

It was true, or at least truth as best as Josh knew how to put it. She tried to reopen their link, but he waved her off, orange frustration rising.

"Okay," she said. "What do you mean?"

He turned into the weaving and weighing of colors, a balance of OACET green against Mulcahy's cerulean blue. "You remember what it was like?" he finally asked. "Back before activation?"

"The brainwashing?" she snapped, only hearing that much-hated word after it sprang loose. "Yeah. Yeah, I remember. Thanks."

"He can tap into that," Josh said. "That…the conditioning. He can put himself back in that empty place. It helps him get through events like this."

She was sitting on the couch again with no memory of how she got there, and wasn't sure whether to thank her feet or curse their timing. "No," she whispered. "He can't do that."

"Yeah, he can. We all can, probably—Pat's just the only one of us who finds it useful. Or the only one who isn't terrified to use it." Sorrowful, stressful yellows and oranges and even the green of guilt as he tried to shoulder some of the burden.

"He can't do that!" she gasped.

"Obviously he can—"

"No, Josh, there's no way he'd do that to himself—not willingly! Put himself back in that living hell?"

"Do you really want him angry?" Josh asked. "You know what he did before he got tapped for OACET. If he loses control, there'd be a body count."

"I think…" she began, before she decided she didn't know what she thought, that maybe Josh was right and it was better that Mulcahy stayed in control.

Patrick Mulcahy hadn't started out as a bureaucrat. The U.S. government had its own internal messaging service, couriers they used to move special packages from Point A to Point B. He had been one of these, instead. When most people learned that he had been a delivery boy prior to joining OACET, they usually laughed and congratulated him on his promotion. When those who had the proper security clearance learned what he had done, they usually needed to sit down and put their heads between their knees for a few minutes. They knew that, if mishandled, some packages tended to die, or explode, or spread little tiny viral pathogens all over the place, and that sometimes these packages needed to be moved behind international lines or through active warzones. The U.S. government's specialized couriers received training equivalent to SEALs and the Green Berets combined, and nobody made too much fuss about their methods as long as the job got done.

Mulcahy had been *very* good at his job.

"Body count, my ass. If he gets pushed over the edge," she murmured, "it'd be a bloodbath."

"And if Mulcahy falls, we all fall with him," he reminded her. "He's made sure OACET stands for honor and integrity. He could get his wife back any time he wants, but there'd be a cost we'd all pay. He's choosing to let diplomacy win out, for us. He's shut himself down, for us."

"Jesus." She flipped off her implant and buried her head in her hands.

"This is what he's got to do," Josh said. "And we all do what we've got to do."

"We can't let him do this," she said, her mind trying to bundle *'all that we've got to do'* into a single idea. It wasn't working—there was too much that needed to fit inside of it, and the details were spilling out from the cracks.

"No, we can't," he agreed. "And we shouldn't stop him."

"This isn't right!" Rachel said, loud enough to start her headache up again.

"If you can think of any way to end this, please do," he said.

Rachel tapped her fingertips on her temples. The blood in her hair had gone hard and crunchy, and it shed tiny shards of dried biocontamination when she moved it. "I need to go see that militia," she said. "The one up in Pennsylvania. That's the only trail I haven't chased yet."

"Right now?"

"Can't. I've got a golf game in the morning" she said.

She felt him nod. Josh was a golfer, too, because help came from the unlikeliest places and there was no better way to forge a lasting relationship than to demonstrate how skilled you were with a bludgeoning weapon while standing in the middle of nowhere. Or something.

She sprawled out across the couch, and most of Josh. He nudged her foot until the toe of her boot stopped poking him in the ribs.

"Going to be tight," he said. "Golf early, Pennsylvania later… We need you back here and rested for the raid. Phil's scans are good, but yours can't be beat."

"I've got that figured out, but I need your help," she said. She told him what she was thinking, and he laughed.

"Sure," he said. "I'll put it together."

"You using your office bed tonight?" she asked.

"Nah, got to go back to my place and feed the cat," he said. "All yours."

"Thanks," she said, and reactivated her implant. She sent a text to Becca that said she was working late and would see her soon, maybe not tomorrow, but definitely after that and they'd have a nice date night. And then she sent a follow-up text to let her know the psychopath was still being watched by the Hippos and she shouldn't worry. And then a second follow-up text that was three red hearts and an emoji of shrimp tempura.

She waited. Three hearts came back across her mind. A moment later, the shrimp emoji followed.

"Becca?" Josh asked, as she smiled.

"Mmm-hmm."

Sleep. The idea was almost intoxicating. If she went to bed right now, she could put on that autoscript that boosted her healing and sleep for thirteen hours. Thirteen full hours of blissful, uninterrupted—

And, just as she began to acquaint herself to the idea that she could look forward to a day in which she was fully rested and ready to take on the world, the sweet electronic voice of a mostly-dead computer swept through her mind.

"Look at me still talking when there's science to do..."

"Aw hell," Rachel muttered. Santino's ringtone, and something was wrong: he had been so distant lately that he only called when it was important. She opened the line and her partner began shouting.

Josh drove her to the hospital. He didn't stick around. Rachel didn't blame him for leaving. There was…quite a lot of blood.

It might not have looked like a murder. Not if the victim hadn't been tougher than hammered nails and unwilling to go down without a fight. The officers had put Fischer in restraints, and had moved him to a bed designed for that purpose, with metal railings bolted to a weighted platform. No chance of flipping this one, or of breaking the leather straps belted around his body and fastened to the railings. But he had fought back so hard that the bed had wiggled nearly a foot away from the wall.

The medical examiner thought the needle from the syringe that had been used to inject him had broken off in his neck. The needle was gone, but whoever had removed it had needed to dig it out with a scalpel.

…quite a lot of blood. Yes. Quite a lot…

"He couldn't call for help," Santino said. "Not with those bandages around his jaw."

"Yeah," she replied. Her voice sounded distant. "Any leads?"

"Jason's going through the security footage now. There's a woman in a nurse's uniform who nobody recognizes, and the officer at the door went on a five-minute break after she said she'd watch him while changing his bandages."

Santino was quiet for a moment, staring at the body of the man they had, however indirectly, helped put on the path to his own death. "Why'd they kill him?"

"Did Hill get a chance to go at him yet?"

"No."

"That's why," she sighed. "Time to find out who this guy is, and where he came from."

"I don't even know where to start with that," Santino said. "Tracking down that handwriting sample will take too long, even for Jason."

"I do," she said. "I need to learn who else is in my foursome."

SIXTEEN

The man sitting beside her had a monster's face, but she wasn't worried—the monster had stolen her friend's face, not the other way around. He was a youngish man with a Texas drawl and a cowboy strut, even though he had never been near a ranch, let alone a horse. A man from a sleepy suburban home, just like hers, with two upper-middle-class parents who loved him, just like hers, and who couldn't understand why their beloved only child had run off to join the circus. Just like hers.

They were sitting on the roof of a mess hall in Afghanistan, watching the stars.

"Sorry," she said, and since this was a dream, he already knew why she was buried up to her neck in a stinking pile of guilt.

"Hell, Peng," he said in the warm sounds of home. "You were a mind-controlled 'bot when I died. You couldn't'a done anything."

"I *didn't* do anything," she said. "Something would have been better than nothing. A phone call, an email…"

He threw her off the roof.

Rachel hung in mid-air: flying in dreams had become much easier since she started soaring around in her avatar. But Wyatt—a Wyatt three years younger than he had been on the roof—was waiting for her on the ground. She landed and felt her body twist into that of an eighteen-year-old girl's, and started crying.

"What's your bitch, kid?"

Younger-Rachel scrubbed at her face, hot with embarrassment at getting caught crying behind the women's privies. "Go away," she snapped.

He called her names until she was mad enough to take a swing at him, and then they pounded the shit out of each other until they were too tired to stand.

"There you go," he told her. "Stay mad. It helps."

They aged a year; the stars overhead stayed the same.

"Criminal Investigation Command." Wyatt's tone was half-scorn, half-anger. "The hell are you doin', puttin' in for CID?"

"I don't have as many options as you." Rachel was throwing rocks into the desert. The moon was just at the edge of the horizon, and huge. She had never seen a moon this large. It was silver and red, and called to the wolf in her. She wanted to race across the desert in the moonlight, but there were landmines out there, right below the sand. "CID is a good start. I can move up in the ranks, build a rep…"

"As a cop," he said, still angry.

"You know what CID does out here?" She flung a baseball-sized rock into the emptiness, and waited for an explosion that never came. "Everything. You and me, we sit around waiting for something to happen, and then it's chaos for a day, maybe two. Then we go back to waiting. CID gets shit done."

And then she started talking about opportunities in the CID, mostly for women, but hell, Wyatt could put in—should put in—for the transfer, too. It was all puzzles and scams and putting things right, and didn't they spend all of their time complaining about how things around here weren't *right*, right?

Another rock. Another two years on their bones. The same stars overhead, the same moon touching where the world dropped off.

"Gonna miss you, y'know." Wyatt was sitting on a flat-topped boulder, a can of beer in his hands. He held the can gently; beer was almost unheard-of around here, a forbidden treasure from home.

"Yeah." Her own beer was warm, old, and skunky, but she drank it anyhow. God only knew where he had found it for her going-away party. "I'll be back."

"As an officer."

"Hopefully," she said. "You should put in. You'd do good at West Point."

Wyatt shook his head in disgust. "Dragging me into CID was bad enough—"

"Fuck, man, you need *some* ambition or you're gonna die a nobody!"

Wyatt started laughing. She couldn't figure out why he found that funny, or why she thought he should be purple. Then the shell of the dream cracked, and she remembered.

"Sorry," she said. She crushed the can down and it became a stone, and hurled this into the minefield.

The dead man shrugged. The beer can from her memory stretched into an ice-cold stein, overflowing with fresh beer and foam. "It's not all bad," he said, as he raised the glass in a silent toast.

"I miss you," she said.

"I'm still around. I'm just harder to reach."

"Stop talking to my inner Catholic."

"Wasn't," he said, and his grin was made of secrets.

"Want me to track down your body?"

"Nah," he said. "I'm not using it any more. Let your new buddy have it."

Light spilled out of the moon as the dream cracked so hard it nearly split open, and she remembered the psychopath in Wyatt's skin.

"What aren't I seeing?" she asked him.

Wyatt pointed.

The moon had grown a shadow: a man, haloed in black against the silver. He was walking down the desert road, head high, focused on what lay ahead of him.

Mulcahy.

And suddenly, she knew the road was full of landmines—so, so many more landmines than in the desert around it!—and he was about to blow himself up.

"Get him off the road," Wyatt said, before he punched her in the face for old time's sake.

She woke in Josh's office, with yet another headache.

Probably the same one, she reminded herself, as she let herself wake up in the dark. *Head injuries, thrown into a wall, late night at a murder scene... At least this one isn't too bad.*

Snoring from two points in the room: Rachel flipped on her implant and went to the loudest source; Josh, asleep on the couch, alone, with a magazine over his face and a hungry cat at home.

She moved to the second source and found Ami asleep beside her. On the other side of Ami was the fake Wyatt, snoring away in duckling-like peeps.

The two of them were naked.

"No. Just no," Rachel groaned, and left the room at a run.

Becca always says I can sleep through anything. She's gonna laugh so hard—

No, it was her autoscript. The one that put her into a deep sleep so she could rest and rebuild. It had to be the autoscript, because there was no way on God's green earth she would have let herself sleep while that was happening beside her.

*Gah! With **him**? What the hell was Ami thinking?!*

Rachel had never been completely comfortable with casual sex. It bashed up against her nature. And with somebody like Wyatt? Not that she was judging Ami, oh no, but...

...okay. This one time? She was definitely judging Ami.

"Could've at least gone somewhere else," she grumbled, her bare feet slapping quietly against the stone floor as she ran out of Josh's office, trying her best to get into yesterday's clothing before she bumped into someone from the FBI. Or worse, Homeland. "Me, right there...*ugh!*"

She found a side door and fled into the night.

Alone in the relative quiet of the city streets, she allowed the dream to set up shop in her head.

Her dreams had never been anything close to vivid, not until she and Santino had fished a piece of ancient history out of the basement of the White House. Since then, they had turned into living Technicolor on top of Technitouch and Technisound, with some Technismell creeping in around the edges.

She had asked her doctor about this, and Jenny had said

that it was most likely that Rachel's dreams were changing as her senses redefined how she perceived the world. Her doctor pointed out that much of the early research on dreaming indicated that dreams took place in black and white; later, it was found that these colorless dreams were attached to kids who had grown up in the era of early cinema. Black and white dreams were the exception, and once television sets got a bunch of extra tubes crammed into their cases, most folks went back to dreaming in full color. As Rachel's subconscious was probably adapting her dreams to align with her new senses, it wasn't anything to be worried about.

Rachel, who still had dreams of being torn apart by small crustaceans on the bottom of the Mediterranean, didn't agree. Especially as every other Agent who had touched the artifact had stopped eating seafood, too.

Dreams weren't just dreams. Not anymore.

A dream about her dead brother-in-arms had turned into a dream about her live superior officer.

"Get him off the road."

Nothing ominous there, nope.

"All right," she muttered to herself, and this time she included that odd triad of her conscious brain, her subconscious mind, and her implant. "We've got a road, we've got Mulcahy, and we've got hidden landmines. Anybody want to dispel the symbolism so I can do something about it?"

Silence.

She yelled at herself a little, then a lot. Nothing. Whatever was rattling around in her head would shake itself out when it was ready. Hopefully.

Maybe.

No more cookies until you cough up something useful, she grumbled at her mental triad. It was a sorry state of affairs when your own augmented brain somehow managed to team up against you.

The city felt warmer than it had during the day, and she put herself on autopilot and let her feet take her to a building ten short blocks from OACET headquarters. It was an old office building, five stories high, granite and brick in the Greek revival style. The windows of the bottom floor were covered in sheets of butcher's paper, with a tasteful new sign for an aikido studio hanging above the front door, the words *Coming Soon!* draped across it on a removable ribbon.

The door had a digital lock, but this popped open before she could activate it. Four floors above, a man with a core the color of quick-brewed tea leaves waved down to her.

She took the stairs two at a time, at least until she reached the first landing. There, she paused, and let her scans wander over a large metal object, beaten from abuse and blackened by fire. It had been a door, once, a fantastic door in the truest sense of the adjective. Here, it was nothing except a memorial: Hope Blackwell, the building's new owner, had rescued it from a maker space that had been targeted by a couple of itty-bitty riots. Hope had it suspended from silver cables running from the walls and ceiling, and had declared that in a year, she wanted the door gone and its component pieces to have been given new life. The last time Rachel had been here, the object had still looked more or less like a door. The artists, vultures all, had been at it—if she turned her scans to the correct angle, it took on the shape of a woman's profile.

Her scans showed the second floor as empty, or at least as empty as rooms could be in a building frequented by those who were driven by creative chaos. The space was gradually filling with project overflow, with signs of temporary residences here and there, backpacks and piles of blankets and the like. Hope hadn't said what she intended to do with the second floor: she said her choices were either turning it into a gallery or apartments that could be allocated to artists like grants, but Rachel knew she was hoping that the owner of the aikido dojo would relent and agree to live on-site.

Unlikely: the third floor was a machine shop, with all of the smells and noise that a machine shop entailed. Most of it was set up for woodworking and metalsmithing (and no overlap between those two in respect to the sharing of power tools, or there would be blood), but a sculptor had recently moved into a back corner. There was always someone active on the third floor; even at this hour, Rachel spotted a man pressing pieces of wood into the lid of a carved box. Across the room, another two forms were sprawled out across the workbenches, their conversational colors slow with sleep.

She crept up the next flight of stairs, quiet as a mouse, and kept her thoughts far, far away from those two men.

One more flight, and Shawn greeted her with a hug.

Warmth flowed from the other Agent into her, and the smell of oil paint and turpentine wrapped around her. She took a moment to take in his emotions—*peace, wholeness, belonging*—before she stepped away.

"Come in," he said, his mental voice gentle, and brought her into his studio.

Rachel loved the fourth floor. It was the dust-free zone, set aside for artists who might kick up a fume or two but otherwise avoided sanding and polishing and all that airborne mess. The center of the room was home to a large bank of computer equipment, walled off in glass partitions. Around the edges of the room were cubicles for those who mucked around in various media. When the sun was up, these studios were awash in light; tonight, a single floodlight over Shawn's studio lit the entire room.

She stepped through the (still depressingly ordinary) door and ran her scans through the building. The floor above them was an apartment, with space for three permanent residents, and a fourth room for a rotating caregiver. Nobody was in the fourth room, but Shawn's bed held the sleeping form of Rachel's doctor.

"Are you here to see Jenny?" he said, a little wistfully.

She sent him the image of waking up next to an assassin and a psychopath in their full post-coital splendor, and he shuddered.

"Yeah," she said aloud. "This has not been the best couple of days. I'm just…here."

"Well, I'm glad," he said. *"We miss you."*

Rachel followed him into his studio. *"I almost never get over to the Batcave,"* she said. *"And Santino's practically living at Zia's now, so I have to call a cab whenever I go anywhere."* The excuses were weak; Shawn knew it, and forgave her in rich reds and purples.

"It's not you," she whispered.

"I know," he replied.

Agents were trapped in the strangest of government employee conundrums. The implants in their heads were quantum organic computers, and were integrated into their hosts at a cellular level. They had been expensive as hell to manufacture, and couldn't be removed and re-implanted in a different brain if an Agent decided to move to another job. When Rachel had enlisted in the Program, she had signed all other career opportunities away—she had known that after the implant was in, if she wanted to quit OACET, she'd have to repay the government to the tune of thirty-seven million dollars. Plus inflation. She could retire at sixty-five with benefits, but until then, the chip in her head was government property and so, by extension, was she.

(No one really wanted to test the clauses in their contracts that covered what could happen if they were fired for due cause. Brain surgery might be involved, followed by severe neurological damage. And there were worse things, such as complete loss of pension.)

Rachel turned her scans to the floor below them, where the two men asleep on the workbench had curled up in a knot for warmth. Adrian and Sammy. The last of the cyborgs who never made it all the way back to their own heads.

They were still on OACET's payroll. Mare had put them in the Public Relations department; Shawn showed up at the Batcave during work hours to file paperwork and answer the phones.

Adrian and Sammy…didn't.

"Do they ever sleep upstairs?" she asked.

"Jenny and I put them in their beds when we can," he said. "Mostly they just build until they crash, and then they wake up and start again."

"What are they working on these days? More robots?"

He nodded, blue wonder coming across his colors. "You should see them—amazing things!"

"What do they do?"

"Do?"

She laughed. "Why are you awake?"

Shawn's colors clouded over. "I...don't know?" He shook himself, and smiled weakly. "Maybe I knew you were coming."

She slipped her arm around his waist. "Show me what you've been working on."

A large space had been set aside for Shawn's studio; the cyborg-in-residence got a full corner of the fourth floor, with shelf space and—*gasp!*—storage racks. A stretched cotton canvas was settled on a metal easel in the pool of light; other paintings in different stages of completion took up the rest of his studio space. One of these caught Rachel's scans as soon as she spotted it: the piece was round instead of square, and painted over wood instead of cotton canvas. The wood had been covered in a thick layer of gesso, and Shawn had been roughing out an image of a lush garden in greens with a palette knife.

"This is lovely," she said, running her scans across the paint. It was dry, not drying; Shawn hadn't worked on this piece in the last few days.

"It's for the baby," he said.

"Who's expecting?" Avery wasn't the collective's only child. She was their first, and forever would be special because of it, but there were nine other joyful rug rats running around these days. Each new child was cause for aggressive, deliberate celebration. Rachel didn't spend too much time at OACET headquarters, but she was sure she would have heard if someone was pregnant.

Shawn went slightly orange. *"I don't know,"* he said, as he fell back in the comfort of the link. *"I just...**know**. I can't remember* *if I heard it, or if I dreamed it, or…"*

"Hey, maybe you can help me," Rachel said quickly. "I had a weird dream, right before I woke up and came over here…" She told him about the dream, and the minefield, and Mulcahy walking straight into danger. "I'm pretty sure I know what it means," she said. "I just don't know what I'm supposed to do."

"Who was Marshall Wyatt?" Shawn asked, speaking aloud again. Rachel exhaled in relief. His bad moments were few and far between these days, but they could turn grim.

"A big brother when I got to Afghanistan," she said. "A little brother when I left."

"Oh." Shawn's colors fell slightly, then rose as he found his footing. "Symbolism is pretty crazy stuff. Even when it seems clear, sometimes the meaning is… Well, come take a look at what I've been working on."

They moved over to the single spotlight. Shawn glanced up, and the light dimmed; he was more photophobic than most Agents. He moved a wooden footstool aside, and let Rachel have center viewing so she could flip frequencies and take in the piece.

She looked. She flipped frequencies, and looked again. Then, she flicked her implant off and on a couple of times, and looked again, as hard as she could, before she accepted there was nothing wrong with her scans.

"Is that supposed to be me?" she finally asked.

Her friend brightened. "You can tell?"

"I'm a little confused. What's happening…with the… Is that a cornucopia?"

"It's not sexual, if that's what you're worried about," he said, in the pure blues of an artist who had confidence in his work. "All cornucopias are symbolic of vaginas."

"Maybe," she hedged. "But not all cornucopias are symbolic of *my* vagina."

She flipped frequencies again, and made herself look away from the central image of the piece. The rest of it was rough brushwork over light pencils; Shawn had barely begin to fill in the forms. There were handcuffs and guns, an owl shaped from green light, a man made of shadows, and more.

"I'm trying to depict hypocrisy," he said, as he picked up a brush and dabbed some paint on the canvas. "It's an interesting idea—we see hypocrisy as evil, right? It's a negative concept; if we're being hypocritical, we're wrong.

"I don't think you were wrong, though, or intentionally doing harm," he said. "So how could it be evil? I've been rethinking it, and hypocrisy is, perhaps, when you make decisions that aren't…authentic."

"Authentic," she said, as she rolled the word around to taste its flavor. "Interesting."

"Not sure it's coming out the way I intended," he said, gesturing towards the painting with the tip of his brush. "The symbolism is too aggressive. I'm thinking something more like Titian's *Venus of Urbino*, with you lying naked on a bed…"

"Um—" Rachel began, and then noticed that Shawn was rippling with purple humor as he held in his laughter. She socked him in the arm hard enough to bump the paint brush across the canvas; he grinned at her as he spun more blue paint across his brush, and then painted over the woman's figure on the canvas in wide strokes.

"You didn't have to wreck it," she protested, rather weakly.

"I did. I think this version is better." He turned the canvas over. On the reverse side, framed by exposed wood covered in canvas, was a white square contrasted against a black square. The edges of these overlapped as if they were becoming as one. "There's a meditation exercise where you have to envision a white shape and a black shape simultaneously. They need to occupy the same space in your thoughts, but not shift into each other, or turn into a single gray shape."

"Sounds impossible."

"It does at first, but it's not. I think it's easier for me than most people, though," he admitted. Two squares of different shades of green appeared in midair as Shawn shaped his digital projection. These two squares slid into each other effortlessly;

he flipped the projection around in the air, and the squares separated. "This is how I think of you. At least, since your confession the other night."

"I don't know how I feel about it," she admitted, as she traced the lines of the green squares with her mind. *Separate, always, even when together…*

"I want to buy this," she decided. "How much?"

He laughed. "Let me flip the canvas and paint over the reverse," he said. "If it comes out clean, we'll talk."

"Keep it the way it is," she said. "You can say the positioning is symbolic of the dual meanings of…hyperbole and…other shit."

"Always the poet," he said, still purple. "I'll think about it."

They left the fourth floor and went downstairs to collect Adrian and Sammy. They were curled up in the center of a table covered in small pieces of metal and electronics; Sammy seemed to be building a robot that looked like a silver block of cheese. They were both wearing clothes, which made it easier; Rachel managed to get Sammy on his feet and walking without clashing up against the mutiny of his mind.

"C'mon, Sammy," she whispered, her emotional scans off and her own sleeves pulled down over her fingers. "Let's get you to bed."

He looked at her with huge brown eyes, and let her lead him upstairs.

"I still think this is dangerous," she said to Shawn, as Sammy leaned against her. She braced him as they climbed to the fifth floor, one slow step at a time. *"Has anyone figured out they're Agents?"*

"Probably," he said. *"But we're all artists now, and artists are supposed to be nuts."* He grinned at her as he kissed Adrian on top of his head.

"Eccentric," Adrian murmured quietly. "We're eccentric, not nuts."

Rachel squeezed her eyes tight as hard as she could to keep herself from crying, and hugged Sammy to her.

She took the bed in the empty fourth room. The sheets smelled like bottled gardens and home, but sleep kept yanking itself away—as soon as she got close enough to touch it, the bed would drop an inch beneath her and she would jolt awake.

Rachel activated her implant and peered through the walls; everyone but her was sleeping in soft cloudy blues.

Instead of activating her healing autoscript, she conjured two squares of different shades of green, and tried to force them to fit together until the sun came up.

SEVENTEEN

It was Rachel's deep and secret shame that she adored golf.
Worse, she was good at it.
Correction: she was great at it.

Had her stars aligned differently, she could have gone pro. But no, they had aligned in such a way that her parents, upstanding suburban white-collar laborers that they were, had seen her aptitude for the sport at an early age and had (horror of all horrors) *encouraged* her. In those days, the Second Coming of Tiger Woods had put them in mind of a daughter who could place in the LPGA and fund a respectable lifestyle on endorsements alone. Her golf bag had been full of clubs with fancy names and space-age alloys, which were replaced annually as she outgrew them. They had made sure she had the best instructors, and sent her to exclusive summer camps to work on her follow-through.

As soon as she had graduated high school, she had gone straight into the Army. It wasn't as if her parents had given her much choice in the matter, right?

These days, Rachel assumed her parents spent a lot of time laughing about the way things had turned out.

Wind, southeast, 5mph. Distance to pin, 130 yards. The autoscript that helped her plan her strokes took her scans down the fairway, exploring the local environment and turning it into advice. She instinctively knew that this hole had been built with an easterly pitch, and the bent grass was still in dormancy. The ball would have a choppy landing.

7-iron it was, then.

Her golf gear was second-hand but decent. Not top-of-the-line, not like when she was a kid, but definitely decent. The 7-iron was easy to find: she used a pink sock with white kittens stitched into the fabric as its cover.

"Agent Peng?" The man's voice was nasal and irritating, even for a congressman's. "You should probably use a different club."

She ignored him.

"Agent Peng—"

The 7-iron came up, paused, then whipped down to strike against the ball with a solid crack! The ball shot forward like a missile until it shed momentum, bounced once, twice, and rolled onto the green. A perfect shot. Even a blind moron (*cough*) could sink it in a single putt.

She smiled politely at the congressman on her way to gather up her bag.

Charlotte Gallagher fell in step with Rachel as they moved down the first greenway. "Remind me to never play you for money," Gallagher murmured.

"Back at you—you're two strokes behind me." Rachel shrugged, settling the heavy bag across her shoulders. "If I'm ever roped into a playing a ladies' tournament, I might drag you along as a partner."

Gallagher laughed, a ripple of purple humor running over her core of dusty pollen-white. "Deal."

The other members of their foursome reached their balls ahead of Rachel and Gallagher. The women fell back to allow their partners to play through, mainly out of self-preservation. Chief Judge Andrew Edwards, current chair of the Joint Committee on Judicial Administration in the D.C. circuit courts, could shank a ball into the rough like nobody's business. He was an absolute menace: since October, Edwards had hit two caddies, four golf carts, a snack stand (the same one twice), and managed to shear the head clean off a Canada goose.

The congressman was no better. Gallagher's partner made a fantastic show of checking the lay of the land, even going so far as to toss a handful of yellowed grass into the air to test the direction of the wind. Rachel and Gallagher each made a conscientious effort to avoid eye contact as he drove his ball straight into the nearest sand trap.

Whatever. It wasn't as if they were there to play golf, anyhow.

Gallagher had been a pleasant surprise. Most of those whom Edwards invited along tended to be like the congressman—there to invest in three hours of quality schmoozing with the judge, the Agent, or both.

(Rachel went along with it in part so she could shut down Josh's lectures on the importance of making and maintaining political connections, but mainly because of Edwards' coveted new membership at the Congressional Country Club. She had been politically ambitious herself, once upon a time, but the paisleys of political ambition clashed hard against a hivemind's houndstooth. Ambition tended to be fairly one-sided, and if you did enter politics for the sake of your people, you tended to end up like…well, like Mulcahy. Sane through force of will alone.)

The women watched as Edwards finally managed to put his own ball in the general geographic region of the pin, and they resumed their walk up the hill.

Gallagher's pace was slow; Rachel hung back and fell into step beside her.

Oranges weighed themselves against professional blues in Gallagher's conversational colors, but Rachel wasn't worried. Edwards had told her that the bidding had been fierce to get into the fourth slot on their Wednesday roster, as plenty of people wanted to the opportunity to talk to Rachel about OACET's position on Nicholson, militias, and similar.

Gallagher had won, and Rachel was glad of it. As one of the FBI's foremost experts on kidnappings—and, by no coincidence whatsoever, sociopaths and psychopaths— Gallagher should have been brought in the moment that Nicholson set up shop in his family's factory. But no, she hadn't been tapped for the Nicholson case. So, here she was, walking up a fairway with Rachel.

Who, also by no coincidence whatsoever, *was* involved in the Nicholson case.

"What's on your mind?" Rachel asked.

The oranges were joined by OACET green, and these pushed back against the blues. A mournful red appeared, but it was hazy, as if Gallagher was viewing it from a great distance. "We had Nicholson's militia under surveillance before he came down to Maryland."

Rachel blinked, and forced herself to keep to their steady pace instead of shouting, oh, perhaps, "Holy *balls*, woman, why didn't you do anything!?" or some other bridge-burning phrase.

"Really?" she said instead, very mildly. "Undercover, I assume."

The older woman nodded, her tight brunette bob sweeping across her shoulders. "It's no secret that the FBI's been infiltrating militias."

"Right. Militias are the new terrorists."

A flutter of purple amusement came and went across Gallagher's colors, but she didn't allow herself to laugh. Terrorism was apparently still not a laughing matter, at least not in public.

"On the record? International terrorists who have set up cells within the United States are still our top priority."

"And off the record?"

"We're broadening our internal definition of what it means to be a terrorist."

"Ouch."

Gallagher nodded. "The memos are starting to slip out. You've probably seen them?"

"Yeah," Rachel said. "Your national domestic threat assessments are bumping up against...Oh, jeeze, I forget the *term du jour*. Are we talking about sovereign citizens here?"

"No," Gallagher replied. "There's some overlap in the ideologies of most militia groups, but members of the sovereign citizen movement share the same basic manifesto. If they've been shown to be aggressive but don't identify as sovereign citizens or survivalists, we usually just call them extremists."

Extremists. Rachel hated that word. Such a mealy-mouthed attempt at pacifying everyone at once, to assure the public that, yes, we're all generally good at heart but *never forget* that one person in a million thinks nothing of setting the world on fire. Oh, and it's partially your fault if we don't catch him before it happens, because we can't be everywhere at once. Now get out there and watch your neighbors.

"Question for you," Rachel said. "Are they still called extremists when there's a couple hundred of them living in the same compound?"

"I'll ask," Gallagher said dryly. "To be honest, we prefer it when they gather in large compounds. Those're easier to monitor than small cells."

"Easier to put a man on the inside, too."

"Yes," Gallagher admitted. "But extremists aren't dumb—most of them aren't dumb," she corrected herself. "And militias run by stupid people don't stay in operation very long. It's relatively easy to get someone inside a militia, but that doesn't mean it's easy for them to gather intel."

"What about Nicholson?" Rachel asked.

"Textbook narcissist," Gallagher replied. "Most militia leaders have some narcissistic personality traits, but in Nicholson's case, it's full-blown."

"That's usually good for getting a man inside," Rachel said. Narcissists tended to underestimate those around them. As nobody could possibly be smarter than they were, these people with excellent dental work and suspiciously useful skillsets couldn't possibly be threats.

The FBI agent nodded. "Except..." That mournful red came into focus and clung to her professional blues.

Rachel felt like eating her own foot, and perhaps punching herself in the face for good measure. "What happened?" she asked.

"We don't know." Gallagher paused, then lowered her golf bag to the fairway. She pretended to look for something in the side pocket; Rachel unslung her own bag and knelt beside Gallagher, their heads nearly close enough to touch. Anyone watching would have seen two women searching through the endless peripherals required for the act of putting a small ball into a hole. "He went missing three months ago."

"I hate to ask, but—"

"It's likely," Gallagher said. "There's no body, no evidence he's been killed, but—"

Rachel sighed. "But three months is three months."

"Yes. It wasn't my case, and everything I've heard has been secondhand..." Gallagher paused as her surface colors roiled; it didn't take her too long to collect her thoughts, and the reds and blues spun themselves into order as she continued. "He was undercover using the alias Kyle Vanning. Young guy, early thirties. Had worked undercover as a vice cop before joining the FBI, so the Sugar Camp militia seemed a good fit as a first field test for him."

"Why? Nicholson seems like a hard first assignment."

"Nicholson didn't run Sugar Camp. In fact, Vanning was at Sugar Camp for nearly four months before Nicholson joined. We were thinking about pulling Vanning out, since he didn't find anything of concern, but then Nicholson showed up and introduced the sovereign citizen rhetoric. Sugar Camp is a more traditional operation, and we decided to keep Vanning in place to see how the new ideology integrated with the old."

"Gotcha." Rachel spilled every golf ball in her bag onto the ground before handing one at random to Gallagher. The other woman began to pack up her bag; Rachel followed suit.

"Except..." Gallagher sighed. "Except Vanning disappeared instead."

"Disappeared? Any idea where he went? Witnesses?"

"We have no real leads," Gallagher said, as she resettled her bag on her shoulders. The two of them resumed their slow stroll up the center of the fairway. "He was last seen at a bar, drinking with another new member of Sugar Camp. The bartender says that the new member was later seen almost exclusively in Nicholson's company."

Rachel felt as if she had been hit in the gut by an invisible sledgehammer. A deep, quiet breath to pull her rush of anxiety back so as not to call attention to herself within the collective... Concentrating on the grass, the birdsong, those brief hints of spring that proved the world was coming alive... "Ah."

"Thought you should know."

Rachel sent an image of Ethan Fischer to Gallagher's cell phone. "This the guy?"

"Vanning? No, it's not him. And we never got a good photo of the new militia member."

"I'll send some files over to you, but it might be a closed case—the man in this photo was murdered last night."

Gallagher whistled quietly. "Is he the one who attacked you?"

"Yup. We think he was operating as Nicholson's second-in-command, but manipulating Nicholson as they went. That's about all we know about him—his history is pretty ripe."

"Where do you go from here?" Gallagher asked.

"I'm interviewing the leader of Sugar Camp Militia after this," Rachel said, as she checked the clock in her head again. She had over three hours before her ride arrived, and was very diligently checking the time at the insistence of the annoying voice in her head that kept chiming *it's all about time...it's all about time...* "I owe you," she said. "Big."

"Pay me back by finding out what happened to Vanning," Gallagher replied.

"Deal."

"Thank you. I don't know where—" The FBI agent stopped. She tilted her head towards the breeze. "Do you smell—"

A gunshot broke the air apart.

Rachel pushed Gallagher towards Edwards and the congressman. "Get them to cover!"

The FBI special agent went one way; Rachel went the other.

There was nothing as unnerving as a sprint across an open space when a gun was in play. Rachel put her head down and charged towards the nearest stand of trees, hoping, praying... Once she hit the treeline, she tucked and rolled, getting as small as possible before she wriggled deep into the well-manicured brush. Then, she threw out her scans—

Sandalwood.

Of course.

(A surge of relief went along with that particular shade of brown, which she didn't want to think about, followed by the realization that the man with the sandalwood core was standing over a body, which she really didn't want to think about but would certainly have to, as bodies were something of a priority in her line of work.)

She stood and ran through the underbrush.

When she broke into a small clearing, Rachel had to cover her mouth to hide her smile. Sandalwood, yes, but sandalwood wearing a white polo shirt and plaid pants? Her fashion sense shied away from the notion that Wyatt might be caught dead in plaid, but her sense of humor hadn't had much exercise over the last few days and was loving it.

"So, whatcha been doing?" she asked, as she threw her scans around to make sure a second shooter wasn't taking aim from somewhere in the trees.

Wyatt pointed towards the body on the ground. It was a woman in her late twenties with dark hair, lying face-down and unconscious. Like Wyatt, she was dressed in golfers' casual; unlike Wyatt, she had the chemical signature of gunpowder residue across her hands.

The psychopath was leaning on a putter in an abusive manner. Rachel would have put money on that club being the source of the divot in the unconscious woman's hairline.

She reached out to Gallagher's cell phone, and the FBI special agent answered on the first ring: "Rachel? Go."

"Shooter is down," she said aloud for Wyatt's benefit. "Apparently, Mulcahy sent backup in case something like this happened."

She glanced at Wyatt for confirmation. He shrugged and made a wavy more-or-less movement with his hand.

"What do you need?" Gallagher asked.

"Paramedics—the shooter was armed and sustained a severe head wound when my backup intervened. Tell them we're near the 13th hole. Look for a grove of cherry trees, then turn east into the pines."

"All right. Send your location to my phone. I'll join you as soon as I can."

Rachel signed off and went to check the body.

"Gimme," she said to Wyatt. He held out his putter, handle first, and she used the club and her feet to roll the unconscious woman onto her back.

"Nice bedside manner, Peng."

She ignored him, and flipped frequencies to take a photo of the woman's face. "Where's her gun? I'm not finding it."

"Disarmed her during the fight. It's over there." He pointed towards the underbrush, where a century's worth of raspberry brambles knotted themselves into a spiky wall.

Rachel stared at him until he sighed and walked off to search the thicket.

Sirens, far in the distance.

She gave her inner prude a professional talking-to, and then scanned the strange woman's body for tattoos and microchips. Neither, nothing, but there were some interesting layers of recent scar tissues on her buttocks where RFID implants might have been concealed and then removed.

Wyatt came out of the thicket, bleeding through his plaid pants and exceedingly grumpy, gun in hand.

"Oh goodie," Rachel said. "A NORINCO semiautomatic pistol. Don't you just love how every giant screaming clue we've found points us straight back to China?"

"I've got no idea what you're talking about," Wyatt said, as he dabbed at his bloody legs with a tissue.

"Agent Peng?"

"Over here!" Rachel called, before her mouth closed with a snap as she realized it might, perhaps, be a remarkably stupid idea to introduce Wyatt to the FBI special agent who had been in charge of the Glazer case. But then Wyatt was greeting Gallagher in his new role as Rachel's long-lost Army buddy, and Gallagher was buying it because there was no reason on earth she shouldn't buy it, and Rachel wondered anew about long cons.

This was followed by the arcane bureaucratic rituals required when a shooter was apprehended on a private golf course that catered to politicians. Rachel swore she would never again be involved in a shooting incident without an FBI special agent present: the paperwork was wrapped up within a half-hour, with Gallagher's assurance that Detective Hill would have the first chance to interview the mystery woman when she woke up.

For her part, Rachel sent the photo of the suspect to Jason, and cross-referenced the serial number of the NORINCO semiautomatic against the master list of stolen weapons that Smith had given to her. Jason said the photo matched that of the woman who had snuck into Ethan Fischer's hospital room (surprise!), and the serial number matched one of the stolen guns on the list (and surprise!).

After that, they rejoined Judge Edwards and his partner and the four of them went to finish their round, because it wasn't the first time any of them had been threatened at gunpoint, and they were playing the coveted Blue Course and it was unlikely that a new club member like Edwards would get the Blue Course again if he rescheduled, and anyhow Rachel and Gallagher were ahead by six strokes and there were some forms of injustice that just couldn't be allowed to stand.

Wyatt caddied for Rachel on the last holes. He was good at it.

At the end of the game, the judge and the congressman settled up. Rachel and Gallagher left for the women's locker room, each fifty bucks richer. Well, Gallagher was richer; Rachel had passed her winnings on to Wyatt as a tip. The psychopath had thanked her as he pocketed the money, bemused grayish oranges hanging across his body like an overladen golf bag.

Rachel folded herself into a fresh business suit and waited for Gallagher by the locker room door. When the older woman appeared, she seemed slightly brighter than she had been at the end of their golf game.

"Good news?" Rachel asked her.

"Does it show? Got some useful information about a suspect for a change."

"Excellent," Rachel said. "This job is hard enough without the occasional break."

"You aren't kidding."

The two of them moved into the bar. It was senselessly opulent. Rachel's boots clicked across marbled tiles with inlayed mosaic frescos. Exposed beams ran across the ceiling and tied into huge wooden pillars, and the far wall was devoted to photographs of famous golfers. She tossed a scan over these and wondered—briefly—about life choices.

"Agent Peng?" Gallagher's colors were threaded with yellow concern, and her voice was just above a whisper.

"Yeah?" Rachel pulled her attention away from an alternate timeline where she played Augusta and Pebble Beach on the regular. "Sorry, went woolgathering. Yes?"

"Do you know anything about Homeland taking over OACET?"

Rachel chuckled. "I know Homeland's wanted to roll us into it since OACET went public. But we're not law enforcement—what I do is just a tiny part of OACET's overall operations. We're mostly civil servants and administrators. If anything, OACET's closest equivalent is that we're the IRS for data systems. Homeland can't make the argument stick."

"That's good."

Ah. Knudson's core of sour raspberries floated around Gallagher's colors. "Did someone from Homeland reach out to you?" Rachel opened her left hand and rubbed the scars across her palm. She had never filed an official complaint against Bryce Knudson for injuring her, which meant absolutely everyone in Washington knew how she got those scars.

"Let's just say that someone would be much happier with OACET if Homeland were overseeing your agency." Gallagher opened the door for her, and they walked outside into the early spring air. "I'm not rooting for him—I'd hate to lose access to those Agents you've loaned me."

"Put in a good word for our autonomy, and you can keep them forever. When did this happen, by the way? After the kidnapping, or before?"

Gallagher did the single-shouldered shrug of women who didn't want their purses to slip down. "Rumors have been floating around for a while."

Knudson, smug in his pinks.

"I'll bet," Rachel said darkly. "Well, if it happens, it's because Homeland's found a way to bully us into joining. And that's not going to happen."

They shook hands and parted ways, Gallagher towards her car and Rachel towards an old unused putting green far behind the clubhouse. Wyatt was waiting for her. He had changed from his golf clothes to his usual rough-and-ready jeans and Henley, with an old baseball cap to complete the image.

"She seemed nice," he said, as dry as the Sahara after a sandstorm.

"You take a lot of chances," she muttered.

"I get bored. Why'd you ask for me to come on the interview? You said there's no way you're putting yourself in a car with me."

Rachel didn't reply, and let him stew until his colors began to run red and beige.

Not that she'd tell him, but her decision to bring Wyatt along to visit a militia had been a stroke of genius. The list of people she was willing to drag into the serpent's den was depressingly short. Other women were out. Just one hundred percent out. Yeah, they probably weren't going to be raped and murdered, but…

The fact she had to add that "but…" was reason enough.

Hill was right out, obviously. Santino and Zockinski, too. She couldn't bring Phil, because Phil was too trusting, or Jason, because Jason was too Jason. If she brought Josh or Mulcahy, they might never come out again for a whole host of reasons including public image, kidnapping, extortion, and the (highly unlikely but still possible) casual murder spree.

She needed someone who looked like an all-American good ol' boy. A former soldier. Someone who was absolute murder in a fight.

Wyatt's colors sharpened as he scooped up an old golf ball and took aim at a turtle sunning itself in a nearby water hazard.

"Do it and I'll break your arm," she warned him.

He threw the ball, missing the turtle by intentional inches. "Is this it for the rest of the day?" he asked. "'cause it seems like you've got better shit to do."

His timing was excellent: she pointed towards the sky.

Wyatt looked up, and began to laugh.

EIGHTEEN

The ground slipped away below them, a patchwork quilt of early spring greens against winter browns. It was lovely, unexpectedly so—Rachel had expected rural Pennsylvania to be more about missing teeth and the passionate romancing of cousins, not these clean squares stitched together by orderly lines of trees.

Live and learn, she told herself. Besides, coal country was out there, maybe just ahead of them, maybe right around where the Sugar Camp Militia was located. A wide open strip mine would set the mood nicely.

Wyatt was asleep across from her. Almost as soon as they had gotten in the helicopter, he had smirked at her in pinks before he pulled his hat down over his eyes. He had gone to sleep as quickly as blinking, his conversational colors popping off like he was his own blown bulb.

Not his first time in a helicopter, then.

Not hers, either. As helicopters went, Rachel had been in bigger, better, and faster. But the model AW109 had been in service for forty years, and was ideal for ferrying her and Wyatt from one of the most prestigious country clubs in the world to a backwoods group of militants. It was quick, light, and sturdy, and (most importantly, from Rachel's point of view) cheap to operate.

The helicopter dipped slightly as it began its descent. Wyatt woke, his colors snapping to attention in camouflage greens as he instinctively reached for a gun that wasn't there.

"At ease, soldier," Rachel said.

He pushed his hat back and sat up with a glance out the window. "Nice country."

"Ever been here before?"

Wyatt shrugged in indecipherable grays.

"Help me out," she said. "You seem like the kind of guy who's spent time in a militia. Are we walking into a war camp or what?"

He pointed to the dossier that Gallagher had provided on the Sugar Camp Militia. "Should be in there," he said.

"Your opinion."

Wyatt's attention moved to the window again. "Depends on who started it, and who's running it now."

The helicopter began its final descent. Rachel pushed her scans down and away... Yup, there was the edge of a quarry, big enough to scar the farmland all the way to the nearby mountains. The hole cut in the earth was hemmed by rows of evergreens along one side, with what appeared to be a series of smallish buildings separated by fences.

Rachel plastered pure boredom to her face and stretched out her legs so she wouldn't have to tug her pant cuffs down once she stood.

"Do I get a weapon?" Wyatt asked.

She reached into her jacket and removed her service weapon from its concealed holster. The gun had come back with her from Afghanistan, and the only time she refrained from carrying it was when she needed to squeeze herself into a cocktail dress. Wyatt recognized it: when she held it out to him by the handle, his colors brightened in interest.

He reached to take it, and she turned and slipped her gun into the helicopter's open lockbox. "Psych," she said, as she punched the digital lock. "Wait, do the kids still say that? Probably not. Seems like they never should have said it in the first place."

Wyatt sat back and fumed in irritated oranges.

"What are we going to find here?" she asked.

"I dunno," he said. "I didn't do any prep work on this place."

"C'mon." Rachel prodded his shin with the toe of her boot. "It's a militia. They're all the same."

Purple humor appeared in his colors. "That's your first mistake," he replied, and wouldn't say anything else until the helicopter's landing skids hit a long patch of dirt road about two hundred yards from the buildings.

Rachel rapped on the partition between the cockpit and the cabin, and waved to the pilot. Wyatt slid the door open and jumped out first; when his head stayed nice and intact, Rachel leapt from the helicopter.

She nearly blacked out from the silence.

"Whoa," she said, as she groped her way back to the helicopter and took a seat on the nearest piece of stable metal.

"Airsick?" Wyatt grinned at her in smug pinks.

She waved him off. "Not sick," she said, trying not to gasp for breath. "Kinda... Kinda the opposite."

There was so little *here*.

She hadn't been out to the country much since she got her implant. The stray bed-and-breakfast with Becca, of course, because Wall Street type-A personalities apparently had to go antiquing in the Poconos twice a year or their licenses were revoked, but the Poconos were infested with cell towers and Wi-Fi. Those trips had set her benchmark for the digital ecosystem. The digital ecosystem—that persistent chatter of the Internet of Things, as well as those non-Things that were offline but were plugged in or battery-powered or hand-cranked or otherwise gobbling and spewing energy—was unavoidable for the Agents. It was as pervasive as cicadas in the summer, and eighty times as annoying. When her implant was active, Things and non-Things *screamed*. Always. They might be a little quieter at night, but they were always there.

Stepping out of the helicopter was like plunging into a void.

"Get your shit together, Peng," Wyatt muttered.

"Yeah," she gasped. "Yeah." She let her fingertips linger on the metal skin of the helicopter as long as possible, as if drinking deep from the machine's EMF, before pushing off and clomping up the dirt road.

A large metal gate lurked at the end of the road. The gate was set into a wall made from steel-reinforced concrete, and chained tight at its break point. Off to the side was a person-sized door, also made from steel, but with intriguing locks and slots that seemed designed for weaponry. It reminded her of an Afghani warlord's fortress.

Except for the small fruit stand sitting off to one side of the main driveway. The building was shaped like a small fairy tale cottage, with an open front and a dozen different kinds of eggs and honey for sale. The woman behind the counter wore a thick cotton and crinoline dress in greens and reds, and had her hair braided with red felt flowers. She smiled warmly at Rachel and Wyatt, even as her surface colors hung around her like a wary gray cloud.

Rachel flipped frequencies to read the sign over the gate: Sugar Camp Christmas Trees.

She turned her implant off and then back on again. Yup. The sign still read: Sugar Camp Christmas Trees.

In a very merry cursive script.

With candy canes on either side.

And a snowman.

"Oh, screw this nonsense," she grumbled under her breath, and then shouted: "Hey! I've got an appointment, and I'm on a tight schedule. Let's not pretend you missed the arrival of the freakin' helicopter, okay?"

The wicket gate in the wall swung open. An older man stood there, with a core the same color green as old-fashioned carnival glass. "Guests knock," he said. "Usually."

"Right." Rachel stepped quickly over the hard-packed earth and stuck her hand out. "Agent Peng," she said. "Office of Adaptive and Complementary Enhancement Technologies."

"I know," he said, as he ignored her extended hand. "I'm Ahren. C'mon in."

With a last almost-wistful scan towards the helicopter, Rachel entered the militia's camp, her personal psychopath following close behind.

"I'm assumin' you've been briefed," the man said.

"No," Rachel said. "I prefer to do cold interviews. Helps me keep my sources of information straight." A total lie, but a plausible one she'd used many times before. And she hadn't been able to do more than skim the file that Gallagher had given her on the flight up.

So she had utterly missed any description of the front entrance of the militia's camp as Santa's workshop.

Becca had taken her to a Renaissance faire right around Halloween, and the two of them had rented sweaty costumes and spent too much money on turkey legs and ridiculous-smelling soaps. The militia's village put her in mind of a small-scale version of that, with five tiny but ornately decorated buildings painted up like Christmas. These were all closed, but her scans told her they had been recently used, with no dust and all products laid out in well-ordered displays.

"...and what is it you do here?" Rachel asked.

"Folks like to come out and cut their own Christmas trees," he said. "Lots of places like ours around, so we give 'em an experience. First o' November through the first weekend of January, we got trees, ornaments, local chocolates. Rest o' the year, we rent the space to vendors. Flea markets an' gun shows, normally."

"Where are the reindeer?"

"Don't keep reindeer." His conversational colors blurred towards orange-gray bemusement. "Critters live where it's cold. They'd suffer down here."

Rachel disagreed. She was getting chilly herself; early spring in the northerly reaches of Pennsylvania was much colder than she had expected. It didn't help that there was a wind ripping through the quarry and back into the mountains. Everything was crisp and smelled slightly of dust and evergreens, with a faintly metallic note beneath that.

"Why Christmas trees?"

"I bought this land, 'bout twenty years ago. Mining company turned it to shit, so I bought it for pennies on the dollar. Evergreens 'bout all that'd grow back then. They like acid soil, you know? Ground's getting better, but I'll be long dead before we can do more than chickens and wildflowers."

Rachel threw a scan over her shoulder. Wyatt was walking about five steps behind them, his focus on their conversation, with long yellow-white sweeps across the buildings as he searched for threats. She could have saved him the trouble: the buildings were empty. The only people within the length of three football fields were Ahren and the quiet lady selling honey in her after-season Christmas costume.

"You're the owner?" she asked.

"Free an' clear," Ahren said, with a strong streak of red pride. "No liens, no loans, just taxes."

"You pay taxes?" The words were out of her mouth before she could strangle her subconscious into silence.

Ahren stopped and looked at her. "Don't you?"

She stared at him. Not her full-bore cyborg's stare, but enough so he began to get wavy and orange around his edges.

He sighed and began walking again. "Yeah, I pay taxes. All of my taxes, an' my tax accountant would be happy to talk to you."

"Not what I meant," she said. "Just that this isn't what I expected from your operation."

"Y'mean, my *business?*" He stressed the last word as the reds around him changed from pride to anger. "We pay our share, no more, no less. I got problems with people who don't." An angry red pointed directly at Southwestern turquoise.

"Oh, right. Here." Rachel pushed a slip of paper into his hands.

"What—" He took a pair of bifocals out of his shirt pocket and perched these on the tip of his nose so he could study the paper. "Is this a receipt?"

"Yup," she said. "Estimated cost for use of the helicopter from D.C. to here, and back again. Paying for the fuel and maintenance costs out of my own pocket. Since we haven't formally charged Nicholson with a crime, my being here isn't part of a criminal investigation. No taxpayers footing my bill today."

"Ah," he said. "I don't see labor costs on here. What about the pilot? Who's paying his salary?"

"*She* is a good friend of Agent Joshua Glassman, and they've agreed to work out payment between them. And no, I intentionally didn't ask for the details so that's all the information I can give you."

He laughed. It was a warm, hearty sound, almost like what she'd expect from Santa Claus if he were a CrossFit enthusiast, and his reds slipped away. "All right," he said. "You came prepared. Good for you."

"Help me out here," Rachel said, as Ahren turned and began leading them towards a large log cabin. "From what I've been told, you're a militia, but you pay taxes?"

"Damn right, I pay taxes. I pay them 'cause I don't want you people comin' in and shooting up my family," he said. "I'm not givin' you an excuse.

"An' I noticed you admitted you're not here in an official capacity," he added. "I'm seein' you because Nicholson is an ass, an' lettin' him spin his lies might get my people hurt. If I'd thought he'd do somethin' like this, I'd never've taken him in."

Ahren opened the door of the log cabin for Rachel, and he followed her inside, the two of them dogged by Wyatt. The office was built like an old-fashioned cabin, the cracks between the exposed logs chinked closed with putty. The beams holding up the A-frame ceiling were draped with furs and blankets, and the windows were hung with large sheets of tanned cowhide in lieu of curtains. Almost everything in the room was yellow-gray from a veneer of cigarette smoke, misted across the walls through years of saturation.

Even the guns.

Rachel had expected some firearms, perhaps the proverbial gun on the mantelpiece or whatnot. But every square inch of available wall space served as a gun rack, or held a windowed cabinet overflowing with handguns and rifles, sometimes stacked two or three deep. There were multiple gun safes against the east wall, each of them much larger than the hidden document safe down in OACET's War Room.

There were guns that were obviously, flagrantly illegal in

many states. Maybe not in rural Pennsyltucky, true, but there were automatic rifles and sawed-off shotguns and—

Oh dear Lord, that's a fucking anti-tank rifle, isn't it. Is that legal? That can't be legal. Not even here.

"Nice collection," Rachel said, as she flopped down in the nearest chair with the silent hope that her scans would warn her if the cushion was stuffed with even more guns. "Love the useless showpieces. Really lovely. Just the nicest fake felony collection I've ever seen."

Ahren feigned confusion.

"Let me guess," she said, as she pointed at each of the big-ticket items. "Critical missing pieces or—" Rachel paused to scan the interior of one of the shotguns. "—molten metal poured down the barrels?

"Hey, what kind of test is this, exactly?" she added. "If you clear up exactly how you want me to react, I'll be happy to oblige."

He laughed again, but this time he trailed off into a long, hacking cough. He took a linen handkerchief from his pocket and coughed heavily into it. Rachel was bemused. She hadn't seen a linen handkerchief since…ever? It struck her as quaint and homey. More quaint than homey, considering its status as a hotbed of germs, but still.

"I said we do gun shows here, yeah?" he said, once the coughing spell had passed. "Dealers know I'll buy broken products. Hobby of mine."

"And no never mind that a huge collection of broken firearms is excellent cover for any working versions you might have on the property?"

The older man waved towards his wall of weapons. "If you see any evidence of that, Agent, lemme know."

"Sure thing."

Ahren took a good, long look at her. It was the same kind of look she gave to suspects before she started to pick them apart. "You one of those liberal anti-gun nuts?"

"Nope," Rachel said. "I'm a cop, and former Army, and I've

been up against too many full-grown infants with automatic weapons to think the world can be fixed with flowers and happy thoughts. I'm about as anti-gun as you are."

"Maybe I think you should be," Ahren said. "Same technology that reads your thumbprint, unlocks your phone? No reason it can't go in a gun."

"Well," Rachel said. "No reason except me."

Wyatt began to laugh in purples.

"I'd love it," Rachel said. "Don't get me wrong. Me and my buddies have to go into a firefight? The enemy tries to unlock their weapons, I shut 'em down before we even get out of the car… Now it's no longer a firefight. From a law enforcement perspective? It's nothing but appealing, and I'd back the shit out of that legislation—pardon my French—but gun companies will never invest in the tech now. It'll be blocked as a Second Amendment issue before it can get to market. OACET's effectively killed the chance of any personal firearms tech that could be used to save lives.

"Sorry," she added.

"Unintended consequences," Wyatt said from his spot near the window.

She shot him a Look: his conversational colors rolled over themselves in a purple-gray sigh, and he went back to pretending to be furniture.

"He's right," she said to Ahren. "For every innovation we introduce, we manage to screw up something else. It's usually unintentional, and almost always because the general public's convinced that OACET wants to dominate the planet. Have you seen the conspiracy theories about how we're murdering people through their pacemakers? Someone's filed a wrongful death suit against us because her husband's pacemaker broke. And she lives in Kansas! *Kansas!*"

Rachel realized she was shouting. Just a little, but a little shouting was usually too much.

"Sorry," she repeated.

Ahren's conversational colors weighed her Southwestern

turquoise against the teal of family and belonging. "Let's talk somewhere else," he said, as the scales in his mind balanced out.

He led them through another door to a wide hallway, and down that hallway to a pair of double doors at the rear of the cabin. Once through, they were behind the second fence, with the Christmas village and its cutesy-twee shops safely on the other side. The doors opened into a small apartment complex, with a dozen two- and three-story buildings on either side of wide evergreen tree-lined street.

Interesting, Rachel thought. The only way into this second part of the compound was through the office hallway. She was sure there was another entrance somewhere (if for no other reason than to move dirt and other farming equipment), but it didn't trip to her short-range scans.

"Can't help but notice that there's nobody here," Wyatt said.

"I sent everyone out," Ahren said. "Free day—no work, no school. Couple of folks stayed behind for the chores that need doin'. There's always chores on a farm."

"I don't see any lights on," Rachel said. Partially true: she was more curious about how there was very little happening in the local digital ecosystem. The buildings didn't have any power running through them. All of it felt lifeless and empty.

"Turned the generators off," Ahren said. "Saves money when no one's around. We'll have a windmill in a few years, if sales stay good, but until then our grid's on during peak hours 'n that's all."

He had much less Good Ol' Boy in his accent than before, and the red pride was back in his conversational colors as he showed off the compound. He paused to yank a weed from an otherwise barren flowerbed, and then took them to where the street ended.

There was a playground, and beyond that and a third layer of fencing, a shooting range.

Rachel sent her scans along the range and drooled.

Sugar Camp's shooting range was finger-kissin' primo *delicious!* It was built with safety in mind, with the quarry to the left and wide open scrublands to the right, and easily a full ten acres to play with in the middle. There were blinds and targets carefully placed to take advantage of the landscape, and two towers of different heights set at different angles about five hundred yards to the north.

The taller of these towers had wide panels set across the top. Rachel recognized the form but couldn't detect the function.

Ahren noticed. "We're negotiating with a cellular service provider," he explained. "The tower's not active yet. But if the deal falls through, we get a great setup for solar power."

She nodded. The cell company had most likely bumped into a possible public relations fiasco when upper management learned that they were leasing land rights from a militia.

"Did you plan for that?" she asked.

He smiled and kept walking.

At the head of the range was a fiberglass pergola frame covered with translucent plastic roofing. One wall of the shelter was made from DIY plywood cabinets. Rachel scanned these and found the usual safety peripherals found at shooting ranges, including some high-end ear protection.

"I was wonderin', Agent Peng, if maybe you could show off for me a little."

"Not all Agents are good with guns," she said, a light poke.

"But you are. I've seen that video. The one with you in the parking garage, takin' down that man."

Wyatt went red at that.

Rachel grinned over her shoulder at him, then smiled at Ahren. "You know who I am."

"Yeah," he said. "You're famous around here. Be a real pleasure to watch you shoot."

She flipped open her suit coat to show him her empty holster. "Unarmed," she said. "Thought you wouldn't appreciate it if I brought a gun along to the meeting. Especially since I'm not here in an official capacity."

"I think we can find something," Ahren said, and his colors came damned close to twinkling in purples.

Five minutes later, a Sako 85 Finnlight was in her hands, a pair of ear protectors clamped around her head. Ahren cupped both hands to his mouth and shouted to nobody: "Clear the range!"

Rachel was pretty sure she was the best marksman in the world. Markswoman. Whatever. Nobody was about to argue nomenclature with someone capable of putting a bullet in their skull from a quarter-mile away, and blindfolded besides. Autoscripts similar to the one which allowed her to assess the lay of the land at a golf course also helped her line up a bullet to a target. And she could pull off trick shots like nobody else. Her ability to see into objects helped her assess density, and density could be used to plot a bullet's ricochet. Not perfectly—ricochets were accidents by definition—but with enough reliability that she could confidently send a bullet into a piece of metal and bank a shot at a predictable angle.

Two years ago, she had crippled Wyatt's Daddy Dearest by bouncing four shots off of the steel and concrete of a parking garage. That had been mostly luck: it had been her first time firing solid metal rounds, and as much as she adored her beloved concrete, it fractured too readily to be of much use to her in trick shooting. Now, two years and close to five hundred hours of practice later, her service weapon was always loaded with custom solid brass rounds so when she did have to use it, she could be sure she wouldn't have to use it to kill.

Rachel sent her scans down the range, just to be sure, and took a test shot to check the quality of the gun. "Whoa!" she said appreciatively, as the Sako bullseyed the target at a thousand feet. "Nice rifle!"

Ahren said something in reply, but she couldn't hear him. It was probably something nice about the gun: the synthetic blacks and silvers of the Sako's stock and the reds of pride were twining together quite nicely.

Four more shots—each of them landed dead-center of the targets as she worked her way down the range and got a feel for the land and the wind—and then the gun was empty.

"Really nice!" She stood from her hunter's crouch and removed the ear protectors. "This is a very decent piece!"

"It's a favorite," Ahren said. "You're an incredible shot."

"One of the benefits of being a cyborg," she said, as she handed the rifle to Ahren.

"She could do this blindfolded," Wyatt said dryly.

Ahren stood a little taller. "'s that true?"

This time, when she shot Wyatt a Look, she nailed him with the full weight of her cyborg's stare. "Oh, it's true," he said, suddenly engrossed with fixing the band on his ear protectors. "She'd never do it in front of a crowd, but since it's just the three of us, you've got no problems doin' a little more showin' off, right, Peng?"

And of course Wyatt had a convenient strip of heavy cloth handy, and it was just about long enough to be a small scarf.

She wound the blindfold around her head, twice, and knotted it tight.

A blindfold.

Oh no, she did *not* want to do this in front of Wyatt. The psychopath already had suspicions about—

Her skin crawled as she saw Southwestern turquoise walking through his conversational colors, surrounded by walls of sandstone.

Oh. Oh, no.

She had left him wrapped up like a sausage in its casing and handcuffed to the radiator. So, naturally, he had escaped and gone wandering around the halls.

A man's scent, his footsteps—

Rachel snatched up the Sako, reloaded it, and fired five shots as fast as the bolt action would permit.

She yanked off the blindfold and shoved the rifle at Ahren. Her ears were ringing; she had forgotten the protectors. "We good?

Ahren blinked, eyes moving between her and the furthest target on the range. He checked the target through the scope, colors swirling into a single razor-sharp point. "Ah…" he began.

"Ah...yeah."

They retired to a patio table beneath the canopy. The table was old, one of those round pieces of tin from the '60s, with a set of matching wirework chairs. The entire thing had been spray-painted in a fresh spring green.

"You smoke?" he asked, a beaten pack of cigarettes appearing in one hand like a magician's deck of cards. He reached down and picked up an old metal coffee can that had entered a second life as an ashtray.

"No," she said. "But I don't mind the smell."

"I do," he said, wetting a finger to test the wind. He decided he was fine with where he was sitting, and lit the cigarette with a cheap plastic lighter. "Bad habit, I know. Too expensive. Been tryin' to quit but I keep pickin' it back up."

He used the cigarette to point at the furthest target before taking a long drag. "That's some impressive shooting, Agent Peng."

"I was a good shot before I got the implant," she said, watching Wyatt. He had moved over to the playground's fence, out of earshot but close enough to respond if needed. "I'm a great shot now—we think the implant creates a biofeedback process that improves physical performance."

"You think?"

"We're not sure. Most of the documentation for the implant disappeared, thanks to Hanlon. But from what we can tell, it wasn't designed for biofeedback," she sighed. "Unintended consequences."

"Can you build more of them? These implants of yours?"

"Not with what's left," she said, thinking of Santino. "It's dead tech until we can reconstruct it, and that might take decades."

He nodded. The two of them watched the birds return to the nearby trees as the memory of gunshots faded.

"What can I tell you about Nicholson?" he finally asked.

"Everything," Rachel said. "Start with your first meeting."

Ahren took a short drag on his cigarette, his colors falling into place as he organized his thoughts. "Guy calls my office up, out of the blue," he said. "Says he's looking for a new life. We get a dozen or so like him a year, folks who say they're tired of society. They're not, you know. They want society—what they're tired of? Bein' told what to do. That's not gonna change, not here.

"Sometimes we take 'em in, if they're harmless enough. They're good for a laugh. One or two might stick around. Most of 'em decide their old life was good enough after I put 'em to work."

"What kind of work?"

Ahren nodded towards the old quarry at the edge of the firing range. "Rocks out, dirt in. Can't work the land if there's no land to work."

"And Nicholson was okay with that?" Rachel couldn't imagine Nicholson working with his hands. Or associating as equals with anyone who did.

"Never put him in the quarry," Ahren said. "He said he was a lawyer. Came in dressed for an interview, sort of."

"Sort of?"

"Showed up in a shiny truck, and a pair of khaki six-pockets so new they'd never been washed. Said he wanted to join."

"And you let him?"

"I got no use for one more useless know-it-all gun freak," Ahren said. "I got all the use in the world for a good lawyer. Told him if he wanted to join, he needed to be licensed to practice law in my state."

"Was he?"

"Nope. Not then. He drove off. Called my office three months after that, said the paperwork had gone through. Wanted to set up an appointment to discuss terms." Ahren chuckled, low and slow.

"This had to be raising red flags with you."

He nodded.

"So why take him on?"

"Free legal advice, m'dear," he said. "And he got my curiosity up, I'll tell you, this rich lawyer who shows up on my doorstep, talkin' to me like I'm dumber than mice. If there's a game goin' on, thought I'd play better if I knew the rules."

"Did you…" Rachel paused, nudging around the edges of what Gallagher had told her. "You've heard about the FBI hiding agents in militias, right?"

This time, when Ahren laughed, it was in short, wheezy bursts. "C'mon," he said. "Credit where it's due, m'dear. I can spot them a mile away. I've been here more 'n twenty years—after 9/11, feds were all the new blood we had."

"How can you tell they're FBI?"

Another gesture with the cigarette, this time towards the quarry. "They'll move rocks all day long without bitchin'."

Rachel made a mental note to tell Gallagher to remind her men to complain more, and then asked, "What did Nicholson do when he showed up?"

"Took a spare apartment. Moved right in, started goin' through my files."

"You let him? Just like that?"

"You keep things from your lawyer, Agent?" He stared at her in curious oranges. "That'll get you in trouble in the long run."

Rachel laughed. "You are not what I expected from a militia leader."

"Militia…" Ahren lit a second cigarette off of the first, and stubbed the old one out in the coffee can. "That's the third time you've used that word, Agent Peng, but I don't remember using it with you."

"What do you call this place, then? A commune?"

"Sugar Camp Christmas Trees," he said with a grin. "Best damned Christmas trees in Pennsylvania. Proudly family-owned and operated."

Rachel shook her head, and asked, "How big is your family?"

"'bout two to three hundred, dependin'."

She turned towards the small apartment complex at the front of the shooting range, which would have housed maybe thirty families. Nowhere near two hundred people could have lived there, let alone three. Ahren noticed and said, "More 'n half of my people live 'n work elsewhere. Some of 'em all the way down in New York, New Jersey... They show up on weekends, 'n pitch tents when they want to stay overnight."

"How many people left with Nicholson?"

"'bout thirty-some men. Almost all of 'em were weekenders, or lived out here in tents."

"And you let him leave? After he saw your files?"

Ahren held up a finger, pausing their conversation long enough to cough into his handkerchief again. His cough was rougher this time, a wet hacking sound that went on far too long. When it was over, he nodded. "Yeah," he said, the handkerchief going back into his pocket. "He was here for six months, and that was six months too long. Laziest shit I've ever met. Talked about nothin' but how good it'll be when we rise up an' take our country back."

"Seems like the kind of topic an upstanding Christmas tree plantation owner such as yourself has probably heard before."

The annoyed oranges in his conversational colors solidified. "You know why I offered to talk to you, Agent Peng?"

"No, sir, I don't."

"There's always a government. There'll always *be* a government. Takin' down the one you've got doesn't get rid of government—it just puts a new one in its place, an' there's no promise the new one will be better'n the old. I want to be *left alone*, Agent Peng, and if that means payin' taxes and makin' nice with the county sheriff, so be it.

"These little turds, the ones who come out here, hopin' for the world to end so they'll rise up 'n take their rightful place as kings? They want the Wild West they see in movies." Ahren turned the cigarette over in his fingers before taking another long drag. "Never stop to think that there were rules in the West. An' the kings of the West? They made 'emselves that way through sacrifice and goddamed hard work."

He paused. "Pardon my French, too."

"You sly silver fox," Rachel said. "You used Nicholson to clean house."

Ahren nodded. "I did," he said. "He was here for six months and spent every hour yellin' about what was wrong with America. Talkin' about armed revolt. I've got children livin' here, Agent Peng. Talk like that makes the sheriff start thinkin' twice about leaving me and mine alone. Makes the sheriff start thinkin' I've got somethin' evil goin' on up here at my little farm. A cult, maybe, or an army."

The cigarette pointed again, this time at the nearby playground. "Nothin' evil about protectin' children, Agent Peng. If that meant chasin' Nicholson and everyone who thought like him out so he became someone else's problem, I was okay with that."

Rachel was so very glad she had left her gun in the helicopter. "Except he took one of *our* children," she said, when she was sure she wouldn't pull a Mulcahy and try to dangle him over the ground by his throat. That wouldn't work for a bunch of reasons, starting with her height and ending with her fingernails digging out his larynx.

"I'm sorry about that," he said, red sorrow hanging around him. "I swear, I thought he was a spoil'd rich kid, no real threat to anyone. I just wanted him gone."

Rachel went over a dozen possible replies, and went with the one that didn't involve beating the snot out of this self-implied king with the butt of his own rifle. "Right," she said, as she took out a photo of Iron Core out of her pocket. "Tell me about this guy."

"Ah." Ahren barely glanced at the paper. "Him."

"Nicholson called him Ethan. His arrest records put him as Ethan Fischer."

"Yeah," Ahren nodded. "That's right. Fischer showed up about three months after Nicholson."

"After? You're sure?"

"Yup. Made friends with Nicholson the day he got here. Nicholson got real mouthy after that—he was bad before, but he started recruitin' after. Always when I wasn't there, always where I couldn't see it. He was clever, all a'sudden, and you an' I both know those new smarts weren't his. Worse, I'm pretty sure Fischer killed a man while he was here."

"Really?" She reached out to her phone in her nearby purse, accessed its memory, and began recording. The conversation would never show up in court, but it might provide Gallagher with new leads, or even closure.

"Yup. Goes to a bar with one of my men. Kyle Vanning. Good guy. I liked him. Fischer comes back to the farm, says Vanning went home with a woman. I never see Vanning again."

"Why do you think he killed Vanning?"

Another long, slow drag. "Well, he was one of yours," Ahren said. "FBI, I think?"

Rachel laughed before she could stop herself, and then groaned silently; Gallagher would kill her for that slipup. "Hard worker?" she asked.

"Yup." Ahren stubbed out his second cigarette and stood. "An' he never made a move on any of the women while he was here."

"Gay?"

"Professional," he said, and started walking back the way they came. "You people don't start what you can't finish. An' the FBI came out a few weeks after he disappeared, askin' questions but sayin' nothin'. No, he's good an' dead, an' I'm sorry for that, too."

Interview, over. She pressed him on the details as they retraced their steps—Where was Fischer from? (Don't know.) Do you have any files on him? (No.) Was Nicholson already a sovereign citizen when he arrived? (Yup.)—and filled in what remaining blanks she could. Nothing stood out as critical.

Once they reached the helicopter, Ahren stuck out his hand. "Been interestin', Agent Peng," he said. "An' while I've got you here, let me say that what Hanlon did to OACET was pretty damned low. Government's been getting in our heads for years. Glad you took yours back."

"Thanks," she said, and decided, hey, why not, she was here and she lost nothing by being the bigger woman. "Hey, you saw what I can do with scans on the gun range? I've got a set of medical diagnostic scans that an OACET physician made for me. If someone were to ask, I could scan them and point out any health concerns that might pop up."

Ahren's hand moved towards the linen handkerchief in his pocket before he could stop himself.

Rachel shrugged, still staring at the far-off too-close mountains. "If I were asked."

He stared at her, suspicious oranges showing in his conversational colors for the first time since the gun range. "Don't think anyone's asked," he said. He took out his pack of cigarettes and tapped it against his hand, hard. One slid into his fingers. "Good luck figurin' out this mess you've made."

He lit his cigarette, turned, and walked away.

NINETEEN

As the helicopter cut its way south through the air, Rachel let her mind wander across the fields below, and over the matter of Ethan Fischer.

Time…

Fischer had showed up at Sugar Camp three months after Nicholson's arrival. Good. That was a point on the timeline. And Josh had confirmed that Fischer had arrived just days before certain politicians working at the Capitol Building had begun discussing their 'holiday plans' in earnest. That was another point on the timeline.

She was pretty sure that the chain of events pointed towards a power grab by those same politicians, and that it started when they sent Fischer into Sugar Camp to take control of Nicholson. She was somewhat less sure that the purpose of this power grab was to divest OACET of its autonomy and bundle the agency into, oh, say, Homeland Security, but that was probably wishful thinking on her part. If OACET lost its autonomy, then everything the Agents had fought to prevent would likely come to pass.

Such as being turned into instruments of war.

Rachel had no interest in being someone else's gun. It was bad enough that she was sometimes dehumanized as part of her job—she refused to be turned over to the Army and sent on missions from the comfort of a padded cell. She would not be the instrument of destruction for China's civic infrastructure, or the reason that Iran's centrifuges melted down and irradiated an entire country. Or any one of the many ways that a clever cyborg could undermine modern civilization.

She'd rather die.

Let's not let it get that far, she told herself. She unclenched her hands and looked at the half-moon circles her fingernails had sliced into her palms. *Let's get off this road before that happens.*

One last wistful scan across the pastoral landscape below, and then she kicked Wyatt awake. The psychopath nearly jumped her; she had her gun out and aimed between his eyes before he remembered where he was and brought himself under control.

"How'd you know?" she asked him.

Wyatt stretched, his hands bumping into either side of the bulkhead. "Know what?"

"That we weren't walking into a hotbed of racist inbred shitheads."

"Might be," he said in purples. "You didn't get the full tour."

"C'mon."

He smirked and settled back in his seat again. "Two things. Guess."

"They were willing to talk to the cops."

"No, they knew enough to get ahead of talking to the cops."

She made a non-committal noise. Made sense. Willingness to talk to cops was one thing; that showed they recognized legal norms. But getting ahead and offering to do the inevitable interview… "What's the second?"

"They're smart enough to know that Nicholson was poison. A bad militia lets anyone stay. Thinks there's strength in numbers."

"And a good one is selective."

"Uh-huh."

"Ahren is a million times scarier than Nicholson," she said. "And a *lot* more dangerous."

"If he wanted to be," Wyatt said. "But he knows that his community is one mistake away from being turned into a crater." He pulled his hat down over his eyes again, but this time he was feigning sleep; his colors moved back and forth across the cabin, as if he was pacing the floor.

One mistake away… That was relatable, even if she was a little itchy about comparing OACET to a decent law-abiding Christmas tree farm made from acidic soil and firearms. Ahren had been helpful, but she still had too many questions. Her subconscious kept nagging her about connections between Fischer and Nicholson. If Fischer hadn't been murdered, she could have asked him—

Oh!

She sat up and kicked Wyatt in the soft spot beneath his kneecap. He winced in reds and cracked an eye at her.

"I'm gonna interrogate you," she said.

He rolled his shoulders one at a time, like a cat making biscuits. "Thought we were past this," he said.

"Not *you*-you. You're roleplaying the dead dude you stabbed with a butter knife," she said. "I figure you're basically his doppelgänger. Hell, we're lucky space-time didn't fracture when you two made physical contact. So I'll ask you the same questions I'd ask him, and you're gonna answer for him."

"No, I'm not," he said, tugging his hat low. "He wouldn't answer your questions. Not unless he had something to gain."

"Do it," she said. "Pretend I've got leverage."

"Fine," Wyatt said, as traces of the warm teal of family appeared in his conversational colors; she filed that tidbit away for later.

"What's your master plan?"

"Fuck, Peng, how should I know?" Wyatt sat up, finally ready to talk. "That depends on who I'm working for."

"All right," she said. Beneath them, the patchwork of soft spring colors rolled by. "Let's pick it apart. Why work with a militia?"

"'cause there's a thousand different kinds of militia, and nobody knows what any one of them is doing," he said. "Like you, walking into that gun show and expecting a bunch of ignorant dicks."

"That's fair," she admitted.

"Militia confuses the situation. Makes you wonder what's possible. If there are limits on how far they'll go."

"Anything else?"

"Good camouflage," he said. "Nobody aligned with a militia

would be working for someone legit."

"Okay, good," she said. "Why sovereign citizens?"

"They're about the best camouflage out there. Nobody understands what the hell they're doing, and they're willing to go the distance. Makes 'em scary as fuck to law enforcement."

"All right. So let's say your real boss is a politician who works at the Capitol—"

"Sounds likely."

"—they see this report from an undercover agent in the FBI. The agent's entrenched in a militia that's picked up a lawyer who's also a sovereign citizen. It's a scenario that's unusual enough that most folks in law enforcement would sit up and notice. So…what? Your bosses decide this is an opportunity they can exploit, and your boss sends you in to infiltrate the group?"

"Wrong." Wyatt said. "The objective is to get to Nicholson. The FBI agent's in my way, and there's a chance he'd recognize what I am."

"Oh God, I don't want to think all of this started with us killing our own," she muttered.

"Why not? It'd be a red flag if they pulled the agent out, and killing him would endear me to Nicholson. Especially if I could get the agent to confess before I killed him. That'd make Nicholson paranoid, and he'd trust me. He'd rely on me to do what needed to be done."

Rachel had the urge to go stand under a hot shower for the rest of forever. "What a lovely and very intentional phrase you just used," she said, as Wyatt grinned at her in pinks. "Why start with a kidnapping?"

"Kidnapping is gold," he said. "People move around. They're easier to steal than anything else. And they get a damned high return on investment."

"Right, but why take Hope and Avery? Why not Josh, or Mulcahy himself?"

Wyatt shrugged. "Josh would fight back."

"And with Mulcahy, it wouldn't even be a fight," she said, as a streak of gray the size and shape of a Desert Eagle appeared and disappeared in Wyatt's colors.

"I would have taken Agent Murphy," he said. Rachel's face must have shown murder, because he added, very quickly: "You asked. She's a soft target, unguarded, but critical to OACET."

Rachel had to give him that one. "Mare would have been the safest bet," she said reluctantly. "I can't figure out why they thought taking Hope was a good idea. Hell, we would have worked just as hard to get anybody in OACET back! But they took a freakin' wild creature and expected she'd do okay in a cage...

"No," she corrected herself, as something Fischer had said in passing blinked into her conscious mind. "No... He didn't expect her to behave."

Wyatt's expression of disinterest fell away. "Whatcha chasing?"

"Fischer didn't know I was listening," she said, mostly to herself. "I went out-of-body to check on Hope, and he said... He said he couldn't wait until he got to kill her."

"Those words?"

"No," she said, tripping back through three days' worth of chaotic new memories. "He said, 'Can't fuckin' wait 'til I get to kill you.'"

"You sure? Those words?"

"Yeah," she said, as the familiar feeling of puzzle pieces coming together toppled into a complete picture. She scooted forward and banged on the cockpit partition. "Hey!" she shouted at the pilot. "Get us back to Washington, *now!*"

Time... her subconscious reminded her. *It's all about time.*

Human beings were conditioned by the idea of clocks and schedules. These imposed order, a sweet routine which let you know that this was when breakfast was supposed to happen, or then was when you went to bed. You expected the workday to begin at nine o'clock sharp, and excitement and impulsivity was reserved for after ten at night.

Giving Nicholson thirty-seven hours to get his shit together was an open declaration of psychological warfare.

Unless someone in his militia had advanced combat training (other than Fischer, who was steadily cooling in a hospital morgue and thus not a reliable source), Nicholson wouldn't realize that thirty-seven hours was the exact amount of time required to render his brain to mush.

It went like this: Nicholson would expect a raid to come on the first night, once it was safely dark. Around midnight, of course, because that's the high time for excitement. The militia would amp themselves up into a frenzy, watching for signs of incursion, invasion, intrusion… Every little noise would be the first sounds of a SWAT unit storming the building.

It helped that Josh had shipped an outdoor movie screen to the police camp in front of the factory, and they were playing military siege movies at high volume. Bit of a risk, considering the sounds of gunfire might mask the sounds of gunfire, but that concern worked both ways.

And then came the food.

The first pizza truck arrived last night at dinner time. Fresh pizzas straight out of the oven, and plenty of bottled water and sodas. A volunteer from the local police department knocked on the door, waited for Nicholson to give the go-ahead, and then drove the truck straight up to a loading dock where five men waited with guns. The OACET Agents whose avatars were stationed around the interior of the warehouse said the next hour was spent subjecting the hostages to random slices of pizza and waiting to see if they'd keel over. After the hostages were well-fed and the pizza had gone bone-cold, the militia members began to eat. They stuffed themselves until someone realized that heavy food might make them slow, so they dropped everything and spent the next few hours ready for the attack.

Dawn came, and with it a catering truck overflowing with coffee and pastries, bells ringing to announce the arrival of another day's worth of calories. Lunch was fresh seafood, with deli sandwiches for those who didn't enjoy lobster. Dinner was more pizza, with an ice cream truck close behind.

Nobody would be the wiser when the catering truck got close enough to disgorge two dozen FBI agents the next morning.

Everything had been put into motion the moment Nicholson walked out of OACET headquarters. The raid was a go—no matter what Rachel did, that wouldn't change.

It was up to her to make sure it was the right kind of raid.

Rachel leapt out of the taxi and barreled through OACET headquarters as fast as the ever-present hordes of FBI would allow. She spared the passing disparaging glare at the agents from Homeland who were starting to sneak in—a few of them noticed her, and flashed Southwestern turquoise and yellow concern—but most everyone else was brushed aside as she raced upstairs to Mulcahy's office.

Wyatt followed her, ever obedient.

The clock was running out.

Get him off the road.

She burst into Mulcahy's office and shouted: "It's about *you*, you son of a bitch!"

Mulcahy glanced up from the architectural blueprints spread flat across a folding table. He nodded towards the raid coordinator from the FBI and said, "Would you give us a moment?"

The FBI agent blushed in secondhand embarrassment, and left the room.

Josh poked his head inside. "What's up?"

"Get in here!" she snapped at him. "And ping Mare. She needs to hear this.

"And you!" Rachel pointed at Wyatt. "Stand guard outside! Nobody outside of OACET comes near this room."

As soon as the door clicked shut behind Wyatt, Rachel spun back to Mulcahy. "They want Hope dead," she said, "because they *want* to push you over the edge."

He stared at her, conversational colors blank.

"Oh, fuck this," she muttered. She grabbed him by the hands and hurled herself into his mind.

Rachel had been deep inside Mulcahy's mind once before.

He had gone robot then, too, when she got too close to learning a secret he had promised to protect and he had to throw her out. She hadn't realized what his cold emotionless state had meant at the time. Today, it was easy to get around his walls: he was unyielding stone, impenetrable metal; she was water and light. He was inflexible, unable to respond; she flowed around his walls as if they didn't exist.

She dumped the relevant details straight into his memory.

Congressional hearings, so many they blurred together: Politicians, shouting about how OACET should be under the direct control of This Agency, or That Department; Agents, fighting back, telling them *No!*, that *No, No,* ***No!*** You have ***no*** legitimate reason to come in and take us over!

The timeline: Nicholson at Sugar Camp Christmas Trees. Fischer's arrival. Vanning's disappearance. Nicholson's move south to reclaim his factory.

The notes: politicians and their strange holiday shopping lists. The back-and-forth of acceptable losses. Consensus on the need to take down the Comptroller before they could buy what they wanted.

Campbell and Gallagher: both worried about how OACET might be pulled apart, but in very different ways.

Homeland Security, skulking through their own halls.

And a man— Fischer—sneering at Hope as he promised to kill her.

"They want you to break," she told Mulcahy. *"They want you to break in a big public way! They need you to snap and go nuts, so they can come in and take over OACET!"*

Rachel released his hands.

For the first time in days, a spark of real emotion flamed within him. It was small but it was there, a bloody, furious red.

"You're leading the raid, right?" she said aloud. "There's never been any real doubt that you'd lead the raid, right? Even if it means invoking the charter and forcing the FBI to run backup?"

Mulcahy nodded, slowly, as the spark began to burn.

"What happens if they kill Hope and Avery in front of you? Everybody who's anybody knows what you used to do! Can you think of a better way to get you to snap and make a lot of really bad decisions in a high-pressure situation? When you're holding a freakin' *gun?!*"

The red spark burst apart, so fast and bright that Rachel thought Mulcahy had caught fire and exploded.

She was half-right.

Well, she though, as Josh grabbed her around the waist and pulled her behind the couch. *Maybe this wasn't the best way to break him out of his trance, but it sure was effective.*

Mulcahy threw the couch across the room and came at them.

Rachel kicked at Mulcahy's left leg, Josh went at his right. Mulcahy leapt up and came down, both feet just missing Rachel and Josh.

"Oh goody," she said, as she scrambled sideways and hid behind a bookcase. *"He's not actually trying to kill us."*

"Let him burn it off," Josh said, as Mulcahy reduced one of the club chairs to scrap. *"He'll be fine in a minute."*

Knobby chair legs flew at her like shotputs. *"Do we **have** a minute?"*

"Consider it your daily workout."

"We've got to keep the FBI out of here," she said, glancing towards the nervous person-sized shapes on the other side of the door. Wyatt didn't have the authority to hold them back, and if he went for a weapon—

"Mare's on it," Josh said, as he dodged a flying guillotine made of elegant woods and leathers. *"Why was this a good idea, again?"*

"Do you think he'll stay in robot mode if they kill Hope in front of him?" Rachel replied, and rolled sideways as Mulcahy seized the bookshelf and began using it as a club. *"I want to snap him back to reality here, where it's safe!"*

"Yeah, right," Josh said, as glass from the antique light fixtures rained down on him. *"Safe."*

Mulcahy abandoned the bookshelf and seized his computer

monitor, and began swinging it around his head by its cord. Rachel jumped sideways as the monitor slammed into the floor, then fell backwards in self-defense as the cord broke and the monitor bounced once and flew at her head.

Stupid thirty-two-inch screen, she thought, and Josh laughed. "Stop enjoying this!" she shouted aloud at him, as Mulcahy roared and threw his desk chair so hard that it cracked the plaster walls.

Mulcahy turned, and the desk was in his way.

That *fucking* desk.

He stopped moving, just for a moment, and stared down at the desk. The red inferno that raged across his surface colors turned inside out—she got a glimpse of what was under it, a blue-black core entwined around his own, with the unmistakable red of heart's blood connecting them—and then the red became a sharpened blade.

He seized the mahogany desk by one end, and pushed.

The carved feet on the old desk slid across the smooth floor. When the edge of the desk met the wall, Mulcahy tipped the desk on one end and lifted it over the sill.

"Don't!" Rachel shouted, out of instinct more than protest.

There was a moment in balance, and then he pushed again.

Breaking glass, followed by an almost-soft crash.

"Shit!" Josh sprinted to the window and looked down.

"It's fine," Rachel said, her scans turned on Mulcahy as if he were a rabid dog who might come at her again. "There're crowd control barriers up. Nobody's close enough to the building to get hurt."

"No! I mean, good, but that goddamned desk is famous!" Josh trailed off, and began smiling and waving at someone down on the street below. "How do I explain this?"

Rachel was watching Mulcahy. He was standing in place, his anger finally ebbing. Apparently, launching a four-hundred-pound weight from the third story of a building was enough to take the edge off.

The door opened. Mare stormed into the office, long red hair ticking like a pendulum behind her with each step. The waiflike woman walked up to Mulcahy and jabbed him in the sternum with her clipboard. "Sign these."

"What?" Mulcahy asked, his voice scraped down to the bones from roaring.

"You remember how you said you'd have to be out of your mind to open negotiations with Senator McKillip? This is about as close as you're going to get. Sign these."

He chuckled. It started small, barely a chuffing sound in the back of his throat. Purples and grays rolled out from his core and covered him, repressed dark humor swallowing him like a fog.

As Mare kept poking Mulcahy with the clipboard, Rachel righted the couch and checked the cushions for broken glass. Mulcahy shied away from the papers, real laughter beginning to spill from him. "No, Mare," he said. "Not even now."

Mare poked him over to the couch and managed to get him seated. "Lie down," she said, still poking away. "You haven't slept in days. You're worthless until you get some sleep."

"Oh, God, what did I do?" he said.

"Nothing you shouldn't have already done," Mare said. "We're all pretty relieved, to be honest. Now, sign these."

Mulcahy pushed the clipboard away, still laughing, but weakly now.

Mare sighed and went to find something to use as a blanket.

"I'm leading the raid," Mulcahy said.

"Sleep," Rachel ordered him.

His hand closed around her arm like a vise. Anger, frustration, and weary relief rose from his skin into her own. *"Promise me,"* he said, as his mental voice began to fall away.

"Nope," she said. *"Not unless it's what benefits OACET."*

She wasn't sure if he heard her before he dropped out of the link, but she thought he might have still been laughing in his head.

"He's got a grip like a freakin' pit bull," she muttered, as she pried his fingers from her arm. "Anybody got any bacon?"

"I'll stay with him," Mare said. She shook out Mulcahy's suit coat and tossed it over his torso. "Josh, honey, go do what you do and make the normals think this is normal."

Josh smiled at her in sweet rose pinks, and left with a smile and a song for the FBI.

"This is good," Mare said, dimples running deep across her shoulders. She tugged up the edge of the rug and rolled it away from her, broken glass and all. She sat on the floor, and her long red hair puddled around her. "Maybe he'll wake up delusional and I can get his signature then."

"Good luck with that," Rachel said, and Mare sighed.

Rachel scanned the new room-sized garbage bin, and began to pick up papers. "I need Ami and Phil," she said. "Can you ping and pull them?"

"Why?"

"'cause until Mulcahy is good to go, I just got a major field promotion. Now," she said, as she rolled up the blueprints and tucked them under her arm, "I'm off to plan a raid."

TWENTY

The relief boat chopped across the surface of the water as a woman shouted at her about neoprene.

"The dry suits will keep you warm, but only if you don't breach the seals!" The FBI's diving instructor checked the cuffs on Rachel's suit; the seals sucked at her wrists and ankles, and the one around her neck was slowly suffocating her. "The suits use a layer of air as insulation. You get water in there, the water'll act as insulation, but once that suit comes off, you're cold and wet!"

Wyatt's black drysuit was worn beneath bemused oranges. Apparently, the original Marshall Wyatt never had any dive training, and this new version had forgotten to write it into his revised history. He feigned intense concentration as the dive instructor talked him through suiting up, and complimented him on how quickly he seemed to catch on.

(For her own part, Rachel was glad that her girlfriend was rich and enjoyed doing the dumb things that rich people pretended to enjoy, such as exploring old shipwrecks off the rocky coast of northern Oregon. But she hoped the FBI instructor would hurry up so they could get in the water—the extra heat that her cyborg metabolism threw off as a waste product was starting to cook her alive.)

"Rebreathers," the dive instructor said, as she handed Rachel what appeared to be a reverse backpack. Rachel slipped her arms through the holes in the rebreather vest so the instructor could cinch her in, and then stood so the rebreather could be settled over her chest and shoulders. The pack was uncomfortably bulky against her breasts, and the dive instructor gave her the usual *Sorry!* shrug she had come to associate among female professionals who didn't design their own gear.

"Never used a rebreather before," she said to the instructor. "Anything I need to know?"

"Try to leave it someplace safe, so we can recover it," the instructor said. "They're expensive."

"Um—"

"You've got a quarter-mile swim to shore in a calm sea," the instructor said. "Stay just below the surface of the water, and come up early if you need to. You'll be fine."

"Right." The relief boat began to slow as it pulled aside one of the cruisers. Ropes were exchanged; FBI and police from the cruisers began to move back and forth between the boats. Rachel nodded to Wyatt, and the psychopath joined her on the far side of the boat.

She opened a connection with his earpiece. *"Check."*

"Received. How do I talk to you?"

"Think at me. Really hard," she said. His colors blanched to yellow. "I'm serious. And stay as close as you can—I've never done this in the water."

As the dive instructor did a final equipment check and positioned their mouthpieces, Rachel began to spin her shield around the two of them.

In theory, there shouldn't be any difference between air and water in respect to her shield. In practice…

Well. Too late to worry about it now. Either they'd make land without tripping the cameras and motion detectors, or they wouldn't.

The factory was a long, dark spread of black and blue on the horizon as she and Wyatt tipped backwards off the boat.

Bright light, all around her, as the kinetic energy of the ocean took her in. She reached out and tapped Wyatt on his shoulder, and the two of them sank beneath the boats. They gave the propellers a wide berth and set out for shore.

She loved night swimming with her implant. Back in the day, night swimming had been slippery terrors, more of a test of will than anything close to enjoyable. Since activation, night swimming had become immersion within…well, for lack of a better analogy, life itself. Water was alive! Not in a filthy germy way, but in the way of the clean press of a liquid jungle, cells within cells blooming, growing, moving from one state to another before dying and repeating the cycle anew. It was a bath in the heart of the planet, not careless but carefree, free from any trivial concerns except the wholeness of just *being*.

And the frequencies!

Water didn't play nice with the EMF. The digital ecosystem was heavily distorted beneath the waves, and the deeper she went, the worse that distortion. Rachel had heard rumors of whales and other squishy mammals beaching themselves as a response to sonar tests, and she believed it—the ocean wasn't pure by any sense of the word, but it was its own true self. The digital ecosystem wasn't welcome here, and those trillions of creatures that lived in the ocean weren't equipped to deal with it when it was forced on them.

Her shield kept its shape as they swam. She had been concerned that it would move with the water, maybe pull thin and dissolve like spun sugar with each wave, but it remained a perfect sphere. It was weaker than she would have liked; some of the frequencies she relied on to block audio and visual frequencies were buffered, and she had the feeling that if they dove any lower, she might lose those parts of her shield entirely. But here, a few feet below the surface, it did its job.

Sure did seem to be attracting a lot of fish, though.

She and Wyatt were still a couple hundred yards from shore, and it was plenty deep. Fish of all shapes and sizes were swimming out of the liquid light beneath them to check out these strange invaders in their realm. Rachel remembered a nature program about how predatory fish navigated using electrical impulses, and was about to make a note to ask Santino about how her shield might play into this when her spinal cord noticed the huge dark shape swimming towards them and crawled straight up its own vertebrae.

Oh, that's right, she thought to herself, as calmly as possible. *Sharks are fish.*

"*Hey,*" she said to Wyatt, her mental voice calm—*so* calm. "*Hypothetically speaking, have you ever fought a shark before?*"

Purple humor colored his sandalwood; he thought she was joking. His was the only color in this bright white expanse of energy. Even the very large dark shape—*ah, yes, that would be shapes, there are two of them now*—swimming beside him didn't give off any emotions other than more of this intense living white.

"*Humor me and get out your knife,*" she said.

His colors took on orange annoyance and rolled like eyeballs as he took out his flashlight instead.

"*Don't,*" she warned him. "*The guards might see it from the shore.*"

He nodded, and they continued swimming.

As they entered the shallows, the fish got bored and swam off, taking the sharks with them. Rachel and Wyatt stopped just outside of the spotlights and stayed low, shedding dive equipment and the diving suits as they moved. The waterproof case which held Wyatt's rifle was clipped to his stomach beneath the suit; same with her own service weapon. Rachel gave the guns a quick scan. "They're dry," she whispered to him. She checked her shield and tightened what she could.

Then they ran.

There was no beach. It was hard-edged rocks and shattered beer bottles and rusty car parts, every inch of it slippery with seaweed. They were on all fours most of the time, tactical gloves and shoes finding purchase in this tetanus minefield. They dodged the arcs of the FBI's searchlights (which seemed focused on the north end of the shore while they ran up the south, *hmm so strange*) and made it to dry land.

Concrete beneath her feet and scans—blessed, shark-free concrete. The last sprint to the side of the building was as easy as a run through a park.

They began to climb.

OACET's scouts had chosen well when they had selected this part of the factory for the ascent. There were window ledges and industrial gutters aplenty, and between these were spots on the wall where enough mortar had fallen out from between the bricks for shallow finger-holds.

They paused before they reached the roof, clinging flat to the black wall in their black suits, so Rachel could run one last scan and make sure they weren't about to leap over the ledge into a trap. Or drop into a hole. Or meet predatory roof-roaming wolves. Rachel was lost in her scans when Wyatt went pale and yellow beside her. She scanned up, then down and around, unable to find the threat she had missed. Wyatt tapped her on her shoulder and pointed towards the ocean.

There, in the pool cast by the FBI's searchlights, swam two dark arrowheaded shapes that were nearly as long as the boats.

Rachel grinned at him and resumed the climb.

The factory's rooftop was a wasteland. It was as close to the minefields of Afghanistan as she'd seen outside of her dreams: mostly wasted rubble with plants struggling to grow, and holes that snuck up on you without warning to drag you down into the hollows. Beneath that was a jungle canopy made of metal, with iron and steel beams twisting every which way.

She and Wyatt chose a nice sniper's perch in the middle of the roof with those holes all around them. The perch had a structural support column beneath it, and Rachel felt relatively sure the support column would keep them from crashing through the rotting roof into the factory below.

Right beneath them were the hostages.

Avery was asleep in the lap of the woman with the copper core. The woman was awake, barely, with the soft colors of sleep dissolving around her like a slow morning mist. There were militia men around them, some sleeping, some keeping watch in drowsy shades of beiges and grays.

They were heavily armed, of course.

Two soft taps on a flap of peeling tarpaper; Wyatt had turned yellow again, but this time it was an inquisitive yellow. The light coming up through the holes in the roof was a cold filtered blue; he could see her, or at least the outline of her, so she shook her head in answer and touched her wrist where a watch would rest.

Wyatt settled himself and started to unpack his rifle. He unsnapped the flaps on his carry bag and stared at the pieces, then began to assemble them, his colors dipping to orange scorn. He hadn't been happy with the idea of less-lethal weapons, especially when he was supposed to be covering the enemy from a distance. Rachel agreed—weapon accuracy counted in a firefight, and while the idea of rubber impact rounds with a pepper spray additive sounded nice and all, she was somewhat concerned about how the enemy carried real guns with armor-piercing rounds.

He finished assembling the odd-looking rifle and lay flat on the roof, gun pointed at the militia members deep inside the factory.

Above them was the night sky, overcast and starting to drizzle.

This was the weirdest sense of vertigo.

Sniper duty with my own pet psychopath, she thought to herself. *How in the hell did I get here?*

(The answer was that she needed a bodyguard while she was in deep scans in hostile territory, and everybody but Wyatt was needed on the ground. Especially as it was safer for the main team if Wyatt didn't go with them, what with his sudden but inevitable betrayal still yet to occur. Plus, she had planned this part of the raid, so she had willingly stuck herself with him. But a good rhetorical question deserved a good rhetorical flailing.)

Below—multiple stories and most of a wastewater system below—Mulcahy opened a link.

"In position," he said.

"Us, too," she replied.

"Report."

"Clear up here," she said. *"One guard on the roof. He's over on the far side of the factory, near the front doors. I think he's watching the movie."* She took a moment to throw her scans to the movie screen below—Sean Connery was busy saving

Alcatraz from Nicholas Cage, or some other equally unpleasant threat—and the guard's colors flickered slightly as the scenes changed. *"Yeah, he's worthless."*

"Worthless? Not if he's up and moving," he said as he pressed back against her mind. *"Focus."*

"You're not as pushy when you're a robot," she replied.

She felt him laugh, quietly. He was so very tired, and his walls were thin enough to tear, but at least he laughed. In exchange, she let him into her scans so he could contrast her rooftop perspective against Phil's sewer-cam.

"Wait," he said. She did; a few moments later, she felt him pick up the threads of her scans and Phil's, and weld them into a single image. Mulcahy was much less skilled at this than she and Phil: Rachel was in two places at once and her dinner threatened to come up and then go down the nearest roof-hole, and that would certainly notify the militia that somethin' sticky was a-brewin'.

Focus, she told herself, in a voice that wasn't quite her own. *We practiced this. Focus.*

Rachel wrapped a lovely cinquain by Adelaide Crapsey around her mind like a Pendleton blanket—

I know
Not these my hands
And yet I think there was
A woman like me once had hands
Like these.

—and let her own body go.

The sights and smells of the open rooftop took a step sideways, and blended into those of the wastewater tunnels beneath the building. Mulcahy was there, and Phil, and Josh, and the Hippos, smooshed nose-to-ass in a pipe so tight that Mulcahy had to keep his shoulders folded in as close he could. They wore black Teflon coveralls over black tactical gear, and the last person in the chain (Ami, who was the smallest and therefore the most maneuverable in that claustrophobia clusterfuck) dragged a long waterproof bag packed with guns and less-lethal ammo.

She felt the Agents in the tunnel take a long drag of fresh air through her senses. She would have given them the sky and the liquid light of the sea, too, except the crushing weight of the tunnel might swallow them whole when she cut her end of the feed.

"Fifteen minutes until sunrise," Mulcahy said, and all the Agents set their timers.

Breathe, she reminded herself. *They're—we're!—the best of the best. All of us combat-trained and ready. This'll go like clockwork.*

Across the link, she heard the tail ends of the others' thoughts, all of them trying to convince themselves of the same thing—

Time… Her subconscious whispered again. *It's all about time…*

"Running deep scans. Ping me when you need to bring me back in," she told Mulcahy, and left their link to concentrate.

She lost herself to her search, stretching her mind to try to get the last part of the puzzle to drop into place. The militia members were well-fed and slow. Dawn was almost there. The catering truck carrying the FBI's tactical response team was cruising towards the crowd barricades…

What about time? she asked herself, as the barricades lifted. *What am I missing?*

Get him off the road, her subconscious said.

I did! She shouted back at herself in her own head, and could have sworn she heard echoes. *He's off the goddamned road! What am I **missing**?*

"What happens to me after this?"

Wyatt spoke so softly that her ears thought she had caught the breeze talking. She hauled her senses back inside her head and turned them on him. "Huh?"

"What are you going to do with me after this?" His head was pointed down, rifle ready. She might have been able to trick herself into thinking he hadn't spoken if his colors weren't bright with yellow curiosity.

"Oh, Jesus," she sighed, and pressed the backs of her gloved fists against her forehead. Train of thought, derailed before the station. Mass casualties, paramedics en route. "I dunno. Depends if you're running a game. You turn on us in here, and anyone who survives will make you suffer."

His conversational colors picked up a great deal of iron, and this was clubbed away from Southwestern turquoise and OACET green.

"Yeah, I know you saved my life," she said. "Honestly? I don't know what to do with you. I don't even know why Adam sent you here. I mean, you're helping, yeah, but…"

Wyatt's colors went slightly purple-gray around the edges, a smooth blue-gray held within this melancholy.

"Is he dead?" she asked.

"No." He shook his head. Truth.

She pushed him anyhow: Adam was his soft spot. "Did you kill him?"

A flash of bright red fury—his eyes moved away from the factory floor towards her.

"Had to ask," she said.

"No," he said, the fury turning to hard gray granite as his eyes moved downwards again. "You didn't."

"Maria Griffin," she said. "Remember her? Nice woman? You cut her throat and let her bleed out on the floor? Not exactly a good first impression."

He nodded, the slightest movement of his chin.

"I don't know you," she told him. "I don't like your methods. All I know is you show up after people start getting hurt."

Wyatt stopped talking. The two of them went back to keeping watch, her slow scans moving across the rooftop and down into the factory, touching on the FBI agents lying in wait in the van outside—

"Saw you in the corridor," he finally said. "That first night at OACET headquarters." His conversational colors turned opaque over his eyes.

"I know," she said. "I don't want to talk about it."

"Your implant was off, right? You're blind without it."

"I *don't* want to talk about it."

He waited a moment before saying, "You ever stop to ask yourself if maybe I'm getting something out of this, too?"

"Yeah," Rachel said. "But I can't figure it out."

"You ever wanted to do the right thing, but have no idea what that is?"

"Always," she sighed. "Case in point—you."

Wyatt's colors rolled over themselves again in a purple-gray sigh of resignation, and he fell silent.

Seven minutes. She ran her scans again. The FBI's coffee truck was still at the barricades, offering coffee and such to the local officers. In the factory below, word was spreading among the militia that breakfast had arrived; the men were beginning to brighten in anticipation, and the slow mass migration towards coffee had begun.

She pulled herself back to check on Wyatt, and felt metal jab at her through her thick canvas pants. The roof of the building was rusted steel, and there was no part of it that wasn't covered in sharp edges; Rachel stopped squirming to get comfortable when she realized that only made everything worse.

"Calm down," Wyatt whispered.

"I'm not a sniper," she muttered. "I'm not trained to lie in one place for eight hours."

"Eight? Try eighty."

"Liar."

"Can be done," he said. "You gotta work in a team, but it can be done."

"Don't see you as much of a team player," she said.

"I always work with a partner," he said. "Always."

There was weight in those words, and his colors had some wine red in them. She had no clue where that sympathy belonged; he wasn't thinking about anything in particular, and the wine red moved into his core of sandalwood.

Three minutes.

The FBI's truck started moving towards the loading docks. Rachel reached out to Mulcahy: *"Status check?"*

"We're at the entrance point. Good to go," he replied. Through his eyes, she saw the last streaks of heat fade from an access hatch, as the plasma torch finished cutting through the locks and hinges.

"Us, too. FBI's almost in position. No movement on the militia."

"All right. Breaking cover."

She felt hands that weren't hers attach a magnet lift to the hatch, and her body complained about lifting something as massive as that solid piece of steel. Below, Mulcahy swung the hatch aside and set it down on the ground, as soundless as snowfall.

Agents poured out of the wastewater tunnel and fanned out, one-third moving to the north side of the factory, two-thirds moving to the south. All carried less-lethal weaponry; all wore gas masks and eye protection.

Rachel took out her own gear from a hip pocket and fixed her mask to her face. Wyatt didn't: snipers liked to keep their field of vision as unimpeded as possible, even if they were shooting a glorified paintball gun.

Ninety seconds.

"Cover me," she said to Wyatt. "This is about to get poetic."

He nodded, his colors locking down into steady professional blues.

She reached out to Phil, still crouching in the cover of the wastewater pipe, and the two of them joined their senses into one. *Focus*, they reminded each other—skin contact made this so much easier, but at least there was no loss of self in this type of link—and stretched their perspective into every nook and cranny of the factory. Rachel began to pare off the extra pieces. There was no need for chemical sensors, or structural assessment, or even the emotional spectrum: these were clutter, a confusing mess to anyone without months of practice in deep scanning. All the Agents needed was the ability to see through walls and machines, and know where the members of the militia were hiding.

Once done, she added some color: red for the militia, blue for the hostages.

"Good?" she asked, once she had removed everything but the most rudimentary form of x-ray vision.

"Yeah. Bring them in."

She did—she offered their perspective to Mulcahy, and she and Phil stepped away from control of their own senses as he joined them to himself, and, through him, the others. Nineteen Agents, online, aware of the location of every human being in the warehouse.

And Nicholson, sitting upstairs with Hope Blackwell in her office prison.

"The poem is 'Dreamers,' by Siegfried Sassoon," she told them, and took Phil and herself into the words of a man long dead.

The Agents began to move.

"Soldiers are citizens of death's grey land..."

Ami led the strike force in the hostage room; Mulcahy led the one to rescue Hope. Twelve Agents, including Josh and the other Hippos, followed Ami. Before they hit the room, they peeled off into three groups; one group raced up the catwalk, while the other two hung back, hidden behind either side of the doorway.

"Drawing no dividend from time's tomorrows."

Mulcahy took his four Agents north. Every member of the militia had a phone: these were taken off of the network with a tug and a thought. There was a guard stationed along the way: he was poking at his useless phone up until the moment Mulcahy crushed his nose and flipped him into an unconscious heap of camouflage clothing. An Agent with a bundle of zip ties lashed the man's hands together, then twisted his thumbs until they popped out of the sockets.

"In the great hour of destiny they stand,"

The catering truck arrived at the loading dock. An FBI agent in a night-black tactical suit shot a couple of tear gas canisters into the building, easy as pie.

But Nicholson was moving; all of the militia men were moving! Something was wrong. The phones! someone thought, and someone else agreed—when all the phones went down at once, the militia knew the raid was on. *Faster*, the Agents agreed, and pressed forward.

"Each with his feuds, and jealousies, and sorrows."

Ami rounded the corner and began painting the militia members with less-lethal bullets loaded with pepper spray. Less-lethal weapons weren't non-lethal weapons; every shot had to be well-aimed for safety's sake, and a second round fired in case the first bullet didn't release its payload on impact. Ami and the others were fast, but the process was slow. The hostages were pulled away from their sleepy community, woken from uneasy dreams to be held in front of the militia men as human shields. Above, Wyatt began firing, shooting men in camouflage with explosive rounds of pepper spray, the steady *prap!-prap!-prap!* of high-pressure air lost in the din below.

Avery, awake—her high child's voice cut through the sound of gunshots as she called for her parents.

"Soldiers are sworn to action; they must win…"

The FBI had reached the south room. Gas canisters flew; the smell of tear gas and pepper spray soared up to the roof and into the morning sky.

Avery—coughing, held close and covered by the woman with the core of copper.

Rachel highlighted the little girl in her scans, a soft green shape amid the hostages and militia men, and Josh's team on the catwalks leapt from covering Ami's team to offense. Josh was a whirlwind: two shots, *prap!-prap!* and another, *prap!-prap!* as he broke through the militia's cover, grabbed the girl, and ran.

The woman with the core of copper screamed for Avery.

"Some flaming, fatal climax with their lives."

Ami took three shots to the chest.

Her body armor ate the rounds and spat them out, but she still went down. Wyatt changed targets and took out the man who shot her—*prap!-prap!*—but the man behind him was still coming, gun aimed right between Ami's brown eyes—

—Wyatt's gun clicked on empty and he went to reload with machinelike efficiency—

—and Rachel broke cover to fire at Ami's assailant. No weak *praps!-praps!* from her gun, oh no. She had the only active service weapon, and was firing solid brass bullets with the traditional ***bang!-bang!*** of serious gunfire. Two shots went into the right arm of Ami's assailant, and it fell apart into so much useless meat.

"Soldiers are dreamers; when the guns begin…"

The militia men were panicking; their lizard brains turned them towards the new noise in the room. Rachel and Wyatt rolled back from the edge as semi-automatic rounds chipped their snipers' nest apart. Wyatt was silent as the roof gave way beneath him; Rachel lunged, caught him by his arm, but still they both fell.

"They think of firelit homes, clean beds, and wives."

Becca's core of smooth green jade flashed in Rachel's mind as she reached out…out… The support pillar was a chunky thing, with steel limbs shooting off like the branches on a tree. Her fingertips grabbed one of these, and she twisted with all of her strength, whipping Wyatt towards the pillar. He wrapped an arm around a branch and returned the favor, pulling Rachel into the limbs of the pillar behind him.

They scrambled down, almost in freefall. Bullets ripped past them. Wyatt took a shot in his leg and fell again, and this time she couldn't stop it. She let go of the pillar and fell after him: they were fifteen feet from the ground, and they landed hard.

Gunfire all around her. There was more to the poem, but she needed to drop the perspective link and start moving—*"Phil!"* she cried.

"Go, I've got this," said the slip of silverlight in her mind, and Phil pushed *calm, control* back at her. She grabbed at these emotions and wrapped them around her, as she severed herself from the perspective link and let her own senses come back

online.

Red, she realized. *We're drowning in red.*

Pain red, panic red, the reds spun into the yellows of bone-deep fear. She had Wyatt's gun with its less-lethal rounds and was crouched over him like a cat guarding her kill, firing those almost useless pepper spray balls—*prap!-prap!-prap!*—at anyone holding a real gun.

Wyatt's leg was bad; blood was beginning to soak through the knees of her pants. But Ami was there; the assassin had recovered from the shock of taking three shots to her chest. She ripped the gun from Rachel's hands, and started laying cover fire. The psychopath was cutting through his own pants leg; Rachel ripped off her belt and cinched it high around his thigh. An instant to scan him with the diagnostic autoscript—"They missed the artery," she told him, and saw some blue relief through his pain—and she started running.

She had dropped her service weapon on the roof: she had nothing but her fists and her feet, and she used these on the first militia man she found. He was bleeding when she was done with him, and she took his assault rifle; she flipped this around and waded into the fray, swinging it like a club which was the *stupidest* thing she could ever do with a loaded weapon and she *knew* that and she was so fucking *mad* she couldn't just *kill* these assholes and be *done* with it!

And then it was over.

Not completely over: there were still a couple of militia men standing, shouting, calling attention to themselves until the *prap!-prap!* of the less-lethal rounds took them down. But the battle itself was done, and Rachel felt herself giggling in relief.

"Status report." Josh's voice, all business. She poked the giggles back down and replied, *"I'm uninjured, Wyatt got hit in the leg. Needs a medic."*

"Sending one over. I need your doctor's eyes."

"Right." She handed her weapon to the nearest FBI agent and shuffled her way towards Josh. Say what you wanted about Chinese manufacturing standards, but NORINCO made good clubs.

Her ankle was in bad shape. She wasn't sure if it had been the fall or the fight, but it was making small screaming noises with each step.

She was within arm's length of collapsing on top of Josh when Mulcahy pinged her. *"Rachel?"*

"...sec," she said aloud to Josh. *"What's up?"* she asked Mulcahy.

A pause, then Mulcahy's reply: *"We have a situation over here."*

TWENTY-ONE

Hope Blackwell had seen better days.

Admittedly, Hope being who she was and all, if she had been having a better week, she'd have probably thought that having a gun pressed against her head made for a pretty *good* day. But she had been in a constant state of battle since Sunday, and Nicholson had managed to drug her senseless when he realized OACET had begun their raid. She was barely able to keep her eyes open—fighting back was not an option.

Nicholson was holding her in front of him as a human shield. As Hope was close to going full rag doll, Nicholson had compensated by propping her up against the window of her office prison. A thick smear of blood from Hope's cheek blurred much of the view from the ground. All that could be seen of the two was the dark outline of Hope's hair.

"Shit," Rachel said aloud.

"Is Hope playing possum?" Mulcahy asked, doing his best to keep his own fear chained down. *"I don't think she is, but—"*

"No," Rachel replied. Hope's conversational colors were trying to lock on furious reds, but every time they got close, her concentration spiraled sideways. The woman was tripping balls. *"She's completely out of it."*

"What options do you see?"

Rachel ran the numbers for the worst-case scenario: an armed sovereign citizen with a hostage, backed into a corner by law enforcement. By now, he had realized OACET had lied to him about the deadline, and had played him for a fool. Nicholson was vividly red in pure hate. There were also…what were those odd-shaped boxes?

"Did Phil say anything about explosives?" she asked.

"Yes. Small charges, just big enough to take out the office.

They've been disarmed," Mulcahy replied, before adding, *"Nicholson already tried to set them off."*

Her heart gave a little jump; she and explosives did not play well together. *"Great. So he's actively suicidal."*

"Yes."

Worst-worst-case scenario, then.

Options... Her service weapon with its solid metal rounds was up on the roof—no trick shooting to win the day. There was pretty much only one way to win this. *...and shit.*

"What've you got?" he asked, the complex colors of hope kindling near his heart as he felt her plan come together.

"When are his thirty-seven hours up?"

"About three hours from now. What are you thinking?"

"That he needs to be reminded that OACET's word is gold, and we're the only ones involved in this mess who haven't lied to him."

Rachel limped forward.

It was still dark within the warehouse. The pre-dawn light was beginning to seep in through the windows, and the place was a very deep shade of blue. Anybody else might say it felt like walking along the bottom of the ocean. Not her, though. She knew the ocean was made of light, and the occasional shark.

Nicholson's colors whipped towards her as she walked to the bottom of the wire staircase. *Okay,* she told herself. *I'm wrong. There're sharks here, too, and this one's a spoiled brat. Time to bleed in the water.*

"Howdy!" she called out. "Remember me? I'm the OACET Agent who works with the MPD? Got your man Ethan Fischer thrown out of the meeting, and then got him killed?"

The reds twisted across themselves as some Southwestern turquoise appeared in his colors, blue-green threads that didn't seem to know where they belonged.

"Bet everything's gone to hell since he left," she said. "Bet you've been giving a lot of thought to how he manipulated you, twisted things around… Turning you into the fall guy for a lot of really despicable shit." She made it to the bottom of the staircase. One foot placed on the first step… Nope. Her bad ankle was most definitely done. "You wanna crack that door so we can talk? Your thirty-seven hours are almost up!"

Rachel leaned against the railing and waited.

The door opened. Not a lot, but enough for air and swear words to pass through. "I want to talk to Mulcahy."

"You're talking to me. You lost your chance to deal with him when you failed to comply with his terms."

"He lied!" Red anger, spliced through with yellow-white panic. "He told us we'd have thirty-seven hours!"

"Thirty-seven hours before he razed this building to the ground," Rachel corrected him. She turned her back to him and sat on the stairs. "Thirty-seven hours where he gave you a choice to have some control over your own future. At what point did we lie to you? We gave you almost a day and a half to walk out of here and surrender. This is as close to the last minute as we could come without endangering the hostages."

Yellow curiosity appeared. Not a lot, but enough to work with.

"Honestly, what did you expect?" she asked. "Your army and ours to meet on the battlefield at high noon to exchange harsh language? Mulcahy said that if you wouldn't surrender, he'd tear this place down around you. Has he done that yet? No. Will he? Absolutely. You've still got a choice in how this plays out.

"Well," she added, "you would have, if it weren't for that ticking bomb you're holding."

Nicholson glanced at his gun.

"No, dumbass," Rachel snapped. "The woman? You *would've* had more than two hours to negotiate, but you had to go and drug her, didn't you? If we don't resolve this before Blackwell wakes up, she's going to murder you, and there's nothing we can do to stop her.

"Oh," she added, "by the way, if you kill her, Mulcahy will burn down this building with you and your men in it. She's what's keeping y'all alive right now, so even if you don't value your own life, think about theirs."

Rachel pointed across the room, to where the militia men

that Mulcahy's team had taken down were kneeling in their handcuffs. They were staring up at the office, sickly yellow terror ripping their conversational colors apart; she doubted Mulcahy had told them the bombs had been disarmed.

"Want to talk this over like grownups?" she asked. "Time's running out. If you want to save your men and this building, we have to work fast."

(She was getting a little nervous about Hope, to be honest. Whatever drug Nicholson had given her was being metabolized at rocket speed, and those furious reds were about to lock themselves down. Rachel figured she had another three minutes at the most before Hope woke up enough to fight back, and God help whoever was in her way when that happened. Nicholson would probably shoot her in justifiable self-defense.)

The door opened a little wider.

"How about this," Rachel said. "I come up there, I tie Blackwell up. Then you have two hostages again."

"No!" Nicholson cried. "She's Houdini! She can escape anything!"

Rachel winced. *Damn it all, Hope,* she thought. *I **knew** that trick of yours would backfire!*

"All right, here's what we can do," she said, as she stood and hopped up the first stair, all slow and clumsy, the decaying iron railing wobbling under her hands. "You can exchange me for her."

Hop.

"Put her outside the office, take me inside, and lock the door."

Hop.

"When she comes to, she's nowhere near you. You're safe."

Hop.

"I'm OACET Administration," she said. "You've seen me during every part of this shitshow. I'm more valuable to OACET than somebody's wife."

Hop.

"Stay where you are!" Nicholson shouted.

"Dude, you no longer have the luxury of *time!*" Rachel didn't bother to hide her frustration. "If you don't get Blackwell out of there, you are *done*, do you hear me? She will kill you, and if she doesn't, Mulcahy will, and destroy this whole factory along with you!

"C'mon," she said, as she put her dignity aside and crawled up the last few stairs to the landing. "I can't freakin' walk. Move her outside, take me in her place, and then we can start negotiations again. *Hurry!*"

Orange confusion wrapped around yellow fear. These snapped into place like a taut string; the door opened, and Hope Blackwell's semi-conscious body was nudged outside. Rachel reached over and grabbed her, and hauled Hope into her lap so the metal of the landing didn't slice up Hope's skin. Hope twitched as Rachel touched her, and Rachel wondered if this was when Hope woke up and began to slaughter everyone in range, which was at this moment a woman with a bummed-up ankle—

"Get inside!" Nicholson was crouched on the floor, using glass walls and the thin metal of filing cabinets as his bunker.

"I met someone yesterday," Rachel said, as she lifted Hope from her lap and gently set her on the landing. "Didn't catch his last name, but I think you know him? Ahren, at Sugar Camp Christmas Trees?

"You should have spent more time with him." She grabbed the railing and pretended to use it to haul herself to her feet, as she scanned along the length of it… *There.* A weak spot in the metal. Very weak, crumbling from fractures and rust. "Or at least listened to him. If he were here, I'd be worried. That guy has his act together."

Hop.

She grabbed the glass door and yanked it open; Nicholson glared up at her in reds. "You don't worry me at all."

Taking his gun away from him was one of the easiest things she'd ever done. He was so low to the ground that all she had to was step on it with her gimpy foot and kick, and it went sailing off of the landing. It hurt, but not nearly as much as what was to come.

"Hi," she said.

Now for the hard part—Nicholson had to go down. In flames. Or, lacking the availability of fire, headfirst from a decent height.

Yup, this was going to *hurt*.

But maybe that was okay. Yeah, that was fine. Good, even. She was long overdue for heavy penance.

She retreated and stuck her butt against the weak part of the railing. "C'mon," she taunted him. "Come out here. Nobody's going to shoot you. We just want to have an adult discussion."

Nicholson retreated behind the door again.

"Coward!" she snapped. "Ahren would have the balls to talk! To stand up to a cop!"

Nicholson's colors rioted. The mingled blues and blacks she had come to associate with death were still heavy on his mind, but now those colors lanced forward, pointing directly at her heart.

The glass door opened so quickly that it slammed against the stair buttress and cracked.

"Nobody move," she said through the coms. *"He's going to try and jump me...suicide-by-cop. He's got a knife and I'll disarm him when he jumps. Stand down—do not shoot. Repeat: do **not** shoot. Confirm?"*

"Confirmed," came an echo of OACET; the FBI agents got the message through their earpieces, and their professional blues strengthened.

"You're under arrest," she said. She was weary, suddenly, bone-weary and ready to sleep for a month or more. A lengthy stay in a hospital bed was beginning to sound like a viable alternative to standing here and arguing with this manchild. "For assault, kidnapping, and...and we'll start with those, because I'm tired and I want to get this over with."

Nicholson began to move, the hunting knife she pretended not to see sliding out of its holster.

She put her weight on her good ankle and pretended to

slump to her side, where the ceramic plates of her body armor would catch the knife and (hopefully) turn it aside. Or maybe just hold it inside her liver. Hard to tell with body armor, really.

"Peng, *no!*"

Wyatt's voice, from *waaaaaaay* across the room.

Four gunshots.

(*Wait, real gunshots?*)

Jeremy Nicholson, white in shock, then slowly fading into that twisting blue-black color of life giving way to death as Wyatt's shots took him in his neck.

(She was extremely angry about having to watch that process again, as every time someone died in front of her, she needed six months and a case of whiskey to scrub it from her mind's eye.)

Then, general pandemonium as Nicholson's body flopped over the railing and landed on its head.

"Huh," Rachel said. She couldn't hear herself over the shouting on the floor below. She grabbed the weak spot on the railing and yanked once, carefully. When nothing happened, she yanked as hard as she could. More nothing.

"Yup," she said, as she sat a safe distance away from Hope to watch the bedlam unfold. She touched her face; it was covered in an unpleasantly sticky liquid that was definitely not sea water. "I'm done."

And, just like that, her brain tipped the last piece of the puzzle over.

It slid into place, and she sent her avatar out, out…out to Washington, to OACET's headquarters, and the War Room in the basement. Then, she reopened her link with Josh, and asked if his helicopter pilot friend was willing to do them another favor.

Five minutes later, the FBI brought Wyatt over to her. The psychopath had the hangdog expression of someone who knew he had fucked up, and the triumphant reds and purples of someone who had scored the winning touchdown at the Superbowl. They left him sitting on the stairs beside her.

"Where's your earpiece?" she asked.

"Gee, Peng, I dunno," he said. "Musta fallen out during the fight."

"Too bad you didn't have it," she said. "You would have heard me telling everyone to stand down while I took on Nicholson."

"Too damn bad," he agreed. An FBI agent appeared with two cans of soda and a pack of Wet-Naps for Rachel; she ignored the soda while she set to work ridding herself of the last bothersome traces of Nicholson.

"I refuse to believe," she said, after the agent had left, "that you had this specific ending planned from the beginning."

"Told you I was here to do the things you couldn't."

"Oh, Lord," she sighed.

He handed her own service weapon back to her, handle first. She grabbed it from him and scanned the magazine; six shots fired. All accounted for.

"Thought this was left on the roof."

"It was," he said. "Ami got it for me. We were on our way to give it back to you when I saw him go after you with that knife. Instinct and training took over."

"Did the FBI buy that?"

"Looks like it."

She held out her left hand. After a moment, Wyatt slipped a NORINCO pistol out of his body armor and dropped it in her open palm.

"What would your story have been with this?" she asked, as she tested the weight of the unfamiliar gun.

"Does it matter?"

"Guess not," she said.

She stood; her ankle screeched like a yard owl, and she took a few wiggly sidesteps to play with her balance before she hopped down the stairs. When she turned around, Wyatt was still sitting where she had left him.

"I've got to go wrap this up," she said. "If you're gone when I get back, I won't look for you."

Purple humor exploded throughout his colors. "Why

wouldn't I be here?" he asked. "Agent Glassman offered me a full-time position working security. I start Monday."

His scans didn't show any signs of lying. She checked again, and then again, looking for the dimples or stray colors to show that he was dicking her around.

"Pick you up for work, neighbor?" he asked.

She flipped off her scans, counted backwards from ten until she could remove her hand from her gun (negative thirty-six), and limped away from the psychopath laughing silently in purples.

TWENTY-TWO

It had taken a couple of years, but the Agents had finally settled on their new logo. Not their official government seal—seals were easy, all add-an-eagle-and-done. But logos? A logo had to be quick, recognizable, an all-purpose image for those many occasions when the formality of an eagle just wouldn't do. None of them had been trained in graphic design, but that didn't mean that they didn't have Passionate Opinions about typefaces, color selection, layout… There had been wars fought over kerning alone, with entire rooms back at their old headquarters turned into a digital battleground over text alignment.

The result was something that Rachel thought looked like a bastardized version of the London Underground logo, but she didn't much care. It was green, it said OACET, the background elements were ripe with technobabble, and it looked less garish on her running shorts than their official seal.

It was also easier to insert RFID chips into a design that already looked digitized.

The War Room's door was ajar. Pretty cartoon ponies glared at her with glassy eyes from over stacks of black canvas backpacks, as the RFID chips yelped at her from within. A haze of dust from disturbed papers poured, slowly, from the doorway into the hallway; it had all but settled, and Rachel doubted anyone could see it but her.

Inside was a splash of raspberry, along with an assorted six-pack of colors she didn't recognize.

"Idiots," Rachel muttered.

Beside her, Mulcahy tensed; this already long morning wasn't over yet.

Rachel laid a hand on his bare arm and pushed iron calm

across to him.

"Let me go first," she told him. *"I know how to rattle this guy."*

Her boss nodded.

Rachel took a breath, and limped her way into the War Room.

"Good morning!" she said, as brightly as if she were the cheeriest diner waitress in the history of strong coffee.

Bryce Knudson froze. Around him, several other Homeland Security agents glanced at him, fingers twitching in yellow-white energy as they thought about going for their guns—

"Don't," said Detective Hill in his best cop's voice. Rachel felt the butt of his tactical shotgun rest against her shoulder as he took aim at Knudson's center mass. As long as she didn't move, Hill wouldn't have to worry about Knudson seeing his stance waver. (And as long as Hill didn't shoot, she didn't have to worry about permanently losing the hearing in her right ear.) "Metropolitan Police Department. You're trespassing on government property."

"They're stealing government property," Mulcahy said as he entered the room.

Knudson's colors snapped and twisted in reds—*Caught!*

She scanned the mess against the far wall. The filing cabinets had been removed, and a new hole had been opened in the wall, roughly the size of a gun cabinet. Behind it was an old-fashioned metal safe, with an external layer of modern digital locks. The door to the safe had been opened, with bare shelves where the files had rested.

"Man," Rachel said, shaking her head. "You guys prepped for everything. Did you bring paint in case you scratched something? I bet you brought paint."

Knudson's team stayed silent, but their yellow caution and orange anxiety twisted over each other and pointed directly towards one of the canvas bags on the floor. Her scans dipped into the canvas bags…

"Yup," she said, as she used her mind to poke around the contents of the cans. "Federal institution beige, green, and cream. Those are about as basic as colors get, trust me."

"Come in, extract, and get out," Mulcahy said. "Leave no trace."

"Leave no leverage," Rachel clarified. "We knew they were down here as soon as they tripped the locks on that safe.

"And yes," she said, "we could have trusted the FBI to arrest you, or called the cops. But right now, it's just us, Knudson. Just OACET and Homeland, having a nice discussion. Plus one cop, who is currently not on duty and decided to come down to the Batcave to see if his friends wanted to get some breakfast, and has found something very odd in the basement."

"You're on their side?" Knudson asked Hill, very quietly.

"I'm on the side of the people who didn't kidnap my niece."

Knudson's colors blanched, and the gunmetal gray that had been swirling around the edges of his attention jumped straight to the middle of his chest.

"Yeah," Rachel said. "You should have done more research.

"Oh," she added, as his attention swung wide as he continued to search for an opening. "Those dudes you had at the top of the stairs standing guard? They're on their way over to Sibley Memorial Hospital."

Knudson went extremely still, traces of red anger starting to work its way into his colors. "What did you do to them?"

"Me? Nothing. OACET? Nothing. The MPD? Nothing. How-*ev*-er…"

Hope Blackwell flowed around Rachel like a wave.

The weird woman had lost weight during her time in captivity, and her cheekbones stood out beneath furious dark eyes. Or maybe that was just the streaks of blood across her face—some were smeared and drying, while others were stark, fresh red. She was wearing what must have been one of her husband's white dress shirts. It hung around her like a smock, untucked and draped over a pair of athletic shorts, with more fresh blood across its front and sleeves.

She was also barefoot, which somehow drove home the fact that she was there for no other reason than to commit unspeakable violence.

"We can either do this on the books, or…" Mulcahy let the offer hang.

Knudson's colors twisted between professional blues and sickly greens.

"Both options have their good points," Rachel said. "If Hill arrests you right now for breaking and entering, Hope can't touch you. But if we do this all casual-like, then we can keep this quiet. Our reporter friends are waiting for an exclusive about the reasons for the kidnapping."

He didn't have to think about it. "Off the books."

"Good," Hope hissed as she moved, sliding to the side of the room. She kept away from the shotgun, stopping just far enough away so she could bring down Knudson if the gun went off. Her fingers knotted and cracked as she stretched them, readied them—

"Off the books means no one will ever know what happens here," Mulcahy said. "Just us, and whomever we choose to tell."

He took a step forward; the men from Homeland began to move. Hope grabbed the nearest by his arm, turned him upside-down, and put his head straight into the floor. The others stopped, and looked to Knudson again as he held up a hand for patience.

Mulcahy took one of the chairs from around the table and handed it to Rachel.

"Thanks," she said, and sat so her screaming ankle was finally able to rest. Hill moved the shotgun accordingly; it dropped a little lower than dead center on Knudson, and the Homeland agent's colors solidified themselves as he accepted the inevitable.

"What do you want from us?" he asked.

"Me?" Rachel lifted her hands. "I'd like you all to go tell your superiors how you fucked up. Hell, I'd like to do this official, myself. Make an example of you. Press charges, drag you out in front of the media. Tell the entire fucking world how you kidnapped a child to get control of OACET."

"But then I wouldn't get the chance to beat the shit out of you," Hope said, her voice ragged and dry. The man lying on the ground before her groaned quietly; Hope lifted one foot and *stomped*.

Knudson glanced at his man, and then back to Hope. "Let us sit down," he said. "We'll answer your questions, and then we'll go. No tricks." Hope lifted her foot again, and he added: "Please."

Mulcahy agreed; the Homeland agents were disarmed and were placed around the War Room's small wooden table, hands laid out flat and empty.

"You're not supposed to be here," Knudson said.

"We're OACET," Rachel said. "We cause more chaos before sunrise than most civil servants do all day."

"I'm aware," Knudson said. Streaks of angry red ran across his colors at her words.

"We're cyborgs, Knudson dear," Rachel said, with a nod towards the files and their RFID tags. "Our security system is the best in the world. We've known you've been snooping around the building since we allowed the FBI full access. We just weren't sure when you were planning to make your move, not until you tried to get into that safe."

"At first, we thought you were trying to get into our databases," Mulcahy said. "But we don't keep anything of critical intelligence in our databases."

"Agent Murphy is just fanatical about paper documentation," Rachel said. "You must have known that—she's monologued for hours about the importance of paper trails. And after that fake break-in where you raided the offices, looking for our intelligence caches? We realized you didn't want any ol' run-of-the-mill documents. You were here for the good stuff. Our rumored Grade-A blackmail materials."

"You waited until our entire security team was at the raid," Mulcahy said. "And then you spent the last hour trying to bypass our codes."

One of the Homeland agents had been flailing in impotent orange confusion. The cell phone in his hand continued to broadcast the supposedly live feed from the factory down in

Maryland. According to the reporter, the Agents were still in the factory, Nicholson was down but his militia wasn't, there would be a press conference as soon as the details were wrapped up—

"No tricks, honey," Rachel said to him. "Reporters are willing to bend over backwards for you when you promise them a really juicy story.

"So," she continued. "What type of story are they going to get?"

"We're not giving anybody up, if that's what you want," Knudson said. "This was all us."

Hope laughed, a harsh, choking sound. "Even I know that's a load of crap," she said, as she pointed to the files.

"It's plausible, though," Rachel said. "I suppose Knudson and his men *could* have planned this alone. They *could* be after these files to ensure that certain politicians would support them when they move to bundle OACET into Homeland. They let the militia do the dirty work, and come in behind them to clean up.

"Pretty clever," she said. The urge to scurry over to Knudson and scream right in his face was slightly—so *very* slightly!—outweighed by the pressure of the shotgun resting on her shoulder. "I'm not even sure if we've got any evidence against y'all."

"Except for…" Behind her, Hill's conversational colors moved in an arrow, pointing towards the safe and the canvas bags full of papers.

"And…" Mulcahy said, as he unslung his shoulder bag and removed a file. He placed it on the War Room's table. "We have this."

To Rachel, it looked like any other standard government-issue file; a little past its prime, a little worse for wear. Maybe a few too many handwritten notes on the cover, but scratch paper was never around when needed.

Knudson's eyes widened as if they had threatened him with a bomb.

"Now," Mulcahy said, his fingers resting lightly on the file's cover. "I'm going to speak in hypotheticals, so as not to place the blame on any one person or organization. Besides, I'm sure that those who orchestrated this scheme left little evidence of their own involvement, and it's not fair to punish those who work under them while letting those responsible slip away."

"I think it's fair," Rachel said, grinning at Knudson. "I really do, but Mulcahy says different. And that's the heart of this whole mess, right? Where Mulcahy goes, so goes control of OACET.

"Now, the only reason I'm not hauling off and beating you until you're nothing but trace evidence?" Rachel said. "You've been used almost as much as we have. Because—and here's the heart and soul of this cockup—it's impossible to get Congress to pay for an unstoppable cyborg army when the country's already got one."

"One that's proven they obey the law," Mulcahy said as he stepped forward, his huge hands wrapping around the back of the nearest unoccupied chair.

Knudson seemed hypnotized by those hands; Mulcahy was grasping the chair like it was mere moments away from becoming two halves of a chair. Two very sharp and pointy halves.

"You can't go after OACET," Rachel said. "Not directly. Senator Hanlon tried that, and we spanked the shit out of him. We're an unimpeachable organization. We've defined ourselves as such. We're aware that any slipup will be an opportunity to take us down, and we behave accordingly.

"So if somebody wanted to take control of OACET, it'd require a two-stage attack. First, you get Mulcahy to make a mistake. An incredibly public blowup that he can't recover from. Then, you get control of the documents that nobody has ever seen but everyone in Congress somehow knows we have. With Mulcahy disgraced and our leverage gone, we'd be unable to defend ourselves.

"You knew Mulcahy's history, how he could break in and rescue Hope and Avery whenever he damned well felt like it. But it's all about public perception, right? Nicholson made sure the standoff was national news. If Mulcahy rescued his wife and godchild, he'd have to leave behind those other hostages while he got them out, and I bet they'd all be in very poor condition by the time he got back to make a second trip."

"Bad press for OACET," Mulcahy said. "Worse for me—I'd probably have to resign."

"Alternatively, the standoff lasts long enough for Hope Blackwell to come down from her meds. Or they give her something else which amps her up beyond what she can manage. She's already in a high-stress situation, and she's the kind of person who fights back.

"Sorry," Rachel added as an aside to Hope.

"Nah," Hope said in her too-hoarse voice. "'s fair."

"If this happened, Hope might get Avery out of there, but she's not trained for covert ops… It's more likely that whatever she did would end really, *really* poorly. It'd be a slaughter. Dead hostages, definitely, and possibly the beginnings of a firefight with the FBI and officers when they reacted to the situation inside the factory."

"Not so bad for OACET," Mulcahy said, as he leaned on the chair. It began to creak and sag beneath his weight. "Very, very bad for me. I'd definitely resign."

"Diplomacy couldn't work," Rachel continued. "Your man inside made sure that Nicholson wouldn't agree to any terms. Once I took him down, Nicholson went completely cheese and crackers. He was an egomaniacal rich kid—he was never someone you could reason with! He thought that once Mulcahy heard him out, we'd be so swept up in how right he was that we'd fall in line. He had no idea what to do once he actually met us; Fischer would have been able to aim him like a gun.

"It was a really good plan, guys. Kudos. You plugged our escape holes ever so nicely. But the one thing I can't figure out?" Rachel leaned forward, hands tented in her lap, as she glared at Knudson. "The China connection. What's going on there?"

Knudson had spent the last few minutes staring into space, his surface colors moving in tempo with Rachel and Mulcahy as they laid out the reasons for the kidnapping. He shook his head. "A distraction," he said. "We got our hands on a few crates of guns stolen from NORINCO, and it turned out they were part of a larger theft. Since Nicholson's recent history included travel to China, we thought you and the FBI would waste time chasing down the idea that China was arming U.S. militias."

Rachel leaned forward so her jaw rested on her hands and tried to look thoughtful, and not completely poleaxed by the realization that if Wyatt hadn't shown up when he did, that would have been exactly what happened.

"Interesting," she said. "And the rumors that China is developing an implant similar to OACET's? Did you put those out there as part of the false trail?"

Red—furious, burning red across the table, as each of the men from Homeland sought to hold their tempers.

"Oh," she said. "Oh, my goodness. *That* got y'all going!"

"Peng?" Mulcahy asked.

"Answer the question," she said to Knudson.

"Those rumors are true." The Homeland agent spoke through gritted teeth, red spinning off of him like gouts of flame.

"Well, damn," Rachel said, as she sat up again. She cocked her head so she could look at Mulcahy. "They think a version of China with OACET's capabilities is a serious threat. I think…" She turned back to Knudson. "…you did this because of national security, right? I mean, there were probably a few suitcases full of unmarked bills, plus the promise of job promotions and all that sweet stuff, but there was some fundamental civic duty in there, too. You did this so you could bring OACET under Homeland and get ahead of the Chinese threat."

Some of the Homeland agents nodded, and Knudson said, "Not just China. If the technology was invented once, it'll be discovered again. We need to get ahead of the threat, not react when it finally happens!"

"I've heard all of this before," Mulcahy said. "A million times over. And our answer is the same: we were not intended to be weapons. We have free will and the ability to use it, and if the situation arises in which we might act as weapons to save American lives, we will address that situation as it comes."

"And that'll be too late," said one of Knudson's team.

Mulcahy picked up the chair, broke it in half, and set it aside with the same casual grace his wife had used to drive a man's face into the floor.

Knudson's professional blues wrapped around himself as protection. "We did what had to be done," he said loudly, calling the center of attention away from his men and back to himself. "You're too powerful to be left uncontrolled. We needed to do this."

"Sure," Rachel said. "Absolute power corrupts and all. Definitely does not set a bad precedent to break into a fellow federal organization that hasn't given you evidence of wrongdoing."

Knudson pointed to the documents from the safe.

"Hey Mulcahy?" Rachel asked, falsely bright. "If those documents contained compromising information, and I'm not saying they do, have you used it?"

"No," Mulcahy said.

"Would you use it?"

"Only—" Mulcahy said, as he prodded the pieces of the broken chair with his toe. "—if pushed to the point when it needed to be used."

"And when would that be?"

"Considering how we've been fighting for three years without resorting to its use? Never, I hope."

"You were played, Knudson," Rachel said. The shotgun resting on her shoulder was becoming annoyingly heavy, and she was still so tired, but this was so close to being finished... "The politicians who could be ruined by what's in those files wanted them back, end of story. Everything else was a nice song and dance about patriotism and preserving the American way to get you to fall in line."

Mulcahy slid the file towards Knudson. "I'm sure you've noticed this," he said.

Knudson swallowed. "Where did you get it?"

"I believe you know her as Agent Johnson? Rachel apprehended her at the Congressional Country Club. Detective Hill spent most of yesterday interrogating her."

The shotgun lifted from Rachel's shoulder as Hill stood. "Ethan Fischer's partner. She slipped OACET once in Maryland, when they tried to arrest her after the meeting with Nicholson. Still, that managed to kill communications between you and Fischer.

"But Johnson wasn't just the go-between for Fischer. She was also the primary connection between you and six men in Congress." Hill pointed to the file. "She said this was yours."

Knudson nodded.

"She's not saying much," Hill said. "Enough to convince me she's not going down alone. She gave up that file as security. It's got your notes on the kidnapping in it, and some of Fischer's notes on the same pages."

"Fischer was good enough to give me a handwriting sample, and tried to kill me to get it back," Rachel said. "I'm sure those pages would hold up under scrutiny."

"I've read your notes," Mulcahy said to Knudson. "You seem to be missing some information. Did you know it was always part of the plan to kill Hope, and possibly Avery and the other hostages?"

Knudson didn't reply, but Hill said: "No."

"Why do you say that?" Rachel asked Hill.

"These guys are law and order," Hill said. "They think they're doing the right thing. They wanted to minimize casualties, not build a plan around them. Tell 'em about the dead agent."

"Right," Rachel said. "Did you know the FBI had an agent inside Sugar Hill? And that he was almost certainly murdered by Fischer to convince Nicholson that he was on his side?"

The Homeland agents turned a deep orange gray.

"What are you going to do?" Knudson asked.

In response, Mulcahy took an RFID sticker in the shape of OACET's new logo out of his pocket, and affixed it to the front of the file. He carried this to the open safe, and set it on the empty top shelf.

"Fill 'er up, boys," Rachel said, and pointed at the canvas bags.

The Homeland agents stood and started loading.

It was a long five minutes before the safe was full again. Rachel scanned the Homeland agents from head to toe, and they were told they had to leave the bags behind, just in case.

Hope escorted them out, dragging the unconscious man across the floor by his arms.

Knudson was the last to leave. As he reached the door, he stopped and turned to face Rachel. "This can't be allowed to continue," he said to her. "OACET can't be left as its own organization. Not with the kind of power you have—the kind of power we *need*. You *have* to come in. There's too much at risk."

Rachel took a long look around the War Room before she met Knudson's eyes. "I'm sure you thought you were doing the right thing," she said. "But I'd shut up if I were you."

Storm clouds of black and red anger rolled across him, and he turned to leave.

"Wait." She held up her left hand, stretching it open as far as the scar tissues allowed. "A child might have died because you were dumb enough to let yourself get dragged into politics. My boss is letting you walk out of here, but do not confuse that with forgiveness."

He glared at her until Hill loomed closer with the shotgun.

And then they were gone, and it was just Rachel and Mulcahy left in the War Room.

She collapsed across the table and thought she might spend the rest of the day right there. Or the week. She could probably get pizza delivered, if she tried hard enough. *"That was close,"* she sighed through the link. *"If Josh hadn't bribed his pilot friend to fly us back here in time, things might have gone sideways."*

"Maybe," Mulcahy said, as he went to reset the locks on the safe.

She sat up. *"What did you do?"*

He grinned. It was the old Mulcahy grin, the one a wolf wears when he's turned a trap on the hunters.

"*What did you **do**?*"

"Scan the wall," he told her.

She did. Cinderblocks over thick unyielding sandstone. But behind that—

Rachel stared at him.

"*You didn't really think I'd keep our best intel in a tiny safe,*" he said. "*Did you?*"

Rachel couldn't help but laugh.

TWENTY-THREE

She was resting her eyes—*not* sleeping, thank you very much, she was not so old yet that she'd accidentally fall asleep at a party—but there was Marshall Wyatt, grinning at her over a Texas-sized steak. Young Wyatt. Her friend. Not the phony older version chatting up Zockinski's wife at the buffet.

"Where'd you get that?" she asked, before she saw a matching plate loaded with steak and accoutrements resting on her lap. "Ah," she said, and she fell upon the golden ear of corn resting atop a mountain of mashed potatoes. She glanced around with working eyes, and saw they were in Afghanistan again. Well, Afghanistan by way of Hope and Mulcahy's colossal private greenhouse: she and Wyatt had never been to a catered function in Afghanistan, and there was that jazz band combo playing on a flat fiberglass rock in the middle of a manmade river. "Another dream?"

"Not for me," he replied. "But the lines blur when you're dead."

She waved a waiter over for a refill on her champagne. And got a second glass for Wyatt, because when your friend comes back from the dead for a chat, it was simply good manners to offer him some champagne.

Wyatt's ghost stared at the fluted crystal as if it were poison. "Beer used to be good enough for you."

"Still is," she said. "But if Mulcahy wants to serve expensive champagne, I'm drinking expensive champagne."

He shrugged, sipped, and his eyes went wide.

"I know, right?" she said, and relaxed against the eucalyptus tree.

"You've got a strange life," Wyatt's ghost said, as a Caspian cobra twisted around their feet. It hissed at a passing koala, who ignored it.

"You get used to it."

"You happy?"

"Yeah," she said, as she watched Becca and Jason on the dance floor. "Most days, I am."

"Good." He nodded towards the fake Wyatt: Ami was twisting the psychopath's arm to get him to dance with her. Literally. "He's sticking around?"

"Yup," she said, as she shook her head in absolute bemusement. "Josh offered him a job working with the Hippos, and he accepted. Officially, he's you, forever."

Wyatt's ghost laughed. "Good for him," he said. "Maybe he can make something out of me."

Rachel kicked the cobra off of her boots. It turned into a giant flying squirrel and scampered up the nearest tree.

"Not okay with that?" he asked.

"Nope," she said. "He's not you. Shouldn't be wearing your face."

"Told you, I got no use for it. Let him have it." When she didn't reply, he added, "Thought you didn't notice faces any more, anyhow."

"It's the principle of the thing," she said, and stabbed at her steak with her knife.

"But you think this is the best place for him," Wyatt's ghost said.

She'd been trying to convince herself of this for days. It was getting easier: they couldn't turn him over to the cops without dangerous explanations, and this way the Hippos could keep an eye on him.

And…maybe…she had finally realized what he had been trying to tell her on the factory's roof. It took her longer than it should have: the poets she loved so much always spoke of a sense of morality, a sense of ethics, a sense of fair play. There was always more truth to be found in words, if you went digging.

Not that she had any sympathy for a murderous psychopath. Really.

"I don't know what else to do with him," she said. "But is this the best option? No. We're letting him walk around free. No punishment for what he's done in the past. Even if we keep him honest from here on out, that's on me."

"You still think he's running a long con?"

No, she thought, but she didn't answer him.

"Well," Wyatt's ghost said, as he finished his champagne, "I'll catch you around, Penguin."

"What, you got plans?" she chuckled.

The ghost grinned. "You'd be surprised," he said, and faded into the tree.

The giant squirrel hung upside-down from a nearby branch and chittered at her.

"Quiet," she told it, and the squirrel disappeared.

Let there be peace, she told herself, as the band played a tune by Miles Davis and the children chased the koala through a field of wildflowers. *Or something like it.*

Across the greenhouse, Hope and Mulcahy sat close beside each other, legs entwined. Hope's bruises would take time to fade. Healing—for both of them—would take longer. They carried reds and grays on their shoulders, and it was only when they were close enough to touch that some of that weight was lifted. They watched the room like wary predators, and when one rose to get a new plate of food or make conversation with friends, the other followed close behind.

Avery's protector during the kidnapping had turned out to be an unemployed single mother of three. The woman with the core of copper had children who weren't much older than Avery, and she had brought them to the party. None of those children, Avery included, seemed to have been affected by the kidnapping: they all screamed in glee as they romped with the koala and splashed in the stream. The woman with the core of copper sat beside Mako and Carlota, the three of them not talking. All three of them wore their heavy cloaks of reds and grays, but while Mako and Carlota shared theirs between them, the woman with the core of copper carried hers alone.

Josh was—

Oh!

Rachel yanked her scans out of the coat closet and made herself wake all of the way up, as quickly as she could, because she had just learned something new about human anatomy and *where* on *earth* did Josh find women who could bend like *that?!*

A half-eaten plate of food slid off of her lap.

She nudged it aside with a sigh, and resigned herself to another year in a starring role in the annual OACET holiday bloopers reel. It wouldn't be the first time someone had filmed her while she was talking under the influence of drowsy.

The greenhouse was much smaller now that she was awake. It held only a small fraction of the party, although the jazz band was real. Everything else was located through the open doors, which led to Hope and Mulcahy's mini-mansion, or to the lawn and the dance floor outside

It was tight quarters all over. Parties with more than two hundred people used to be the norm for OACET in their mansion out on the Potomac River. There was nowhere to hold large events these days, and she felt the loss.

She touched the stone in her necklace. It was a pink sapphire set in gold, and she only wore it for special occasions, or endings, or both.

She knew it was selfish, but she was so tired of the constant loss of small things.

The bone-weary exhaustion that had swallowed her at Nicholson's factory hadn't faded with time. It was hard to move. Hard to pull herself forward. Hard to think about anything but blue and black, and Nicholson tipping over into—

How long are you going to allow yourself to sit here like a useless shit on the floor?

She stood and tested her ankle. Five days after Nicholson's death, and she was able to limp around without crutches if she wore an ACE bandage under heavy leather boots. Becca's core of jade green was out on the lawn, moving beneath a galaxy of twinkling string lights as she swayed to the music, and Rachel wanted nothing more than to steal her away and go home and curl up in her arms—

"Hey."

Santino was standing a few feet away, uncertain in oranges. He was holding a small potted begonia.

"Got a minute?" he asked.

"Yeah," she said, and used the tree to lower herself back down to the ground. She had a feeling she knew what was coming, and a few more minutes of being a useless shit on the floor seemed appropriate.

"Can I sit?"

"What is with you lately?" she snapped. "Of course you can sit."

Her partner folded his long legs up and dropped to the ground, several feet away. The orange grew deeper, and it started to push the Southwestern turquoise away—

Santino thrust the begonia at her. "Here," he said. "I think this belongs to you."

She didn't move. After a moment, he set the begonia on the ground between them.

"Could you stop running emotions?" he said, almost sadly.

"Yeah," she said, and snapped off her scans altogether. Whatever was coming, she didn't need to see it.

"I'm moving in with Zia," he said.

"Yeah." She nodded; no surprise there. "Is it because of Wyatt?"

"What? No, why?"

Curious, she activated her scans again and flipped frequencies until she could see Santino's face. He was older than she remembered, with crow's feet beginning to crack around his eyes. "Figured Wyatt was the last straw," she replied. "I pushed you hard last year—this was worse."

"No!" He laughed, and the crow's feet crinkled. "No, it's got nothing to do with you."

"Then why?" she asked, before she could swallow her words and keep herself from sounding like the world's biggest self-pitying teenager.

"I really liked living with you," he said. "Big yard, finally got the garden the way I wanted…"

"Shut up," she said, smiling, and picked up the begonia. "Is this what I think it is?"

He nodded. "Yeah. It's not rooted yet, so be gentle. But you used it to fight off a trained killer, so it's yours by right of conquest."

Rachel stroked the plant's soft leaves. A single flower remained; a bud had survived the beating and had coaxed itself open despite the stress. "Thanks," she said.

"I want to tell you something," he said in a rush. "But you've got to keep it a secret for another few weeks."

"What—" she began, and then whipped her scans around to find his girlfriend in the crowd. She flipped the emotional spectrum back on, and honed in on Zia's violet core.

Zia was carrying blue around in that core—a babysoft blue, with the seafoam greens of dreamless sleep.

"You son of a bitch," Rachel said to her partner.

"Most people lead with 'congratulations.'"

"You could have told me!"

"I *am* telling you!" He rose up on his knees and hugged her in blues, purples, reds, and the most joyous yellows she had ever seen, colors brighter than the sun, or maybe the bottom of the ocean. A whole future cascaded around them in rainbows. "We wanted to wait until we were safe in the second trimester," he said. "But you'd know, so we're asking you to keep it quiet.

"Oh, that reminds me," he added. "Want to be my best woman at the ceremony?"

"You are *such* an asshole," she said.

Acknowledgements

There've been a lot of jokes about how 2016 was an especially wild year. All I know is that I had a decent chunk of *Brute Force* written before Ammon Bundy and his militia took over the Malheur National Wildlife Refuge. When that happened —January 2, 2016—my draft of a handful of madmen with a vendetta against OACET became too tame for a work of fiction. I spent the next nine months expanding the plot to keep ahead of current events, and sent the final draft out to my copyeditor during the first week of November.

…yeah…

A wild year, indeed.

Sovereign citizens shouldn't be overgeneralized: I hope I haven't done that here. They are a highly diverse group with no central governing structure, and are only loosely united by a broad view of government corruption. Some of their members are, however, a serious threat to law enforcement. The FBI has identified "sovereign-citizen extremists as comprising a domestic terrorist movement," especially during confrontations with law enforcement. If pushed, sovereign citizens will push back.

Three works of poetry appeared in this novel. These were, in order, Carl Sandberg's "Prayers of Steel," "Amaze" by Adelaide Crapsey, and "Dreamers" by Siegfried Sassoon. Rachel never got to recite the second part of Sassoon's poem:

> *I see them in foul dug-outs, gnawed by rats,*
> *And in the ruined trenches, lashed with rain,*
> *Dreaming of things they did with balls and bats,*
> *And mocked by hopeless longing to regain*
> *Bank-holidays, and picture shows, and spats,*
> *And going to the office in the train.*

It's a shame she didn't have the chance to introduce the other Agents to these lines, as I feel they would have embraced Sassoon's tribute to mundane normalcy.

As always, this book wouldn't be possible without the goodwill and support of my husband, Brown. As always, this book would have been finished much, much more quickly if it weren't for my dogs. Thank you for purchasing a copy: you've helped offset the cost of their numerous vet bills and the three windows they've broken.

Thanks goes to my beta readers, Fuzz, Gary, Kevin, Tiff, Joris, and Cora, for their critical and necessary feedback. To Danny and Jes, thank you for the copy edits. And to Rose Loughran of *Red Moon Rising* for the fantastic cover art.

Finally, *Brute Force* is set in a larger fictional universe. Patrick Mulcahy's story is free to all readers, and is in graphic novel form at agirlandherfed.com. The novels in the Rachel Peng series, fill in the five-year gap between when Mulcahy discovered the purpose of their implants and when he was finally able to establish OACET as an independent federal organization. Please excuse the talking koala; he has a good heart.

You can find updates on current projects and novels at kbspangler.com and agirlandherfed.com. Thanks for reading!

Rachel and Santino will be back!

Made in the USA
Columbia, SC
02 October 2018